song *of*

sorr◯w

state of sorrow

song *of*
s o r r o w

MELINDA SALISBURY

■SCHOLASTIC

Scholastic Children's Books
An imprint of Scholastic Ltd
Euston House, 24 Eversholt Street, London, NW1 1DB, UK
Registered office: Westfield Road, Southam, Warwickshire, CV47 0RA
SCHOLASTIC and associated logos are trademarks and/or
registered trademarks of Scholastic Inc.

First published in the UK by Scholastic Ltd, 2019

Text copyright © Melinda Salisbury, 2019
Map illustration by Maxime Plasse

The right of Melinda Salisbury to be identified as the
author of this work has been asserted.

ISBN 978 1407 18028 1

A CIP catalogue record for this book
is available from the British Library.

Printed by CPI Group (UK) Ltd, Croydon, CR0 4YY
Papers used by Scholastic Children's Books are made
from wood grown in sustainable forests.

1 3 5 7 9 10 8 6 4 2

This is a work of fiction. Names, characters, places, incidents
and dialogues are products of the author's imagination or are used
fictitiously. Any resemblance to actual people, living or dead,
events or locales is entirely coincidental.

www.scholastic.co.uk

Svarta

Jorea

Skae

Nyrssea

Rhylla

Adavaria

Ceridog

North Marches

Meridea

West Marches

Istevar

East Marches

Prekara

Rhannon

South Marches

Asha

Astria

Laethea

PART ONE

For us there is only one season, the season of sorrow.

—*Oscar Wilde,* "De Profundis"

A Dream Realized Is One Ended

Sorrow decided her first official act as the chancellor of Rhannon would be to outlaw the word "congratulations".

"Congratulations on your victory, Chancellor!"

"Many congratulations, Miss Ventaxis!"

"Sorrow! You did it! Congratulations!"

That wretched word. Repeated until it made no sense at all, melding into a jumble of sounds that left her feeling ashamed, and sad, and scared. It got so bad that every time someone said it – often giving her a pat at the same time, as though she was a prize horse that had performed well – she had to fight to keep herself from either screaming, or swearing at them; neither of which were acceptable responses for a chancellor, even a newly minted one.

In the aftermath of the election result, Rhannish citizens surrounded her, their faces a blur, words a senseless roar as she moved from stranger to stranger, all determined to say they were there, in the front row on the day everything changed. She'd fought for this moment; she'd almost died for it. They wanted to celebrate it, and they wanted her to celebrate it too.

She saw the amused looks people exchanged, as she stood frozen before them; how they'd assumed she was shocked, overwhelmed, humbled, even. Delighted by her reaction, they congratulated her again, adding how proud and happy they were, loudly announcing they had voted for her (of course), claiming their spot in her history.

Each word was a nail in Sorrow's heart. Each clap on the shoulder felt like a blade, cutting her to the core. They didn't know what they were saying. They couldn't know what they'd done by choosing her. What she'd done.

For Sorrow, the worst thing of all was that part of her was thrilled by it. Because it meant she'd won. After months of trying, and fighting, and wanting, and working, she'd done it: Rhannon was hers. She couldn't help the pride that thundered through her when someone called her "Chancellor". Even if it was immediately followed by guilt and terror.

Yes, Sorrow would ban "congratulations"; excise it from the language and establish her own special police force to punish anyone who said it.

She wouldn't, of course. She had enough problems with the current special police force that now fell under her command. But, stars, how she wished that she could. And, to cap it all, the next two weeks would be full of congratulations. Sorrow already felt trapped by them, the feeling compounded by the very literal pins holding her in place at that moment, thanks to Ines, her personal tailor, who was busy draping swatches of fabric over Sorrow's body.

"You must have *some* preference as to the colour," Irris said, peering at her friend from her position on Sorrow's bed, flat on her belly, propped up on her elbows.

"I really don't," Sorrow replied. "I'll be happy with whatever Ines designs."

"It's your ball. To celebrate *you*."

Sorrow raised her fist in a mock cheer. The motion caused a length of chartreuse silk to fall to the floor, and Ines tutted softly as she snatched it up and repositioned it once more.

Irris frowned at Sorrow. "What about blue? You love blue."

"Blue is fine." Her tone indicated the shrug her shoulders were denied.

Irris opened her mouth, but then snapped it shut, chewing her lip thoughtfully, before saying, "Ines, could you give us a minute?"

The girl didn't need asking twice, hurrying from the room in silence, leaving Sorrow stranded on the stool she stood on, with no escape from Irris's piercing gaze.

"All right, Chancellor Grumpy. What's going on?" said Irris, the moment Ines had closed the door behind her. "And if you say 'nothing', Ines left more than enough pins to torture it out of you."

"Nothing," Sorrow dared, drawing an exasperated growl from Irris. "Really. I'm just not that into clothes."

"You're lying. And not even as well as usual," Irris said. She sat up, kicking her legs off the bed and considering her friend. "You liked getting all dressed up for Rhylla."

"Yes, and look how that ended. I slept with Rasmus, was almost murdered, and found out my advisor was a crime lord."

"But you looked great the whole time," Irris quipped.

Sorrow allowed herself a small smile. "I did, didn't I?"

Irris grinned, then her expression became serious once more. "I mean it, Row, you've not been yourself since the final presentation. Is it Mael? You still haven't told me what he said to you in the corridor, after. Was he awful?"

Sorrow closed her eyes as she remembered. Mael, his expression raw and wounded. Mael, who she'd hated when he'd been the golden boy miraculously returned from the dead, her long-lost brother stepping into the story just at the moment Rhannon most needed him. The man she could not bring herself to trust, for fear that he was an imposter. Only, all that time, she was wrong. *She* was the imposter.

And Vespus Corrigan knew it.

Vespus had been seeking land in the north of Rhannon for decades, first through war, then by manipulating Harun – the man Sorrow thought was her father – before he'd finally found the greatest prize of all: her.

He would give her his silence – about her identity, and her relationship with his son – if she would give him that land. And she'd had no choice but to agree. Not to protect herself; if she was the only casualty, she would have cheerfully told him where to go. There were nights where she imagined it before she tried to sleep, replaying the scene in his room where he revealed what he knew, and instead of crumbling, she laughed in his face.

"Tell the world," she dreamed of saying. "Do your worst."

But it would only ever be a dream. She had to protect the country she'd fought for. To protect the people she loved.

Exposure would mean Rasmus's head on the block; Vespus had made it clear he wouldn't spare him, and death was the price for a Rhyllian caught in a relationship with someone Rhannish. It wouldn't matter that they'd parted, and promised to stay apart: Rasmus would still die for it. Sorrow wouldn't risk it. She'd done enough to Rasmus as it was.

Then there was Charon. Sorrow was angry with him for keeping who she really was from her, but he'd raised her, cared for her, which was more than Harun had done. She loved Charon – the idea of him suffering on her account was unbearable. At the very least he'd be arrested if the truth about her came out, if not worse. After all, he'd urged her to depose her father while he lived, knowing full well she was an imposter. The Sons of Rhannon had already sown seeds to make the people question the Ventaxis right to govern. Rhannon was still too fragile to survive another war, civil or otherwise.

Vespus had her exactly where he wanted her. Winner of a hollow victory. Puppet ruler. Not worthy. . .

"Row?" Irris's voice snapped Sorrow from her thoughts, and her eyes focused on her friend, now standing in front of her, concern drawing her features tight. "Talk to me. What did Mael say?"

"Oh." Sorrow shook her head. "No, it's nothing to do with him."

"Then who? What? The look on your face. . . You're scaring me."

Sorrow was scaring herself. She felt the heaviness of Rhannon settling on her shoulders, more and more as each moment passed. It weighed on her like a cloak; the lives and hopes and fortunes of the millions of people she now led. And she was the only thing standing between them and Vespus's ambition. "I'm just . . . tired. I'm so tired." It was half-truth. "It's been non-stop."

Irris's gaze was searching. Then she nodded. "You need

a day off. Tell my father you need some time before the tour starts. He'll arrange it."

"When?" Sorrow held her hands out, a waterfall of teal velvet slipping off her body. "I'm being dressed like a doll all morning, and then I have to write to the Jedenvat formally inviting them back to the council, and the ambassadors to their posts too – not to mention we need to choose our foreign ambassadors to send across Laethea. There's dinner with the Jedenvat tonight, the swearing-in tomorrow, another bloody dinner, then we're off around Rhannon. I don't have a day. I don't even have a minute. Stars help me if I need to go to the bathroom."

"That's what I'm trying to say." Irris spoke slowly. "Ask for one. We can make it happen. You're the chancellor. You're the last word on everything."

"I might be the chancellor, but I still have to obey the laws of time. The ball is two weeks from now, and it can't be moved – people are coming from across all of Laethea. And before then I have to meet with all the districts. If I cut even a couple of hours from one, they'll either see it as a snub—"

"Arran wouldn't. The East Marches wouldn't."

"—or they'll think I'm weak, like Harun. Shirking my duties after only a few weeks," Sorrow continued, ignoring Irris's attempts to be helpful. There was no way to explain it to Irris, but she didn't want to be helped.

Sorrow wanted the chance to be openly annoyed about something. She needed to get her feelings out before they poisoned her, and this – raging against nothing in particular – was the only thing she'd come up with that kept everyone she loved safe. She'd briefly considered violence, indulging in a splendid fantasy in which she'd knocked the living daylights out of Balthasar Lys, but she didn't think Vespus would take kindly to her beating up his lackey. And again; it was hardly appropriate for a chancellor to abuse her staff, any more than screaming or swearing was. Which left her with this. Being annoyed at little things instead.

Irris shrugged. "All right. But you could ask my father if he'll write to the Jedenvat and the ambassadors, and take the afternoon off, at least. You can sign the letters before dinner."

"They'll know it's not my handwriting."

The look Irris gave her would have soured cream, and Sorrow knew she deserved it.

"Sorry," she muttered. She climbed off the stool, pins raining to the floor. "I know you're trying to help and I know I'm being a brat. Like I said, I'm tired. A little overwhelmed. And my courses are due."

Irris raised her brows, forgiveness still withheld. "That's all? Truly?"

Sorrow racked her brain for something to offer Irris that might satisfy her. "Well – I suppose Mael *has* been on my mind. I'm worried about him."

"Why?" Irris was puzzled. "He's not your concern, Row."

Sorrow swallowed. "But he is. He's Rhannish, isn't he? And he's here because of me. Besides, he's alone, Irri. Vespus has abandoned him. He has no one else."

"So what are you saying?" Irris crouched to collect the pins, and Sorrow bent to help her.

"I— I want him to live here." As soon as she said it, Sorrow knew that it was true. It was the only thing she could do to stop feeling so awful about the way she'd treated him. And how Vespus had treated him, because of her.

9

"What?" Irris winced as she stabbed herself with a pin, but her attention remained on Sorrow as she straightened slowly. "You don't owe him that. He's not really your brother. He's not really Mael."

And I'm not really Sorrow.

Sorrow stood too. "The whole country believes he's Mael Ventaxis – *he* believes he's Mael Ventaxis – until Vespus admits otherwise, or we miraculously find proof, he might as well be. And he's no threat right now – but he might be, if someone decided to use him to form a rebellion. Better to have him onside than as a rallying point for my enemies."

Irris looked thoughtful. "I suppose when you put it like that, it can't hurt. Shall I have him found? Do you have any idea where he might be?"

Sorrow shook her head. "No. But he's not cunning enough to hide, or at least not for long. We should find him. It's the right thing to do."

"It also makes you look good. Generous and forgiving. Luvian would approve, I think."

Something in Sorrow's chest tightened painfully at the mention of her erstwhile advisor, Luvian Fen. She hadn't seen him since those few brief glimpses in the crowd on day of the last presentation; as far as she knew he hadn't been at the voting results, and he hadn't written to her either. She had no idea where he was.

She'd forgiven him for lying to her about who he really was; it would have been the height of hypocrisy to rage at him for that, given her own circumstances. And so what if he'd been born a Rathbone, youngest son in a dynasty of criminals and thieves? He wasn't like them, and that wasn't just affection talking. He'd turned his back on them long before he met Sorrow, he'd risked everything to bring her the truth about Lamentia, and how her father had died, walking into the lion's den without knowing how she'd react. She trusted him.

And she missed him.

Missed how irrepressible he was, missed his optimism and determination. He had a way of making the impossible seem likely, and she needed that right now. She needed someone in her corner whom the Graces favoured. And the Graces were surely in love with Luvian Fen. Or Luvian Rathbone. Whoever he was.

"He still hasn't been in touch?" Irris asked quietly.

"No."

"Maybe he's waiting for his pardon before he reappears."

"More likely he's waiting for the most dramatic moment to make his entrance," Sorrow replied darkly.

Irris laughed, the tension lifting from her brow.

And in turn, Sorrow straightened her back. She still had a country to run. She had to remember that. She couldn't be like Harun, and forsake Rhannon for her own demons.

"Call Ines back and let's get this over with," she said, forcing the corners of her mouth to lift.

Irris smiled in reply, teasing, "Such a hardship, having beautiful gowns made for you."

"If I were a man no one would make me dress up. There would be no fuss about my clothes then."

"Tell that to Luvian. He'd die on the spot if he knew you were turning down tailoring," Irris called over her shoulder as she moved to the door. "Sorrow..." She paused, turning, fingers resting on the handle. "You would tell me if there was something really wrong, wouldn't you?"

Sorrow looked her dead in the eye. "Of course. Of course I would."

For a moment, Irris watched her and Sorrow's pulse hitched. But Irris simply nodded, opening the door. "Ines, the chancellor is ready for you now," she said.

Sorrow plastered a grin to her face as the girl returned.

"I've had an idea," she said as Ines entered. The tailor's scepticism was plain on her face, but Sorrow continued. "What if we work through the rainbow – seven districts, seven fancy parties, seven colours? Starting with red tomorrow, for the swearing-in, and the dinner here, ending in violet for the West Marches."

Ines's eyes narrowed. "And for the final ball?"

It was a test.

"White," Sorrow said. "The opposite of black. The opposite of mourning."

Irris and Ines nodded approvingly and relief melted Sorrow's bones. Finally, she'd got something right.

The fitting took the rest of the morning, as Sorrow had predicted, but she bore it with grace, laughing and joking; daring Ines to put a slit up to her thigh in her dress for the event in Asha, doing impressions of how Lord Samad's eyes would bulge in outrage.

After the dress fitting was finished and the three girls had eaten a light lunch, she and Irris had gone down to Sorrow's office so Sorrow could write to the Jedenvat. Before she'd won the election, Sorrow had been toying with the idea of retiring half of the council and finding younger replacements, but Vespus's blackmail had changed that. For now, it seemed wiser to keep the current senators as they were, rely on their experience to keep Rhannon ticking over while she dealt with

Vespus. Then, later, when she had all her power, she'd decide who should stay, and who should go.

The chancellor's office – now hers – had been updated during the great restoration, and Sorrow didn't know whether she was relieved or saddened by it. The desk was the same one she'd known all her life, where her grandmother had once sat, but the chair was new. Out with the old, sturdy one – cushion worn at the seat and arms from generations of Ventaxises sitting in it, the back stained dark where the heads of former chancellors had rested against it – replaced instead by a friendlier, cosier-looking seat, cushioned in blue. The curtains and rugs were new too, soft golds and duck egg, echoing the bronze wall sconces. She had the sneaking suspicion Charon had ordered it this way for her, anticipating her win.

Sorrow stood at the window, peering out into the gardens, as Irris began to flick through the stack of letters that were waiting on Sorrow's desk. Sorrow had briefly looked through them already. There were cards and notes from across Laethea: more congratulations, enquiries from people hinting they'd like to be considered for roles in her government, or as ambassadors, requests for confirmation that trade agreements would continue, and suggestions for new ones.

Irris began to sort them into piles. She let out a soft laugh and Sorrow twisted to look over her shoulder.

"Kaspira wasted no time," Irris said, holding up a piece of paper. "'A plea to command the Decorum Ward to round up and exile the Rathbone family from Prekara, on the grounds of disturbing the peace.'"

"Disturbing Kaspira's peace of mind." Sorrow smiled as she looked back to the gardens. "Maybe I should. Have my

13

revenge on Arkady for trying to kill me. And it might tempt Luvian out of hiding if I send them all packing to Asha. There's no way Luvian would survive in the desert. His hair would flop terribly."

Irris was still laughing as she tore open the next one, but her grin turned to a grimace as she read it. "Ugh. Vine wants to meet with you about the future of the Decorum Ward."

Sorrow watched a spider as it dropped suddenly down the window, suspended on an almost-invisible strand of spider silk.

"They don't have one," she replied, not taking her eyes off the spider as it swayed like a pendulum in the breeze.

"A future?" Irris asked, sounding confused.

"Exactly. As soon as we're back, we'll start dismantling them."

Irris's pause was heavy. "Row, I have no love at all for Vine or his people, but Rhannon needs a police force."

"Exactly. A police force. Not a militia. I want them gone. Next."

"Sorrow. . ."

"Next," Sorrow said again.

She felt her friend's stare resting on her back, but when she did speak, it wasn't at all what Sorrow expected.

"Oh. This one is from Vespus."

Within a second Sorrow had crossed to the desk and snatched the envelope from Irris's hand. It *was* from him; his handwriting, his version of the Rhyllian seal, the Alvus tree, and bridge of stars bordered by vines. Sorrow tore it open, her fingers fumbling as they shook with fear.

But it was only a request to remain in the ambassador's quarters in the Winter Palace.

A simple request. Or not so simple. From inside the Winter Palace, Vespus could watch Sorrow. Make sure she wasn't trying to wriggle out of her side of the terrible bargain they had struck. She shivered.

"Graces, tell him no," Irris said, reading over her shoulder. "None of the other ambassadors are going to stay in the palace, so why should he? He can go and live in one of the ambassadorial town houses like everyone else."

"He won't like it," Sorrow said, folding up the note and replacing it in the envelope.

"Who cares what he likes? The ambassadors don't need to stay here any more; we're not at war. The houses exist for a reason and he can't be the only one staying in the Winter Palace. Think of the message it will send if you keep Rhylla in your house and rest of Laethea outside."

Sorrow said nothing and dropped the letter on to the table. If Vespus wanted to stay, he would. She couldn't stop him. Besides, it worked both ways. He might want to stay to watch her, but she could also keep an eye on him if he was close.

Irris worked through the rest of the messages, sorting them into piles of varying urgency, as Sorrow began the process of offering the Jedenvat their jobs back.

Inviting Bayrum, Tuva and Arran to return to her council was easy; she couldn't imagine governing without them. But others were harder. Lord Samad was one of those she'd hoped to replace.

Kaspira, too, was a conundrum, although Sorrow had softened a little towards the Prekarian senator, especially now she knew exactly what she was up against with the Rathbones. It was they who'd formed the Sons of Rhannon, tried to kill her twice that she knew of, and sabotaged her election campaign.

Sorrow's list of people she disliked was getting longer by the day, and Arkady Rathbone was high on it.

But thinking of Arkady led Sorrow straight back to Luvian. Where on Laethea was he? Was he safe, at least? Waiting quietly somewhere for her to pardon him?

Sorrow still hadn't come up with a convincing reason why the warrant for his arrest should be withdrawn. The way she saw it, if she told Charon who Luvian really was, he'd never be allowed near her again – reformed Rathbone or not, Charon would think it too dangerous. And even if she told him Luvian had discovered the truth about Lamentia, it would lead to Charon confronting Vespus, and that was the last thing Sorrow needed. So Luvian remained a wanted man. And Sorrow couldn't imagine that sat well with him.

"What is it?" Irris asked, interrupting her. "You look moony."

Sorrow shook her head. "I was thinking about Luvian."

"Oh, *really*?" Irris drawled, stretching the words, her eyebrows raised suggestively.

"Funny," Sorrow said, rolling her eyes. "It's just… It's not like him to be quiet. I feel like he should be harassing me night and day for his pardon."

Irris looked thoughtful. "It *is* strange. He's not the backstage, avoiding the glory type. And you're sure he wouldn't have gone back to his family?"

"I'm sure. But we should try to find out more while we're in Prekara."

"Agreed. Are you almost finished?" Irris nodded at the paper Sorrow was signing with a flourish.

"I just have Balthasar and your father left."

"Tell me you're not keeping him?"

Sorrow smirked. "I don't know, as vice chancellors go he's been all right."

"Now who's funny?" Irris smiled. "Seriously, you can't keep Balthasar. He's hideous. And he doesn't do his job – he spent most of last year taking Lamentia with your father. You should get rid of him. And, come to think of it, Vespus too." Irris sat up straight. "Never mind him staying in the palace; he shouldn't be staying in Rhannon. He's not fit to be ambassador. The election is over, Sorrow; you can tell everyone now that he set out to corrupt your father. We agreed that."

Sorrow's heart stuttered. "I can't," she said finally.

"Why not?"

Sorrow scrambled for an answer. "Diplomatic reasons."

"Such as?" Irris's eyes narrowed.

"His sister is the queen of Rhylla."

"Half-sister. And so what? It didn't stop your father from firing him. You have proof that he brought Lamentia into the palace."

"No. I have proof that Starwater becomes Lamentia, that's all. The fact that he makes Starwater doesn't prove he introduced Lamentia to the palace – especially because Lamentia only appeared after he left. And I can't start throwing accusations around without proof; as you say, he's the half-brother of the Rhyllian queen. We need proof. Real proof. And in the meantime, I want him where we can keep an eye on him. Balthasar too." Sorrow glanced at the clock and stood up so fast she almost knocked her seat to the ground, relieved to have an excuse to leave. "I need to get ready for this dinner. If you see your father, tell him I'll give him his formal invitation to be my vice chancellor tomorrow – explain why it's late."

"Tell him yourself at the dinner."

"I doubt I'll have a chance," Sorrow hedged.

Irris raised her brows. "He thinks you're avoiding him."

She was, but she could hardly say that aloud. Sorrow couldn't get past the fact he'd lied to her for her whole life.

Sorrow wanted him as her vice chancellor, but she wasn't ready to trust him again. Or even really to talk to him. So she'd done her best to make sure they hadn't been alone since she'd won, coming up with some excuse or another to buy her time to figure out how she felt.

Apparently, her best hadn't been good enough. . .

"Row. . ."

"I'm going to have a bath. I'll see you in the morning."

Irris gave a long sigh. "See you then."

Sorrow sped from the room as fast as she could without running, her heart beating uncomfortably hard. She hadn't fooled Irris; she knew that. She wouldn't be able to avoid dealing with Vespus for ever.

"Sorrow?"

She hadn't heard him approach. For a moment she considered pretending she hadn't heard. Then she sighed, and turned.

"Charon."

He pushed his wheeled chair to where she'd stopped at the bottom of the stairs. His dark eyes sparkled as he drew the chair before her, the skin at their corners crinkling. He was happy to see her. Stars, she wished she could say the same.

"I was hoping to catch you before the dinner," Charon said as he pushed the brake and locked the chair in place.

"I'm just on my way to get ready."

"Perhaps you could spare a moment?" It was a request, not a demand. Respectful of her new position. Sorrow appreciated

18

it, but that didn't mean she would grant it.

"Is it something urgent? Only I really am running late."

Charon's eyes dimmed, but he nodded. "Nothing urgent. I merely wanted to check on you."

"I'm fine. Never better."

Charon looked at her – looked through her – as though he could see the lie, and Sorrow instinctively took a step back, putting distance between them. When Charon's gaze fell on the steps – a place he couldn't follow – Sorrow felt like the worst person in the world. She hadn't meant it like that.

But he sounded calm as he said, "I'll leave you to it, then. Perhaps we can talk at dinner?"

She nodded and turned, taking the stairs two at a time, aware of his gaze on her the whole way up.

She dismissed the servants waiting in her parlour, heading straight to her bedroom. She'd draw a bath, and let her mind wander. Hopefully it would find its way to a solution about—

She opened her bedroom door. Vespus was sitting at her breakfast table.

2

War Games

"What are you doing here?" Her hands fluttered to her throat, shock like ice water freezing her in place. "Who let you in?"

He was dressed for travelling in chestnut-coloured leather boots, a midnight-blue cloak thrown over a sharp Rhyllian suit of the same colour, a small case at his feet. His moonlight hair was braided in a thick rope over one shoulder, though a few strands were loose around his pointed ears. He smoothed them back now as he smiled silkily at her.

"I let myself in."

"How?"

He turned to where her wardrobe door lay open. "The passage, of course."

Sorrow looked between him and the door. "I didn't know you knew about that."

"Obviously. Won't you sit?" He gestured to the chair opposite him, as though it was his room, and she his guest.

Sorrow crossed slowly to the table and sat on the other chair. She left her bedroom door open, wanting an escape route at her back.

"What do you want, Vespus?"

His answering smile had no humour in it. "I suppose we're way past honorifics, aren't we? Very well, Sorrow, I'm here to let you know I'm taking leave, during the fortnight you're away. I'm sorry to miss your swearing-in, but I'll be back for the ball, two weeks from now."

Surprise flickered through Sorrow. "Where are you going?"

"Aren't you bold? Don't tell me you're going to miss me?" When Sorrow remained silent, her gaze stony, he continued. "I'm going back to Rhylla. I have business there, at my estate."

"I see."

"I doubt it."

Sorrow bit the inside of her cheek. "When do you leave?"

He looked at his cloak, and then raised an eyebrow. "Imminently," he said. "I need to make sure I have a stock of seeds here, ready to plant, when the land becomes available. You hadn't forgotten our agreement, had you?"

"How could I?" she asked, her voice bitter.

"Well, you seem very busy; *dressing like a doll, writing to the Jedenvat, then dinner with them. The swearing-in tomorrow* and, what was it? . . . *another bloody dinner, and then off around Rhannon.*"

His mimicry was spot on and his recall was perfect.

The skin along her shoulders contracted as horror engulfed her. "You were listening? How?" She realized in that instant. "From the passageway."

21

"Not intentionally. I was waiting for an opportune moment to see you."

"You had no right—"

"Report me, then."

Sorrow's shock turned to fury. Stars, she hated being caught in his web like this.

"Get to the point," Sorrow ground out through clenched teeth.

His smile vanished. "Very well. As I said, I'm going to collect seeds. When I return, I want to begin planting them."

"In two weeks? But you said I'd have months to arrange things. We agreed."

"I've changed my mind. Winter is snapping at our heels; I want my saplings strong enough to withstand it."

"It's not enough time."

"For what? For you to come up with a plan to defeat me, as though we're in a storybook? Or for you to break down and confide in Miss Day?"

"I have no plans to tell Irris anything else."

She realized her mistake a moment too late.

"Anything *else*?" His head tilted as she stared at her. "Anything else. And what, pray tell, does she know now?"

Sorrow swallowed. "She knows Lamentia is a by-product of Starwater, and that you make Starwater. But I told her that before we made our . . . bargain." The tips of Vespus's pointed ears turned red, his jaw tightening. "I've told her nothing since, and I wo—"

"You're damn right you won't." Vespus leant forward suddenly, gripping both of Sorrow's wrists and pulling her halfway across the table, so his face was close to hers. "Hear me, Miss Ventaxis. You made an agreement with me. And you will see it through. I will have my land, and I will grow my trees. Nothing and no one will stop that, not now."

He pulled her closer, until all she could see was a blur of deepest blue as his violet eyes swam before her own, his cool breath caressing her face.

"I have worked too hard, and for too long, to fail. When you return from your little tour, you will give me my land. The lives of your people and your loved ones depend on it. You know enough of me to understand murder is very much within my remit. Don't make me start working through your friends and loved ones to prove I mean this. Because I will. Beginning with the knowledgeable Miss Day."

He released her, and Sorrow stumbled back into her seat, almost knocking it over. She caught the table to steady herself as Vespus watched her.

"Do I make myself clear?"

She couldn't speak. Her stomach felt loose and slippery, her knees shaking with terror. Wave after wave of fear pummelled her, knocking away any thoughts and instincts other than that she needed to run. Yet she couldn't, locked in place by his gaze.

He was waiting for her to reply, she realized dimly, and she nodded; the most she could manage in that moment.

It was enough for him.

"Good." He rose, smoothing down his cloak. "Then I look forward to hearing your ideas two weeks from now. Congratulations again on becoming chancellor, Sorrow Ventaxis. Enjoy your tour."

He left her the same way he'd arrived, vanishing into the wardrobe, leaving behind the scent of earth and green things.

Sorrow lowered her head to her knees, fighting to steady her breathing. Her heart thundered wildly behind her ribs, seemingly with no plans to return to normal. She tried to pace her breaths and force herself calm, but every time it felt as though she was getting somewhere, her body rebelled and began to panic again. Finally, she tasted something acrid in the back of her throat and bolted to the bathroom, emptying the contents of her stomach into the sink. It was only then, as she lowered her trembling form to press against the cold tile floor, that she felt herself begin to calm, as though she'd needed to expel her fear before she could move past it.

She rolled on to her back and stared up at the ceiling. Her mind raced with a thousand thoughts, but loudest of all was the one insisting she protect Irris. How could she have been so stupid as to open her foolish mouth and put Irris at risk? Vespus knew now, he had that over her too.

Then she remembered the rest of the threat. *"Don't make me start working through your friends and loved ones."* Irris wasn't the only one at risk. There was Charon, Arran... Mael should be kept away too. Far, far away.

Something occurred to Sorrow. Maybe Irris should be kept away, too, out of Vespus's reach. Sorrow could send her somewhere for a while – Meridea? No, Svarta. The top of the world, miles and miles from anywhere.

She knew even as she thought it that Irris wouldn't leave her. Not unless Sorrow forced her to.

And how could Sorrow manage without her? Bad enough to have lost Rasmus, and Luvian; to lose Irris would be catastrophic.

But sending her away was the only thing Sorrow could think of that might keep her friend safe a little longer. Long enough for Sorrow to come up with a way to stop Vespus once and for all.

Sorrow spent the next precious hour barricading the passageway, piling trunks against the entrance. It was a rather empty gesture, but she had to sleep in that room, and the idea of waking up to find Vespus leering over her whilst she was abed was too much.

She managed a quick wash before she pulled on her dress for the night, a sky-blue sheath that made her look more capable and mature than she felt. She pulled her hair into a knot and applied a little make-up, lining her eyes and rouging her cheeks. It did nothing to hide her haunted expression, nor the occasional tremor in her hands as Vespus's words replayed in her mind, but it would have to do. Then a servant was knocking her door, and she pushed away the encounter and squared her shoulders. It was time to work.

The dinner was an uneasily tense one, but only for Sorrow, and, she suspected, Charon. Despite agreeing they might talk, Sorrow had chosen to sit between Arran and Bayrum, ignoring the momentary shock on Charon's face when she didn't take her customary place beside him. He covered it well, turning to Kaspira, but Sorrow caught his eye as she reached for her drink and saw the pain there. He knew what she was doing. And why. It hurt him.

The rest of the council were jubilant, all pleased to be invited back to the Jedenvat; even Lord Samad smiled at her. Well, almost all of them...

Balthasar was behaving as he always did, supercilious and superior, but every now and then Sorrow glanced at him and saw his mask had slipped, revealing a face taut with worry. Though he was pretending to the others he'd received his invite too, beneath his act he was plainly terrified. And that gave Sorrow a fierce burst of joy, finally, to have something to hold over him.

Is this how it feels to be Vespus? she wondered as the table raised their glasses to her in the final toast of the night. To have the ability to humiliate and crush on a whim? To keep a person like a mouse dangling from a paw, not knowing whether murder or mercy would come, unable to do anything but squirm and hope? That thought ruined any pleasure she had in making him wait, no matter that he might deserve it. She might despise Balthasar, but she didn't want to be like Vespus.

Though she came close to it when, after the dinner was over, Balthasar followed her out, trailing her far past the point he should have turned to his own rooms, forcing her to stop and confront him.

"What is it, Senator Lys?" she asked, too tired not to be direct.

Balthasar's lip curled.

"I assume once you've had your fun I'll have my invitation to my role?"

His scornful tone lit a fire in Sorrow. "Excuse me?"

"I'm the only member of the Jedenvat to have not received one."

"Then, *technically*, you're not a member of the Jedenvat, are you?" Sorrow snapped before she could think better of it.

He froze, his lips parted.

"Don't tell me you're worried?" Sorrow said, smiling humourlessly. "After all, surely you have other options. I'm hardly your only master."

"I don't know what you're talking about," he said stiffly, not meeting her eye.

But she was sure he knew exactly what she meant. He'd been the one who brought Lamentia into the palace, the one who'd given it to Harun, on Vespus's orders – Vespus had told her so.

"Oh, I think you do."

He blinked at her for a moment, frozen, and then drew himself up to his full height, his handsome face blank as he looked down at her. "Am I relieved of my duties, Your Excellency?"

Sorrow itched to say yes.

But she had to deal with Vespus first. What was it Vine had said to her, all those months ago – he wanted the organ grinder, not the monkey. So did she. Balthasar could wait.

"No," she said finally. "I ran out of time earlier, that's all. I didn't manage to write to Lord Day either, though he's not stalking me through the corridors. You'll have your invitation in the morning, before the swearing-in."

Balthasar looked startled, and then shrugged. "Good. Fine. Well, I'll bid you goodnight, then."

He turned and walked off. With a sigh, she made her way back down to her office. She would write the letters now, start afresh tomorrow.

She signed and sealed them, leaving them on Charon's and Balthasar's desks when she found the doors to their offices unlocked.

A headache beginning, Sorrow returned to her rooms, almost falling over the great pile of trunks by the door of her parlour.

Her stomach lurched and she hurried into the bedroom,

throwing open her wardrobe door.

The wall she'd built earlier was gone; the back of her wardrobe exposed once more. For a moment her blood froze. And then she realized, it must have been the servants; of course they'd packed her trunks while she was at dinner. She closed the door and grabbed one of the chairs from her breakfast table, wedging it under the handle. Just because Vespus had said he was leaving that night didn't mean he would.

She changed into her nightgown and climbed into bed, closing her eyes, willing herself to sleep.

Dawn was a long time coming.

She didn't sleep at all; every bump and creak had her convinced Vespus hadn't left, and was coming through the passageway to threaten her again. At five, she got up and ordered a pot of coffee, calling for a second barely an hour later, relieved when the caffeine finally kicked in, even though it left her feeling as though her insides were shuddering. She was awake, at least.

That would do for now, she told herself as she dressed. She only realized her tunic was inside out when Irris came to fetch her, and pointed it out.

"You shouldn't change it," Irris said, as Sorrow reached for the hem. "It'll change your luck and you don't want that just before you're sworn in."

Sorrow tugged the garment over her shoulder and righted it, before slipping it back over her head. Irris watched her but said nothing else, at least until Sorrow yawned.

"Late night?"

"Balthasar stopped me after the dinner in a snit because

28

he hadn't had his invitation. I ended up writing it before I went to bed."

"You're really keeping him, then?" Irris said.

Sorrow bit back a sigh. "Who do I replace him with?"

"Literally anyone. A street dog would be a better choice. Certainly more loyal."

"Rhannon has been through enough, lately," Sorrow replied. "I don't want to cause any more upheaval."

Irris shook her head as Sorrow spoke, bewildered by her decision, and her logic. "So you'll keep a senator who doesn't do his job, and an ambassador who helped kill the old chancellor?"

"Irris—"

"Forget it. It's your call. I came to tell you they're ready, that's all. I'll see you there."

Irris turned on her heel and left, Sorrow following her. *Look on the bright side*, she told herself; *if Irris isn't speaking to you, at least she'll stop asking questions you can't answer. You won't have to send her away; she'll leave.* But it wasn't a comforting thought.

The swearing-in, for all its importance, took a matter of moments. In the Round Chamber, witnessed by the Jedenvat, and Irris, Sorrow stood before Charon Day, placed her hand on the original Charter of Rhannon, the document her regicidal ancestors had drawn up after their coup, and vowed to serve and protect Rhannon until the day she died. That was it.

Years of dread as she'd watched Harun drive the country into the ground, knowing one day it would be hers. Months of campaigning, and planning, of being threatened and attacked by the Sons of Rhannon. For this: a hand on an old scroll that was mostly illegible now, and a scrawled signature on a newer one.

In less time than it took her to brush her hair, she became the official and sworn leader of Rhannon. And she had just two weeks to find a way to save it from Vespus Corrigan.

3

End of the Rainbow

The North Marches were beautiful in autumn, the light warm and buttery, deepening to caramel as the sun began to set. It turned the white walls of the buildings they passed to slabs of toffee, gave the people a burnished golden glow as they reached out with tokens, flowers and food for Sorrow.

Her country was beautiful. Her people were beautiful. They glowed with health and life, and Sorrow's heart ached at the sight of them. Not one of them cowered like a kicked dog as her carriage rumbled slowly through the streets. Now they were straight-backed and smiling, meeting her gaze with hope. Before they'd left the first village Sorrow's carriage was full of gifts: bangles hammered from silver with the date of the election engraved on them; scented pillows stuffed with herbs, her name embroidered in curling letters on the front; endless packages of cakes and pastries that Dougray – her

31

new bodyguard – warned her in a low voice she was not to eat.

As if they would poison her. They loved her.

When Sorrow left the carriage, children clamoured around her, shy and smiling; their mothers and fathers ushering them forward to meet her, presenting babes in arms and beaming as Sorrow pressed her lips to their foreheads, inhaling the milk-and-honey smell of them. At points the streets were lined two or three deep; people told her they'd come from all over the North Marches to see her; some had even come from the East and West Marches to be there at the beginning of the tour.

Bunting hung along the route, the entire district scented with sugar, fried dough, and cinnamon, tempting her enough that she broke Dougray's order and pinched pieces of pastry from a peach tart when he wasn't looking. Music wound out of every corner; a reed flute played a climbing melody, lost as the carriage moved on, replaced by violin jig, which gave way to a trumpet fanfare. Drums beat under it all, wild as a happy heartbeat.

It was so different to how it had been before. Sorrow could scarcely believe just half a year ago these same people would have been clad in grey and black, their faces lowered to the ground. Instead of singing they would have been silent; instead of smiling their mouths would have remained stiff, their eyes deadened. They'd embraced joy so easily, opening their arms to it, as though it had always been there inside them, beneath the grief and the despair. It was exactly what she'd wanted for Rhannon, exactly what she'd hoped to build.

It broke her.

Not outwardly; before them she kept her mask in place,

her smile a rictus grin, eyes unblinking as she thanked them, over and over, shaking hands until her arm ached and Dougray insisted she leave. But inside she was shattering, piece by piece.

These were the very people Vespus wanted her to displace, so that he might have their land. These people, who jostled to be near her, who urged her to dance with them, eat with them, be one of them. Olive farmers, winemakers, schoolteachers, artisans and poets.

The young, who saw themselves in her and trusted her for it; seeing what they could achieve if they dared. The elderly, who'd believed before Sorrow that they'd go the Grace of Death and Rebirth without ever smiling publicly again. They smiled at her now, mouths pink and gummy, proud of the brand-new lines that creased the corners of their eyes. Every smile was a needle in her skin, until every inch of her felt as though it was bleeding.

When she greeted Bayrum at his manse, his face glowing with pride and joy, she could barely look him in the eye. But she did, lifting her head and grinning, laughing as he swung her around, ignoring the frowns of her bodyguard.

Sorrow wore a flowing orange gown to the dinner, and beamed the whole way through it, dancing with Bayrum's eldest son, Shar, pretending to be embarrassed when Bayrum said how well they danced together.

She doubted very much they did – they'd both been born under Harun's mourning rule, and it was the first time either of them had danced in public. Irris had given Sorrow hasty lessons she'd cobbled together from books, and Sorrow assumed from Shar's rigid stance he'd had instruction too. His movements were beat-perfect but stiff, as though all his focus was on the dance; twice she caught Shar counting steps, his expression pained with concentration, and she expected her own was the twin of it.

Sorrow drank and ate everything put before her, ignoring how her stomach churned with fear and self-loathing as she accepted yet more praise and congratulations. She acted her heart out, behaving as though she didn't have a care in the world, and her attitude was infectious, the room full of laughter and chatter, everyone feeding on the energy she forced into the room.

Irris didn't join in. Sorrow could feel her watching; every spin she took in Shar's arms, every glass of sparkling wine she poured down her neck, Irris catalogued it all. There was something about the way she sat with Bayrum and his wife that made Sorrow feel childish, as though they were the adults sitting watching the children run wild, and Sorrow railed against it. The more she felt watched, the louder Sorrow laughed, the more fun she pretended to have. However, when she caught sight of her friend's face, she saw Irris didn't look convinced.

She stayed until Sorrow left the party in the early hours of the morning, shadowing her though the hallways to the upper floors, to the room beside hers.

"Goodnight," Irris said, hovering outside her door.

"Night," Sorrow replied without looking at her.

The closing of Irris's door was nothing more than the quiet click of a latch, but it echoed through Sorrow like a thunderclap, and she told herself again this was for the best. She had to protect Irris. She had to protect everyone. It was her job.

They didn't speak at all the next day, somehow managing to get through breakfast, the departure from Bayrum's home, and the journey across the North Marches to Prekara in silence. Sorrow felt the absence of conversation, how unnatural it was for them, and she hated that it had to be that way. They should have been gossiping – Irris should have been teasing her about Shar, and mocking her dancing. But she wasn't; her head was buried in a book, shutting Sorrow out.

The crowds in Prekara were as large as those of the North Marches and just as joyful. Sorrow visited a newly opened brewery, a school, the temple for the Grace of Family and Kinship, before heading to the main square to give a speech. From there to Kaspira's town house in the merchant quarter, overlooking the main canal.

The quarter was a strange mix of architecture, everything built with white Rhannish stone, but the abundance of canals and waterways meant the houses were tall and narrow, reminding Sorrow of her journey through the streets in Adavaria. Which made her think of Luvian, and how she was in the district his family called home.

Kaspira's town house was too small to hold any kind of event, though Sorrow, her bodyguard and Irris would be staying there. The reception to welcome Sorrow to Prekara was in a refurbished dance hall – not, Sorrow noted with relief, the one where she and Mael were attacked.

She wore a gauzy yellow vest with thin straps and matching wide-legged pants to the party, piling her hair atop her head, working her way around the room until she was dizzy. She met fisherfolk and merchants, tradespeople, and even, Dougray told her in a furious tone as they returned to Kaspira's town house, a suspected crime lord. Not a Rathbone, much to her disappointment.

She'd half-hoped Luvian would do as he'd done at the

Gathering, and sneak in to see her. Every time someone tapped her shoulder she turned, already smiling to see him, only to have to fix it in place as she was disappointed.

How to get him back? She could hardly announce she'd decided to forgive him for being involved, however loosely, in Arkady's attempt on her life. Well, she could – she was the chancellor, she could actually do what she wanted – but she didn't want to set that kind of precedent, especially after Queen Melisia of Rhylla had offered a reward for his capture. If she was to pardon him, she'd have to claim new evidence had emerged to prove his innocence, and she was at a loss as to what that evidence could be. Ironically, she was sure Luvian himself could have come up with something plausible. If only she knew where he was. All she knew was he wasn't there and she needed him.

When she finally collapsed on to her bed, she heard a rustling beneath the sheets, and as she pulled them back, she found a note, signed in a familiar hand.

I wish I could have seen you tonight, but I couldn't, because you still haven't pardoned me.

That's a lie. I did see you tonight. You just didn't see me. Because you still haven't pardoned me.

Yellow suits you.

Know what suits me? Amnesty. Clemency.
REPRIEVE.

Stop torturing me and let me back into your life. My world is meaningless without you. And it's not fair I don't get to go parties after all the work I did.

L

Sorrow stared at the note for a full minute before she threw herself at the window, hauling it open and leaning precariously over the sill to peer out.

"Luvian?" she whispered. "Luvian?"

Far below, the canal was ink and shadow, rimed by the occasional glint of light as whatever stirred down there disturbed the surface. There was no sign of anyone still around, or that anyone had been there at all.

She drew back, fetching the gas lamp and using it to examine the window. No fingerprints on the glass, no footprints on the sill. Perhaps he'd come in some other way, through the front door, in disguise, or snuck through a lower window.

Why hadn't he waited to see her? He could have stayed, could have hidden. At that thought, she darted to the wardrobe and opened it, hoping that he was in there, fallen asleep. But there was nothing aside from her clothes for tomorrow, hanging forlornly, as though they knew she was disappointed in them for not being what she wanted to see.

She returned to the bed, pulling the window shut on the way, and read the note again. She fell asleep with it crumpled in her hand.

The East Marches were next, and Sorrow spent the afternoon exploring the northern coast, and meeting the business owners who wanted to share their plans with her. She nodded dutifully as they told her how they would build inns and cottages for holidaymakers, how they planned to mimic Meridea, and its famed riverside resorts, surrounding the beaches with restaurants and theatres and pleasure gardens. Through it all Sorrow smiled, promising to come and open them, even stay there, on holiday herself.

They moved inland, to visit the wineries and vine growers, all thrilled to be able to grow grapes that did not leave a bitter taste in the mouth, like those Harun had permitted. As she toured the vineyards all she could see was what Vespus would do with the land in the North Marches, how he could use his ability to alter the landscape. Would he? she asked herself. And would a parcel of land in the North Marches be enough? What if he wanted more? Of course he'd want more, people always wanted more.

She still had no idea how to stop him. Time ticked on, the days passed into night with indecent haste and she was no closer to a solution.

Unless. . . Could she kill him? She closed her eyes, trying to imagine it: sneaking through the passageway to his rooms, holding a pillow over his face and pressing down. Which would be fine, as long as he lay there silently, hands folded on his stomach, allowing her to murder him.

She couldn't stab him; she didn't think she'd have the nerve to do it – stabbing someone felt, well, *personal*. Not poison, either, he'd be too alert for it, although the justice of it would be poetic. The thought of it made her smile darkly. It would be fitting.

An accident, though, cunningly arranged? Or an assassin? How did one find an assassin? Luvian would know, she thought, and her smile widened, a hand moving to the pocket where his note hid. She imagined his face if she asked him to set up interviews with Laethea's premier hired killers.

Then she remembered the weight of Arkady Rathbone bearing her down into a bath full of water, the fire in her lungs as she tried not to breathe, not to drown, and the tiny amount of happiness slipped away.

38

There was Rasmus to consider, too. Could she kill his father?

"We're here," Irris said as the gates to the Days' estate were drawn back, the first words she'd spoken directly to Sorrow since the North Marches.

"It's nice to be back," Sorrow replied.

"I think Arran is putting us in the same suite we used last time."

"Good. I know where that is, at least."

"There's a surprise for you," Irris said softly. "At the house."

"What kind of surprise?" Sorrow asked as the carriage drew to a halt.

"You'll see," Irris said, following Dougray out of the carriage. Arran Day – Irris's older brother, and the senator of the East Marches – came bounding down the steps towards them, long legs taking two steps at a time, his face – so like his sister's – splitting into a wide, boyish grin. He embraced Irris, whispering something in her ear, before releasing her. Irris shot Sorrow a glance that was almost shy, and then left them.

"Chancellor," Arran said, holding out his hand to Sorrow.

She took it, barely beginning to shake it before he pulled her into a hug too.

"We have something for you," he said, guiding her to one of the lower parlours, the bodyguard trailing them.

"Irris said. Do I get a clue?"

"It's something you wanted."

"That hardly narrows it down," Sorrow replied.

"Greedy," Arran laughed. "Close your eyes," he added as they paused outside the door. Sorrow obediently did so, but he put his hands over them anyway.

She heard the door open, and Arran gently urged her forward.

"Surprise!" he cried, freeing her.

She blinked, and saw Mael standing before her.

"*No*," she whispered, before she could stop herself.

She heard Arran's indrawn breath as Mael, whose face had briefly lit with hope, staggered back as though she'd struck him.

"No, I didn't mean ... I meant..." She meant that things had changed. That he wasn't safe as long as Vespus was there. In all of the awkwardness between her and Irris, Sorrow had forgotten to tell her not to find Mael.

But she couldn't tell them why. And she couldn't take it back.

She glanced at Irris, at the hurt on her face. Mael was meant to be a peace offering, Sorrow realized. A way for Irris to show she trusted Sorrow's decision-making.

"You told me to find him," Irris said, confusion and irritation in her voice.

"I know. And I meant it." Sorrow just hadn't expected it to happen so fast. She turned to Mael. "I wanted you found. Truly." She took a step forward, stilling when he took one back.

"I think we'll give you two some privacy," Arran said, grasping his sister's arm and pulling her with him. "The reception starts at eight."

Sorrow nodded, watching them go, before looking back at Mael.

There was stubble on his chin and cheeks, shadows beneath his eyes. His clothes hung loose, as if he'd lost weight, though only two weeks had passed since she last saw him. Worst of all, he smelled stale – when she'd moved closer Sorrow had caught

40

it – like he'd been wearing the same clothes for days, perhaps even sleeping in them.

"Do you want to sit?" she asked.

He followed her to a set of sofas, sitting opposite her, folding his arms over his body.

It disturbed Sorrow, the way he shielded himself, head ducked as if he was braced for a blow. "How have you been?" she asked in a soft voice.

"They said you wanted to see me," he said, ignoring her question.

"Yes. I did. I do."

His voice held no trace of affection, or happiness. There wasn't even any real curiosity in it as he replied. "It doesn't seem like it."

Sorrow's mouth had turned dry, and she swallowed. "No. No, Mael, that wasn't... I'm not... I'm sorry," she said, fumbling through her sentence. "Mael... Where have you been?"

"With friends."

"What friends?" Sorrow was puzzled. She'd been under the impression he knew no one. "Here in Rhannon?"

When she realized he wasn't going to reply, she continued, the words tumbling out like a waterfall. "I did want to see you. I wanted to find you, to ask you to come home."

"Home?" He looked at her, frowning.

"To the Winter Palace. But ... things have changed." Her mind filled with Vespus, and his threat to murder those she loved. "I don't think it's a good idea for you to be there right now, but that doesn't mean I don't want you around."

"I don't understand."

Sorrow shook her head. "I can't explain. I need you to trust me, though. Please?" She tried to catch his eye. "I'm ashamed,

41

Mael. I'm ashamed of the way I treated you – the same way Harun treated me. I know how awful that is. I want you to have a place there. I want you to feel like you belong."

"Just not right now." He lowered his head.

Her heart was beating fast in her chest, nervous sweat beading her chest and shoulders. Sorrow didn't know what she'd expected, but it wasn't this. There was no trace of the warm, eager boy she'd met just a few months ago, and guilt pulled at her. If the boy was gone, it was because she'd banished him, and it was up to her to bring him back.

"Please," she said, leaning forward and laying a hand on his arm. "Please believe me."

He looked at her, his expression unreadable. "All right."

If she hadn't been sitting already, the relief that crashed through her would have knocked her from her feet. It wasn't the enthusiastic response she'd hoped for, but she could work with this.

"So, when should I come?" Mael spoke again.

Sorrow hesitated. "I can't say. But I hope soon," she said. "Very soon. And I'm sure Irris and Arran won't mind if you stay here, until then. There's a party tonight..."

His eyes narrowed. "Your victory party? No."

His tone made it clear there was no point in trying to convince him, and they lapsed into awkward silence, Sorrow not daring to speak for fear of saying something wrong, which seemed likely. She'd been worried about him the last time she'd seen him, but now she was terrified for him. Everything about him had changed; his fundamental, earnest Mael-ness had been squashed out of him. It had warped into something sour and strange; who were these "friends" he'd stayed with, or was he just saying that to save face?

"I think I'll go to my room." He rose, still not looking at her. "You should start getting ready. You can't be late to your own party."

Sorrow had the strangest feeling that if she didn't do something, right now, she might never see him again.

"Mael..."

He paused, turning to her.

"I'm sorry," she said.

His gaze flickered briefly to hers, and she thought she saw a flash of something there. Then it was as though someone behind his eyes had pulled the curtains.

He gave a brisk nod, and left her in the Days' parlour. Sorrow blinked away the stinging in her eyes.

That night she wore green, a dress that clung to her hips and flared like the caudal fin of a merrow at her feet. She danced with Arran, and anyone else who asked, shook hands with everyone who offered, ate and drank whatever she was given. She was the belle of the ball; to look at her no one would think she had a sorrow other than her name. But inside she keeled like ship in a storm. She caught the hand of Arran as he spun her around and wondered what the next week would hold, and if it could be any worse.

The next morning dawned grey and overcast, a pall hanging over the estate; Sorrow could feel it before she even got out of bed, lethargy weighing her limbs down, making her want to burrow under the quilt and stay there, cocooned in her room. When she finally made her way down to breakfast, she found Irris there, alone.

Sorrow paused briefly in the doorway, long enough for Irris to note her hesitation, then crossed to the table.

"I can leave, if you want," Irris said. "I've finished eating."

"No, it's fine. You don't have to leave. I don't want to drive you out of your own breakfast room." Sorrow sat opposite her, pulling a pot of honey towards her.

Silence thickened between them. Irris was watching her, and Sorrow refused to meet her eye, instead focusing on the honey.

Irris put her cup down, hard enough to startle Sorrow. "OK, enough. I'm sick of this. Two weeks ago, you were fine. We were fine. Then we got back from the final presentation, went to bed, and the next morning you were a wreck. It was as though someone had drained the life out of you overnight. And now this? Keeping Balthasar? Letting Vespus stay? That's not you. I know it isn't. I know something is wrong."

"I... It's..." Panic deadened Sorrow's tongue, leaving her stammering while Irris fixed her with curious eyes.

"You can either tell me, or I'll find out by myself," Irris threatened. "You know I will. Starting with Balthasar and Vespus."

As terror clutched at Sorrow's heart; she realized she was out of time. If she wanted to protect Irris from Vespus, this was it.

"I'd like you to be the Rhannish ambassador to Svarta."

Pure shock wiped Irris's face free of expression. "What?" she said, her voice small in a way Sorrow had never heard before.

Sorrow nodded.

"I need an ambassador there and I think it should be you."

"What on Laethea makes you think that? I don't speak Svartan. I don't know anything about Svarta. Why me?"

For Irris's sake, she had to make it good. Make it something Irris couldn't argue.

Make it something Irris wouldn't want to argue...

"Because I need some time apart from you." Sorrow's heart fractured, but she continued. "I need space to learn how to be chancellor without you telling me what to do."

Irris stared at her, her mouth open.

"Let me get this straight: you're banishing me to the top of the world because you think I'm controlling?"

"No, of course not. I just. . ." Sorrow stopped, unable to continue.

Irris was looking at her as though she'd never seen her before. "Wow. So, when am I to go? Do I finish the tour with you? Or shall I start packing now? I suppose I should be grateful you told me to my face, at least."

Sorrow tensed. "What does that mean?"

"When you were finished with Rasmus, you let him figure it out through overhearing Bayrum. Nice to know I warranted more." She shoved her chair away from the table so hard it fell to the floor, slamming the door on her way out.

Sorrow was frozen. She knew she was hurting Irris and she knew she deserved to be hurt back. She just hadn't expected it.

The following day, when the carriage left the East Marches, Irris's absence was everywhere; the space where she ought to have sat, the gap by Sorrow's side where her best friend had always been. The lack of her presence swallowed Sorrow whole, and she had to battle against herself to keep from having the coach return to the East Marches and telling Irris the truth.

In Asha she met quartz miners, and engineers, and those who worked the border between Rhannon and Astria. This far south the sun was still merciless, even in autumn, and when she returned to Samad's palatial villa she'd caught the sun, drawing out freckles on her nose and burning her shoulders.

The following night, she wore a demure blue gown with a high neckline that irritated the sunburn, worsening her mood. There was no dancing – Sorrow was one of the only women in the room, the other being Samad's silent wife – instead they had a formal dinner, and listened to a sombre reed flute concert that sent Sorrow into a trance. She was glad Samad hadn't asked her if she'd enjoyed the night, because she didn't have the will to lie to him.

Then to the South Marches, and the home of Balthasar. Sorrow remembered a time when he'd been sallow-skinned and dull-eyed, gripped by the Lamentia he'd secreted into the Winter Palace for Vespus. The man who welcomed her to his home was a stark contrast to that memory – colour high in his cheeks, his eyes sparkling – and Sorrow soon found out why. Rather than meeting farmers, or merchants, or tradespeople, he'd arranged for her to visit the prison there, and the local headquarters of the Decorum Ward. His agenda for the trip was clear; she would be bold to challenge decades-old tradition. Bold, and foolish. His confidence had clearly returned now he was officially back on the Jedenvat.

In the Decorum Ward's headquarters, the Ward had smirked at her, calling her "Miss Ventaxis" instead of "Chancellor", until she corrected them, which only made them smirk more. And, just when Sorrow thought the trip couldn't be worse, Meeren Vine arrived, invited by Balthasar to conduct the tour of the prison.

Vine cheerfully pointed out everyone who was imprisoned because of him, his fleshy lips a curving leer as Sorrow tried to hide her discomfort.

"This is the murky side of governing," he said as they passed a cell occupied by a man screaming repeatedly. "Reality as opposed to glamour. The opposite of your balls and parties. Why you have me. To be your hands in the dark. To remove the things that make your life less rosy, and hide them away. Without the likes of me, Rhannon's dirty laundry would be there for all to see."

She heard a threat in his words, as though he knew what she planned for the Decorum Ward. But if anything, what he said cemented her belief she was right to disband the Ward and replace them with something more just. Vine's justice was brutal, and unforgiving. Sorrow wanted more for Rhannon than that. Democracy, like Meridea and Rhylla had.

But there was a part of his speech she kept coming back to: the hands in the dark, the concealer of the unpleasant. . .

There was something in there, she could feel it, scratching at her brain, burrowing in and refusing to let her move on. Hands in the dark, keeping things hidden. . . It went around and around in her head, even as she dressed for the evening. She put on full make-up, each stroke of a brush an act of war against her enemies.

Balthasar didn't deserve the indigo dress she wore to his soirée, even though his was the most lavish one so far. Champagne flowed freely, waiters travelling the room with decadent morsels: rare roast beef on black salt bread, crab in saffron cream on butter puffs that melted the moment they hit the tongue. His food rivalled anything she'd eaten in Rhylla, anything she'd eaten anywhere. It was a beautiful, elegant night, and yet completely without soul. Sorrow spent the entire time wishing she had her back to the wall, sure that if she wasn't careful someone would stab her in it.

She also missed Irris.

Finally, the West Marches; the former creative heart of

Rhannon, eagerly coming back to life, where she met singers, and dancers, and a troupe of actors, who'd written a play about her.

"About me?" Sorrow was stunned. She looked at the leader, a young woman with shining eyes, a strip of her hair dyed bright gold, wondering if she was joking.

It seemed not. "Yes, Your Excellency." The woman nodded eagerly. "I wanted to record what you've achieved, and what you've done for us."

"You gave us back our art," another woman piped up, wrestling her way forward to beam up at Sorrow. "It's what sets us apart from animals. Being able to write, and play instruments, and dance, and paint. To make stories out of chaos. And you gave us that back. You said especially you wanted those things to be taught. You're the new mother of Rhannish art. That's why we're called Sorrow's Players, and it's our great honour to perform for you."

Being called the "Mother of Rhannish art" both pleased and embarrassed Sorrow, and she fanned herself, flustered. She turned to her left, only to falter when she remembered Irris wasn't there.

"I've never seen a play before." Sorrow turned back to the players and forced herself to smile.

"Then we're doubly honoured."

They led her to the best seat in the house, a glass of champagne slipped into her hand, as the curtains rose on the freshly painted stage and the play began.

Sorrow was flattered, and touched, though it was a little awkward to watch the events of the last few months acted out onstage, especially as the play turned out to be a musical. A few times, she turned to catch Irris's eye, needing someone to giggle with, only remember once again that Irris had gone.

It sobered her, even as the actor playing Sorrow gave a rousing interpretation of the time when Sorrow had visited the stone mine. She was glad Mael wasn't there, because he was the villain of the piece, creeping about the stage. Though she understood why they'd done it – after all, they didn't know about Vespus – it made her uncomfortable to see her own, old feelings manifest in the show.

Still, she applauded loudly, getting to her feet as they took their bows, and at the party afterwards she'd told them all how brilliant they were, asking them to sign her programme. She'd worn the last of her rainbow gowns that night, a strapless violet piece with a gauzy skirt that fanned like petals around her, and she'd drunk date wine with the company until the early hours.

"I bet you can't wait to get back to Istevar. You must be tired to the bones," Tuva said the following morning as she walked Sorrow to her carriage.

Sorrow stopped dead as something inside her mind clicked. That was it.

The bones.

Hands in the dark, hiding the terrible... Yes. It was the only way to defend herself against Vespus. It would not be pleasant, but Sorrow knew what she had to do.

4

The Proper Season

Sorrow returned to Istevar like a conquering general; to streets full of people cheering and – in absence of real flowers being in season – throwing homemade, fabric blooms in front of her carriage. Lovely as they were, they were also a problem, catching in the spokes and around the horses' hooves, needing to be cleared before the carriage could move on.

It amused Sorrow to see the Decorum Ward forced to clean the roads so she could pass; her only regret was that Vine wasn't there to join in too. She would have liked to see him with a broom in hand, clearing the way for her to get to the Winter Palace.

They drew to a stop outside the gates of Istevar's cemetery to allow the Ward time to clear the final stretch to the palace. A better, more dutiful daughter might have taken the opportunity to go and pay tribute to her parents at the Ventaxis monument...

But Sorrow was not Harun and Cerena's daughter. And though she planned to visit them, very soon, it wouldn't be to honour them.

She needed to remove the bones of the real Sorrow. She had to be the hands in the dark that hid away the things that could hurt Rhannon. The bones, innocent as they were, could be that instrument in Vespus's hands. They had to go.

As long as the bones of the real Sorrow lay with Cerena in the mausoleum, the proof was there for the taking. If she moved them she could call Vespus's bluff; refuse him the land and tell him to expose her, if he wished. He could make the accusation, but he'd have no evidence. He could call for a search of the tomb, but there would be nothing there. He'd look like a liar, and Sorrow could send him away, if Melisia didn't summon him home first for shaming her. It would be over.

It wouldn't be that simple. Removing the bones would be a mission that only she could undertake. She could trust no one else, which meant sneaking out of the Winter Palace – no easy feat for the chancellor.

Then there was the question of her real parents – could Vespus use them against her somehow? Sorrow thought not – at least, not without the bones. If he'd thought for a second they might have any leverage over her, he would surely have dangled them in front of her already.

Unless he hadn't found them, yet. Or even thought to – he might believe he'd done enough to secure her obedience. He might not have considered using her birth family.

It was a long shot, but she had to make sure he never could. She needed to find out who and where they were, and destroy any records of them, make it impossible for him to trace them.

She needed Luvian. The thought slipped into her mind,

unbidden. But Luvian would likely ask why she was looking, and she couldn't risk him digging further, and doing as she'd done and realizing what had happened. Instead, she'd have to ask Charon.

As the carriage lurched to life once more, Sorrow continued waving absently at the people.

She tried not to think about her real parents, because she couldn't keep a grip on her feelings. They changed daily, slick like eel skin and slipping from her grasp.

Sometimes she missed them, which was impossible, considering she'd never known them. There was a small part of her that still, despite everything she'd fought for, wished she could forge her own path – as the child of commoners, she could have done that. Her grandmother hadn't just stolen a baby, but a whole destiny.

Then there were the times that she hated them. For allowing her to be stolen. She knew that was irrational, but it made no difference. She hated them for losing her, and for not seeking her out. Or if they'd tried, for not trying harder. She hated them for being strangers to her, and for having lives that had nothing to do with her now. She might have brothers and sisters; she might be an aunt. She knew nothing about them, and she blamed them for it.

Mostly, thinking of them made her sad. Because Rhannon's survival meant they could never know who she really was. They would always have to be strangers, and she had to destroy the proof they were more. Otherwise, she would never be free of Vespus.

But it would be worth it, to save Rhannon. That would be worth anything.

The carriage juddered to a halt again and shook Sorrow from her thoughts. They were back at the Winter Palace.

She followed Dougray out of the carriage. No one was waiting for her – she'd expected Charon, at least, to be ready to welcome her home. But the steps were bare, and Sorrow's spirits sank lower as she mounted them and entered the palace.

Dozens of people milled about, all laden with items for the ball that night: armfuls of taffeta and silk, piles of candles for the chandeliers, barrels of oil for the gas lamps. Servants hurried past with vases full of flowers that must have been imported from hot houses in Meridea, men and women balancing trays of glassware, walking deliberately, determination and fear tautening their faces. Dougray stayed close to Sorrow as he escorted her through the scurrying workers, into the main foyer.

Curiosity made her follow the staff, eager to see the changes they'd made to the ballroom. She expected something beautiful – maybe not as magical as the ballroom at Castle Adavaria, but the Rhannish version of it.

When she got there, it looked as though an earthquake had struck the room. The chandeliers were on the floor, their ropes slack beside them, as servants used knives to remove the old candles. Tables and chairs were stacked in the corner, vases of flowers lining the walls like sentries, dusty footprints covering the floor. As they realized the chancellor was there everyone stopped working, rising to face her and bowing their heads.

"It looks . . . great. Carry on," she said, before fleeing back to the foyer, her cheeks hot.

Charon wasn't in his office when she arrived there, though he'd left a small pile of things in hers that needed her approval. She worked slowly through them, then made her way to the

53

window. Her spider friend was there, fat in the centre of her web, waiting for her prey to come to her.

Clever, Sorrow thought. Set the trap and wait. Not like Sorrow, scrambling frantically to stay afloat, banishing her friends and alienating her allies.

By now Charon would know she was sending Irris to go to Svarta. Perhaps that was why he hadn't been there to meet her; maybe he'd begun avoiding her.

She knew it was stupid, but she was annoyed that no one had thought to welcome her home. That no one was there to ask her how the trip had been, or what she'd seen and done. What, if anything she'd achieved, or learned, or decided while she'd toured Rhannon. Sorrow caught sight of her reflection in a mirror on the opposite side of the room, her lips pursed petulantly, and it made her smile.

"Chancellor for two weeks and already you're in a mood because the sun isn't orbiting around you," she murmured.

"Pardon, Your Excellency?"

Sorrow jumped as Dougray spoke. She'd forgotten he was there, waiting beyond the doorway, still not used to having a bodyguard inside the palace. "I. . . Do you know where the vice chancellor is?" she fudged.

"I don't – I can have someone find out."

"No, it doesn't matter. I'm finished here."

Dougray shadowed Sorrow all the way to her suite, dodging the harried staff rushing about on the way. The doors to Irris's rooms were closed as she passed, and Sorrow didn't pause outside them, heading straight to her own. She left the bodyguard in her public parlour and retreated to her bedroom.

The first thing she did was open the wardrobe and check the passageway for any sign Vespus had used it. She didn't know what she was looking for, but none of her clothes seemed to have been disturbed, and the air that washed over her as she opened the secret door was cool and scentless. No hint of plants, or earth.

As she turned to leave the wardrobe, she saw it.

A dark blue garment bag hanging on the back of the door.

Sorrow lifted the navy velvet to reveal an expanse of ice-pale silk that seemed to glow, lit from within like a pearl. Her dress for the ball. Even from that small glimpse, she knew it was something extraordinary – more than the gowns she'd worn on the tour, even more than the honey-and-gold dress she'd worn in Rhylla.

She longed to try it on, to lift her mood, but she stopped herself. She needed to bathe first, wash the sweat and dust from the road off her skin. She was lucky she hadn't marked it with her hands. Carefully, she pulled the velvet back over the dress.

She checked the bathroom twice before she locked the door and put a chair under the handle, only then climbing into the bath. It was too hot, but she relished the burn, forcing herself to withstand the heat as though it was scouring her clean, watching her limbs and stomach redden. When it had cooled a little, she took a deep breath, lowered her head beneath the water and opened her eyes, looking up at the rippling world above.

Sorrow did this every time she bathed now. She climbed in, and then she forced her head under, holding her breath for as long as she could count, staying a few seconds longer each time. She knew it wasn't the same when she held herself under, remembered all too well how instinct had taken over when Arkady Rathbone tried to drown her, how she'd thrashed and panicked. But to Sorrow this felt useful. Every extra second she could train her body to survive this was a second longer she would live if it happened again.

Sorrow resurfaced and gasped, gripping the sides of the bath as water sluiced down her face, steam billowing from her hair. When her breathing had returned to normal, she leant back and closed her eyes.

Ines arrived with uncanny timing, just as Sorrow stepped out of her bath.

Sorrow watched in silent awe as Ines removed the cover with expert hands and laid the dress on the bed, lovingly spreading the skirt. It was white – whiter than the still-fresh paint on the outer walls of the palace, whiter than cream, or the blossoms of starflowers. She wondered at the lustre of it as she reverently ran a finger over the skirt, how the light chased across it, reflecting gently so the dress seemed to glow. Both girls stared at it for a moment, Ines with a satisfied smile at the corner of her lips, and Sorrow decided whatever she was paying her, she'd double it. This wasn't dressmaking – it was spellcasting – witchcraft – like in a story. Ines had woven magic into this dress.

First, Ines insisted Sorrow do some of her own magic with her hair and face.

"I'll be forced to kill you if you spill anything on the dress before it has debuted," she said, leaving Sorrow in no doubt she meant it. "Once everyone has seen it, go wild. Fling red wine and saffron salad all over yourself. But before that, the dress stays as virginal as Namyra was on her wedding night to King Adavere."

"Where in the legend does it say she was—"

"Make-up!" Ines interrupted Sorrow with a grin.

*

Ines buffed Sorrow's nails and painted them with a pale pink paint. She watched critically as Sorrow applied a sheer layer of dewy oil to her face, blending rouge into her cheeks and outlining her eyes. When Sorrow brushed her hair out, intending to leave it down, Ines simply said, "No," and took over, gathering Sorrow's hair into her hands and deftly arranging it into a large knot atop her head. "Trust me," the dressmaker said. So Sorrow did.

Her stomach tightened with anticipation as Ines stitched her into the gown. It was strapless, the front of the bodice high and demure, cut to skim her collarbones. Ines had beaded it with patterns wrought in pearl – the Rhannish flag, Sorrow realized, as she lightly traced it, a crown over her breastbone, a beaded heart beneath it, and thorns winding up over Sorrow's hips and chest. The back of the bodice, however, dipped to the base of her spine, leaving her back bare, and Sorrow understood now why Ines had insisted she wear her hair up. Ines had left part of the fluted skirt unstitched until it was on, protecting Sorrow's dignity by fitting it snugly against her skin, leaving no room for mishaps. It was clever, and daring.

"Has anyone else seen it?" Sorrow asked, as Ines bit the thread and then tied it off.

"No. I wanted you to be the first." She stepped back, eyeing Sorrow critically. "You're ready."

Ines walked her to the mirror as though she was leading her down the aisle at her wedding, and Sorrow couldn't help but gasp.

She looked like a promise. The moonlight gown brought out the gold of her skin and lit her eyes, making them sparkle. When she twisted, she saw the long column of her back, exposed by the dress, the hint of the dimples that lay at its base.

"You're lucky that there's never been a female chancellor before," Ines said, glowing with pride. "It means you don't have a template to follow."

Sorrow turned and swept Ines into a hug, managing to embrace her for merely a second before Ines wrestled free, immediately checking over her work.

Satisfied, she stepped out of reach. "Don't you dare hug anyone else," Ines said. "Not until—"

"Everyone's seen the dress, I know, I know." Sorrow's joy deflated like a soufflé. "I don't think we need to worry about me hugging anyone," she added.

Ines cast her a puzzled glance but said nothing.

"What time is it?" Sorrow asked, turning to the clock on the mantelpiece to answer her own question. "Time to go," she said.

Ines appeared behind her. "Is someone coming to walk down with you?" she asked.

Sorrow swallowed. Irris had been invited, before everything went so wrong, but Sorrow doubted she'd come. And she didn't know which would be worse – if Irris came, she'd be in Vespus's sights, reminding him of his threat. But if she didn't, Sorrow would lose her chance to try healing things between them before Irris left for Svarta.

"No. I'm the chancellor," Sorrow said finally. "I escort myself."

She carried herself, upright and regal, from her rooms, skirt held in her hands, relishing the surprise and awe that crossed Dougray's face as she emerged. She told herself it was because

58

ballgowns were still such a novelty to the Rhannish people, but she knew it wasn't the whole truth. She looked magnificent. She felt magnificent as she swept down the stairs, for a brief moment forgetting everything that troubled her as she relished the susurration of fabric in the otherwise silent halls.

Through the frosted glass in the doors to the ballroom, she could see golden light, and the ghostly silhouettes of people moving inside. Music escaped from the small gap between them, a violin that made her heart contract with the memories of both the ball in Rhylla and the time Vespus and Mael had played together in the Summer Palace.

Sorrow had had no hand in arranging the ball – chancellors might throw parties but they didn't arrange them, which was lucky for Sorrow, as she didn't know the first thing about it. She had known only that she wanted something like the ball in Rhylla. The sheer amount of detail – decorations, lighting, food, drinks, music, security, who to invite, deciding the order people would arrive in, hiring extra staff to work – had turned her brain to soup and she'd been more than happy to leave it in the hands of those who knew what they were doing. One of the perks of her job at least was getting to delegate.

Her only stipulation was that there would be no formal sit-down dinner, but that was mostly to give herself a chance to escape to the bathroom if she needed to. It was hard to slip out of a state dinner when everyone rose when you did and remained standing until you sat once more.

But tonight would be different. People would mingle, and circle the room. Ambassadors and representatives from every country, her senators and their chosen deputies and guests. Leading physicians, lawyers and ranking members of the Decorum Ward – Irris had refused to let her snub them, even as she planned to disband them.

Then there were the artisans and performers who'd so recently re-emerged. Those who'd already risen to fame or acclaim were there, as well as those who been famous before Harun banned pleasure. Among the celebrated were people whom Sorrow had met on her journey to leadership: Mael Braith, who'd guided her in the mines, and Malan, the giant man who'd mocked and then coached her down there. Teachers and nurses she'd spent time with, acolytes of the Graces. She'd wanted the party to feel as inclusive as it could, and she knew across Rhannon tonight other parties would be held, celebrating her.

After tonight, it was down to business. A smile curved her lips as she imagined dealing with Vespus. Freeing herself from his hold. Telling him the land he craved would never be his.

Sorrow was smiling as the doors to the ballroom opened, the music giving way to a fanfare, announcing she was there. She stepped into the room and turned to look at all her guests.

The smiled slipped like hot butter from her face as her eyes met Rasmus's.

5

Three Dances

He stood motionless beside his father as the room erupted into applause and cheers. Sorrow blinked, as though the tiny action might banish him – but he was there. Here. Vespus had brought him back with him.

That bastard.

Rasmus smiled, his face lighting at the sight of her, but Sorrow couldn't return his smile. Instead she shuddered with foreboding. He shouldn't be here.

As though he knew what she thought, Vespus smiled, dipping his head at her, before looking deliberately at his son. The message was loud and clear. Rasmus was here as a hostage. He just might not know it.

At the sight of Vespus's sickle-moon grin, Sorrow rallied herself. She'd wipe the smirk from his face soon enough. She could be a good puppet until then.

Sorrow stepped into the centre of the room, the movement commanding every eye remain on her. Her guests stepped back as she did, forming a semicircle around her. The skirt of the miracle-dress fell like a waterfall from her hips, whispering around her legs, while the bodice gently reflected the light from the chandeliers. She marvelled once again at the power of clothes and make-up to lend her a persona that wasn't truly hers. She hadn't planned a speech, but when had she ever stuck to a plan? She raised her voice.

"Welcome to this celebration of our new Rhannon, and our future. It brings me so much joy to know across Rhannon my people are celebrating tonight too. And I'm delighted you all could be here to celebrate with me."

She kept her eyes on the crowd as she held out a hand to the right, and sure enough, a waiter darted forward, bringing her champagne. "To Rhannon," she called, raising the glass as her words echoed back at her, repeated by her guests. She took a sip, nodded at the musicians to resume playing, and began to make a circuit of the room.

The ballroom looked lovely, as if the chaos from earlier never was: the chairs and tables, covered in snow-white clothes, glass and silverware gleaming atop them. She greeted everyone generously, taking the time to clasp their hands and ask after their families, accepting the hated "congratulations" with a wide smile. But as she worked her way through the room, the feeling of strength began to change to anxiety, turning tight and sharp behind her ribcage, painfully aware that every face she smiled at, every word she said was a countdown to when she'd reach the ambassadors and have to face them. Him.

The last time Sorrow had seen Rasmus had been the night she had told him they could never be together again. And that time, she'd meant it. Because the moment he'd touched her all logic flew out of the window, the need to be close to him overwhelming all sense and reason.

The pull of his skin – the ability that made him able to calm her worries, soothe her pain, and ease her – had come close to being an addiction. Hiding in his arms had always been too easy, and Sorrow feared the time would have come when she lost the power to refuse him, becoming like Harun, in thrall to a drug she thought she needed to survive. Sorrow would be forever grateful that Rasmus was so good, so full of integrity. In his father's hands that power would be devastating, a thousand times worse than Lamentia ever was. She thanked both the stars and the Graces that it was his son who wielded such a gift.

Sorrow felt Rasmus's eyes on her as she slowly made her way from the civilian guests, to where the ambassadors were waiting, and her stomach churned, her palms clammy. She didn't know what to think; she couldn't be glad to see him there, but she'd never be sad to see him either. A familiar knot of confusion rose in her stomach.

She tried to concentrate as she embraced Stile of Svarta, Magnas of Skae, and Krator of Meridea, accepted the gloved hand of Petyr of Nyrssea, and the apologies of a mere envoy from Astria. She knew the Astrian king wouldn't send a proper ambassador to a country controlled by a woman; it was a mark of reluctant respect he'd sent anyone at all and it pleased her.

Then it was Rhylla. Vespus stepped forward, arms wide, and Sorrow bit her tongue as he held her. His fingers were cool and light on the exposed skin of her back, his lips just as delicate as he bent to kiss her cheek.

"Welcome home, Chancellor," he said, his voice smooth with triumph.

"Thank you, Ambassador Corrigan," Sorrow replied with as much grace as she could muster, mindful of how the entire room watched her.

"I brought you a gift," he said, gesturing to his son. "Or rather, I'm returning one to you."

She turned to Rasmus and felt her heart break a little more.

He was breathtakingly beautiful, his pale hair – almost the same colour as her gown, she realized – half-tied back in a knot, the rest flowing over his shoulders. His outfit was the same mesmerizing violet-blue as his eyes, the coat trimmed in silver cord, the trousers fitted to his slim hips, making him seem taller and more elegant than ever.

His gaze was soft and full of love as he met Sorrow's eyes, his smile open and genuine. Like his father, he embraced her, though he placed his hands on her hips, where the gown covered her skin so his ability wouldn't affect her. A lump formed in Sorrow's throat.

"Hello, Sorrow," he said, when he released her. "Or, Chancellor, as it should be. You look so very beautiful."

His Rhyllian accent was more pronounced now than it had been last time she saw him.

She peered into his eyes, trying to read his thoughts, to divine whether he was unhappy to be there, what he was feeling. As though he knew what she was doing, his lips curled, and he gave her a swift wink.

"I'm happy to be back in Rhannon," he said.

"You're welcome here. And Sorrow is fine. You don't have to stand on ceremony with me."

"You do look stunning," Vespus said, drawing their attention back to him and causing Rasmus to glare at him. "Radiant, even. Such a daring dress. I can only imagine the reports the Astrian envoy will be sending home."

Sorrow ignored the provocation. "How was your trip home, Ambassador?"

"Good. Excellent, in fact. Though I haven't returned alone."

"So I see." She smiled at Rasmus.

"Ah," Vespus said. "But I meant my wife."

"Your wife?" Sorrow was stunned. "You're married?"

"I am indeed. While I was at home, I married."

"Aphora?" Sorrow looked around for her. She had no liking for the woman who had long been Vespus's companion. It was Aphora's ability to communicate with birds that had given Vespus his opportunity to blackmail Sorrow.

"Ah, now this is awkward." Vespus didn't sound the least bit put out. "Aphora and I parted ways. Don't worry." He smiled. "We're still very good friends. You haven't met my new bride, Taasas, but I do hope you will like her."

Sorrow blinked. She'd never heard of this Taasas before, was sure she'd never been mentioned. So how had Vespus married her?

Sorrow looked at Rasmus for explanation, but his expression was unreadable.

"Where is your wife now?" Sorrow asked. She'd seen no other Rhyllians there.

"Resting, in our chambers. She found the journey here a little taxing – it's her first time outside of Rhylla. But I'm sure you'll meet her soon enough. She's looking forward to meeting you."

Was that a threat, somehow? It was Vespus, so it was likely. Sorrow fought a shudder.

Vespus smiled a close-lipped smile, as though she'd amused him. "I fear I'm taking too much of your time, Chancellor," he said. "You should share your favours with your other guests. We'll have plenty of time to catch up, now we're both back."

Before Sorrow could protest he took her hand and kissed it, then bowed, dismissing her.

Smiling tightly, she nodded to Rasmus, and moved to where the Jedenvat were waiting. Well, most of them, at least.

Arran stood beside his father's wheeled chair, listening intently to whatever Bayrum Mizil was telling them. And with them was Irris. She'd come.

Irris lowered her gaze to the floor as Sorrow approached, and Sorrow's stomach churned with anxiety and regret.

"Vice Chancellor, it's good to see you. Senator Mizil, Senator Day. Irris," she added, her voice softening as she said her best friend's name.

By contrast Charon's voice was almost hard as he said, "Welcome home, Chancellor."

They stood in uneasy silence, until it seemed Irris could bear it no longer. "If you'll excuse me," she said, not waiting for an answer as she walked away. Sorrow watched her go, her pulse rising as she saw the crowd move and Mael appear. He'd come too.

Irris went straight to him, and the two stood close to each other, talking, Mael reaching to rub Irris's shoulder. The sight of their heads bent together sent a poison dart of jealousy through Sorrow.

"I hear you want Mael to live here," Charon said, his eyes also on the pair. "Among other new living arrangements."

Sorrow turned back to him, heart sinking lower. "Eventually." Charon's mouth was a thin line; it was clear she was out of favour with the Days. She looked instead at Bayrum, and pasted a smile on. "I'm happy to see you again,

Senator Mizil. How was your journey?"

"Rather fraught actually. I was just telling Charon and Arran I passed not one but two house fires on the way here."

"Goodness," Sorrow said, jumping on the subject change. "Two fires? Any idea why?"

"Villagers lighting fires in fireplaces that haven't been cleaned properly," Charon said. "Winter is drawing in, the nights are getting chilly. People build fires in chimneys that have half a year's worth of debris and birds' nests in them. It happens every year."

"We should put out some kind of bulletin, in the circulars, reminding people to properly clean their chimneys," Sorrow said, and Bayrum nodded at her. Then she turned to Charon. "I tried to find you earlier but you weren't in your office. Or your rooms."

He nodded curtly. "I was in Istevar town, dealing with Vine."

"What did he want?"

"More money. Less work. And more power, as ever."

"He's in for a shock when he finds out there's soon to be no money or power for them at all." Sorrow spoke without thinking, only to spin on the spot as Charon's eyes widened at something behind her.

Balthasar Lys had been creeping closer while they'd been talking. Close enough to hear.

"Did you want something, Senator Lys?" Sorrow asked.

"The first dance, if I may?" His response was smooth and immediate, an elegant hand extended to her. "I believe the music is about to start up again."

"I'm afraid I've already claimed that honour." Arran stepped forward, placing a possessive arm around Sorrow's shoulder.

"Too slow, Senator Lys," Sorrow replied, not bothering to feign regret. "Perhaps the next one."

"Indeed." Balthasar gave a shallow bow and stepped away as music began to flow from where the band sat.

"We'd better dance, then," Sorrow said to Arran, smiling at the others before she allowed Arran to lead her to the dance floor.

"I promise to step in every time he tries to dance with you," Arran said as they stepped on to the floor.

"He won't try again, unless I'm whispering in a corner and he wants to know what's going on."

"Ah, then I should confess my motivations aren't entirely pure either," Arran said. "I want to know what's going on with you and Irris. Svarta, Sorrow? What can she possibly have done for you to want to send her there?'

Sorrow pursed her lips. "Arran—"

"OK, none of my business." He paused as she twirled away from him, waiting until she was back in his arms to finish. "But she said you've all but exiled her."

"I haven't exiled her. It's just. . . It's for the best."

"How is you two being apart for the best, Row?"

Across the room, Sorrow saw Vespus watching her. Sorrow knew he was assessing Arran. Trying to decide if he had a use. And that was exactly why Irris had to be kept away. Until the threat of Vespus was gone, Sorrow had to hold her nerve.

"I don't know what to say," Sorrow finally replied.

Arran frowned. "I feel like there's more to it than either of you are letting on. And she won't say anything other than you're sending her to the north."

"So you thought you'd try me?"

"Did it work?"

"No." She smiled. "But it'll be fine soon," Sorrow assured him.

"I hope so."

They were silent for the rest of the dance, and Sorrow allowed her attention to wander.

She watched Balthasar approach Vespus, her scowl freezing as the Rhyllian turned away and began talking to the man on his right, the envoy from Astria, ignoring the senator for the South Marches completely.

Balthasar frowned at Vespus but continued to hover, not taking what Sorrow could see was a very obvious hint. Even as Vespus angled his back towards Balthasar he stood, waiting for Vespus's attention.

Vespus didn't so much as look at him as he ushered the envoy away to where a waiter stood with a tray of canapés. Balthasar watched them go, a bewildered expression on his face.

She looked away before he saw her watching, smiling up at Arran as the dance ended and he released her. Only for Magnas of Skae to take her hand, spinning her around with such vigour the room continued moving even when the song ended. After that, Sorrow turned down other requests to dance, instead moving to where Krator of Meridea was leading a lively conversation about the industrial age that had gripped the neighbouring country. Sorrow asked Krator if it would be possible to set up some kind of visit for Rhannish scientists to learn from the Merish, and she seemed flattered, promising to write to the duke in the morning.

Sorrow moved through the room like a bee in a flower garden, never lingering too long with one group, but giving a moment to all. She joined circles of teachers and doctors, artists and artisans, introducing them to each other when she knew who they were, accepting their introduction when she didn't.

She mimicked how Queen Melisia had behaved at the ball in Rhylla, listening more than speaking, keeping a soft smile at her lips, even as she made endless notes in her mind of things people said they wanted, or needed, things she needed to talk to the Jedenvat about. These were the things she had to focus on once Vespus was dealt with. The promises she'd made to win the vote.

As the night drew on, the servants doused the gas lamps on the walls, leaving only the light from candles in the chandeliers above. The party got louder as people drank more than they ought to, the room full of noise and laughter. Slowly, the older generations left, leaving the younger to debauch themselves peacefully. Sorrow's evening moved from diplomacy to ceaseless dancing, no matter that her shoes rubbed and pinched, and that she desperately needed both the bathroom and something to drink. She danced on and on, until Arran once again came to her rescue, whisking her to the sides and pouring her a glass of water, which she drained in three gulps, holding it out for a refill.

She sipped the second one slowly, watching Mael and Irris as they took to the floor, moving together with ease. They were still deep in conversation, Irris talking and Mael shaking his head. Then, as though they could feel her watching, they both looked at her in the same moment, and Sorrow almost dropped her glass.

"Is there something going on there, do you think?" Arran asked, his eyes following hers.

Sorrow shrugged. Though they hadn't discussed it, she always had the impression Irris wasn't interested in romance. And she had no idea what Mael was interested in, if anything at all.

She opened her mouth to say as much, snapping it shut as Mael and Irris parted and he began walking towards her with purpose.

He paused in front of her. "Hello, Arran. Sorrow, may I have this dance?"

She nodded, handing the glass to Arran and taking Mael's arm.

He placed one hand on her waist, using the other to take hers, leading her in an accomplished waltz. His time at the Rhyllian court showed – he flowed from move to move, not counting steps, nor checking his feet. Instead he kept his gaze on hers, his face impassive. He looked better than he had last time she'd seen him, but there were still hollows under his eyes, and this close she could see the faint pinkness to them, bloodshot from sleeplessness, or stress.

"I didn't think you'd come," Sorrow said.

"Because you didn't invite me?" he replied. "I'm Irris's guest. You forgot to disinvite her."

Sorrow flushed. "It's not—"

"Are you really keeping Vespus?" he said abruptly. "After the campaign? After everything?"

Sorrow stopped so suddenly that another pair bumped into them.

"Sorry, sorry," she apologized, pretending her shoe had come loose until they moved along. "Did Irris put you up to this?" she whispered.

"No. I'm asking because you can't really expect me to come

and live here if he is. Or is that why you told me not to come right away?"

"Mael..." She couldn't tell him that she hoped Vespus would be gone before long. She couldn't say a word.

He read her silence as a confession. "So, you are keeping him. For all your talk of wanting me here, it's clear you don't – how could you, if he's staying? I wanted to believe you, but I was a fool. When will I learn?"

With that, Mael stalked off, leaving Sorrow alone, her mouth open in shock as she watched him go.

"Here." Rasmus appeared beside her. Once again, he rested his hands on her hips as they began to dance, lending an intimacy she could have done without, but it was better than his hands on her naked back. "Are you all right?"

"Fine." Sorrow's voice trembled, and she fought to master it. "He's just ... upset. He doesn't want to be here if your father is."

"Can't blame him. I feel the same way." Rasmus gave a wry smile.

"Who is this wife of his?" Sorrow asked, ignoring the glares she could feel Charon directing at her.

"Taasas? You know as much as I do. The last I knew he was with Aphora – all he'd say was that they ran their course."

More like she'd served her purpose, Sorrow thought darkly. It sent a shiver down her spine; if that was the case, then what could this Taasas do that Vespus needed? Control the weather so his trees would grow even faster? Make water flow from her fingertips? Clearly something more valuable than what Aphora could do, and so she'd been discarded – Sorrow had no doubt it was Vespus who'd ended the relationship. Perhaps that was why he was shunning Balthasar too – he'd outlived his usefulness, now Vespus himself was back inside the Winter Palace. Interesting.

"Are you really all right, with my being here?" Rasmus lowered his voice, interrupting Sorrow's thoughts. "I know it must be strange, but I do want us to be friends. I think I can be your friend now. If you still want to be mine."

"Yes," Sorrow said at once. "Yes, absolutely." She gave a shaky laugh, realizing that she was speaking the truth. She did want to be his friend. *Just* his friend. "You're right, it's a little weird, but you'll always be one of my best friends. And I'm short on them right now so I'm not going to turn anyone away."

Rasmus laughed.

They danced on. Sorrow knew they must make an incredible sight; the tall, pale Rhyllian with his pointed ears and silvery hair; and she, golden-skinned and curved, dressed in white, spinning in his arms. She knew she was right when the number ended and spontaneous applause broke out around them.

"Should we go again, give the people what they want?" Rasmus asked.

"I'd like to cut in, if I may," came a smooth voice behind them. "I must be one of the only men here who hasn't danced with the chancellor yet."

Vespus. Sorrow swallowed down her distaste as he stepped in front of his son, placing his hands on Sorrow's waist. She had little choice but to move hers to his shoulders, and sway with him as the band took up once more.

"You've got a nerve," Sorrow said, a fake smile plastered to her face.

"This is your job, Chancellor. Think of it as the reaffirming of old ties. Talking of, you and Rasmus looked good together."

73

"Stop."

"I'm simply saying – it's a shame about the law. You make an attractive couple."

"It's over. We both know that. It has been for a while. And it will stay over," Sorrow forced out behind curved lips. "So if you thought to bring him here to dangle him before me like a carrot to a donkey, you're out of luck."

"I've never relied on luck, Sorrow. Only planning. And precision. Luck is for the lazy." He spun her in a series of circles before lifting her lightly, setting her down and waltzing with her again, not missing a beat as he said, "Though ... I have need of a favour."

Sorrow laughed. She couldn't help it. The nerve of him.

"Are you mad?" she asked.

"Would it make it easier if I was?" he mused, continuing before she could answer. "I have my seeds with me. I need somewhere to start them. It needs to be dark, and private – they can't be disturbed during the first two weeks of growth, or even my ability won't help them. At home I use my cellars. I'd like to use yours."

"The kitchens here use the cellars. I can hardly clear the palace's supplies for you."

"The dungeons, then? Surely they're not used."

They weren't. They sat abandoned, beneath the barracks for the palace guard. The last person to occupy one had been Balthasar, and afterwards the guard had advised her that people shouldn't be kept down there again. They were a relic from the time the Winter Palace had been a castle for kings. There was no place for a fire, no natural light. Inhumane to hold someone in them.

They sounded like exactly what Vespus wanted.

Sorrow was loath to give it to him, however temporarily.

He read her hesitation and smiled, as though she'd amused him. "Why don't you bring me the keys tomorrow? Have no fear – I'll be discreet; I promise no one will know I was ever there."

There was little point pretending she wouldn't do what he wanted. She gave a terse nod, and his smile widened.

"Excellent. Can I assume you've found a way to give me my land in the North Marches?"

Sorrow matched his footwork, step for step, schooling her expression into careful blankness. "I have an idea, yes. I'll need some time to set things in motion."

"I'm sure. How much time?"

"A month?" That would give her plenty of time to get to the crypt and deal with any records on her birth parents.

Vespus laughed, exposing white teeth and pink mouth as he threw his head back.

The music picked up, the crescendo approaching, and Vespus lifted her again, spinning them at the same time. "No," he whispered in her ear as he lowered her. "I can't give you a month. I just told you, the seeds need two weeks of isolation. After that, they'll need the sun."

Her plan made her bold. "Then I can't give you the land."

As the melody reached its peak and the music crashed to the finale, Vespus dipped Sorrow backwards, lowering himself over her as he said, "I don't need you to *give* it to me, Sorrow."

He hauled her back up, holding her close as she staggered in his arms. The song finished, and those watching applauded, louder than before.

"One more thing." Vespus bent his mouth to her ear. "Rasmus isn't staying in his old rooms so I suggest you don't look for him there. I'd hate to give my wife the wrong idea if you came sneaking in during the night. And, unlike my son, I prefer my own kind."

He kissed her on the cheek and released her.

The moment she was free she fled the dance floor. Suddenly she'd had enough of the party, of the people. And yet she couldn't leave. It was her job to stay there.

"Sorrow?" Irris was beside her, her eyebrows raised in concern, as though they'd never fought. "What's wrong? What did he say?"

Wordlessly, Sorrow shook her head. The memory of Irris, her head bent close to Mael's, rose in her mind, poisoning her. "I'm fine," she said stiffly.

Irris made an exasperated sound. "For the Graces' sake, Sorrow, I wish you'd—"

"I said I'm fine," Sorrow snapped.

Irris glared at her, then turned on her heel. She crossed the room in a few seconds, Mael following behind her. No one else seemed to notice, too deep in gossip and wine to pay any real attention. Sorrow realized with a sinking heart that there were still hours of socializing ahead. Dancing, laughing and talking. Even the thought of it exhausted her.

As she watched the staff trying their best to clear away empty glasses and plates in the dim light, she had an idea. Beckoning a waiter over, she kept her voice low as she asked him, "Could you find one of the gas lamp attendants and ask them to relight the lamps, but slowly, subtly? I have a lot of work to do tomorrow…"

The waiter nodded, understanding at once, and Sorrow was pleased to see one of the lamp tenders appear a few moments later, making his way around the room, relighting a lamp every few minutes.

Feeling a little more in control, Sorrow walked to the musicians and asked them to play slower, less boisterous songs. After that, she summoned the waiter again, this time tasking him with getting his colleagues to return to the kitchens, out of sight of the revellers.

It soon had the effect Sorrow desired; as the wine stopped flowing and the music became more sedate, people stopped dancing and sought out seats. The growing light exposed torn stockings and stained shirts, smudged make-up and glazed eyes, and the spell of the party broke.

Slowly, the room began to empty. Sorrow stayed until all the guests had gone, graciously thanking them.

She sagged the moment the last one had left, bending to pull her shoes off. Barefoot, she made her way out of the ballroom, Dougray following behind, turning towards the stairs.

Only to find Rasmus sitting on them, waiting for her.

Dougray stepped forward, but Sorrow stayed him with a hand.

"It's all right," she said.

As the bodyguard stepped back, giving them space, she looked at Rasmus. "I don't want to talk, Ras."

"What did my father say to you?"

"Nothing. I'm just tired."

"Liar."

"Go away, Rasmus." Sorrow turned to him. "Can't you see I want to be left alone?"

"I don't think it's a good idea to leave you right now."

Tears pricked Sorrow's eyes.

"Are you. . . Row, don't cry." He reached for her again, and then stopped, helpless.

"Please, just go away, Ras." Sorrow fought to keep her voice from cracking.

He looked at her, shaking his head slightly. "All right. If it's what you want." He nodded and left her.

Forgetting she wasn't alone, she raised her hands to her face and covered it, using the heels of her palms to push her tears back in.

"Is everything all right, Your Excellency?" Dougray asked, his voice soft and unsure.

"Fine." Another word Sorrow wanted to exile from language.

She felt enormously grateful for the way he didn't ask more questions, just fell in step behind her, escorting her all the way back to her rooms in blessed silence.

6

Burn

Sorrow was still awake that night when she heard footsteps rushing through her suite, doors slamming against walls as whomever it was burst through them, desperate to reach her. A chill bloomed at the base of her spine, creeping upwards, extending icy fingers over her shoulders and making her skin tight with apprehension. She put down the papers she'd been working on and stood, straight-backed, then turned to face the door.

"What is it?" she asked the girl who'd crashed into the room after the briefest of knocks.

The girl tried to speak, and immediately began coughing. She shook her head, too winded to talk, holding up a finger to beg Sorrow to wait as she gulped air into her hungry lungs. Sorrow waited without protest, feeling strangely calm. It was as though she was at the eye of a cyclone, the only fixed point in the world, everything else spinning madly around her.

"Your Excellency. Miss Day asks that you go to the Round Chamber immediately."

Sorrow blinked in surprise. "Miss Day sent you to me?"

"Yes, Your Excellency. She said I was to wake you at once."

"Did she say anything else?"

"She said not to delay. It's an emergency."

Sorrow was about to ask what kind of emergency, but the girl looked close to tears, clearly unused to having to race through palaces and then undergo interrogations. Sorrow bit back the rest of her questions.

"Thank you. I'll be right there."

Obviously relieved, the girl hurried from the room, and the numbness Sorrow had mistaken for calm punctured like a balloon. Her heart punched against her ribcage; sweat soaked the back of her nightgown. She was frightened. Frightened of what could be so urgent that Irris had sent a servant to summon her in the middle of the night.

Sorrow dressed hurriedly, pulling on soft blue trousers to match her tunic, twisting her hair into a swift chignon and jamming her feet into beaded house slippers.

When she arrived at the Round Chamber, nerves jangling like a bell, she found Balthasar and Lord Samad already there, sitting in their usual seats as if this was a scheduled meeting.

She gave them a brief nod, and made her way around the table to the chancellor's place.

Her place, now.

The thought made her hesitate, though if anyone had asked, she couldn't have explained why. She'd sat there before, many times in fact, while she'd covered for her father. It was quite possible she'd sat in it more than Harun ever had. But this felt different. It felt ominous that her first time officially occupying that seat should be in the dead of night.

She rested a hand on the battered old chair but didn't pull it out, instead leaning on the back of it as she caught her breath.

"Where's Charon, and the others?" she asked coolly.

"Coming, I expect," Balthasar answered. His eyes were bloodshot, and he was still wearing the outfit he'd worn to the ball, though now it was rumpled, and stained. "After all, this is a serious situation."

Sorrow waited for him to continue. Balthasar remained silent.

"What is?" she ground out from between closed teeth.

His mouth formed an "O" in a parody of surprise. "You mean you don't know?"

Sorrow's eyes narrowed.

"Oh, I don't know either," said Balthasar, smiling. "I'm merely making the assumption, given it's not every night we're forced from our beds to attend meetings." He paused, and then continued, an edge to his voice. "It would seem, then, that only Miss Day is in the know, despite no longer being on the Jedenvat. Interesting, that. In fact, I wouldn't be surprised—" He stopped as Charon appeared in the doorway, Irris and Arran behind him.

Charon wheeled himself to the spot beside Sorrow. "What wouldn't surprise you, Senator Lys?" he asked.

"I was just saying to the chancellor I was surprised your daughter, who is no longer on the Jedenvat, summoned us." Balthasar stared at Irris. "And here she is again."

Irris ignored Balthasar and held out a rolled note to Sorrow.

"I was awake and in the hall when the messenger arrived," she explained, her eyes not meeting Sorrow's.

In silence, Sorrow unrolled the note, and read it.

It was brief, and perfunctory, but even more chilling for it. It explained the fires Bayrum had seen earlier. They hadn't been the result of blocked chimneys.

It was plague.

People had begun setting their own homes ablaze to try to halt it.

Sorrow read on. It had started three mornings earlier, while she'd been in South Marshes. In a small village just south of the Humpback Bridge a young man had woken feeling under the weather. He'd worsened throughout the day, becoming lethargic and dazed, before falling into a coma-like sleep that night. His family had been unable to rouse him the following morning and had rushed him to hospital, where doctors had been baffled by his condition.

The following morning all four members of his household had fallen ill with the same symptoms: his parents, a younger sister, and a cousin who had been staying with them. By nightfall they too were unconscious. Then more cases were reported – not just friends, men he'd worked with, and neighbours, but strangers, people who hadn't been in contact with any of the sick. And worse, another village near the Summer Palace was reporting victims too, five: all with the same symptoms.

The head physician at the hospital in the North Marches, who had written the note, was telling Sorrow she believed it was a state of emergency, and over fifty cases were confirmed across the two villages.

Sorrow looked at Charon, who had been waiting for her

to finish reading. The look on his face told Sorrow he already knew what it said.

"Well?" Balthasar asked. "Are you going to tell us?"

Sorrow swallowed, forcing the words out. "It's a plague. In the North Marches."

A chill seemed to move through the room and Sorrow locked eyes with Charon. Whatever awkwardness had been between them faded as Charon gave Sorrow the slightest of nods, and she returned it gratefully. She didn't want to face this without him.

"Do we have any idea what it is?" Samad asked.

Sorrow slumped into her chair. She knew what it was. Or at least, she suspected. Vespus had as good as told her earlier, at the ball. He'd said he didn't need her to give him the land. He hadn't needed her to give it to him, because he'd already begun to take it.

She ignored Samad's question, asking one of her own, though she already knew the answer. "And it's only in the North Marches?"

"Yes. So far." Charon paused as Kaspira, Tuva and Bayrum arrived.

All three stopped in the doorway, held fast by the expressions of the others.

"What's going on?" Kaspira asked, ever to the point.

Sorrow looked at Bayrum Mizil as she spoke. "There's been an outbreak of some kind of plague in the North Marches. Fifty victims so far. The fires you passed were people trying to cleanse their homes."

"Dear Graces..." Kaspira raised her hands to her mouth as Bayrum sagged against the door frame, his eyes wild and lost. Tuva moved to hold him up, though she wasn't even half his size.

"If I'd known..." he muttered as Tuva guided him into his seat.

Sorrow put the message down and stared across the room, at the map of Rhannon, locking on to the still vandalized Humpback Bridge as she tried to make sense of it all.

If this was Vespus – and she was sure it was – then it wasn't a disease. He wouldn't risk a real illness, because it could spiral from his control. This must be a poison. What was his aim – to clear the land of people by making them run for their lives from a plague?

"Your Excellency?" Charon said, breaking into her thoughts.

Sorrow turned to Charon. "Yes?"

"We need to come up with a plan," Charon said. "Before it spreads further."

"Yes." Sorrow nodded. "We need to isolate and contain it." She realized she was stating the obvious, but her thoughts were focused on one single task: the need to find Vespus. That was her plan. She shook herself, and continued. "The first step needs to be setting up a quarantine zone around each of the affected homes, and the hospitals. No one in or out. Dispatch as many of the Decorum Ward as we can to the North Marches at once, to keep people in their homes. Then we'll see how it spreads. If it spreads." She had a hunch it wouldn't, at least not in a natural way.

Charon nodded. "Whatever this sickness is, it's fast. We'll have to move faster to stop it tearing through the country."

"How likely is that?" Lord Samad asked, and an uneasy silence fell.

"We don't know," Sorrow said. "And we won't until we see how the quarantine holds. I think that's all we can do for now," she added. "I'll go and speak to the Rhyllian Ambassador. The

North Marches borders Rhylla at the bridge and the bridge is close to the first infected villages; they need to know."

Charon didn't hide his relief at her decisiveness. "We should inform Krator of Meridea too – they share a land border with us at the west, and one of the villages affected is only a few miles from the district line with the West Marches."

"I'll write to her after I've seen Vespus. Is there anything else?" she asked, looking around at Samad and Balthasar. They shook their heads, and Sorrow noted that Balthasar seemed as stunned as anyone. He hadn't known Vespus's plan, then. "All right. We'll meet again later, say, fifteen chimes, to check in?"

Charon nodded.

"Meeting over," Sorrow said, and went to find Vespus.

She should have sent for him, but she knew Vespus would keep her waiting, drawing it out as long as he could, enjoying the thought he was riling her. Instead, she decided she'd find him, giving him no choice but to talk to her.

He wasn't in the Rhyllian ambassador's office when Sorrow arrived, which wasn't that surprising, given the hour, though she'd held out hope that he might be. She didn't want to go to his private rooms, especially after his parting shot at the ball, but she didn't see what choice she had.

So it was with gritted teeth she used the passageway from her rooms to go to him, shoving down the memories that rose at the familiar sound and feel of her knuckles against the wood as she knocked briskly at his door.

It seemed Vespus wasn't prepared for visitors, or wanted it to appear that way; his brows rose in a very good impression of startled when he opened the door and saw her standing there, arms folded.

He was dressed, but only partly, a green vest unbuttoned over his shirt, the sleeves rolled up, revealing lean, muscular forearms. His pale hair was in a scruffy knot atop his head, exposing his long pointed ears; there was earth beneath his fingernails, a smudge on his cheek. Surprise, it seemed, made him look younger, and painfully like his son. Sorrow couldn't bear it, balling her hands into fists, fixing her gaze on his collar.

"Good morning," Vespus said, peering behind her. "This is unexpected. I didn't think you'd bring the keys at the crack of dawn."

Sorrow cursed inwardly. She'd forgotten he'd asked for the keys to the dungeons. "I'm not here about the keys."

He inclined his head. "Then you'd better come in." He stood aside, nodding for her to enter.

She stalked past him into his small parlour, noticing the half-eaten meal of bread and fruit on a small table, two still-steaming cups of black coffee and a paper in Rhyllian folded over beside the plate, and she quickly scanned the rest of the room.

He'd left the door to the bedroom open, and Sorrow was grateful to see he'd replaced Rasmus's old sleigh bed with a traditional four-poster – the thought of Vespus sleeping in Rasmus's bed had made her feel ill. It was also empty; it seemed his new wife wasn't there.

But the biggest changes were the plants. Save his breakfast table, every surface in the parlour was covered in pots bursting with greenery at various stages of growth; vines wound their way around the legs and arms of his sofas, and a row of miniature orange trees tempted her from the coffee table, bearing fruit the size of her thumbnail.

Through the open bedroom door she could see more vines woven into a canopy over the bed, even the rug beside it seemed to be made of moss. He'd replaced the fabric hangings at the window with a curtain of ivy; rows of young shoots lined the sill behind it.

Beneath it was a long table, filled with seed trays and pots, some empty, others not, and Sorrow realized that's what he'd been doing when she knocked – repotting plants. It was such an innocent thing to do, and Sorrow's anger sharpened and honed itself at the unfairness of someone like him being able to control something so lovely

"I'm afraid you just missed Taasas," Vespus said. "She likes to exercise in the gardens as the sun rises. Some Merish stretching and balancing thing; I'm afraid I don't understand it."

Unable to sheathe her temper any longer, Sorrow unleashed it. "There's an illness tearing through the North Marches. Sickness, fever, then coma, striking within hours. Except it isn't an illness, is it?"

Vespus moved to the table and lifted one of the coffee cups. He took a long sip, and when he spoke, it was with an air of infinite patience. "No. I decided it was time to put our plan in motion."

She stared at him. "Our *plan*?"

"You agreed to the terms. You could have said no."

"I didn't agree to this. I agreed that you'd stay on as ambassador, and that after a few months – *months*, Vespus – I'd find a way to give you the land. I didn't agree to you unleashing a plague on my people three weeks after the election."

Vespus put the cup down, considering her. "That's fair. I can see how the surprise of it is upsetting."

Sorrow bit her tongue to keep from screaming.

"But I did tell you I wanted to begin when you returned. I was very clear," Vespus continued. "And, if I'm truthful, I believed it pertinent to act before you did." He paused, and smiled at her almost fondly. "A knife in the night, perhaps a poison of your own, slipped into my cup. It would have occurred to you to try killing me eventually, if it hasn't already. I know what desperation drives people to, in the end."

Blood pooled in Sorrow's cheeks at his words, and the kernel of truth in them.

He went on. "When you've had time to calm down, you'll see this is for the best. It needed to be something that would drive the people away – make them afraid, and ensure they wouldn't want to return. A sickness accomplishes that perfectly. It was one of the ideas I mentioned at the time."

"A faked one," she spat. "That's what you said."

He dipped his head, conceding the point. "I did say that, you're right. But it wouldn't have been enough. To force people to leave their lives, and homes and businesses – their whole history – they need to see horror. They need to see the people they love suffering, and be afraid for them. They need to believe that staying is worse than leaving."

She swallowed. "Will it kill any of them, this . . . poison of yours?" she asked him.

"I can't say." Vespus spread his hands wide when she narrowed her eyes at him. "Truly, I don't know. If they're weak, or already ill, perhaps. The very young, the very elderly are most at risk. The healthy and hale should be fine, once they wake, though the weakness may persist for a while."

"What is it?"

It was his turn to be quiet then, as he decided what, if anything, to tell her.

"I call it Hellfior," he said finally. "It's a compound made from two plants, Hellia and Fiorosa. It's my own creation." He couldn't disguise the glint of pride that lit his eyes as he admitted it. "I was trying to recreate Rasmus's abilities."

Sorrow was horrified. "His ability takes away pain."

"Now, you of all people should know it's more than that. He soothes both physical and emotional turmoil – I believe my son's gift is the closest to Adavere's Laethea has seen in some time. That's what I wanted to replicate. Hellia is a natural painkiller, Fiorosa a tranquilliser for the mind. I hoped by combining them I'd have it. However, they reacted and made something else. Instead of calming, it made people severely ill, followed by a deep, unnatural sleep."

"And when will they wake?"

"That I'm afraid I don't know. My Rhyllian subjects rallied within a day or two. The Rhannish are a different race. There's no telling."

"Is there an antidote?"

"I'm working on one. It's difficult. The usual counters won't work, because Hellfior is something new. I'll find one." He smiled. "Probably."

Sorrow made a sound of disgust. "You unleashed something you couldn't undo?" She rose, shaking. "I *command* you to end this."

He stared at her, tall and pale as a silver birch, his violet eyes cold. "Don't be such a child, Sorrow. And don't attempt to command me. This is just – politics. You scratch my back, I scratch yours. I keep your secrets, you keep mine. There is no moral high ground for you to take." He turned and stroked long fingers along the leaf of a spindly plant.

"If anyone dies, I'll reveal who I am," she said, forcing herself to keep her voice steady. "Better that than standing by while you kill them, and doing nothing. Will you risk it, Lord Corrigan? Because I will. I'll end this whole thing now."

She saw his shoulders rise, and braced for his wrath.

"Do you know what power is, Sorrow?"

"Don't patronize me."

"I don't mean to patronize you, Sorrow. What I'm trying to explain is that power is temporary – even the most zealous dictator knows it. Power is a vampire, a tick that attaches itself to a host and sucks the life from them. The only question is how long you can keep the tick on your vein. How long can you hold on to power? Long enough, if you have the right allies. Look at your father – he managed to cling to his seat for eighteen years with you, Charon Day and the Jedenvat propping him up. Because they needed him to keep their power, as he needed them to hold his. He only lost his hold when they tried replacing him with you."

She let out a bitter laugh. "So which one of us is the tick and which one the vein?"

He ignored her. "I have power, only so long as you give it to me. For us power is symbiotic, Sorrow. And that means we stand a good chance of holding on to it. Passing it back and forth. Like I said, you keep my secrets, I keep yours. We're both siphon and reservoir. But it only works if we work together." He paused, looking at his plants and then back to her.

"I'm not a bad man, Sorrow. And I'm not your enemy – or, at least, I don't have to be. There's no reason for us to be at war over this. All I'm doing is using the tools I have to achieve my goals. The possibilities for Starwater are huge and I can't allow my half-sister to stand in the way of progress. Or you. The end justifies the means. So, you need to decide once and for all where you stand. With me or against me."

7

Taasas

"This is what will happen next." Vespus took her silence for agreement. "First, if you haven't already given the order, you will demand the places affected be quarantined. A week from now you will have a change of heart, and begin evacuating them. You should precede it by making a speech about the cruelty of condemning people to suffer by keeping them there; the public will love it. Those evacuated will all be found reassuringly healthy, fear not," he said, as she opened her mouth to protest.

"After the land is cleared, you'll decide to cordon it off, just to be on the safe side." He stopped, and looked at her expectantly. "All right?"

He'd stolen the time she needed. Instead of dealing with bones and records, she'd be fighting to keep Rhannon calm every moment of every day until his plague vanished. And it would only do that once he'd got his way. If he'd known what she'd planned to do he could have hardly stopped her more soundly. She couldn't focus on herself while he struck down her people.

She spoke quietly. "How could you do this?"

"To lead means making tough decisions, Sorrow. And you'll benefit from it, ultimately. Within weeks of becoming chancellor, you'll have saved hundreds from a hideous sickness and found them new homes. The leader they dreamed of for eighteen long years. That they deserve."

"And then?" Sorrow asked.

"Then you continue governing Rhannon as the hero whose swift and decisive actions may have saved the entire population."

"What about us?" Sorrow asked, her jaw clenched.

"So you'll admit there is an 'us'?" Vespus smiled silkily before he continued. "We're done, if that's what you want. Despite your girlish need to cast me as the storybook villain to your poor damsel in distress, I'm only interested in the land. It's business, Sorrow. I've bought the land in the North Marches from you with my silence about your origins. So you don't need to worry about me, once I have it. Your part is done."

She laughed disbelievingly. "You'll ask for nothing else? No more land? No favours? You'll leave me, and the rest of Rhannon, alone?"

"As I said, if that's what you want."

"Would you resign as ambassador?"

"No, no. Sorrow, try to remember I could be a powerful ally to you. Things will change once I have a steady supply of Starwater. You could benefit from keeping me onside."

"I don't want to benefit from the drug that killed my father."

Vespus tutted, as though disappointed. "Then rest assured I'll consider our business concluded once I have the land."

Bile rose in her throat, bitter and thick, and she dropped her chin to her chest.

Once Melisia found out Vespus was growing Alvus, source of Starwater, she would declare war on Rhannon again – she'd have no choice; it would appear to all of Laethea that Rhannon had collaborated with him, against his queen's express wishes. The Rhyllian queen knew what he wanted the land for; by granting it to him it would seem Sorrow allied herself with him and his cause.

But if she exposed Vespus now, without moving the bones, she would expose herself. There would be an uprising. The fragile peace of the last eighteen years would disintegrate, along with her government.

So either way, as things were, there would be war.

If Sorrow had to choose one, though, she would choose honesty. She'd submit to a trial, allow herself to be imprisoned or exiled. It wasn't too late. No one else had to be hurt.

Sorrow sat up straight, steeling herself to tell him it was over. That she quit. That he could tell the world what he knew and she'd take the consequences. Alone.

Like he said, power was symbiotic. And that worked both ways. Rise or fall together. She chose to fall.

She cleared her throat to speak, and Vespus turned to her, his eyes alert. But just then, the door opened behind her.

A woman, ageless in the way mature Rhyllians were, entered. She was tall, as ice-pale as a Svartan, her hair a soft brown that fell in loose waves to her chin. Her beauty was angular and glacial, something cold and fathomless in her large hazel eyes, reminding Sorrow of an insect.

She looked from Sorrow to Vespus, and closed the door behind her.

"This is Taasas," Vespus said, gesturing for the woman to join him. "My wife. Taasas, this is the woman whose home and land we owe so very much to. Her Excellency, Sorrow Ventaxis, Chancellor of Rhannon." Taasas moved to Vespus's side, and he slid an arm around her. "Taasas knows everything. And I mean everything. You don't need to be coy in front of her."

"I interrupted, I think," Taasas said. Her voice was deeper than Sorrow had expected, musical, a storyteller's voice; but something about it made Sorrow's skin crawl.

Vespus fixed his gaze on Sorrow. "Yes. What were you about to say?"

Sorrow looked between them, and steeled herself. "That I'm done. Tell the people what you want. I won't be part of this."

Vespus and Taasas exchanged a look, and then Taasas began to speak. Her voice was low, amused.

"In Rhylla, we have a game we like to play, a kind of thought experiment to entertain ourselves after dinner. It's called the Carriage Problem. Do you know it?"

Sorrow shook her head. What was this? Her heart was thudding in her chest. This woman frightened her in a way that Vespus never had.

Vespus stood, walking past her to his table, scooping a handful of earth from a bag and depositing it in one of the larger pots as Taasas continued.

"In the game, you are the driver of a carriage, containing some of the most important people in your world. Let's say a doctor who has developed a cure for a deadly illness. A scientist on the brink of discovering how the universe works.

A philanthropist whose knowledge could eradicate crime, and poverty. More than that... Perhaps there's a vice chancellor, whose loyalty is unparalleled. A lover, who cares only for you, who would do anything you asked, no matter the cost. And, finally, a young woman who is the best friend anyone could hope for. Irreplaceable."

The hair on Sorrow's arms rose as a chill snaked beneath her skin. She knew exactly who Taasas was talking about.

Her Rhannish was flawless, almost unaccented. If it weren't for her pointed ears and the whiteness of her skin, she might have passed for native. Where had Vespus found her?

"You're driving your carriage, and come suddenly to a fork in the road. There is no time to fully stop the horses. The fork to the left will lead the carriage straight over a cliff, killing all of your passengers, and you. But a child, happily and obliviously playing, blocks the path on the right. They have no idea of the peril they're in. If you continue to the right, you'll run that child down, killing them before they even know you're there. But those treasured, vital people would survive. If you turn to the left, then they, and you, will die."

Vespus gently plucked one of his seedlings from its tray and held it up. It was a delicate thing, the stem still translucent, the roots fine. Sorrow couldn't take her eyes from it as Taasas stepped closer, continuing.

"One child. Versus all of that experience, and knowledge. All of that loyalty."

"The child might grow up to surpass everyone in the carriage." Sorrow's voice was almost as low as Taasas's.

"Or they might grow up to be a monster. Or nothing. Nothing at all. You're gambling potential, over solid ... ability, for want of a better word. I won't deny the death of the child would be a pity. But the death of the others... That would be a tragedy." She stepped closer. "Especially as they'd *know*. They'd know that you, as the driver, chose to kill them. They'd know it was your choice."

Without warning Taasas darted forward and gripped Sorrow's wrist.

And Sorrow was there, in the driver's seat of a carriage.

She could feel the reins biting into her fingers as she gripped them, the vibration of the carriage beneath her, could smell the horses and the dust.

Ahead of her she saw a fork.

Just as Taasas had said, beyond one path was a sheer drop. And on the other, a little girl no older than three, her hair in bunches, sat in the road using a stick to draw in the dirt.

"Move..." Sorrow tried to shout, but the word wouldn't come; she couldn't make a sound and the child couldn't hear the horses.

She heard screams from inside the carriage. Irris – it was Irris, screaming.

Rasmus, calling out over the drumming hooves of the black horses, imploring her to turn.

Charon, beating the roof of the carriage, begging for his life.

And the little girl played on, unaware that death was bearing down on her.

Sorrow tried to pull the reins but the horses wouldn't halt, galloping on, and she had to choose, she had to decide...

The child turned so Sorrow could see her in profile. She was smiling as she drew, chubby fingers clenching the stick as she dragged it through the dust.

Sorrow was close enough now that she could see the girl was drawing a picture of a family.

A mother, a father, two children...

Before she realized she'd decided, Sorrow jerked the reins, guiding the horses left.

Then the carriage was falling, the world was tumbling, and Sorrow felt her neck snap. She died.

Though that didn't stop her being able to see her friends; Rasmus's silver hair splattered with gore, a dark hole in his skull; Irris's beautiful face caved in, recognizable only by the outfit she was wearing. Charon shattered completely, his chair in pieces around him.

Then the scene changed; she was back at the Winter Palace and she was standing up, alive again.

But her friends weren't.

Irris was still dead, only this time she hung from the balcony of the Winter Palace, twirling gently in a macabre dance, her head mercifully bowed so Sorrow couldn't see her face. The rope around her neck creaked like a mast in the wind, her orchid-pink dress floating dreamily around her stiff feet. Sorrow turned away, gagging, only to see a hooded man run across the room, a spear in his hand. As she watched he released it, and it soared through the air before landing in Charon's chest, the force pushing his chair backwards into the wall, blood spilling from his mouth.

She staggered away, tripping over something, and when she looked down saw Arran, eyes wide and unseeing, his throat cut. There was Tuva, dead. Bayrum, dead. All of them dead.

Hooded people were everywhere, armed with hammers and pikes and lengths of chain, cutting down everyone that moved: men, women, children. They threw the servants and guards down the stairs, where their fellows waited to finish them off. Others held torches and they set fire to the curtains and the carpets, chanting, "Death to the overlords," over and over.

Then they turned and saw her.

Sorrow screamed and the men were gone. The bodies were gone, the fire was gone, and she was back in Vespus's bedroom, sweat pouring from her, her hands clawing her face. Taasas had released her, and stepped back.

"Why don't you think on it? Come back to us with an answer," Vespus said, sprinkling loam around the base of the repotted shoot.

"What was that?" Sorrow's throat was raw, and she wondered if she really had been screaming.

Taasas moved the table and picked up the second coffee cup as Vespus replied.

"I told you my sister kept some gifts hidden. Taasas's is one of them. Have you ever had a dream, and even though you know it isn't true, you can't help believe it?"

Sorrow said nothing, still sick with terror and horror.

"That's what Taasas does. She makes you dream, while still awake. Makes you live things, in your own mind."

Sorrow gagged.

"And so now you've seen what will happen if you defy me."

"It's not real," Sorrow gasped. "You just said that. It's a waking dream. Not a prophecy."

"It will be real, though." Vespus finally looked up at her. "Everything you saw will come to pass. You know it will. It wouldn't hurt so much otherwise. And now you've seen the cost of your nobility. Still want to give yourself up?"

"You're monsters," Sorrow whispered.

Vespus shrugged and rubbed his hands together, sending earth falling to the floor. Taasas crossed to him, sliding her arms around his waist, and lifted her face for a kiss. He obliged, as though they'd forgotten Sorrow was there.

Sorrow had seen enough. She fled to the door, freezing when he spoke again.

"I'll protect you, afterwards."

"What?" She turned to him. Taasas began kissing his neck.

"My half-sister won't be happy when she finds out you've helped me," Vespus said, his gaze on Sorrow. "But I'll protect you, and Rhannon. I won't forget that you helped me, whether under duress or not. I won't allow her to harm Rhannon. Or you. Don't forget to bring me my keys, will you?"

He lowered his mouth to meet Taasas's and Sorrow left, using the passageway to return to her room. Then she sank, shaking, to the floor and wrapped her arms around her knees, willing herself still.

She saw now the true dilemma of her problem wasn't in deciding which the right way was, but in understanding and accepting there wasn't one. Whichever path she chose, there would be suffering and agony, and she would be the one to cause it. All that remained was for her to decide which one she could live easier with.

Of course, on only one path would she live at all.

Broken Things Heal Crooked

Sorrow had dreamed once that Rasmus kissed another girl, some faceless, nameless other person. She knew the moment she woke that it was a dream, but that didn't change how angry and hurt she felt. When she saw him next, the false memories bombarded her, and she had taken it out on him. Snapped at him, sent him away.

Later, she'd snuck into his room and confessed in the dark why she'd been so mean. He'd been baffled and, to her annoyance, amused. "It was just a dream," he said, but it didn't matter that she *knew* that – she couldn't make her feelings obey her rational mind. It felt real. Her heart hurt, her stomach ached, and it took a long time for the sense of betrayal to fade.

It was the same now. She *knew* what Taasas had shown her wasn't true, but it didn't matter. Her pulse still raced as though it was; bile still rose in her stomach as she thought of it. In desperation, she grasped at the science of it, trying to figure out how it worked and how she could stop it. Did Taasas choose the images she wanted Sorrow to see, or did they come from her own fears? Was there some way she could defend herself against future attacks, some kind of wall she could build in her mind to repel it? Touch was obviously part of it – she'd stay out of her reach from now on – but would that be enough?

She thought bitterly of her plans – to trace her parents, to remove Sorrow's bones from the crypt. It was as though Vespus had known she'd found a way to disarm him, and had moved to stop her before she could.

Sorrow sent for tea, too fraught for her beloved coffee, and paced until she'd burned off most of the adrenaline that surged through her. When she'd finally calmed enough to stand still, Sorrow paused by the window, putting her thoughts in order.

Idly she pulled one of the tasselled curtain ties from its hook and slipped her hand in the loop, tightening it like a noose, until an image of Irris pirouetting in mid-air sprung into her mind and she dropped it, returning to pacing.

She missed her friend. Her heart ached for her.

When the bedroom door knocked Sorrow was convinced it was Irris. She opened the door, apologies burning on her tongue.

"Rasmus."

"Do I disappoint?" He raised a pale brow at her surprise. "Were you expecting someone else?"

"No. No. Come in – actually I'll come out." She slipped out of the bedroom, into the private parlour. He gave her an amused look and followed her to the sofas, sitting opposite her.

"I'm sorry about last night." Sorrow spoke before he could. "I shouldn't have snapped at you. You were being kind."

"You don't have to apologize to me. It's all right."

Sorrow smiled humourlessly, and Rasmus continued, looking around the room.

"Thank you for receiving me so graciously. Despite everything," he said, "it is nice to be back. I thought of this place as home."

"It was your home," Sorrow said. "And I told you that you were welcome here."

Rasmus gave her a long, piercing look. "Actually, that's why I wanted to see you. I have a question."

"What kind of question?" Sorrow said, her eyes narrowing.

"The awkward kind." He smiled. "My father implied I was more than welcome. He said you wanted me here. He insisted on it, though I was sure he was lying."

"But you came anyway."

"Of course I did. So, did you? Ask for me?"

Silence stretched between them as Rasmus waited for her reply. Sorrow knew what he wanted her to say and she couldn't. But nor could she bring herself to tell the truth.

"That's a no, isn't it?" he said, his voice low. "You didn't ask for me."

Sorrow shook her head. "That doesn't mean I don't want you here."

He sighed, shaking his head. "I should have known. I should have written to you."

"Ras... Really, I'm glad you're here. I could do with a friend."

His gaze sharpened and he leant forward. "What's going on with you and Irris?" he asked.

Immediately defensive, Sorrow crossed her arms. "What makes you ask?"

He shrugged. "I passed her just now in the corridor. She said she was leaving."

Sorrow was on her feet and out of the door instantly, charging through her rooms, out into the wing. She heard Rasmus calling after her but she didn't stop, bolting down the corridor; the guards barely had time to open the doors at the end before she burst through them, skidding on to the landing, then leaping down the stairs two at a time, momentum the only thing keeping her upright.

She ran through the hallways, out of the main doors, on to the steps, looking down into the courtyard.

Irris stood there, with Mael and Arran, before a carriage laden with trunks. The driver was already seated, whip in hand, the horses pawing the ground, eager to ride on.

All three gaped at her as she made her way down to them, gasping for breath, a hand pressed against the stitch in her side.

"Sorrow..." Arran began.

Sorrow ignored him, her focus on Irris. "You're leaving."

"Of course I am. At your orders. Home to pack and then off to Svarta I go."

Rasmus appeared at Sorrow's side, annoyingly serene considering he must have just run from the other side of the palace too.

"No," begged Sorrow. "No, you don't understand."

"You keep saying that," Mael interrupted. "But I think

we understand just fine. You want us to like you, just from a distance. Consider this your wish granted. Goodbye, Sorrow."

"But. . ." She was going to cry. She could feel the telltale tightness in her throat, the burning in her chest.

She bit down on the inside of her cheek. She was the chancellor, she couldn't cry.

And this was what she wanted. Her friends away from Vespus. They weren't safe here, and they needed to go.

So why did it hurt so much?

"Fine." Sorrow forced the word from her mouth.

"That's all you have to say?" Irris looked at Rasmus and threw her hands in the air. "See?" she said, turning her back on them and climbing into the coach.

Mael followed her, giving Sorrow a disappointed shrug as he did.

She didn't wait to watch the carriage roll away, turning on her heel. She knew without turning that Rasmus was behind her, but she didn't expect Arran to follow.

"I told them to go straight back to the estate. No detours. They won't be near the infected zones." Arran reached for her arm, gently drawing her to a stop.

"What infected zones?" Rasmus asked.

Sorrow rounded on him, pouring out her fury. "What did she mean by 'see?'" she said coldly.

He sighed. "She's worried about you."

"And you know this how?"

"We spoke, last night," he admitted. He never could lie.

Sorrow shook her head. "And that's the real reason you came to see me earlier? To get information." She laughed bitterly. "Well, I've changed my mind. I don't think it's a good idea for you to be here."

His eyes widened in shock, immediately shaming her, then his expression hardened. "Is that really what you think?"

Pride made her nod.

"Then I'll say goodbye. Chancellor."

He spun away, his hair whipping behind him like water, striding away from her, leaving Sorrow staring after him, her stomach twisting itself into a knot of anxiety and regret.

"What on Laethea was that about?" Arran said, startling Sorrow. She'd forgotten he was there.

"Nothing."

"Your Excellency?" A liveried servant edged towards her, his head bowed, a silver tray in his hands. "A message. It's marked urgent."

Sorrow took the envelope and opened it, dismissing the servant. It was from Meeren Vine, telling her the quarantine was in effect in the contaminated villages and the hospitals. No one allowed in or out while his Decorum Ward were monitoring the border. She screwed up the paper, folding it into a clenched fist, her heart thudding like a drum between her lungs. Vespus's Grace-damned plague would only serve to reinforce Vine's sense of self-importance, and his demands for more money. He'd screwed her twice over.

A headache began to tiptoe over her skull in heavy boots, and she closed her eyes, massaging the bridge of her nose.

"Sorrow?"

Arran watched her, concern written across his handsome features.

"It's an update from the North Marches. The quarantine has begun. If you could tell the others. I shall be in my office for the rest of the day."

*

She fantasized about writing to Irris, to Mael, to Rasmus. Explaining everything, begging them to understand. But most of all, she thought of writing to Luvian. She still had his message from Prekara in her pocket. She told herself it was safer there, less likely to be found, but she knew that was a lie, even if she couldn't quite admit it. She wanted him close, in some way, even if it was just words on a page.

She thought the note was flirtatious; but then the boy was a born flirt. There had been a moment in her room before the election, just after he'd brought the Lamentia to her, when the world had felt like a spinning coin, both of them watching which way it would land. But the coin had kept spinning, and the only things that had changed were Vespus's power over her, and how much she despised herself.

Pushing away those thoughts, she pulled a file towards her and tried to lose herself in the safety of bureaucracy, plunging herself into a world of budgets and resources, relishing the controllable.

An hour before dinner Charon wheeled himself into her office, neither knocking nor waiting to be invited.

He spoke without ceremony. "The Jedenvat have all left, save Arran, who's asked for leave to stay here and support you."

"That's fine," Sorrow agreed.

"May I have permission to speak to you frankly?" Charon asked in a cold, clear voice. "Not as your vice chancellor, but as the man who helped raise you."

She had known this was coming. She schooled her face into blankness, giving what she hoped was a dignified nod.

He took a deep breath. "I don't know what is going on with

you and I don't care. But it stops. Now. You and Irris can fight, you and Mael can fight, but you do not do it on the doorstep of the palace where anyone can hear you. You are the chancellor of this country and it has just been plunged into crisis. And as for Master Corrigan—"

"He's leaving," Sorrow protested.

"He's already gone," said Charon drily. "It's not diplomatic to fight in the halls with the son of the Rhyllian ambassador."

He'd left. He'd really left. Despite the fact she'd told him to – despite the fact he'd said he would – she realized she hadn't believed it.

She'd finally succeeded in pushing him away, too.

"Sorrow?" Charon's anger mellowed into concern. "Are you all right?"

She nodded. Swallowed, and nodded again. "I'm fine. I know where my attention needs to be. Believe me, it's all I'm thinking of."

Charon gave her a long, steady look. "Good. Good. And, Sorrow?" He paused, licking his lips before speaking. "I gather I'm at the end of a long queue of people saying this, but I'm here if you need me. I know things have changed since Rhylla, and what you learned. But nothing has changed for me. I am still behind you; I always will be. You'll find me a lot harder to push away. Take your time. I will wait."

Sorrow forced the lump in her throat down and gave him a benign smile. "Everything's fine, Charon. I'm fine."

His expression was unreadable. "As you say."

He turned his chair sharply and wheeled away, leaving Sorrow hollowed.

She rose on shaking legs, and closed the door. Then she leant against it, face shining with the tears that poured from her eyes, her fist crammed in her mouth to keep her from sobbing. Luvian was missing. Mael had gone. Rasmus and Irris were gone. Even Charon had taken her at her word she was fine.

For the first time in her life, Sorrow was truly alone. And it was all her own fault.

The following day, Sorrow released a statement, telling the people there was no cause for alarm; so far the illness was isolated to the North Marches and they were doing all they could to establish the cause of the plague and find a cure. It was politic, and placatory, and rendered immediately pointless by the announcement that a third village had found victims in its midst.

Sorrow hadn't given up on her plan to move the bones, but every time she cleared her desk and turned her mind to it, some new fire sprang up, demanding her attention and forcing her to shelve it once more. She was spending eighteen, sometimes twenty hours a day working, dashing between the Round Chamber to consult with the Jedenvat, then back to her office to go through the endless accounts and messages that had arrived in her absence.

She read the reports from each village with mounting horror. New victims were still being diagnosed, but the older ones showed no sign of waking. To keep them from wasting away as they slept, their terrified families were dribbling milk and honey down their throats, even as they feared catching the illness themselves. It didn't help that there seemed to be no way to predict who would succumb.

Sorrow went to Vespus again.

"Vespus, you have to stop. Or at least give me the antidote. They're starving to death."

He shook his head. "They'll wake once their bodies have processed it. They won't die."

"How long—"

"I've already told you, I don't know," he snapped, cutting her off. "I would have expected them to have woken by now."

The admission surprised her. Then terrified her. "You don't have any idea what you're doing, do you?" she said, hiding her horror with a sneer.

"Be careful," he barked. "You might have sent my son packing with your sharp tongue but it won't work with me."

Taasas slunk into the room on silent feet, startling Sorrow as she moved to Vespus and rested her hands on his shoulders.

"Hello, Sorrow," she said. Between her eerie, placid countenance and the anger rolling from Vespus, Sorrow decided it was time to take her leave. Besides, it was clear that Vespus wasn't going to tell her anything. She'd have to figure it out herself.

9

To Scythe and to Rake

Vespus had lied.

Mila Stenzon. Avis Block. Carr Vixel.

Those were the names of the people his plague killed. They could have been mothers, fathers, brothers, sisters, friends, lovers, life partners. They were people – the people she'd sworn she'd do her duty by – and they'd died, and it was firmly on her account.

Sorrow wrote down their names on a piece of paper she carried in her pocket, next to Luvian's letter.

Mila Stenzon. Avis Block. Carr Vixel.

These were the lives she had stolen by agreeing to Vespus's terms.

Vespus had looked startled when she had told him, but he refused to acknowledge her distress. He was in an excellent mood; apparently when he'd checked his seeds in the dungeons that morning he'd sensed them quickening. That was the word he used – *quickening* – as though they were a child in a womb. His face was manic with joy as he ushered her into his rooms.

"It means the worst part is almost over," he said.

"'The worst part'?" Sorrow was incredulous. "People are dead, Vespus."

"Three people, Sorrow. Three. Out of a hundred. Winter chills kill more people than that. You're overreacting. Besides, we can use the deaths to our advantage. People will be desperate to leave now. Announce the evacuation of the area, effective immediately," Vespus went on. "And order that a fence be built, to keep anyone from straying into it."

"A fence?" said Sorrow dully. "We didn't agree on a fence."

"Sorrow, think, for once in your life." He spoke slowly, enunciating every word. "I told you there would be a cordon. I'll need to clear the land before I can plant my seeds, and I can hardly do that with an audience. People will have questions if they see their homes and businesses destroyed and a forest springing up in their place. I need a fence to keep your people, and mine, from seeing it."

He stood, crossing the room to an ornate chest of drawers and pulling out a map. He pinned it down on the table, pointing.

"You'll invite me to use my ability to fence off the land, protecting the people from the horrors within, and I'll graciously accept."

Sorrow stared at him. He had wanted more, after all. Not just the villages but the farms, meadows and natural forests between them. The Summer Palace fell in the area he wanted.

"I can't do this. . ." She felt weak, and unmoored, as though

112

drifting away from herself. "It's too much."

"I assure you, Sorrow, you can. And you will. I just told you the Alvus are quickening. Soon they'll need to be planted in the ground. So get me my ground."

Sorrow couldn't stop thinking about the people who'd died. In her mind they took on the characteristics of people she knew; Mila Stenzon took on the face of her grandmother, stately and stern, but with kind eyes; Avis Block had Irris's heart-shaped face and quick wits; Carr Vixel was bespectacled, with neatly styled hair and a wry smile.

Their imagined faces haunting her, Sorrow turned all of her attention to the plague. If Vespus wouldn't give her the cure, she could at least try to make sure no one else fell ill. She spent every waking hour poring over the medical reports the doctors sent her, looking for a link. There had to be one – something they'd eaten, drunk, some place they'd been, something that told her where and how he was poisoning them.

Sorrow wrote to Vine, telling him she needed him to investigate the common factors between the villages – the layouts, the kind of homes people had, what plants and trees were nearby. She was searching, desperately, for a clue. She knew she would be unlikely to succeed without Vespus's help. But she had to try. She owed the people that.

Vine's reply arrived just two hours later, saying he didn't have the resources to be a detective as well as keep the quarantine maintained. He told her she should have listened to him when he asked for more money in the first place, and asked again for it.

For a split-second, she was tempted: pay him to get the answers she wanted. But Irris would have advised her not to;

Sorrow knew that as surely as if Irris was there in the room. She'd tell her she couldn't buy her way out of the problem. And Sorrow knew any extra money would go straight into Vine's own pockets and he *still* wouldn't do what she'd asked. He'd never respect her; stars, he'd even addressed the letter to "Miss Ventaxis" and not "Chancellor". If she wanted this done, she'd have to go there herself. So, seething with annoyance, she replied to say there was no more money, and he needed to get that into his head. She sent the message before she could think better of it.

When word reached her the following morning that Vine had beaten a young man severely for trying to "escape" the quarantine, Sorrow knew it was because of her. She had had enough. She might not be able to stop Vespus right then, but she could stop Meeren Vine. That, at least, was in her power.

She returned to the library and pulled down different books: histories of Rhannon, Rhylla, Meridea, even Svarta. She forgot lunch, forgot dinner, forgot everything that wasn't the task she'd set herself. Finally, as the clock chimed eleven bells, she put down her pen.

Rising stiffly from her desk, she hobbled across the room on the dead legs of someone who'd been sitting in the same position for too long, and she threw open her office door. "Find out if the vice chancellor is still awake and if he is, ask him to join me," she demanded of Dougray.

He nodded, and vanished at once. Sorrow made her way back to her seat, rubbing her calves, waiting.

Charon, bleary-eyed and suspicious, stared at her across her desk. It had taken him half an hour to arrive, leading Sorrow to think he'd been in bed, and had got back in his chair for her.

She felt guilty, but only for a moment, then she told him her plan. He ran his tongue over his teeth before he spoke, buying time to choose his words, his hands clasped tightly in his lap.

"You can't go to the North Marches. What if you catch this illness? People have died, Sorrow."

"I won't."

"You don't know that."

She would have laughed, if it had been at all funny. "I'll take precautions. A room at the Summer Palace will be all I need."

"Sorrow..."

"I want to see the victims. I want to see the families of the dead. And I want to get to the root of this." *Roots. Plants. Vespus.* She fought a bleak smile at the unintended pun.

"Ask Vine to investigate it."

"I have. And he's still singing the same old song about money. Which leads me to something else..." She paused. "When I get back from the North Marches, once this plague has been dealt with, I want to call the Jedenvat back for a vote. I want to disband the Decorum Ward."

"It's not pos—"

"It is," Sorrow said, pointing to the books on her desk, the piles of paper. "I'm not suggesting getting rid of the police force, but getting rid of the Ward itself. Vine has too much power and control. He's corrupt, and he corrupts them. To begin we'll pass legislation that makes them Lawkeepers, not the Ward. They all keep their jobs, but not as the Ward. As of that moment, the Ward no longer exists. They no longer wear those badges, and they wear blue, or grey, something less intimidating than the black. I want to set up proper, regulated training places for them, where they're held accountable. Where we have some control."

Vine wouldn't like it, but he could quit, if he wanted. It's what she wanted; she knew she couldn't fire him. Yet, at least.

"I want us, the Jedenvat, even Vine and a few of his commanders to amend the legislation. I want to implement a system of trial by peer. The Ward, or the Lawkeepers, even, won't get to pass judgement any more. Everyone arrested by them gets a fair hearing."

Charon gave her a long look, followed by a resigned shrug.

"This won't happen overnight."

"I know. I know that. And I know it won't be easy. But it won't happen at all if I don't do something. Don't you see? I have to do something. It's my job. They're my responsibility."

"The plague isn't your fault," Charon said softly.

Sorrow stilled, watching him across the table.

"You're our leader. It's natural for you to feel helpless when things happen that you can't control, and I understand the need to do something – anything – to try to help Rhannon. But this is a lifetime role, Sorrow. There's time for you to allow the dust to settle before you tear the rulebook up and write a new one."

Sorrow was silent for a moment.

"My mind is made up," she said softly. "There is something else, though." She took a deep breath; she might as well ask now. "I need to know if any records of my birth parents exist."

"Why?" Charon's face blanched.

"I just want to know."

"You want to know if they're victims of the plague?" Charon guessed.

It seemed easier, for now, to let him believe it. "Partly. And also I want to know who they are, Charon. I deserve to."

For a while he said nothing, and Sorrow waited.

But when he replied, Charon had no more questions. "I'll look into it, discreetly."

"I appreciate it. And I'm sorry to keep you up so late."

"I'm worried about you," Charon said, watching her as she stood.

She walked to the door and held it open, making it clear the meeting was over. "You really don't need to. Everything will be better soon."

He rolled past her in silence, and she repeated it to herself. *Everything will be better soon.*

It had to be.

The Decorum Ward were not pleased to see Sorrow when she arrived at the border they'd set up around one of the affected villages – Inarz – in the North Marches. Charon had insisted on coming with her.

They waited outside the border, an invisible line marked only by the presence of the cold-eyed men and women in black, the fist-over-iron-heart displayed proudly on their chests. They all gave Sorrow the curtest of nods when she met their eyes, which she returned with as much disdain as they did. Stars, she'd be glad when their time was over.

Inarz was a small village, home to only four thousand people, a mile from the Summer Palace. Once it had served as a satellite village for workers there; cooks, footmen, guards and gardeners, maids, maintenance workers and serving staff, but after Harun stopped going there, those who'd stayed had become smallholders, most moving to find a living elsewhere. On the great map in the Round Chamber, back in Istevar, Sorrow had marked all the affected villages, and she knew

Inarz was at the edge of the area Vespus had chosen.

"It's not too late to change your mind," Charon murmured as they waited for one of the physicians to brief them. "You don't have to do this."

"Yes, I do."

She smiled as the doctor approached, a mask over her nose and mouth, obscuring her own smile, which Sorrow read in her eyes. She wore gloves too, made from some kind of thin, translucent membrane. She didn't offer Sorrow her hand.

She spoke in a muffled voice. "Forgive me, Chancellor. I'm Dr Kenra, we've been corresponding. I have no new findings for you. We still have no idea how it's transmitted."

"I would like to enter the affected zone nonetheless," said Sorrow, and the doctor nodded. Four other masked people stepped forward, each holding a pile of what appeared a set of folded leaves and a bowl of steaming water.

Sorrow looked at Charon, who nodded for her to go first, so she did, first washing her arms in the hot, oily-feeling water. She let them drip dry, stopping short of shaking them when the steely-eyed assistant shook her head, and took the first folded leaf from the pile. Inside she found a pair of gloves similar to the ones they all wore.

"What are they?" she asked, holding them up to the light. They were thin, membranous, and felt delicate, though they held as she pulled them on.

"The skin of the Esafish."

Sorrow grimaced at her hands as Dr Kenra continued.

"They're a Merish invention. We're very behind here in Rhannon." She paused, her eyes widening as she realized what she'd said, and to whom, but Sorrow nodded for her to continue, dangling the face mask in her hands. She'd wait to hear what that was before she put it near her mouth. Dougray had the same thought, holding his mask away from himself as subtly as he could, though Charon had already put his on.

"The skin is an excellent barrier, and it never fully dries out," the doctor said. "It remains pliable, even after death. They're a fascinating species; they return to the Archior after mating at sea to die, and when their bodies wash up on the riverbanks, the skin is harvested. We bought as many pairs as we could when the plague broke out."

"And the mask?" Sorrow asked.

"Just cotton, Your Excellency. Boiled and then soaked in frangipani to keep it protected."

Sorrow heard Dougray sigh in relief, and both she and he covered their noses and mouths.

Dr Kenra took them on a tour of the village, deserted as the people remained in their homes. It was eerie, how quiet and abandoned it felt. Even during Harun's time, the villages had pulsed with life when she'd passed through them, though it was a subdued, resentful sort. This was frightening, as though Hellfior was a god and the people were hiding, afraid to draw its eye. Every now and then Sorrow would see a face in a window, and she raised a hand to wave, but the people never waved back. They just watched, solemnly, as she passed by, before disappearing once more. They weren't masked, Sorrow noticed, and she asked the doctor why.

"We don't have the resources to provide them," the doctor said. "We don't even have enough for the Ward at the border. They stay outside the line and rely on their batons to protect them," she added grimly. "We've asked everyone to stay in their homes as much as possible, to keep the risk of infection down.

It seems to be working too; there have been no new cases in the last three days."

"Good. That's good. And do you know yet where it originated from?"

"We don't. It's puzzling. Everyone uses largely the same resources: water, food, the same small school and shops, but there doesn't seem to be a pattern. Some entire families seem to fall ill, sometimes only one of them does. It's like the sickness just fell from the sky, infecting those it landed on, forsaking those it didn't."

"I'd like to visit some of the victims," Sorrow said.

"I'm still not sure that's a good idea." Charon had been silent until then, propelling himself along beside them.

"I'm safe enough, with the mask and gloves, aren't I?" Sorrow asked the doctor.

"In theory, yes. . ." Dr Kenra replied. "But I agree with the vice chancellor. We know so little about this."

Guilt dug its spurs into Sorrow's flesh. She could tell them it wasn't an illness, but a poison. Perhaps they could create an antidote if they knew that. Though if Vespus hadn't been able to – or so he said – it was unlikely anyone else could.

"I understand. But I would really like to," Sorrow repeated. "They're my people."

"Sorrow, I must advise you against this in the strongest possible terms." Charon pulled the mask from his mouth so she could see how set it was, his lips a line of disapproval.

"I know. But I have to do it. I have to see." She looked back at Dr Kenra, who nodded at her from the door of a cottage. She could go in.

She looked at the steps leading up to the front door, then at Charon's chair. "You'll have to wait here," Sorrow said. She turned to Dougray. "You don't have to come, either."

"I do, Your Excellency," Dougray said.

She left Charon staring after her, his gaze burning a hole in her back as she approached the house. The Esafish gloves made her hands clammy, sweat sticking them to her palms, and she longed to take them off, to dry her hands on her tunic, pull the mask from her face.

Sorrow smelled the sickness at once, even through the mask: a sweet, almost alcoholic scent, as though fruit had been left to rot and ferment in the summer sun. She heard a choking sound behind her and turned to see Dougray pushing his way out of the house, hand over his mouth. She didn't blame him.

There were two victims here, a man and a woman, perhaps a decade older than her, both wearing plain silver bands on their ring fingers, lying side by side on a double bed. It was clear at once to Sorrow that they weren't just asleep. She could see their veins beneath their papery skin, green and rotten-looking. Their chests rose and fell not with the depth and rhythm of real sleep, but with the shallow labour of the suffering. The worst of it was their expressions: twin grimaces that were tight and pained, as though they were lying trapped beneath their own faces, fighting to get to the surface. They looked as though they battled every moment, and the horror of it made Sorrow step back.

"Can they hear us?" she asked.

Dr Kenra moved to her side.

"We don't know. They don't seem to respond to our voices, any more than any other stimulus, but until someone wakes and tells us, we're in the dark."

The phrase sent chills down Sorrow's spine. Were they in the dark? Was that what it was like for them? Prisoners inside their own bodies, blind and dumb, held hostage by Hellfior.

She didn't stop to ask advice, or permission. Instead, she cleared the room in two strides, taking the hand of the female patient and sitting beside her on the bed.

"If you can hear me, I want you to know I'm sorry. I'm sorry this happened to you. I'm – we're – doing everything we can to help you get better. You will get better, I promise you," she said. "I promise."

She squeezed the woman's hand, desperate for some sign she'd been heard, but her fingers remained limp in Sorrow's, no indication she knew the chancellor of Rhannon, or anyone else, was there at all.

It was the same story with the rest of the victims, thirty in this village. Sorrow insisted on seeing every single one, telling all of them the same thing. The children almost brought her to her knees, their peachy skin drawn taut over small bones. She stayed the longest with them, only moving on when the insistence of the doctors overwhelmed her.

She couldn't speak when she got back to the carriage, devastated by what she'd seen. What she'd done. Charon gave her a soft smile as she and Dougray climbed into the carriage, where he'd retreated to wait for them.

Though she'd taken off her gloves and mask to be burned, and walked through a tray of boiling water to sanitize her boots, she could still smell the sickness clinging to her hair and clothes. It wasn't her imagination, either, as Charon wrinkled his nose when she moved to open the window.

"I need that information I asked for," she said, trusting he'd know what she meant without her having to spell it out.

"It should be at the Summer Palace before we leave," Charon said. "I wrote this morning and asked for a list of all the records for the pertinent time to be sent there with haste."

The coach began to move, and Sorrow nodded. "Good. Thank you."

Sorrow sat back, her jaw set with determination, as she watched the countryside roll by. All this land. She wouldn't let Vespus have it. Not one single inch would she yield to him.

The carriage slowed, and then stopped abruptly, and the driver pounded the roof violently.

Sorrow leant forward to peer out of the window, but Dougray pushed her back, leaning out himself.

He withdrew within a second and turned to Sorrow.

"Get out. Run," he said as he drew his sword in the small space of the carriage. "They're coming."

"Who?" Sorrow stared at him.

"The Sons of Rhannon."

PART TWO

A man who is master of himself can end a sorrow
as easily as he can invent a pleasure.

—*Oscar Wilde,* The Picture of Dorian Gray

10

Against the Fortress

Dougray pushed the door open and swung out of the carriage in a swift, clean motion.

"Go. I'll hold them off," Dougray said. "Go!"

He darted out of sight.

How could it be the Sons of Rhannon? They didn't exist any more. They'd been disbanded, Luvian said he'd tell them to leave her alone—

Sorrow looked at Charon. He wouldn't be able to escape without his chair.

"Don't worry about me," he said, looking fiercer than she'd ever seen as he read her thoughts. "Get out of here. Take one of the horses and ride."

"I can't leave you. . ."

"Then we're both dead," he barked.

Outside the carriage came shouts and the sounds of men

fighting. Something hit the side loudly, hard enough to rock it on its wheels.

"Please," Charon said, sliding across the seat and reaching forward to open the door on the opposite side. "Sorrow, go."

She gave him one final, desperate look, and scrambled out.

Sorrow rolled under the carriage and saw immediately that Dougray had been right. There was no mistaking the enormous hooded figures that were fighting her bodyguard and the poor coach driver. Five, no – *eight* of them, two fighting Dougray, while the others tried to edge around the perimeter the coach driver was creating with his whip.

As Sorrow watched he sent it cracking through the air, forcing them back. One of the Sons was gripping his forearm as blood dripped to the ground.

Good, she thought, scrambling out.

As she did, one of them whistled, and all of them turned to her, like wolves homing in on their prey. Those trying to get past the whip backed off at once, fanning out to prevent her from finding a way past. Adrenaline and fear lanced through her body, and she cast around for a way to escape.

Sorrow looked to where the two roan beasts were stomping, blind to what was happening, thanks to the blinkers over their eyes, but able to hear and smell the blood and fury on the Sons.

She edged along the carriage, her heart pounding, reaching for the flank of one of the beasts, intending to soothe it, only to fall back as the horse tried to rear, terrified at this new, strange touch.

"Shush," Sorrow tried, but the horse wouldn't calm, and every time it shied the other horse panicked too, jostling the carriage, where Charon was helpless. She needed to find another way.

Sorrow turned, intending to start running back along the track towards the village they'd just left, when the coach driver gave a strangled cry and fell to the ground, his forehead bloody from the rock one of the Sons had thrown.

Without stopping to think, Sorrow lunged, skidding under the bellies of the horses before they knew what she'd done, grasping the whip the fallen man had dropped.

A split-second later she was on her feet, spinning the leather in her hand, even as Dougray screamed at her to run. There was no point in running now. There was only fighting.

She snapped it out at the first of the men to try reaching for her, bringing her arm back and swinging it forward with as much force as she could. She made contact with his wrist, heard the slap of leather against flesh and felt a buzz of triumph as he cried out and dropped back, clutching the wound she'd given him.

Feeling bolder, she advanced, flicking the whip before her.

Dougray was trying his best to get back to her, but his sabre was in his left hand, his right dangling uselessly by his side as he battled two of the Sons alone.

One of them had snuck closer while she'd been distracted, and she flicked her wrist, sending the strap snaking towards him, missing him by inches as he ducked and rolled. He came up on her left and she went for him again, aiming lower this time. He jumped as the leather shot beneath him, and, believing himself safe, rushed her. But Sorrow pulled the whip back towards her and caught his ankle, sending him stumbling in the dirt. She raised her arm again, ready to take him out of the fight.

She realized her mistake too late.

While she'd concentrated on the one nearest her, the others had moved to the right, cornering her, the carriage at her back leaving her nowhere to run. She spun and cracked the whip to drive them away as the man she'd been focusing on dived at her, tackling her to the ground.

The impact forced her breath from her lungs as instinct kicked in. *Not again.*

She drove her knee into his groin and shoved him off her, kicking out at another as he tried to get a grip on her, connecting with his knee and sending him sprawling. Staying low and pivoting on her left ankle, she spun, sweeping a third off his feet before she straightened.

They'd surrounded her.

For all her efforts, there were too many of them. They closed in, moving as one, and she summoned a last burst of strength to make sure it wasn't easy for them.

She kicked, punched and spat, refusing to give up. Some fool moved his hand too close to her mouth and she bit down, clamping on through the glove until he screamed and she still wouldn't let go, not until a pair of rough fingers pinched her nose.

Even then, she refused to release him until the urge to breathe became unbearable, all those times pinning herself beneath her own bathwater paying off as she held him in a terrible grip, her lungs ready for it.

She knew she'd broken the skin. She hoped the bite got infected.

Then a hood was over her head, filling her nose and mouth with a bitter, herbal scent. A drug of some kind, she realized.

Sorrow understood then, with crystal clarity, that they

hadn't come there to kill her. They'd come to take her away.

Somehow, that scared her more.

Once again she held her breath as she tried to shake the hood off, while her captors forced her hands behind her back and tied them. She almost succeeded – tipping forward until the hood fell and she sucked in a lungful of fresh air.

"Hood's off!" a man to her right said, and Sorrow flinched because she knew his voice. The last time she'd heard it she'd been gasping for breath too.

"Arkady, you coward," she screamed.

Someone picked up the hood and sprayed the insides of it with the contents of a small bottle, reaching for her. Sorrow threw herself backwards, knocking the man still holding her hands, and herself, to the ground.

They hauled her to her feet, and the last thing she saw before they pulled the hood over her head was Charon Day, pale and terrified, watching helplessly from the carriage.

Sorrow fought it for as long as she could, taking tiny breaths only when her lungs forced her to. But slowly a fog appeared in her head and bloomed, her limbs turning heavy and loose, unable to hold her up. She slumped in her kidnapper's arms, desperately trying to cling to consciousness.

And then there was nothing, and she was gone, floating away into darkness.

When Sorrow woke, the hood was off, and she knew, instinctively, that she wasn't alone. Her head was a bell and it was ringing, pain deafening her as it beat against her skull. It tried to pull her down, and she was happy to follow, welcoming the darkness that crept in and promised to take her away from the agony. To think this was the result of some drug – why on Laethea would anyone voluntarily do this to themselves?

Through the merciful blackness, she thought she heard someone speak her name, and she moaned her refusal, though her eyes blinked open regardless. She was lying on her side, apparently on a bed; she could feel the softness of a pillow beneath her cheek, the gentle dip of a mattress under her legs. Her hands were still tied. She kept herself still, staring at the expanse of the grey wall before her. The Sons of Rhannon had kidnapped her and brought her . . . where?

Sorrow could sense someone was there, tell from a heaviness in the air, the way the silence wasn't quite silent. She didn't know how many of them watched her. She didn't know what they might do if they realized she was awake. She kept her breathing slow and even, resisted the urge to shift, although her right shoulder ached, and tried to listen.

She could hear water, she was sure of it. The faint rushing sound of waves. Wherever she was felt steady, though, so she wasn't on a boat. So still on land, but maybe near the river then? Somewhere further north. . .

Then something so obvious occurred to her she realized she must still be under the effects of the drug not to have thought of it sooner. She was somewhere in Prekara. Prekara was where the Rathbones held their own tiny republic of criminals; it was their seat of power. And Prekara was riddled with waterways.

That was a start.

She moved on to wondering how long she'd been unconscious. Gas lamps lit the room, she could smell the faint tang of them, and the light had that hazy yellow quality the lamps emitted. So perhaps it was night? Aside from her sore wrists and throbbing head, she seemed to be unharmed. And alive.

What did they plan to do to her?

After several more moments lying still, eyes fixed on the wall, Sorrow realized the only way she was going to get any answers was by turning over and facing whoever was there, watching her. So far, they hadn't moved, hadn't sighed, hadn't given themselves away at all.

Silently, she counted to three and rolled over.

The room was empty.

Quickly, Sorrow scanned the whole room, but there was no one else in the small space. Nowhere for anyone to hide, either. Surprised, she hauled herself up and surveyed it. It was windowless, all four walls grey, and tiny. The only furniture was the small bed she sat on, and a stool by the bed that she assumed was to act as a table. That was it. No bucket for a latrine, nothing else, save a door opposite the bed that looked as though it was made of metal. There was a small dark square in its centre, around head height, and Sorrow frowned at it. What was that?

She shuffled to the end of the bed and put her feet down. The first time she tried to stand her legs would have none of it, and she toppled back on to the bed.

Sorrow sat up sharply as she heard someone giggle, and then the hiss of shushing. So she was right – someone had been watching her, but from outside the room. The dark square was some kind of glass that hid the viewer, on one side. Whoever was on the other side of it, they were watching her now, and they weren't alone.

She tried again, slowly, pushing down through her soles, lifting herself to standing and locking her knees. She cleared

133

her throat as quietly as she could, wanting to be sure she sounded strong and clear when she said, "I know you're out there, I can hear you. So why don't you just come and face me?"

She cocked her head, listening.

"What have you got to be afraid of?" she asked, her courage growing a little as the voyeurs remained on the other side of the door. "I'm alone, and bound. And no doubt still suffering from whatever you drugged me with. Don't be a coward, face me like a—"

The door opened, and a startled Sorrow fell back on to the bed once more.

Two people stood in the doorway, and to Sorrow's immense relief neither was Arkady Rathbone. One was a young girl, aged around nine or ten, her hair in two long plaits, reaching down past her waist. The other was older, mid-teens or thereabouts. Her hair was short, cut in a sharp bob that fell in line with her pointed chin. Both of them had the golden skin and dark eyes of the Rhannish. The elder one held a tray, and Sorrow raised her eyebrows.

Neither of the girls said anything.

"Is that for me?" Sorrow asked finally, using her head to gesture to the tray.

The two silently conferred, and then nodded in tandem. The elder girl held it out, as though inviting Sorrow to take it.

"You're going to have to bring it over." She smiled. "I'm a bit tied up right now."

Again, they looked at each other, and the younger one gave a blunt nod, as though she was in charge.

A split-second later, Sorrow realized she *was* in charge, when she pulled a wicked-looking knife from behind her back and held it in a steady hand.

"Our papi says if you try anything I have to cut you. I don't want to," she said solemnly. "But I will."

Sorrow swallowed, and by way of answer, moved on to the bed until her back was flush with the wall. Any thoughts she'd had of trying to subdue the girls fled at the sight of the weapon clutched confidently in the girl's small but firm grip.

Appeased by her actions, the older girl crossed the room, flanked by her tiny bodyguard, and placed the tray on the stool. Sorrow saw now that it contained what seemed to be a change of clothes, a large jug of water, a cup, some flatbread, and olives, and a small pot of a creamy-looking paste.

"I'm not trying to be a nuisance," she said, addressing the youngest girl. "But how am I supposed to eat that with my hands tied?"

"I'm allowed to cut the rope for you," the girl replied. "Papi said."

"Right. Good. May I ask who 'Papi' is?" Sorrow tried.

The girl looked at her blankly, and Sorrow sighed.

She kicked her legs to the side and drew herself up on her knees, twisting to expose her bound wrists to the child. The bed dipped as the girl climbed up, and then there was a moment of pressure as she took the rope and cut it in one stroke. Sorrow swallowed again; the knife must be wickedly sharp.

Sorrow turned slowly. The older girl was waiting in the doorway, the younger one backing away from Sorrow, the knife glinting dangerously in her hand.

"Thank you," Sorrow said, deciding it couldn't hurt to be nice to her.

The girl smirked, as though she knew what Sorrow was doing.

"You're supposed to eat. And get changed. Someone will be

135

along for you soon," the older girl said, her voice soft and husky.

"I'll just wait here, then," Sorrow said.

Her captors looked at her strangely, apparently not getting the joke, and then left, closing the door with a gentle clang.

Sorrow didn't hear the sound of a lock, but didn't find that reassuring. For all she knew there was an army of children out there, all kitted out with knives. At least for now she had a bed and food. The last time she had encountered the Sons of Rhannon, things were a lot less civil.

She hoped Charon and the others were all right. The entire Decorum Ward were probably tearing the country apart trying to find her. But they would have no idea where she was.

She reached for the flatbread, and then paused, her hand hovering in mid-air. Irris. Irris would know where to find her. Irris knew who the Sons of Rhannon were, and where they came from. She'd know Sorrow would be somewhere in Prekara – she'd tell Charon and the Ward that.

Sorrow changed out of the dusty and torn outfit she'd worn to the village and into the clothes they'd left her. They were men's clothes, the buttons on the tunic on the wrong side, and they were old, the material soft, as though it had been washed many times. She combed her hair through with her fingers, then used a little of the water to wash her hands, before eating the food she'd been left. She wasn't worried about poison. They had her captive; they didn't need to sneakily murder her. They could do it openly. Brazenly, if they liked.

They wanted something, Sorrow decided. That's why she was still alive.

The door opened again.

There were no girls this time, with knives or otherwise. Instead, a giant of a man occupied every inch of space in the doorway. He looked like Luvian, if Luvian was made from mountains and moons, and other things larger than Sorrow thought any person had a right to be. This man's eyes were the same shape as Luvian's, though without glasses; he had the same high cheekbones and pointed jaw, albeit under a layer of scuff. Luvian, but with rougher edges.

So this, finally, was Arkady Rathbone.

"Hello, Arkady," Sorrow said.

"Wrong."

His voice matched his form, gravelly and deep, rumbling like an avalanche. But he was telling the truth; he wasn't Arkady. Arkady's voice had haunted her nightmares for long enough for her to know it.

Luvian had three older brothers; the eldest, Sumner, was in prison, as far as she knew.

"Lawton?" she said.

From his shrug, she assumed she was right.

"Come," he growled.

Silently, Sorrow slipped off the bed. There was no point disobeying him, even less in trying to fight. "Where are we going?" she asked.

He said nothing, gesturing for her to follow.

And because she had little choice, she did.

11

Something Rotten in Rhannon

Fighting to remain calm, Sorrow followed Lawton out of the room into a narrow, windowless corridor. For all her efforts, her legs were shaking, mind racing. Arkady Rathbone surely wouldn't want her to walk out of this alive. Wherever he was taking her, she didn't believe she was supposed to survive it. But then why feed and clothe her? It didn't make sense.

She trailed Lawton down the passage and they passed a row of doors that looked like hers. Cells, she realized. This was a prison block. She didn't know what had happened after she'd been knocked out, didn't know if they'd taken anyone else. Charon would be easy to detain; Dougray might be here, too.

She stepped up to the glass panel in one of the doors and peered into the cell. It was empty.

Sensing she'd stopped, Lawton turned and raised his eyebrows.

"Please," Sorrow said, all pretence of composure gone. "Is anyone else here? Any of my friends?"

Lawton said nothing.

"Please, just tell me. I'm begging you."

After a long moment, he replied. "You'll see. Come on."

He started moving again, giving her no choice but to follow.

It was just as Vespus had predicted: another coup against the ruling classes, another dynasty eradicated. And as he'd said, this time a Ventaxis was on the losing side.

Ah, but she wasn't really a Ventaxis, was she? Despite the dire situation she was in, she almost smiled. What would they make of that, if they knew?

Lawton stopped, and she almost walked into him. His elbows were wide, bowing out from his sides, and it was only when Sorrow heard a creaking, grating sound that she realized he was undoing a lock, winding it around like a wheel.

One final wrench and she heard a deep boom as the lock slid back and Lawton opened the door.

"In there," he said, opening the door before him.

Sorrow squared her shoulders and prepared to face her captors.

The room was cavernous, cold and dark, the only light coming from what seemed to be a fire in the far corner. It smelled pungent and musky, and she wrinkled her nose.

There were shadowy shapes in the centre, hanging from the ceiling, and there was a horrible moment where Sorrow thought they were bodies, before she realized they were large bags, suspended on chains. Around the edge of the room were other things she couldn't make out – benches and items that were stacked – but the light was too dim and she was too frightened to pay them more attention.

"Go," Lawton said.

Sorrow hesitated. He hovered behind her, blocking the doorway. Leaving her no choice but to walk towards the flames.

As she got closer, she could make out the shadows of people sitting around the blaze. There seemed to be four of them, in a semicircle around the fire, backs to her, either unaware she was there, or ignoring her. When she was just feet away, she heard laughter, soft and familiar, answered by a smooth, deep voice. She couldn't make out the words, but she recognized it.

That was Arkady Rathbone.

She recognized the other voice too. "Mael?" Sorrow called, not trusting what she'd heard.

The silhouettes turned to her, and one rose, tall, slender, elegant as a willow tree.

His movement unblocked the light, and she could see them all.

Though she didn't need the light to know him. She could have picked him out of any crowd.

"Rasmus?"

The Rhyllian stepped forward, his face fully revealed. "Hi, Row."

"What... What..." Sorrow couldn't get the sentence out.

"Sorrow. We're so glad you're here," Mael said.

Arkady Rathbone, sitting beside Mael as though it happened all the time, gave Sorrow a stiff nod, and she stared at him, mouth open, the sound of blood rushing in her ears. She had to be dreaming. That must be it; she was still asleep and the drug they'd knocked her out with was playing havoc with her subconscious. This wasn't possible... This couldn't be...

"I think she's going to faint."

Irris.

And sure enough Sorrow's knees buckled, though she stayed conscious.

Someone caught her – Lawton, she assumed, for she'd seen no one else – grunting as he did, while Sorrow stared at the unlikely group before her. Her ex-lover, her best friend, her imposter-brother. Barring Arkady Rathbone, it was everyone she cared about most.

Together.

"What is this?" she asked, trying to struggle out of Lawton's grip, though he held her tighter, his arms leaner than she'd first thought.

"An intervention, of sorts," Irris said. "And before you start shouting, it wasn't my idea." She looked behind Sorrow and smiled.

"Whose was it?" Sorrow said.

"Who do you know who'd think an elaborate, public kidnapping might be the best possible way to liberate a young woman from the clutches of an evil and manipulative diplomat? No offence to your father, Rasmus," said the man holding her up.

Who Sorrow now realized was not Lawton. Obviously it wasn't Lawton.

"Luvian?" she said, not daring to turn, as Rasmus murmured, "None taken."

"Is this real. . . ?" Sorrow whispered. Where had he come from?

He spoke directly into her ear as he said, "In the flesh, my dearest Sorrow. Surprise! Welcome to my home."

It was too much. For the first time in her life, Sorrow fainted.

When she came around she was on her back, and four familiar, concerned-looking faces were peering at her.

"She's awake," Luvian announced, pushing his glasses back up his nose before they fell on her.

"You don't say," his brother replied from somewhere close by, causing Luvian to scowl.

"How are you?" Irris, Mael and Luvian spoke together.

Sorrow stared at them. She wasn't all the way back yet, her mouth still disconnected from her brain. Unable to do anything other than blink at them, she looked between the last people she'd expected to see. Her gaze lingered on Arkady, who'd loomed into view behind Mael, unable to understand why he was here with the others.

"I think we should give her some air," Rasmus suggested.

"Yes," Mael agreed.

But none of them moved until Sorrow struggled to sit up. Then there was a glass of water before her, someone was rubbing her back, someone else patting her arm gently. The only person who hadn't rushed to nurse her was Arkady, crouched on his haunches, watching her.

Asking what was going on didn't seem like a big enough question, but she asked anyway.

"As I said, an intervention," Irris said, standing up and holding out a hand.

Sorrow took it, allowing her friend to pull her up.

"By kidnapping me?"

She let Irris lead her towards the fire, guiding her into a battered chair with a tall back and two curling arms and handing her a stoneware cup. Sorrow took a small sip, recognizing the bitter taste of coffee.

"What have you done?" she said, her voice hoarse.

Luvian pulled a stool to her side, leaning on the right arm of her chair. "Sorrow, everything is fine." -

"Everything isn't fine. I'm the chancellor of Rhannon, you can't just kidnap me. People will be looking for me. Charon. . . Vespus. . ."

She froze in horror at the thought.

"My father managed to keep Harun's addiction secret for years. I think he can handle hiding your whereabouts for three days," Irris said.

"Though your mention of *my* father brings us neatly to why we're here," Rasmus said.

"In a nutshell, we all agree that there's something rotten in the Republic of Rhannon and we think, despite all appearances to the contrary, it's not you," Luvian added.

"Talk to us," Irris finished.

"I can't believe you're part of this. *You*, I expect this from," she said to Luvian, who looked pleased with himself. "It's not a compliment! Irris, you have to send me back. This could ruin everything." Sorrow shook her head. Dread coursed through her, turning every limb to lead. She couldn't be away now – there was no telling what Vespus would do. If he thought it was some kind of trick, or scheme. . . "You don't understand. . ."

"Then tell us," Irris cried. "You're pushing me away, Ras away. Sorrow, you're not acting like yourself and you're scaring all of us."

Sorrow flinched at Irris's outburst, and Luvian patted her arm.

"Maybe we should tell her what we know first," Luvian said. "Let's sit down, everyone. And calm down while we're at it."

But Irris wasn't done. "No. I'm sick of this. We've spent the last two weeks planning and working to get this together – to save her – and she wants to go back."

"You're not saving me, Irri," Sorrow said desperately. "You're making it worse."

"Making what worse?" Irris shouted.

"Enough," Rasmus said, moving between them and clasping Irris's elbow. "Row is, understandably, shocked. Why don't we give her a moment to take it all in and then we'll sit down and talk?"

Irris nodded dreamily, then her features sharpened and she looked down at where Rasmus was touching her. Instantly he let her go, his face downcast. He'd used his ability on her, and they both knew it.

He stepped back, but then Irris reached out, this time touching his covered arm, drawing him away. Arkady and Mael followed and Sorrow watched them go, momentarily distracted by their apparent friendship.

None of this made sense to her, and she turned to Luvian. He alone had stayed with her.

"Hey." He crouched in front of Sorrow and took her hands. "How are you?"

Sorrow shook her head. Words were pointless.

He seemed to understand. "Let's just talk. We'll all say what we need to, and then if you still want to go after that, I'll take you back tonight, OK?"

Sorrow sucked in a deep breath, releasing it through her mouth. "Fine. I'll give you an hour. And then I need to go."

"Good," he said, gesturing to the others. They all grabbed the stools they'd been sitting on and formed a semicircle around her, with the exception of Luvian, who sat on the arm of Sorrow's chair.

"Before we begin," Luvian said, looking directly at Sorrow, "I just need to know, on a scale of one to 'I wept constantly and eschewed all nourishment', how much have you missed me? No need to play it down."

"Luvian!" Sorrow and Irris chorused.

Luvian kept his eyes on Sorrow as his mouth widened into a thrilled, sunny grin. It pulled at her, tugging the corners of her own lips despite herself. His hair had grown since she last saw him, long enough to stick out at haphazard angles. It gave him a curiously manic look, highlighted by his glittering eyes behind those silver frames. He looked very pleased with himself. More so than usual.

She'd missed it.

Skin heating, she glanced away, and caught Rasmus watching her with a tight expression.

Sorrow squared her shoulders.

"All right then. Tell me. What on Laethea possessed you to do this?"

It was Luvian who replied. "Desperation. You didn't reply to my letters—"

"I didn't get your letters!" Sorrow protested immediately. "Well, I got the one you left in Prekara. But no others."

"I got that eventually. After I contacted Irris. That's when she told me you were sending her to Svarta."

Irris's tone was soft when she spoke. "We knew something was wrong – we had to convince you to confide in us—"

"And to do that we realized our best hope was to liberate you using a crack team of Rhannon's finest. And Arkady," Luvian interrupted.

Sorrow bit back an involuntary smirk as Arkady growled, "Watch it."

"And then I overheard a conversation between my father and new stepmother," Rasmus added. "About keeping you in line..."

Sorrow's heart was in her mouth as she looked from face to face.

"And?" she managed finally.

"Well, we don't know," Luvian admitted. "We were hoping you'd tell us. That was rather the point of the kidnap."

Sorrow shook her head.

"This is madness. People will be looking for me, even now—"

"We've covered it," Irris said. "Arran is helping us."

"Arran?" Sorrow couldn't believe it.

"Why do you think he decided to stay after the rest of the Jedenvat left?" Irris's tone was wry. "He's been keeping us up to date on your plans. It's how we knew where you'd be today. We left a ransom note with my father. It says the Sons of Rhannon have you and are demanding a ransom for your release, but no one else is to be told you're missing. Not even the Jedenvat. We didn't want it to get too out of control."

"Ha," Sorrow said faintly. This was impossible.

"The people will be told you are in quarantine for observation following your visit to the infected area. No one else will ever know the truth. Or even the lie we told my father. It's foolproof."

It was a good plan. Great, even. But Sorrow knew it was doomed to fail. Because...

"*He* won't believe it," she broke out, frustrated.

"Of course he will."

"I don't mean Charon," Sorrow cried.

"Then who?" Mael said, leaning forward.

Sorrow swallowed. She couldn't tell them the truth – not

146

the whole truth. If they found out who she really was, it would all fall apart. But she could tell them some version of it – they'd all already said they suspected Vespus's involvement. She could give them something...

Sorrow looked at Rasmus, offering a silent apology for what she was about to do.

"You're right, about Vespus holding something over me. He discovered something I did and he's using it blackmail me for land in the North Marches. He's been trying to get it for over twenty years. And because of me, he can finally get it."

Rasmus muttered a curse in Rhyllian, and Irris closed her eyes.

"Do you remember the woman he was with, at Aralie's Naming Gala?" Sorrow said, as Rasmus moved to stand at her side, opposite Luvian. Sorrow looked up at him. "Her name is Aphora. Her ability is being able to communicate with birds. She used them to spy on me. And they saw . . . us in Rhylla."

Luvian leant forward. "Saw what?"

Sorrow took another deep breath, using it to steel herself. "I had a relationship. With Rasmus. Vespus found out."

"But that's illegal," Arkady said, sounding much younger than his years, his eyes saucer-wide.

"It is," Rasmus said calmly.

"Well, well, well." Arkady grinned. "I didn't think you had it in you."

Sorrow looked at Irris, but found she was watching Luvian carefully. She turned to him to see his expression frozen, mouth parted slightly.

"That'll do it," he said faintly.

12

Poking the Hive

Luvian's face was utterly blank, his shoulders pulled back. His gaze fixed on a spot near Sorrow's right temple.

"It's over now," Rasmus said. "Was over then, really. And there are other factors." He looked at Sorrow before he continued. "My ability soothes pain. Not just physical but psychological and emotional. In short, it means my touch makes you feel good."

"I bet," Arkady snickered. Mael thumped him lightly, as Sorrow flushed.

"Like Adavere," she snapped. "Like a drug."

Rasmus looked pained at the description, but nodded. "That's why it was illegal for Rhannish and Rhyllians to have relationships. Because even our most benevolent abilities could potentially compromise someone Rhannish. I compromised Sorrow."

"And in their case it's compounded by the fact they're both from powerful families. The Rhyllian queen's nephew having an advantage over the chancellor of Rhannon would cause outrage. Possibly another war, if it escalated far enough. So . . . yes. Valuable information for someone with an agenda to have," Irris explained to Arkady, Mael and Luvian.

Sorrow nodded, ignoring her tightening chest at Luvian's reaction. He hadn't said a word, holding himself rigidly. "We all knew Vespus had an agenda. I was just stupid enough to supply him with a means to achieve it."

"Not stupid," said Mael softly, and smiled at her, a sympathetic, supportive smile. She found herself wishing once again that he was her brother. She could use a brother about now.

"Why didn't you tell me?" Irris said.

Sorrow shook her head. "That's not all. There's more, and it affects you. And Charon, and the whole Jedenvat. Vespus threatened to tell everyone about my father and Lamentia, and the fact that everyone was covering it up."

"But he supplied the drug," Irris said.

"Would anyone have cared?"

"No. They'd be too focused on the fact the chancellor was a drug addict, while the whole of Rhannon was kept in mourning," Luvian finally said, taking his glasses off and beginning to clean them.

Sorrow nodded. "That's what Vespus said. And thanks to you," she shot at Arkady, "and your stupid terrorist group, he's probably right. Anyone involved in the cover-up – which is everyone on the Jedenvat, and everyone who worked in the Winter Palace – would be a target. That's what Vespus said he'd unleash if I didn't do as he wanted. He'd give you your coup. Death to the Ventaxises, and all who support them. Everyone in this room, except you."

"You should have told us," Irris said, but the sting was gone from her words. She returned to her position in front of Sorrow, taking her hands once more. "You didn't have to bear this alone. We could have helped you."

"I thought I could handle it," Sorrow said. "I thought I could deal with it, and him, before it got this far."

"Vespus must be furious about the plague, then," Arkady said. "It's contaminated his precious land."

Sorrow stiffened. She couldn't meet anyone's eye.

"It's not a plague, is it?" Irris said, her voice soft with understanding. "*He* did it." She looked at Sorrow for confirmation. "And you knew." Irris stood, folding her arms around herself. "Three people died and you knew it was him all along. You let him do it."

"No!" Sorrow sat up straight, eyes locking on Irris's. "I would have confessed to all of it rather than that."

"But you realized it was him at some point?" Irris pressed.

Sorrow swallowed. "He said he needed to clear the land – I thought he meant by a rumour. By the time I realized it was too late. I confronted him, of course. He said that it had to be real – frightening enough to make people believe they had no choice but to move. And I begged him to stop. Of course he wouldn't."

"How did you let things get so far?" Irris said, and Sorrow hung her head.

"I thought I could buy some time. I never expected him to move so fast."

"I still don't understand why you didn't tell me?" Irris said. "I already knew about the Lamentia, and about you and Ras.

150

So did my father. We could have helped."

"So everyone knew," Luvian said faintly.

Sorrow couldn't look at him.

"He made it very clear if I acted against him he'd hurt people I loved." She spoke to Irris instead. "And I was scared. He made the plague – it's a poison, not a disease. I didn't want him to use it on anyone I cared about."

"But it was OK on strangers?"

"Irris, that isn't helpful," Rasmus snapped.

Irris gave him a long look and shook her head. Sorrow twisted to watch her stalk from the room, through an exit Sorrow hadn't known was there until then.

"Row..." Rasmus's voice was soft. "She just needs time. For what it's worth, I don't think it's you she's angry with. She's angry with my father. And at herself, for not guessing. She's the big sister; she thinks she's supposed to protect you. You trying to protect her won't sit well with her."

Beside Sorrow, Luvian was nodding.

Rasmus continued. "I don't think we should do anything else. Today has been intense, and we all need some rest." He rose, and Arkady did the same, slapping his knees as he did.

"I'm hungry," he said. "Drama always gives me an appetite."

With that he left, Rasmus and Mael following. Mael rubbed Sorrow's shoulder as he passed.

Then she was alone with Luvian.

She'd wanted – dreamed of – this moment for weeks. But when she turned to him, he gave her a pinched smile, his glasses resting on his knee. Without them, his gaze was slightly unfocused, and she wondered how well he could see her. Maybe he didn't want to.

"This didn't go how I thought it would," he said at last.

"How did you think it would go?"

"We knew Vespus was holding something over you. So I thought you'd tell us, we'd gasp at his devilry, and then come up with a clever plan to take him down. Instead we've got . . . this."

"This," Sorrow repeated dully.

"Yeah," Luvian replied. "Even I'm going to have trouble spinning it."

Going to. He spoke in the present tense.

A small part of the knot that had been tangling itself inside Sorrow loosened at that. He was still with her, then. For now, at least.

"I'm so, so sorry, Luvian. I've made so many mistakes."

He made a strangled sound, somewhere between laugh and gasp. "As ever, you're the master of the understatement." He finally replaced his glasses and met her gaze, his expression resolute. "We need to come up with a plan. I just don't know what it should be."

"Maybe I shouldn't go back at all," Sorrow said, only half-joking. "Maybe we should pretend the Sons of Rhannon killed me. It's pretty clear I'm a liability. We could end it all now. I could disappear, stay here with you."

It was a neat solution. Vespus would lose his ally and therefore his leverage. She wouldn't be able to hurt Rhannon any more.

Luvian reached out, twining his fingers with hers and leaning in.

"Listen to me, Sorrow. We can fix this." He pulled a hand free and held a finger to her lips to stop her protesting.

She frowned at him, but he continued.

"This is, to be blunt, shit. By far and away the worst

152

situation we've been in. But I believe that every decision you made came from a good place. Yes, you've been naive. Some might even say stupid." He smiled. "But not bad. Vespus is decades older than you are, a hardened politician, and an utter bastard. No matter what you'd done, he would have outclassed you. As he outclassed your father, and grandmother, Graces rest them. He's been working towards this for a long time." He frowned. "I just wish we knew why."

Sorrow sat up straight. "But I do know why. Starwater – it's more than just a drug. It strengthens abilities. Any ability. The possibilities for Vespus are endless."

Sorrow told him about Taasas and what she'd shown her, the Carriage Problem, how Taasas had made her live it. She explained that there were other Rhyllians with terrifying abilities, hidden by Melisia to reassure the world the Rhyllian abilities were benign and unthreatening.

"But even the most innocent ones wouldn't be with Starwater," Sorrow explained to Luvian. "Never mind people like Taasus; say he finds someone with the ability to make it rain. He can give them Starwater and they could cause a flood within a few hours. Or sustain a drought long enough to bring a country to its knees. It gives him more power than any other Rhyllian – than anyone else on Laethea."

It wasn't often Luvian looked anything other than perfectly composed, but Sorrow saw his eyes widen as she talked.

"So, if he can produce a lot of Starwater. . ."

Luvian understood.

"His options are unlimited. Sell it to the highest bidder; form an army of people who want to benefit from it; overthrow his half-sister – Melisia famously doesn't have an ability. Then there's Taasas. What if she could spin a vision big enough to fool whole groups of people? She could convince the Nyrsseans we were attacking them, or that someone had committed a crime. And we don't know who else he has hidden away and what they can do."

"Exactly."

"Well, we knew he had big plans. . ." Luvian said in a quiet voice. Then he rallied. "All this does is prove you couldn't have stopped him alone. To beat him you need someone who *can*."

"You?" Sorrow guessed.

"Graces, no." He somehow managed to look delighted and disdainful at once. "Write to Melisia. She's his half-sister, his queen, and soon to be his enemy if he carries on. He's committing treason, and so is Taasas. Probably. We'll let Melisia decide that. Write to her. As you said, both of our countries – the whole of Laethea – is at risk if he harvests this stuff. She needs to hear it from you so she knows you're not part of it. That it's against your will."

Sorrow looked down. She was relatively safe. But what might it mean for Rasmus?

Sensing her hesitation, Luvian leant forward. "I think her half-brother and his creepy wife potentially plotting to seize her throne will overshadow any outrage about what her nephew and you got up to. Especially given you were both minors when it happened. She's not going to execute her nephew for being a hormonal seventeen-year-old." He frowned then continued. "Seriously, you have to talk to her, and soon. Before she puts two and two together and makes five." He raised a hand to cup her cheek. "Trust me on this."

Her stomach flipped as his palm curved under her face. One of them, she wasn't sure who, leant in, leaving a space the size of a clenched fist between them.

She recalled someone once told her that her heart was the size of her fist. She remembered a younger version of herself holding up her clenched hand and wondering how something that small could power her whole body. Rasmus – he'd told her that fact.

Rasmus.

"There has to be a way to protect Rasmus in this," she whispered.

Luvian sat back and pinched the bridge of his nose. "Carry on."

Sorrow swallowed, bewildered, but continued. "Do you think it's possible we can persuade her somehow not to go public with it?"

"How?"

"By agreeing to do the same. We won't tell the other world leaders Starwater exists and what Vespus plans to do with it. What Melisia has been keeping from them."

Luvian crossed his arms. "Blackmailing a queen, Sorrow? Isn't that almost exactly how Vespus is playing you? You'd be using your knowledge to get her to do what you want, just as he has."

"It's not blackmail." Sorrow was outraged. "We all benefit from this."

"I'm sure Vespus thinks that about your deal with him."

Sorrow shifted uncomfortably. Vespus had said as much. "He's hurt people. Killed people. He did it to get land. I don't want anything, other than him gone. I want the opposite of what he wants. If we can get rid of him, I can fix everything."

"I just don't think you should threaten her."

Sorrow blinked, rapidly scrolling back through the last few moments, trying to understand how they'd gone from joking, to this. "I'm not threatening her. I thought you were on my side."

"I am. Always. But being on your side doesn't mean blindly following wherever you lead. It means calling you out when you're going to do something stupid, and not letting you hurt yourself. I was your advisor once, so let me give you some advice now. Don't poke beehives, Sorrow. Queens don't like it, and angry bees sting."

"But Rasmus..."

"Would agree with me. I'm sure of it. Write to Melisia and tell her what's going on with Vespus. She'll treat you fairly, if not kindly." He gave her a rueful smile.

Fairly might not be enough, Sorrow thought darkly. The moment Vespus realized his Starwater harvest was threatened he'd lash out, not caring where the blows landed.

She remembered the bones then. If she moved those before she wrote to Melisia.

Insurance.

Something very similar to hope began to stir gently inside her, like a bear waking after a long winter. It was a thin, malnourished sort of hope, but it was there.

"What's that look?" Luvian asked her.

"I need you to help me get back to Istevar."

The Point

To his credit, Luvian didn't ask any questions. Not straight away, at least. His only comment was to ask if they could eat first.

He took her hand as they left the room.

"This is new," she said, swinging their clasped palms.

"I don't want you to get lost," he said, without looking at her. "Dangerous criminal types live here."

Sorrow didn't reply, content to hold his hand, content to be reunited with him. She knew she'd missed him, but here, now, she understood just how much.

They left via the same door the others had gone through, and Sorrow found herself in another windowless corridor, only this one ended with a steep staircase. Luvian kept hold of her hand as they descended.

"What is this place?" she asked, her voice echoing.

"Home," Luvian said. "This is where I grew up. It's called the Point."

It wasn't exactly the crime-lord stronghold she'd expected. She'd pictured something a little sturdier, some towering citadel or fortress. Perhaps apartments over illegal gaming halls. What she'd experienced so far didn't match up with what she'd imagined of Rhannon's first crime family. If Luvian had said it was a holding area, or warehouse, she would have accepted it. But this. . .

"*This* is the seat of the infamous Rathbones?" Sorrow said, before she could stop herself.

He chuckled. "You sound disappointed."

"No." She flushed. "But *what* exactly is it?"

By now she'd realized it was no ordinary building. From what she could tell, it was set across one level, but the space it occupied was huge; the walk from her cell to the meeting room had taken at least five minutes, by her estimate. Since they'd left it, they'd been walking for around the same time, in what Sorrow could only assume was a different direction, the walls either side occasionally studded with a door, always closed, betraying no sign of what lay behind them. There were no windows, which gave Sorrow the sense of being underground... But she'd been down in the mines of Rhannon, deep beneath the surface, and the Point didn't feel like that.

The walls were wooden, the grain and patina, colour and texture altering every few feet, as though new parts had been added when needed. The Rathbones' empire ran from this labyrinthine, hodgepodge place. More warren than bastion.

"It's . . . difficult to explain from the inside. But just as hard to understand from the outside, unless you've been inside."

"Helpful," Sorrow said.

Luvian squeezed her hand. "I'll show you when we leave. Then it'll more make sense. We've just passed a bunch of storerooms, and right now, we're heading towards the private heart of the Point. If madam would look to her left, she'll see doors that lead to offices. My mother's, father's, Arkady's, Sumner's, Lawton's."

"Yours?"

"Hardly. As the official black sheep of the Rathbone clan, my office was turned into a supply closet. Which is largely what it was before, except it had a desk in it. I say desk; it was a crate I found, and Arkady smashed it when I was fifteen." He fell silent for a moment, before continuing brightly. "Anyway ... the room we just left is kind of a recreation room. It's where we train. By 'we', I mean my brothers. They do weights down there, teach punch bags what for, and so on. Being built like a kraken takes work, Miss Ventaxis. None of them were born half-man, half-monster." He paused. "It's also where they take people to beat them up, if they wrong us. Technically, the place you woke up in was a kind of cell block."

So she'd been right about that. She shuddered at the image of Arkady Rathbone hitting the punch bag and wondered how many he'd split, or knocked clean to the ground.

Luvian mistook her silence for anger.

"It wasn't my idea to put you there," he said.

"Whose was it?"

"My mother's. She's not keen on strangers."

Sorrow felt uneasy. "Your mother? Is... Is she here?"

"Yeah. Erm... Actually, she wants to talk to you."

"Oh."

Beata Rathbone was rumoured to be the most violent and brutish of the Rathbones, though she'd married into the family. Luvian hadn't said much about her, but he'd revealed she used to call him "runt". It had struck Sorrow as being monumentally unmaternal, which was a big thing, coming from a girl whose so-called mother had cursed her moments after her birth.

Sorrow didn't relish the idea of meeting Beata. And nor could she understand why Luvian seemed so relaxed about it. About being here at all.

"Why did you come home?" she asked quietly.

Luvian shrugged. "I had nowhere else to turn. Neither did your maybe-brother. I was hoping for a pardon, so I could come back to you," he said. "But then the plague, as it was, broke out, and I knew you'd be too busy to deal with it. As for Mael. . . We found him after the election and we brought him here, until Irris wrote."

"You were the friends he'd met."

"He was worried about you."

"Yes, I can tell from the way he joined the organization that spent months trying to kill me, immediately after the election." She was only half-joking.

Luvian gripped her hand tightly. "It wasn't like that. Once he heard you wanted him, he couldn't leave here fast enough." He glanced at her. "He cares about you, Sorrow."

She sighed. "Fine. I'll talk to him. And I'm sorry I didn't get you your pardon," Sorrow said. "I started it, but things escalated. As soon as I go back, I'll do it. I'll make it really grovelly."

"I should hope so. But I understand you were somewhat busy, what with being blackmailed and all." They walked on, fingers loosely twined together. Sorrow found a callus on the side of his middle finger, just below the nail, and she rubbed it. It was from writing, she realized.

"So, I assume there's an appropriately secret way out," she said, breaking the silence.

"Out of where?" He frowned.

"Here. To go to Istevar."

"There is." He looked at her suspiciously. "But I'm not showing you until we go tomorrow."

She shook her head. "It has to be tonight. And you're not coming. I need you to cover for me here."

"No chance." He stopped, blocking her way, and Sorrow pulled her hand from his.

"You don't get to tell me what I can and can't do."

"I'm not telling you; I'm advising you. This is a stupid idea."

She took a deep breath. "Then I thank you for your advice. But it needs to be tonight, and I need to be alone."

The tips of Luvian's ears turned red. "We all risked our lives for you – me, Mael, Irris, Rasmus. We're not going to throw that away. *We* are going tomorrow, or you're not going at all. I'll have Arkady put you back in the cell if I have to."

"You wouldn't."

He took a step closer, so they were almost nose to nose. "To save you from yourself? Yes, I would. And more. Hence the kidnap."

Emotions flashed though Sorrow faster than she could catalogue them: shock, fury, joy, the feelings salty, spicy, sweet. She focused on fury; it was less confusing.

They glared at each other, neither willing to back down, and Luvian's glasses began to fog up from their mingled breath.

"I'm coming with you, tomorrow night, and then we're both coming back here," Luvian said finally, taking a deep, shaky breath before stepping away, pulling his glasses off and wiping them on his shirt. "And that's that." He shoved them back on his face.

161

She knew she'd lost. The strange thing was, she wasn't sure that she minded.

"You can't tell anyone. I mean it, Luvian. I know keeping secrets got me into this mess, but this *has* to stay a secret. I need you to trust me."

"Always." His dark eyes bored into hers.

The moment stretched, spinning out like flax over a loom, and Sorrow felt as though she was spinning too. Luvian was breathing heavily, as though merely standing in front of her was a great trial.

Somewhere ahead of them a door banged as it opened, breaking the spell, and Sorrow felt like laughing, though there was nothing funny about it.

"Come on," Luvian said, and turned. This time he didn't offer his hand, and Sorrow didn't reach for it.

She followed him, keeping a body-sized space between them, down corridors that showed heavy signs of wear and tear. Patches of the floor were worn to a shine from the passage of feet; the walls were dark with stains from fingers trailed along them. She could smell food, clean laundry – domestic smells – and her nerves returned.

As though he sensed her worry, Luvian paused.

"Almost there. Just around this corner. It'll be—" was as far as he got before a stern voice interrupted him.

"I said six sharp. You're late. Which is disappointingly predictable."

Luvian swallowed, then smiled brightly. "Hello, Mother," he said.

14

The She-Wolf

Beata Rathbone moved her attention from Luvian to Sorrow, looking her up and down, clearly unimpressed.

It seemed impossible this woman could birth sons the size of Arkady and Lawton. Beata was tiny, a full foot shorter than Sorrow, and reed-slim, dressed in a demure pink tunic over loose trousers, a stained white apron covering her front. Her eyes were grey – unusual in someone Rhannish – her curled hair streaked with the same steely colour.

Everything Sorrow had heard about Luvian's mother led her to expect Beata to be a giant, literally as well as figuratively. She was the real thug of the family, the muscle as well as the brains – Luvian himself had all but confirmed it. But right now, rather than looking like the ruthless head of a crime family, Beata merely looked exasperated by her son. Which was a feeling Sorrow could identify with, given it was how Luvian made her feel half of the time.

"If you're waiting for a written invitation you're wasting your time. Move," Beata growled, sounding slightly more like the woman Sorrow had expected. "I'll deal with you after."

With no way of knowing which of them she was talking to, Sorrow followed Luvian and Beata around the corner and into the dining room.

It was dominated by a huge, scarred table, and it seemed they really were late, as everyone else was already sitting around it, their mismatched wooden bowls filled with some kind of stew.

"Sit," Beata ordered from behind them.

Rasmus was a jarring sight, blond and elegant, sandwiched between Arkady and Lawton, though he didn't look uncomfortable, gesturing a greeting with his fork as he swallowed what was in his mouth. Mael was beside Arkady, Irris beside him. She gave Sorrow a short nod, and then returned her attention to the bowl before her, and Sorrow's heart sank. Next to Lawton sat the girl with the knife, the older girl on her left, and Sorrow assumed they were his daughters – funny, she'd never pictured Luvian as an uncle. Then there were three spaces, one for Luvian, Sorrow and Beata. Beata made her way to the seat beside the oldest girl, leaving Sorrow with a choice. Beata or Irris?

Luvian decided for her, seating himself next to his mother. Sorrow slid on to the stool beside him without a word.

The casual homeliness of the setting made it feel as though she was attending a family dinner, the sensation compounded when Beata slopped a delicious-smelling stew into the bowls before Sorrow and Luvian. Neither complained when some splashed on to their laps, and Sorrow took Luvian's cue and began eating immediately.

Beata's stew was rich and fragrant: thick chunks of lamb,

164

juicy sultanas, apricots, aubergine, and chickpeas in a spiced broth, sweet almonds flaked over the top, and the first spoonful Sorrow had was like waking up after a long sleep, her taste buds finally remembering what they were for.

When Luvian offered her a plate of flatbread she took some, using it to soak up the juices, then abandoning her spoon and scooping the stew on to it as the others did. Flavours burst across her tongue: cinnamon, ginger, paprika and cayenne. She hadn't enjoyed a meal so much in weeks, the whole thing made more pleasant by being at a table with others, even if some of them didn't want her there. She ate, enjoying the moment, aware that when the meal was over she would have some questions to answer.

Her instinct was right; when she put her spoon down, unable to eat another bite, Beata stood and said, "You, with me."

With that, she strode from the room. There was no mistaking who she meant by "you" this time, and although she was the chancellor of Rhannon, and had been raised to give orders, Sorrow immediately pushed her chair back and followed Beata.

She waited in a small parlour, as sparsely decorated as it seemed everywhere in the Point was. There were two high-backed armchairs in soft blue velvet facing the fireplace, similar to the one she'd sat in in the rec room, a long-legged table between them with three paperbacks and a tea tray on it. A roll-top bureau against the far wall, and the fire. No pictures hanging, nothing displayed on the mantle.

Sorrow knew enough about power plays to know that there were ways and means to display your status, and prove to your that audience you held all the cards. Vespus was a master at it. But Beata seemed uninterested in that kind of posturing;

instead of seating herself throne-like in a chair, or even standing dominantly by the fireplace, she crouched in front of it, sweeping out ash. Again, the homely act threw Sorrow – surely she had people who could do this for her? What was she trying to prove by doing it herself?

Sorrow closed the door behind her, hoping to preserve some dignity, watching as Beata cleaned, then laid a new fire, actions Sorrow knew from watching servants do it – even in Istevar, they needed fires in deepest winter. Sorrow wasn't sure if she'd be able to build one herself, though. It was only when flames crackled merrily in the grate that Beata stood and faced her. Soot covered her apron and there were smears on her face, but Sorrow got the impression she didn't care.

"Luvian said you wanted to speak to me," Sorrow said, when she couldn't bear the silence any longer.

Beata walked right up to Sorrow, looking her up and down once more.

"You and your family have caused me and mine no end of trouble," she said. "But then, you know that."

"Yours haven't exactly been a gift to us, either," Sorrow said, matching the other woman's straightforward tone.

Beata barked out a laugh.

"Is this the part where you show your mettle, proving you're more than just a girl, more than a match for me, and I bestow my reluctant respect on you?" she said, still smiling, though it was not a kind expression, her eyes lupine gold in the firelight.

Sorrow understood then where Luvian got his clever tongue. She swallowed. "I don't have to prove myself to you."

"Agreed. You've already proven yourself as contemptible as the rest of your family."

Sorrow's pulse fluttered in her veins as outrage built in her chest, the fire of it burning her furious response from her throat.

Beata continued. "Your father, the addict. Your grandfather, the warmonger. Your great-grandfather, the philanderer. Before him, the zealot, and the profligate, the skinflint. The alcoholic, the idiot, and the deluded. All the way back to the original dissenter-turned-kingslayer. Now you, the puppet. But you're not the only ones with monikers that betray your character." Beata's iron eyes pinioned Sorrow in place.

"They call me the she-wolf, because I protect what's mine. The survival of the pack above all – that's my job. You're a threat to me and mine, Sorrow Ventaxis. You were a threat before, when I worried your idealism might kill our way of life, hence sending my boys against you. But you're a bigger threat now your idealism has made you the marionette of Vespus Corrigan. And I respond to threats with swift action."

Sorrow watched in silence as Beata poured herself a cup of tea from the tray on the table. She didn't offer Sorrow one.

Twice she'd referred to Sorrow as a puppet of some kind, which led her to wonder if Beata would offer help if Sorrow agreed to do what she wanted.

The same old show but with a new director.

Only Sorrow wouldn't perform.

"Where are you going with this?" she said. "Because I won't be your puppet."

"You might," Beata replied. "I have enough dirt on you to make it happen. But I don't want a pet chancellor, thank you."

"Then what do you want?"

Beata gave her an appraising look. "A promise that you'll do nothing. No matter what Kaspira Blue – or anyone else – says,

167

you won't attempt to evict me and mine from here. It stays exactly as it is."

Sorrow watched her. "That's it?"

The older woman almost smiled. "Well, now you mention it, I wouldn't be unhappy if the Decorum Ward vanished into the Archior."

"We share that aim."

Beata nodded. "Good."

"And that's really everything?" Sorrow was wary. "You just want me to leave you alone?"

"This is our home. My sons were born here. My granddaughters were born here. My husband was born here. I want your word we'll get to stay, as we are, doing as we do."

"I can't give you permission to keep committing crimes."

"I don't want permission. If you catch us, fair enough, that's on us for being sloppy. All I want is your word you won't use the sanctuary my son has offered against us. You won't take it from us."

Sorrow met the hard gaze of the Rathbone matriarch once more, unable to believe what she was hearing. All of this, just to keep her home?

"You don't get it, do you?" Beata said. "Even now." She lowered her teacup. "You fought for your home; why is it hard to believe I'd fight for mine?"

"Because . . . I fought for what was right."

"And how's that working out for you?"

Touché, Sorrow thought.

"Why give up a chance to have power over me?" she tried instead.

"I have plenty of power," Beata laughed. "This is my republic, I'm the chancellor here. I don't need or want yours. I like my life, Sorrow Ventaxis. I want it to stay as it is. I'm not a greedy woman. I don't want more than I need – that's the trick to holding power. Only take what you can comfortably manage. I'm managing fine."

Sorrow thought of Vespus's words, that power was a parasite jumping from host to host, seeking the biggest meal. Beata wanted a different sort of power. A sort she could hold on to, live with. Vespus had said symbiotic, but hadn't meant it. Beata really did.

"What about Arkady?" Sorrow asked. "Will he be satisfied with this?"

"You can consider Arkady leashed," Beata said, with a smirk. "Do we have an agreement?"

Sorrow lifted her chin. "Are you going to help me get rid of Vespus?" she asked.

Beata gestured with both hands to the walls around them, as though to suggest she already had. Which, Sorrow realized, was true. She'd allied her family with Sorrow.

Beata smiled. "I've said all I needed to. You can go now."

The dismissal was clear, but Sorrow had one more question for Beata. Taking a deep breath, she began.

"I want to ask you something." She leant forward. "You're driving a carriage, and your sons and your granddaughter are in it. All the people you care for most. You come to a fork in the road and down that road is a little child, playing in the dirt. Taking the right-hand fork of the road would mean killing that child. But taking the path to the left of the fork would mean the carriage plummeting into a ravine, killing you all. Which path would you take?"

Beata looked at her over the rim of her teacup. Then she snorted.

"I'd turn the carriage around and make my own damn path. What kind of a fool would stay on the path if they're the only options?"

"I see that now," Sorrow said, smiling as she turned to leave.

"Wait," Beata said, "there is something else."

Sorrow had the sense that there hadn't been, until she'd mentioned the Carriage Problem.

She looked back at the she-wolf to find the woman appraising her. When Beata spoke, she spoke quietly.

"Be good to my son."

15

Soul May Fix

Luvian was waiting for her outside, cheerful once more. "I thought you might like the tour?" He smiled in a way that made her instantly suspicious, lips curved like a new moon, sly and gleeful. Nothing good could come of a smile like that.

"Am I allowed a tour?" she asked, eyes narrowed. "This is a criminal base, isn't it?"

"Oh yes."

Luvian's wicked grin widened, and a prickling feeling warned her they were being reckless. She ignored it, raising a single eyebrow in challenge, delighted when he laughed.

She followed him out of the dining room, through a door on the opposite wall that led to another corridor.

"These are the Rathbone dynasty's private quarters," Luvian told her.

Nothing about the corridor suggested it was any different to the others, though perhaps the rooms beyond were cosy and personalized.

Suddenly she wanted very badly to see his space and how he fitted it. "Is one of them yours?" she asked as they approached the end of the corridor.

He shook his head. "I don't sleep down here."

But he didn't say where he did sleep, or comment any further, leading them out of the corridor and into one that, unlike the others, seemed made of metal, iron bolts marking lines that she ran her fingers over as they walked. Their footsteps echoed as they travelled; even when she tried to walk on softer feet each tread boomed.

As with the other corridors, doors peppered the walls, but each of these was visibly secured, multiple keyholes and padlocks giving the unmistakable impression they were not to be opened.

"Where are we?" Sorrow whispered, wincing when it bounced back at her.

"These are the vaults. . ." He stopped, and turned to her. "Where we keep our stolen goods."

"I'm the chancellor of Rhannon," Sorrow pleaded. "Don't show me this stuff."

"Maybe there's a method to the madness. Maybe this is part of a plea bargain I'm planning. When everything is settled, you use what you've seen to jail my whole family, and I get immunity for my invaluable help."

"You don't want me to jail your family."

Luvian said nothing, beginning to walk again. Sorrow followed.

"What's in them?" she asked, drawing level with him.

"Right now, I don't know. In the past we've had all sorts of things: art, money, gemstones. For a while we had a consignment of Astrian lemons, which we managed to get hold of during a shortage. Nyrsseans have a thing for them candied; we turned quite a profit. We've had quickfire, alcohol. Drugs, though nothing as bad as Starwater – Mother is very anti-substances. Just the odd batch of sleepweed." He raised his eyebrows. "Do you want to look?"

"Do you have keys?" Sorrow couldn't imagine the size of the bunch needed to get into any of these doors.

"Keys are for the uncreative." Luvian drew a slim roll of canvas from inside his pocket and pulled the ribbon fastening it. It opened to reveal a set of lock picks. "I carry them everywhere."

Sorrow reached out, touching one of the long slim silver picks with her forefinger. "That's how you broke into the registry in Castle Adavere?"

"Locks are the same the world over. It's just a matter of charming them."

"Charming them?" She looked up at him.

"It sounds nicer than picking."

He rolled the pick holder up again, and put it away, then led her back the way they came. Sorrow was confused.

"Was that all of the tour?"

"Yes. I might have overstated how much there was to see. You've seen it all."

There had been no sign of anyone else there, save the Rathbones and Sorrow's people.

"Are we the only ones here?"

"Right now. Usually there are more people about, coming and going. Growing up I had about forty burly criminal aunts and uncles at any given time. But when we decided to bring you here, Mother told everyone that wasn't immediate family to vacate for a while. And, well, you've met her. She inspires obedience."

"Apparently not in you."

"I'm a maverick, beautiful. I live by my own rules."

For reasons neither could understand, they both blushed.

Sorrow rallied first. "It's just not how I pictured a criminal lair."

Luvian laughed. "What did you picture?"

She'd expected shadowy corners, weapons, *bloodstains*. Not dining rooms and common spaces. Not home-cooked meals and an underworld crime lord lighting her own fire in a parlour that could have been in almost any home in Rhannon. And certainly not children. Not even knife-wielding ones.

"More ... danger, I guess. It's just like a regular home, aside from the architecture."

"Most of all it is a home."

She nodded. "Your mother made that very clear. I suppose I hadn't really thought about the human side of it. I'd focused more on the theft and murder. I'd forgotten you were a family, too."

"I promise if you ever come back I'll make sure there are lots of hideous sights to behold."

Sorrow smiled. "Are we underground? In some kind of drain system?"

He barked a short laugh. "Not quite. I really think you'll appreciate it more once you see it from the outside. You know I hate to brag, but it is impressive."

Sorrow laughed and the two of them made their way back towards the dining room. It was the most relaxed Sorrow had been in weeks.

The feeling turned to smoke when they opened the door

and found Irris there, sitting at the table, playing with a fork someone had left after dinner.

She stood up when they entered, narrowing her eyes at Luvian.

"I'll go and see my mother," he said, knocking at the room to Beata's small parlour.

They all waited, but there was no answer, though from what Sorrow had seen of Beata, that didn't mean she wasn't in there, so much as she didn't want anyone else in there.

"I'll go and see somewhere else," Luvian said. He shot Sorrow a sympathetic look, and left her with Irris.

"I'm really angry with you." Irris wasted no time, speaking the moment the door had closed behind Luvian. "For so many reasons. I don't even know where to begin."

She lifted the fork and then put it down, repeating the motion. Sorrow stayed quiet, letting Irris gather her thoughts.

"I'm angry that you didn't trust me enough to confide in me," Irris said finally.

"I do trust y—"

"Don't," Irris said. "I know you trust me. And I know you love me. But not enough," she emphasized. "You didn't let me in."

The accusation stung Sorrow. She'd done what she did *because* she loved Irris so much. It had been to protect her. She told her as much, but Irris shook her head.

"You don't protect people by hurting them and making them want to leave you. You should have told me what was happening. You especially should have told me if you thought I was at risk. You should have let me decide whether I'd be safer in Istevar or Svarta. And Svarta, Sorrow. Seriously? You were going to send me to the top of the world?"

175

"To keep you safe. I couldn't put you at risk."

"At risk of what?"

"Vespus threatened you. He threated to kill you. He meant it, Irris. He would murder you to get me to do what he wanted."

Irris blinked, and then said shakily, "Even so. . ."

"And then there's Taasas. Vespus's wife. She can *do* things, when she touches you. Make you see things. She showed me you. Dead. Twice. And Charon, and Arran, and Tuva. Bayrum, Ras, the servants. . . She showed me what Vespus said would happen if I didn't do what he said. I lived it, Irri. I lived seeing you dead and knowing it was because of me."

"Row. . ." Irris shuffled her seat closer and took Sorrow's hand. "You should have told me at the time, and let me make the choice. You took the decision from me. That's not what friends do. They don't leave people to shoulder problems alone. And they don't assume they're better off alone either."

"I really thought it was for the best," Sorrow said miserably.

"I know. Believe me, I know. Do you see now, that it wasn't?"

Sorrow nodded. Irris was right, as she usually was, and Sorrow was embarrassed that she hadn't seen it. She had thought she would be better off alone. So that she couldn't hurt anyone.

Sorrow, for that is all she brings us. She didn't want to think it. But somehow, she always did.

"You're not cursed," Irris said gently.

Her words startled Sorrow from her thoughts. "What?"

"What Cerena said when you were born was a terrible thing to say, but that is all it was. Words. It wasn't a curse."

"I know." The lie was automatic.

"Do you? Because it doesn't seem like it to me. You have

176

to let go of this idea that you're some kind of black cloud, or harbinger of doom. You don't let people in. You never let Ras in. When it counts, you don't even let me in."

"I do," Sorrow said. "I always confide in you."

"Clearly not always," Irris said, and Sorrow's face flushed. "I don't want to fight with you," she continued. "That's not why I came here. I want to talk this out. Because that's what best friends do. We're stronger together and you know it. No more secrets," Irris said, the words firm, though her tone was soft. "No more lies. Promise me."

Sorrow looked at her friend. Irris's heart-shaped face was unusually serious, her lips pursed. Sorrow wanted to promise her, but if she told her the truth she might lose Irris – she might lose everything.

"I have to keep one more secret from you," she said at last, "for one more day. And I'll have to lie to Vespus when I go back."

Irris frowned. "What's the secret from me?"

"Tomorrow night I have to do something, back in Istevar."

"No—"

"I have to. But I promise once I'm back, I will tell you everything. Irri – I have to do this. You'll understand why afterwards. I just hope you still want to be my friend when you know it all."

Irris sighed, shaking her head slightly. "You're scaring me," she said.

Sorrow snorted softly. "You have no idea."

"All right," Irris said. "The day after tomorrow." She stood, and gave Sorrow a hesitant look, before opening her arms.

Sorrow was on her feet and hugging Irris in a blink. As she did, a weight lifted from her chest. The weeks of living without her best friend, knowing she'd hurt her, had been a burden she hadn't realized she was carrying.

They released each other, and Irris smiled, her resemblance to Charon striking in that moment. Sorrow felt a pang of guilt.

She'd have to talk to Charon when she went back. Properly. She should tell him the truth too – Irris was right, they were stronger together. She had amends to make – not least for the kidnap.

"Where does your father think you are?" Sorrow asked her.

"Still in the East Marches, packing very slowly for my sojourn to the north."

"What if he checks?"

"Arran is keeping an eye on things – he's refusing to leave his side, so if my father does anything unexpected, Arran will either talk him around, or at least give us a warning. I suspect all his attention will be on getting you back from the Sons of Rhannon safe and sound."

"We should tell him it's not real," Sorrow said. "At least to stop him from worrying."

"And if Vespus intercepts the message?"

"No, I mean when I go back. We should tell him I wasn't in any real danger."

Irris grimaced. "He won't like it."

"If I'm being honest, I'm being honest with everyone," Sorrow said.

"Fine. Just do it before I come home so he has time to calm down. Come on. Let's go and find the others. When I left, Arkady was destroying Mael at cards and I want to see if he made a comeback."

*

Luvian was in the recreation room with everyone else, though he sat alone curled up with a book, so engrossed in it he didn't look up as Sorrow approached. Rasmus, Mael, Arkady and Lawton were playing some kind of complicated card game, which, Sorrow judged from the pile of wooden tokens in front of him, Arkady was definitely winning.

The four men looked up at Sorrow and Irris, but quickly returned their attention to the cards, and Sorrow didn't blame them. Mael and Rasmus were clearly fools for gambling with the Rathbones.

She unhooked her arm from Irris's and approached Luvian, sitting on the arm of his chair, surprising him.

"Hey," he said, his face lighting up as he saw who'd interrupted him. He folded the corner of the page and put the book down. "How did it go?"

"All right. We're good again."

"I'm glad."

"She knows I'm going to Istevar tomorrow. She isn't happy about it, but I told her what I told you – I have to. And," Sorrow took a deep breath, "I told her I'd explain why afterwards. To both of you."

Luvian's eyebrows rose.

"But right now, I'm tired, and I want to sleep. Where shall I go?"

"The others are sleeping in the cell block, at Mother's request," Luvian said.

"I'm fine with that," Sorrow said.

He stood. "I'll walk you there."

"Is there a bathroom I can use? I'd really like to wash my face, and brush my teeth."

"Not in the cell block. We're not big on creature comforts

for our enemies. We'll have to go back to the family quarters. Or there's the cottages..."

"Which is closer?"

"The family quarters."

She turned to say goodnight to the others, and found Rasmus watching her. He smiled when he caught her eye, and she returned it.

"Night," she called.

"Goodnight, Row."

Mael and Arkady glanced briefly at her, and Irris, who'd somehow taken Lawton's place, waved, then all three returned quickly to the game.

He showed her to the bathroom, where she cleaned her teeth with a finger and gave her body a cursory wash. The water was warm, at least, and there were clean towels in a cupboard.

Then they were outside her cell door, and Sorrow felt strangely nervous.

"Goodnight, then," she said.

Luvian nodded. "Yes."

They both stood, staring at each other, butterflies making Sorrow feel fidgety and anxious, suspended somewhere between yearning and dread. She felt certain he was about to say something very important, and she both wanted and feared it.

Luvian leant forward.

Then stopped.

"Night," Luvian said suddenly, spinning on his heel and leaving Sorrow feeling confused, and strangely cross. He didn't look back, vanishing around the corner, and Sorrow slipped into her room, though it was a long time before she was able to sleep.

*

Word came from Arran the next morning. His note said everything was going to plan – aside from Arran himself, and Dougray, who'd been there too, witnessing it, Charon had told no one Sorrow had been kidnapped. He'd done as asked and put out the story that Sorrow had gone to the Summer Palace in self-imposed quarantine. To support the ruse, the Summer Palace had been cleared of all staff while she was supposedly there, so there was no one to prove otherwise. Arran had convinced Charon they had to carry on, business as usual, so as not to alarm the Sons of Rhannon and risk Sorrow's safety.

Sorrow read the note, feeling sick. Charon's fear for her bled from every word, even through Arran's writing. She couldn't get the image of him telling her to run out of her mind, all his worry for her. They were right not to have drawn him into the plan – Charon would never have gone along with it, she knew that. But the idea of him terrified on her behalf was a lot for Sorrow to bear.

Then there was Vespus. Sorrow knew his scheming mind would be suspicious of the kidnap. She'd have to work hard to convince him when she returned.

"What's wrong?" Irris asked.

In the spirit of her new-found honesty, Sorrow replied, "I'm worried about Charon. And Vespus. And what they're both thinking right now."

Irris have her an appraising look. "You need a distraction. Come on."

They collected Rasmus and Mael, and spent the rest of the day teaching Mael the games they'd played as children in the Winter Palace. They stopped often to tell him a story about some trouble they'd got into, or some adventure they'd gone on, the three of them seamlessly slipping between

181

the narration in the way only long-term friends could, each knowing their part.

Mael seemed delighted by them, pressing for details, and it pained Sorrow how he soaked them up, his hunger for their memories obvious. She suspected he was keeping their stories for later, so he could imagine himself as part of them instead of their audience, and she was expansive, generous, making jokes with him, drawing him into their circle.

She could change. She would change. She wouldn't be like Harun and push people away, too busy being trapped in her own mind. The only person cursing her, she realized, was herself. So she had to break it.

The afternoon turned into evening before Sorrow was ready; suddenly it was time for dinner, all of them gathered around the table as though they'd been doing it for years. It was informal, and messy, people reaching across each other to grab salt, and bread, and water. Sorrow loved it.

Across from her, Mael was recounting some of the anecdotes Sorrow, Irris and Rasmus had told earlier to Arkady, who listened raptly, barely remembering to eat. On his right, Beata talked to her granddaughters, asking about their day, and what they'd done, and the two girls kept up a steady stream of chatter as they shovelled food into their mouths. Lawton and Luvian were talking about a book, apparently disagreeing, and beside Sorrow Irris sat, asking Rasmus about the library systems in Rhylla.

Sorrow ate her food – a gooey, savoury rice pudding, flecked with sweet squash and mushrooms, golden from saffron, soaking it all in. She tried to seal it all in her mind, as Mael had earlier. If tonight went well, this time tomorrow Irris and Luvian would know the truth of who she was. Her heart palpitated as she looked at them all, wondering if this might be the last time she spent a happy evening with the people she loved.

No, she told herself. *Have faith. Trust them. And for the Graces' sake, stop cursing yourself.*

Then the meal was over, and Luvian was looking at her pointedly. It was time to go.

"You've been quiet," Irris said, raising her voice a little, her eyes widening with meaning. "Do you have a headache?"

"No," Sorrow said. Then she realized what Irris was doing. "I mean, yes. I do actually." She raised her hand to her forehead and rubbed.

"Let me..." Rasmus began and then stopped, his eyes widening. "Never mind."

Sorrow gave him a sad smile.

"I have painkillers in the cottage," Luvian said smoothly. "You could rest there, if you like. It'll be quieter."

"Excellent idea," Irris said.

Then she and Luvian were hustling Sorrow from the room.

"Good luck," Irris said, as the three of them stood there. "Be careful."

"I will. And tomorrow..."

"Tomorrow," Irris said. She drew Sorrow, then Luvian, into brief hugs and returned to the others.

Sorrow released a ragged, nervous breath. Then she followed Luvian, out of the Point, back into the world.

16

A Disappointment of Ventaxises

When Sorrow finally saw the outside of the Point and realized what it was she'd been inside, she was astounded.

It was a dock. The Point was inside the skeleton of the docks on the Archior estuary. An ancestor of Sorrow's – the profligate; she smiled as she remembered Beata's words – had spent a fortune on creating the docks and commissioning boats, intending to explore as many nations as he could get to. Sadly for him, though not the rest of Laethea, he'd died before his dream could be realized, and his successors – the skinflint, philanderer, and so on, as Beata had called them – hadn't been interested in continuing it.

Even Reuben, the warmonger, who could have used it to build a navy and launch seaboard attacks on Rhylla during the war, hadn't tried. The Rhannish, for all their long eastern coast, weren't a seafaring people. They liked to visit the beach, and a few would fish off the coast, or sail the estuary between Prekara and its Rhyllian opposite, Mantious, but dipping a toe in the seas during the warm season was enough for most of them.

The docks had foundered, and the half-built boats rotted... On the outside. Inside and beneath, however, an empire was forming. This apparent ships' graveyard masked the Rathbones' base of operations. This was what Beata had meant when she'd asked for Sorrow to leave Prekara, and the Rathbones, alone. She wanted her to do as her predecessors had and ignore the docks, leaving the place intact for her and her family to continue living and working from.

The entrance was through one of the old harbourmaster's cottages, which were the official residence of the Rathbones.

They'd emerged from the Point into the garden of the cottage Beata used as her legal address, through a tunnel hidden beneath an authentically reeking compost heap. Sorrow had gagged as she'd emerged into the night, her stomach rebelling again as rotting food, fertilizer, and worms rained into her hair.

At least now, she understood what Luvian had meant when he'd said it was difficult to understand it – never in her wildest imaginings would she have thought those three salt-battered cottages were the gateway to a world hidden underground.

She looked down at the hole again before he covered it once more, and then turned to where the moonlit hulls rusted gently. There were no lights visible, nothing to suggest there was a sprawling world inside the docks that held them. Sorrow knew the recreation room was behind the cement casing of one of the docks, the cell she had woken in in the belly of another. As she watched, she saw the shadow of a large person snake down the side of the marina – Lawton, or Arkady.

Then it was gone, and Luvian was hissing at her from the other side of the fence, urging her to hurry. She dropped to her belly and wiggled under the fence, out of the Rathbones' territory and into Prekara.

"We need horses," she said, as they made their way towards the narrow streets that defined the north-east district. "We can't walk to Istevar."

"We're taking the stagecoach there," he said. "I booked us passage on it earlier."

Sorrow stopped. "Are you mad? I'm supposed to be in quarantine. I can't just hop on to a public stagecoach for a four-hour trip."

"Of course you can."

"Yesterday you wouldn't let me go because it was too risky and now we're getting a public coach? Luvian, no way."

"Hiding in plain sight is the best kind of cover. It's a thirty-hour walk to Istevar from here, and the nearest horses will be in the North Marches. If you want to get there tonight, it's the coach. Besides. . ." He peered around, and then pulled her into a doorway.

"What are you doing?"

"Magic."

He took something from his pocket and moved behind her, pushing the hood down and lifting her hair from her neck. She stayed still as he pinned it up gently, her eyes on the sky above, holding her breath. When he was done, he turned her to face him, and pulled a pair of delicate spectacles from his pocket.

"The lenses are just ordinary glass." He slid them on to her face, hooking the arms over her ears. "Now put this on."

He handed her a lipstick.

Sceptical, she opened it. It was bright scarlet.

"Trust me."

Sighing, she applied it, running a finger around the edge of her mouth to clean the excess off.

Once she was done, he pulled her over to a shop window and as she stared at her reflection in the dark glass, she had to admit she was impressed.

He'd tucked her hair under and pinned it in place, to give the appearance it was chin length, and her face looked rounder without the length of her hair against it. The glasses altered her further, and the lipstick drew all attention to her mouth. In her borrowed clothes, and her makeshift disguise, she had to admit she didn't look like herself. And he was right – the last thing anyone would expect would be to see her running around Prekara at night.

Still, it didn't stop her keeping her head down as she followed Luvian through Prekara. It would have been impossible to navigate without him; the streets weren't signposted, and they didn't seem to follow any usual planning rules. The buildings were all several storeys tall, haphazard and leaning, looming over her like giants. It felt like every twenty paces they had to cross a bridge over an inky canal, boats slipping beneath them, the rowers silent and shadowed.

"Don't stare," Luvian whispered as Sorrow watched a boat dock and a man begin to unload. "You really don't want to catch anyone's attention here. Even with me."

She looked away, but not before she caught the malevolent glint in the eyes of the man she'd been watching.

Sorrow kept her gaze to herself after that, only looking up when they arrived at the stagecoach post.

"If anyone asks, we've been visiting an aunt in Prekara and are heading home to Istevar," he said low in her ear.

"Right. Is anyone likely to ask?"

"We'll find out," Luvian said, ushering her forward as the stagecoach pulled up beside them and the other four passengers jostled to climb in.

Sorrow and Luvian were last. Luvian smiled politely as he settled himself between a well-upholstered older woman, whose scent was overpowering, and a reedy young man who jiggled his leg nervously. Sorrow took her place between another woman, who'd already leant against the side of the carriage, her eyes closed, and a young man who gave her a curt nod and pulled a book out of his pocket.

The stagecoach pulled off with a sharp jerk.

Luvian held out a book to her.

"What about you?" Sorrow asked.

"I'll nap. Wake me at the change point," Luvian said. With that, he slumped down, extending his legs and crossing them at the ankle, and settled into an apparent easy rest.

Sorrow turned the book over. It was fiction, at least twenty years old from the dated art on the cover. It featured a man dressed in a long cape, holding a woman in a red dress close to him. A romance novel. Sorrow looked over at Luvian once more, but he truly seemed to be sleeping. She mulled it over for a few moments, but she had two hours to kill, and the book would at least stop anyone talking so her. She opened it.

"We're here." Luvian loomed over Sorrow, looking amused.

"Huh?" she said, blinking at him.

"We're at the change point." He grinned. "You were supposed to wake me. How's the book?"

Sorrow shrugged as nonchalantly as she could manage. "Fine, I suppose."

"You were sighing on average once every four minutes."

"I was not," Sorrow replied indignantly. "Anyway, I thought you were asleep."

Sorrow hustled out of the carriage. She stretched her legs as she made her way to a water fountain, drinking from it heartily. She hadn't realized she was thirsty, or that she needed the bathroom, while she'd been reading. The book wasn't as bad as she'd expected. In fact, she couldn't stop reading it.

She'd never thought of herself as a big reader – the library in the Winter Palace wasn't exactly stocked with much aside from historical and geographical tomes; Harun had outlawed fiction after Mael's accident. Irris loved to read, and had smuggled books in for Sorrow, but she wasn't a fiction fan – and especially not of the kind of racy romance it seemed Luvian carried around. Sorrow was surprised to find all she wanted was to get back in the carriage and continue.

She met Luvian outside the bathrooms and they made their way to the second coach, which would take them to the heart of Istevar. Their travelling companions hadn't returned yet, so they settled themselves back into the coach.

"You have to sit where you were before," Luvian told Sorrow as she slid over to the window.

"Why?"

"It's etiquette."

Sorrow slid back to the middle seat, her expression mutinous.

"The last coach back is at midnight. So I hope you can get your business completed before then," Luvian said.

"I should be able to."

"Are you going to tell me where we're going once we get there? Please don't say the palace."

Sorrow glanced around. "The cemetery."

Luvian's eyes went wide behind his glasses.

"Why?"

"I need to go to the Ventaxis mausoleum. More than that I can't tell you."

Their fellow travellers returned, the stout woman and the nervous man sandwiching Luvian once more, as the reader took his place beside Sorrow. The carriage moved off and Sorrow stared at Luvian.

"The other woman didn't come back."

"Maybe she's where she wanted to be."

He lunged across the carriage as Sorrow slid into the newly vacant space, landing on her lap and almost crushing the book, as the older woman tutted at them and the reading man looked scandalized. Sorrow shoved Luvian to the side, into her old place, and smiled beatifically at him. In response, he snatched the book from her hands.

"You can't read *and* have the window seat." He turned to the man beside him. "You obviously can. She can't."

"That's not fair," Sorrow said.

The older woman muttered something about mothers and manners and both of them had to stifle a laugh, causing the woman to glare at them.

Then Sorrow realized they were being foolish – drawing attention to themselves, making themselves memorable. She shot Luvian a warning glance and he closed his eyes in understanding. Silently, he handed her the book and Sorrow lowered her head, opening it once more. For the rest of the journey they were quiet and well behaved, neither speaking again until the coach rattled into the inn in Istevar. As luck would have it, Sorrow was just finishing the book, and she closed it with a satisfied thud before following Luvian out.

"What did you think?" he asked her as they hurried away from the brightly lit coaching inn and towards the street.

"It was . . . kind of silly, in places. And surprisingly . . ." She didn't think she could say "sexy" to Luvian. The realization he'd been going to read it while she was there made her stomach swoop. ". . . good. And I didn't see the end coming. I thought she'd choose the other guy."

"Really?" Luvian frowned. "I thought it was obvious they were supposed to be together. They had so much more in common."

"Like what? Being from the same place? That's not important. It's about values. Shared dreams. A connection."

Luvian looked thoughtful and took the book from her when she offered it, shoving it into the back pocket of his trousers.

"Thank you," she said. "For letting me read it. I didn't know you liked those kinds of books."

"I'll pretty much read anything with words in," he said, his tone suspiciously casual. "Which way is the cemetery?"

Sorrow paused, turning on the spot, trying to catch her bearings. The coaching inn was a mile from the palace, to the west. She hadn't been there on foot before, but the temple for the Grace of Death and Rebirth, which housed the Ventaxis mausoleum, was a straight shot from the palace, around half a mile away. She turned to the left.

"This way," she said. "We need to head towards the Winter Palace."

"Oh, joy," Luvian said, but he took her arm and they began to walk.

The people of Istevar were making the most of their evening. Light and noise spilled out of taverns as Sorrow and Luvian passed them, the patrons enjoying themselves. Sorrow was trying to act nonchalant, trusting in the night, her disguise, and the sheer unlikeliness of her being on the streets, but every time someone called out, every time a door flew open, her heart jumped into her throat and choked her with terror.

She reminded herself with every step, with every breath, that she was fine; no one would ever know she was there, except Luvian. And she could trust him. Trust him to help her, and trust him not to ask questions. Trust him with everything.

Even so, she didn't relax until they'd climbed over the fence, dropping into the cemetery on light feet, a few pins falling from her hair as she did. Sparing a glance for the temple, all monochrome moodiness in the moonlight, she wound her way through the graves, towards the large white building at the rear.

The Ventaxis mausoleum. Inside were the bones of every Ventaxis – chancellors, wives, sons and daughters. And the bones of the real Sorrow Ventaxis, who'd never taken a breath.

She stopped outside the door, and read the great stone tablets either side that detailed every person who'd been laid to rest there. Starting with Harforth Ventaxis, the first chancellor, all the way through to her father, her grandmother, and her mother just before him. Above Cerena's name was a scar in the stone, and Sorrow realized it was where Mael's name had once been. Someone had removed it.

"That's a lot of Ventaxises," Luvian said, looking between the stones. "I wonder what the collective noun for a group of Ventaxises would be."

Sorrow thought again of Beata's words about her ancestors.

"A disappointment," she said, only half-joking. "You need to stay out here. Keep watch. I mean it, Luvian," she added sternly. "I want you to promise you won't come in."

"I promise," he said solemnly. "I'll stay here."

You trust him, Sorrow reminded herself. "One more thing," she said.

"Go for it."

"I need you to pick the lock. I don't have the key with me."

He smiled and pulled the thin cylinder of fabric from inside his jacket, kneeling down before the door. He unrolled it and examined the keyhole carefully before selecting two of his tools, then immediately set to the lock, lining up the picks in one hand and inserting them all at once.

He used his left hand to alter them, inside the lock, pressing and testing, and she watched for a moment, fascinated by the motions and the delicacy and precision.

"How do you do it?" she asked.

Without looking away from his task, he spoke. "This is a lever lock. Inside there are levels, sometimes two in old locks, sometimes as many as five in newer ones. I need to use the picks to lift each level, and once they're lifted, the bolt will spring back."

He returned to work, and she watched carefully as he used first one, then two, then three picks in the lock, positioning them carefully. He paused, nodding to himself, before pulling out a fourth, inserting it upwards. Without warning, she heard the sound of a bolt release and the door opened, bathing them in the cool, musty air from inside the crypt.

As Luvian rose to his feet, she met his gaze. He smiled at her, and it could have been for reassurance, or courage, or even permission, but whatever he'd meant by it, it gave her the strength to enter the mausoleum.

"You'll have to lock me in," she said as she turned to face him. "If someone comes and they see the door is open, they'll know something's wrong. You can let me back out after."

He gaped at her. "You seriously want me to lock you in a crypt?"

"Are you afraid you won't be able to unlock it again?"

"Trying to goad me into doing it by insulting my skills? Cheap," Luvian joked, though it didn't quite mask the worry that lit his eyes. "But effective. Fine. I'll lock you in. And then I'll unlock it even faster, to protect my honour."

"Good man. Listen for my knock?" she said, stepping away from the door.

He nodded, and closed the door behind her. The last thing she saw was his anxious smile.

There were oil lamps along the walls. Sorrow knew the acolytes of the temple made sure they stayed lit night and day, so it was easy to see where she needed to go. The mausoleum was organized by the generations of chancellors; at the very end of the corridor was Harforth and his family. Her parents – or rather, Harun and Cerena – were housed three quarters of the way down, and she headed towards their own tomb, passing the empty ones, one of which, she realized with a shiver, would be hers. When she died, she wouldn't be interred with Harun and Cerena, but in her own tomb, as the 105th chancellor of Rhannon. Assuming Vespus didn't tell everyone otherwise.

She put him out of her mind as she reached Harun and Cerena's tomb and, as carefully as she could, pulled the door open.

The corridor might be lit, but the tombs weren't, so Sorrow took one of the lamps from the wall inside with her.

In the centre of the room were two stone sarcophagi, their wooden lids inscribed with the names and birth and death dates of their occupants. On the right, Harun. And on the left, Cerena.

Sorrow placed the lamp on top of her father's tomb and crossed to her mother's. *Not your parents*, she reminded herself. But how could she think of them as anything else? She might not have their blood, but she couldn't reverse the lifetime of connection she felt to them. Especially without knowing who her real parents were. The list that made her realize who she was – or rather, wasn't – had simply stated "baby girl, missing shortly after birth". No names. Neither theirs nor hers. Perhaps they hadn't even named her yet.

Something strange happened then, as she stared at the twin coffins, imagining herself with another name. For the first time, she didn't like it. She *was* Sorrow. That was *her* name. Suddenly she didn't want to know any other name she might have had.

She stared at the final resting place of the woman who'd named her, for better or worse, and then forced the lid of Cerena's sarcophagus aside.

Sorrow turned away to avoid the burst of rot she'd anticipated, and was surprised to find it absent. A vaguely vanilla-like, papery scent rose up briefly, then there was nothing, save for the silk-wrapped bones of Cerena Ventaxis. The dark fabric hadn't rotted, treated with some compound

Sorrow didn't understand to keep it intact, even as it helped the body inside to decay. She almost missed the shape tucked into the crook of Cerena's arm, also wrapped in black.

For some reason it jarred; the tenderness with which it seemed the remains of Cerena cradled her daughter. After all, she'd used her last words to curse the child she'd thought she'd had. It didn't feel right to Sorrow that she held her close to where her heart had been.

It was that thought that gave Sorrow the strength to reach down and take her.

"I'm doing this for Rhannon," Sorrow whispered, her voice sepulchral soft. "I'm sorry. I hope you'd understand."

Gently, she lifted the bundle into her arms, feeling the bones shift inside their silk wrapping, and she cradled it against her, though nothing had been able to hurt it for a long time. She laid it down beside the lamp with infinite care before closing Cerena's casket, and then stopped.

She hadn't thought about what she'd do with the skeleton of the dead Sorrow once she'd retrieved it. Now she was here, it felt horribly wrong to take it anywhere else. These bones belonged here, with her parents. But where could Sorrow put them to keep them safe, and to keep herself and Charon safe too?

She lifted the lamp high and left her parents' crypt, walking the hall down past her grandmother and Reuben's tomb, past his mother and father. The bones of a hundred dead Ventaxises lay down here, and Sorrow shivered. If she failed, or if Vespus exposed her, what would happen to them? Legend had it that when her family took power they ransacked the Lys mausoleums and threw the bones into the Archior. She wondered if they'd do the same again, and throw her in afterwards.

She reached the end of the crypt, stopping outside the tomb of Harforth Ventaxis and his wife, Janella. The first chancellor – he'd sentenced the former king and his family to death. Perhaps even dealt the death blow himself, depending on which account you believed. Age had crumbled the facade of the tomb, and when Sorrow reached to touch it, it disintegrated, a cloud of dust blossoming over her boots. Not there, Sorrow decided.

She began to walk back, reading the names etched into the stone, recalling childhood history lessons as she did. Not Cesare, not Linos, not Benyan . . . Rohir. . . Who was he? Rohir Ventaxis, her grandfather nine generations back. He wasn't any of the men Beata had referenced. . . She tried to think, but could come up with nothing. Rohir the Unremarkable. . . Could she place the remains with him?

She reached for the door of his tomb and it gave way with surprising ease. Holding the lamp, she entered.

There were a dozen caskets, two large, and many, many smaller.

Then Sorrow remembered who he was. He and his wife had lost over fifteen children, some before they were born, most after. The Jedenvat had tried to push him to leave his wife, Shira, for a more fertile bride, but he refused. He remained with her, going as far as to say if they died childless then the vice chancellor should step up and govern, their family become the new ruling dynasty. It had never happened; Shira finally had a son who'd grown to adulthood and continued the Ventaxis line.

Not Rohir the Unremarkable – Rohir the Loyal. Rohir the man who put his love for his wife and the promise he made to her above his career. Here was a good place to lay the bones to rest. Here with other lost Ventaxis children.

Sorrow hurried back to the bundle, carrying it down to the open vault. She didn't want to disturb the other coffins, but she had little choice. She glanced around, and chose one that looked somehow friendlier than the others did. None of the names were legible any more, so Sorrow didn't know whose casket she was borrowing. Muttering a constant stream of apologies under her breath, she put the real Sorrow down on top of Rohir's casket and opened the friendlier one. Again, the scent of old paper and dust rose from it, but this time when Sorrow looked inside, it was empty.

Or so it seemed.

Whether it was the age, or a fault, the silk had corrupted. Instead of helping the flesh to fade and preserving the bones, it had failed, rotting, the centuries' old bones within doing the same, leaving only dust. It was a terrible shame, but Sorrow had to admit, it was also the perfect solution. She could lay the other Sorrow here, and even if anyone looked, they'd find nothing unusual.

"I'm going to place you here, with your cousin," Sorrow whispered, feeling both foolish and superstitious as she lowered the bundle gently into the dust. She took an extra moment to make sure the shroud was secure, not wanting her other self to suffer the fate of the forgotten Ventaxis child. Then, before she became too maudlin, she pulled the wooden lid back over, and was about to leave when she had a thought. She bent, and scooped a handful of dust from the floor, scattering it over the coffin lid to hide her activity, before leaving. She did the same in her parents' crypt, masking the signs of her being there. Then, with a final glance, she closed the door.

Sorrow could still feel the tiny bones in her hands, shifting inside the silk. She didn't think she'd ever forget the sensation.

It's over, she told herself firmly.

If Vespus ever told anyone that the real Sorrow had died, and her bones were secretly buried with Cerena, Sorrow could call his bluff. If anyone looked, they'd find nothing. All she had to do now was write to Melisia. Then she could finally concentrate on putting Rhannon back together – starting with curing the plague victims.

She made her way back to the door and knocked lightly, waiting for the sound of the picks in the lock, bending her ear to the keyhole. Silence.

She knocked again, louder.

Still nothing.

The door was too thick for him to hear her, or vice versa, but that didn't stop her trying.

"Luvian?" She pressed her lips to the keyhole and spoke into it. "Luvian, if you're messing around, I swear..."

But she knew he wouldn't. Not here, like this.

It's fine, she told herself. *Relax. He's probably hiding because someone came – that's exactly why you wanted to be locked in. It was part of the plan.*

It did nothing to calm her. Suddenly the tomb didn't feel so serene, and safe. Suddenly she was aware that there was no other way out. What if he wasn't hiding? What if he'd been caught? What if he'd been attacked? What if—?

"Stop it," she said aloud. The words echoed off the walls; they were so close, why were they close? When had the passage become this narrow?

Sorrow pounded the door hopelessly, panic rising.

She was trapped.

Trapped until the acolytes came to make sure the torches were lit.

What if they didn't come?

Her mind raced on again – what if they forgot, and she was stuck in here? How long could a person survive with food and water?

She sank to the ground, her breathing shallow. She'd never had a problem with small spaces before, had cheerfully been using the secret passageway in the Winter Palace for years, but this was different. She was locked in with the dead.

Like one of Taasas's visions, Sorrow pictured Cerena, furious she'd stolen her daughter's place in both life and now death, rising from her coffin and hunting her. She heard the scrape of the coffin lid as the dead First Lady rose from her grave, the hissing of the shroud as it brushed the stone floor.

Sorrow covered her ears, but she couldn't hide her mind from the images it showed her: Rohir coming to avenge the child whose casket she'd borrowed; Harun seeking her, the cuckoo in the nest, the changeling who'd tried to overthrow him. . .

She saw him as he'd been that last night in the Summer Palace, gaunt and grey, shambling towards her, a skeletal finger outstretched. She pressed herself against the door, hands over her ears, face buried in her knees, chanting, "No, no, no," desperately aware he was getting closer and closer. . .

When his arms wrapped around her she screamed.

"Shut up!" Luvian clapped a panicked hand over her mouth. "Graces, Sorrow, do you want to get caught?"

The terror that had almost consumed her receded, and she looked up into the concerned brown eyes of her friend.

"Where were you?" she said.

"I had to hide. A pair of acolytes came through the grounds. Are you all right?"

"What time do the inns close?" she asked.

"Around three. Why?"

"I could really use a drink."

17

Out of the Woods

There was a roar of noise and warmth, and an earthy, beery smell washed over Sorrow as Luvian pulled her to a corner table in a small tavern, ushering her into a seat, using his body to block her from sight as he surveyed her.

"Stay here while I go to the bar," he ordered. "Where are the glasses I gave you?"

Sorrow pulled them from her pocket and put them on.

"Pull your hair all the way down, use it as a curtain. Damn, I've lost the lipstick." He sounded annoyed with himself. "Don't look at anyone. Don't talk to anyone."

She had no intention of it, but obediently bowed her head as she pulled the pins from the tangles of her hair, eyes tracing the graffiti carved into the surface of the table, trying to be as unobtrusive as possible.

They drank quickly, and the warmth from the beer

restored Sorrow's nerves. She followed Luvian out into the night, retracing their steps to the coaching inn.

But when they arrived the whole place was dark. No lights in any windows, no coach being prepared, no horses with nosebags fuelling up for the trip. It looked deserted. It looked closed.

"Where's the coach?" Sorrow asked, peering around.

"I don't know..." Luvian said. "It was definitely midnight. I asked at the change point."

"Wait – was it midnight from here? Or midnight from the change point?"

Luvian opened his mouth and then snapped it shut, his eyes closing in frustration. "I assumed... This is the terminus... We're in the capital..." he began, and then stopped. "I'm so sorry. So, so sorry."

Her anger faded when she saw how distraught he was.

"Hey." Sorrow squeezed his shoulder. "We'll just find somewhere to lie low until morning. Maybe a stable, or something? You have your lock picks, we'll be all right."

Luvian shook his head. "We won't. In the morning this place will be filled with people going about their business. It's one thing to hide in plain sight at night, when you're wearing a disguise. But your disguise is shot, it won't hold up under daylight. And we're in the capital – the chances of being seen by someone who actually knows you are too high."

He was right. "What can we do?"

He chewed his lip. "We have to get out of Istevar. We could walk to the changing post. The first coach from there is at four. If we move fast, we'll get there early enough to reach Prekara while it's still quiet. So long as we stick to the backstreets and keep our heads down, we might be all right."

He paused. "I think it's our best option. In fact, it's our only option."

They kept their talking to a minimum, saving their breath to drive them onwards. An hour later, they'd reached the suburbs of Istevar, passing houses and local stores, schools and businesses, the people sound asleep inside, unaware their imposter chancellor was rushing past. Sorrow wasn't used to this much walking, especially after weeks of only moving between the Round Chamber, her office, and her bedroom. But she didn't want to make a fuss, so she pressed on, ignoring the stitch under her ribs and the tightness in her calves.

It was as they began to leave the district of Istevar, about to cross briefly through the East Marches, that Sorrow became aware someone was behind them. She'd paused for a moment to give her agonized feet a break, perched on a wall, kicking her legs back and forth when she turned and noticed a silhouette, trying to blend in with the shadows. A burst of shock blitzed through her, but she looked away, as though she'd seen nothing, continuing to stretch. She turned again swiftly, in time to see the figure duck back out of sight, and the hairs along her arms stood on end beneath her tunic.

As casually as she could manage, she hopped down and jogged until she was level with Luvian.

"We're being followed," she said in a low voice. "Just one person, I think. I don't know how long they've been there. But I'm sure they're following us."

Luvian gave a short nod, and discreetly moved a hand to his pocket, pulling out the lock picks. He bumped Sorrow's shoulder, using the motion for cover as he passed one to her.

"Let's disappear for a minute," he said.

Sorrow nodded.

They turned down the street at the same pace. Then Luvian grabbed her hand and began to run, dragging her with him. Sorrow spotted a doorway and pulled them into it, hiding as far back as they could.

Her chest was flush against his back; she could feel his heart pounding as he held himself taut, ready to fight. Her own pulse was hummingbird fast, and she took deep, silent breaths, trying to slow it, her free hand gripping the back of Luvian's tunic, the other holding the lock pick.

Something hard was pressing into her hip, and she shifted. It was the book he'd lent her.

There was a scene in it where the heroine and her lover were being chased through a bustling market and they'd hidden in a doorway, kissing to throw their pursuer off. Even as she'd been reading it, it had seemed a ludicrous thing to do, and now she was in a similar position, even more so. Kissing would blind them to any danger coming.

And she'd be kissing Luvian.

Which didn't feel like a ridiculous thing to do.

She jerked in shock as her mind presented her with that image.

"What's wrong?" Luvian whispered.

"Nothing," Sorrow replied in an equally low voice. Then, before she could stop herself, "It's like in the book. When they're being chased and kiss as a kind of disguise. Stupid thing to do. It would never work."

When he replied, his voice was low, and tentative. "If only for the timing, we could find out. For science."

Sorrow's jaw dropped, but before she had time to think of

a reply, Luvian continued hurriedly. "What kind of second-rate stalker is this person? You'd think he'd have heard us..." He trailed off, and they waited in silence.

For several long moments neither moved, nor spoke, remaining coiled, spring-tight, waiting to see if they were discovered. Sorrow found she was still holding his tunic, the fabric fisted in her fingers. She also realized she didn't want to let go, though she couldn't quite account for why.

When it felt as though they'd been in the porch for at least a year, Luvian turned to the side, not quite meeting her eye.

"I'm going to look. Stay here."

Sorrow reluctantly released her hold on him, curling her hand into a fist as he slipped away. Her knees felt shaky, and she had the sneaking suspicion it wasn't completely because of their pursuer. She forced her mind back into the moment. She had to be ready. If anyone surprised her, she'd aim for their eye. Lock pick to the eye, knee to the groin. That would be enough to take them out.

She was so intently rehearsing the motions in her mind, imagining her fist arching forward towards an assailant, her knee rising, that she almost hit Luvian when he returned. She stopped herself before she made contact, dropping her hand.

"Sorry."

"No, it's good you were ready," he said, sounding amused. "There's no sign of our mystery pursuer, though. Probably just some chancer looking for an easy mark."

Sorrow nodded. "Let's go." She edged past him and back on to the street.

They walked on, leaving the village behind and following the open road.

The moon was waxing, growing fatter in the sky, surrounded by her courtiers of stars. The longer Sorrow looked up, the more of them she could see, not just white, but pastel pink, faint lavender, ice blue, pale gold, all glittering away above them.

"The staging post is the other side of the woods." Luvian gestured ahead of them, drawing her thoughts back down to earth. "About an hour's walk, I think."

"We have to go through the woods?" Sorrow said.

"We did on the way here. If you'd looked up from the book, you'd know that." He tried to sound light, but Sorrow could hear the strain in his voice.

She understood; she was tired too, energy bleeding from her with every moment she remained on her feet. Even so, Sorrow didn't want to travel through a woodland. Forests were made entirely of plants. It would feel like running past Vespus himself. Not to mention the big cats, snakes, and whatever other beasties haunted the forest.

"Can't we go around?"

"We don't have time, Sorrow," Luvian said gently. "If anything tries to eat you I'll offer it my body first."

In what seemed to be becoming a habit, they clasped hands, only letting go as they clambered wearily over the stile that separated the forest from the road, linking them again the moment they were both over and heading into the woods.

They had to plot their path as the moon allowed, using every patch to move forward. Each snag and snarl in her trousers and tunic felt deliberate, as though the foliage was plucking and pinching her out of spite.

She told herself she was being stupid, that roots weren't rising to the surface of the forest floor to trip her, and that the scraping of twigs against her hair and face was her fault, not theirs. She fought not to cry out, biting her tongue, trying not to squeeze Luvian's hand in panic, concentrating instead on the lock pick she still clutched in the other, and the damage she could do with it if she had to.

On and on they went, one foot in front of the other, until Sorrow was nothing but the journey. The forest was so dense, and her tiredness so great, she had no idea how much time had passed until Luvian spoke.

"We're almost there."

Sorrow looked up, and through the trees she saw lights; the glow of gas lamps in windows, and she pinched herself to make sure she wasn't hallucinating. But the smell of dung and the warm, fresh hay scent of the horses as they drew nearer was enough to convince her it was real. They were the first people to board, and Sorrow slid straight to the furthest corner, resting her head against the cool wood. The last thing she heard was Luvian asking the driver to wake them at Prekara, and then she was gone.

She woke when the carriage halted and the driver bellowed, "Prekara," thumping the roof for good measure. Luvian had been asleep on her shoulder, and he sat up, gazing around with wide eyes, his glasses askew.

The Graces must have been smiling kindly on them, because not only were they alone in the carriage, but the narrow streets of Prekara were mostly empty, only the most industrious or unfortunate citizens forced to abandon their beds so early, their misery blinding them to Sorrow and Luvian as they ghosted past them.

As they neared the docks, and Sorrow could see the

208

sheen of the sea in the distance, Luvian led Sorrow down a narrow alley. He crouched over a circular grate in the ground, digging his fingers into the holes and lifting, reddening with the effort, until he could slide the grate away, revealing a hole.

"Ladies first," he said, gesturing at it.

Sorrow peered down, at a ladder that seemed to be made of rods embedded in the wall. "I don't think I have the coordination for that right now," she said.

"Take it slow. Yell when you reach the bottom. And hurry. It'd be annoying to get caught so close to home."

Sorrow lowered herself on to the ladder, and began to descend.

It wasn't as bad as she'd thought; the handholds were sturdy, thick, and evenly spaced, so she soon found a rhythm. Once she reached the floor, she wiped her hands on her tunic and called to Luvian to come down.

"Where are we?" she asked as he dropped beside her.

"Drains," he replied, his voice echoing.

"What?"

"Not domestic ones. They were built for the harbour. To give the water somewhere to go during high tide, so it wouldn't flood the district. But because the harbour wasn't finished, they were never needed. Until I found a use for them."

"How did you find them?"

"Hiding from Arkady."

Of course.

Their footsteps echoed dully as they walked beneath Prekara, emerging a short while later in the tunnel than ran between the Point and the cottage gardens.

209

She made to turn towards the Point, thinking fondly of the bed in her cell, but Luvian took her hand and pulled her towards the cottage exit.

"You're supposed to be resting in the cottage," he reminded her.

Sorrow needed to brush her teeth and wash her face. In fact, she needed a bath. But the moment she saw Luvian's bed she knew it wasn't going to happen. She forgot her curiosity about his room, too, in the face of a mattress and blankets, though she blurrily registered that it was just as chaotic as she'd expected. And full of books.

She had her boots off and was under the covers within seconds.

Sorrow felt a tug as Luvian liberated one of his pillows from beneath her head, and then she was hurtling gratefully towards sleep.

She woke slowly, her body peeling itself from rest bone by bone, until her eyes fluttered open. Then she frowned, sitting up, trying to gauge where she was.

To her surprise, Luvian was on the floor beside the bed in a nest of blankets, sleeping on his back, one arm crossed over his stomach, the other thrown wide. He'd taken his glasses off and placed them neatly on the cabinet beside the bed. He also appeared to have changed his clothes before he'd slept, and Sorrow was impressed at his fortitude.

There was no clock in the room, and she might have been asleep for two hours, or twenty. However long it had been, though, she felt rested. She toyed with the idea of getting up and finding a bathroom, but despite what Luvian had said about no one using the houses, she didn't want to run the risk of meeting Beata or Arkady. Instead she leant back on her elbows and studied the room.

It was like a library with a bed and a desk in it – reminding her for a chilling moment of Charon's room at Castle Adavaria, and she looked to the window, relieved to see gauzy curtains drawn across it. Three of the four walls were made of shelves, and double lined with books. But these were no matching leather-bound tomes. They were a mix of paperbacks, thick hardbacks, battered bound manuscripts, and old boarded manuals. She saw stories she suspected were in the vein of the romance she'd read during the coach ride, if their titles were any indicator, but there were also history books, books for children and adults, books in Rhyllian and Merish, books about customs in Svarta and Skae.

There were art books too, so many art books, a whole wall dedicated to them: techniques, histories of styles, biographies. He loved art, she remembered, had wanted to be an artist when he was growing up. It showed.

As she leant forward, she saw he really did have a guidebook about Castle Adavaria, and she couldn't help but smile.

"If you want to borrow one you have to see the librarian."

Luvian's voice startled her, and she turned to him.

"Morning," he said, the end of the word lost to a yawn as his arms rose into a stretch that saw him punch the wall, and then wince.

"Morning," Sorrow said, feeling suddenly self-conscious. She ran her hands through her hair as casually as she was able to. "Who's the librarian?"

In response, he sat up, leaning forward to tug one of the books from the nearest shelf and tossing it to Sorrow.

It was a children's book, about a pair of crocodiles who

went on an adventure. She shrugged, and opened it, to find a card stuck to the first page.

"The Luvian Andearly Rathbone Library?" she read.

"Making me the librarian." He mock-bowed. "You may borrow it, for a week. If you don't return it in that time, it's a crown per day, until it's returned. And I'd need to make you a library card."

"That's adorable." Sorrow smiled, her grin widening as Luvian ducked his head and rubbed the back of his neck.

"Ha. I read about libraries, and there weren't any real ones, so I opened my own. With all those. Most of them used to be in the Point – contraband. But I brought them up here after your father died."

Sorrow's smile faded. "Maybe I'll name the first new public library in your honour."

"Maybe you should." He grinned. "Sleep well?"

"I did. But now I'd really like to wash. And . . . can I borrow some clean clothes?"

At that, Luvian looked as flustered as Sorrow felt, but nodded, hauling himself from his makeshift bed and leaving her. By the time he returned Sorrow was standing, working the kinks out of her neck, trying to act casual, as though she hadn't woken up in his bed. He handed her a pile of clothes.

"I didn't know what would work so. . ." He shrugged. "Bathroom is the second door down from here. There's no bath, but a water shower – just turn the wheel and stand under it. I left towels."

"Thank you."

They performed an awkward dance, getting in each other's way, laughing nervously, until Luvian moved aside and gestured for her to pass him.

She stepped back into the courtyard she'd paid little attention to when they'd arrived, and paused, taking it all in. Growing up in a multi-storeyed palace, she'd never been inside a traditional Rhannish house, so she was enchanted by how pretty and peaceful it was.

The rooms were all set off a bright main courtyard that formed the centre of the house. The ceiling was glass, and the roof could be opened, if the owner wished, to let the warmth and sunlight in, blinds ready to cover it and provide shade if that same sun became too harsh. The floor was made of thousands of red hexagonal tiles that were cool under her toes, and she crossed them to peer into an indoor pond where golden fish darted between water lilies.

Either side of it were long, soft-looking sofas, bookended by tables piled with yet more books, and Sorrow pictured Luvian sitting there, reading quietly. When she went over and flipped the covers, she saw each one was a "library" book, and it made her smile. It was tranquil, and pleasant, and if she wasn't conscious of the fact she really needed to bathe, she might have lingered. Sorrow turned towards the room Luvian had mentioned, and began putting herself back together.

Voices pulled her from the bliss of the water shower. She'd never used one before, but the sensation of warm water gently pummelling her back and shoulders was heavenly. Best of all, no one could hold her under. She hadn't relished the idea of bathing knowing Arkady was nearby, even though they were at peace now. The water shower meant she didn't have to. Once she was back home and everything was settled, she'd look into having them installed at the palace. Baths were fine, but this was much better.

Reluctantly turning the water off, she dried herself quickly and pulled on the tunic and trousers Luvian had given her. The clothes were comfortable, the tunic soft blue and sleeveless with large pockets. It reached her knees, which was a mercy as the trousers were indecently tight over her buttocks and thighs, though the length was at least perfect; she didn't need to roll them up. Towelling her hair, she pressed her ear against the door and listened, opening it when she recognized the voice.

"Mael," she said, folding the towel. "Hello."

He and Luvian stood in the courtyard. Luvian looked her up and down, assessing her in his clothes, as Mael said, "Hi. I thought I'd come and see how you were feeling."

Sorrow was confused, until she remembered her "headache". "Much better, thank you."

Luvian spoke then. "I'm going into the Point. I need to check in with Irris and make sure everything is on track. You know the way back?" he said to Mael, who nodded. "Great. I'll meet you there."

He gave Sorrow a reassuring smile and vanished, the door clicking closed a moment later, leaving her alone with Mael.

18

The Death of Secrets

Sorrow and Mael stood, examining each other.

It had been hard to tell, deep in the Point, but here, in the mellow afternoon sunshine that lit Luvian's courtyard, she saw he looked better than he had in Istevar. Less drawn, less anguished. His cheeks were full again, olive skin glowing and clear. He was dressed in a loose, casual shirt and trousers, and his posture was relaxed, arms at his sides, gaze soft. She, she suspected, appeared significantly tenser.

"Vespus is a piece of shit, isn't he?" Mael said, breaking the silence.

The word sounded wrong from his lips, like he was a child trying to impress her by swearing. But she nodded. "He is."

She lowered herself on to one of the plump sofas and Mael moved to sit opposite. They both watched the fish in the pool between them, waiting for the other to continue.

Mael plucked up the courage first.

"I wasn't very fair to you, when I saw you in the East Marches. Nor at the Winter Palace. I had some things to work through."

"With the Rathbones?" There was no accusation in her voice, but he flushed.

"Meeting them was . . . unexpected. I meant about Vespus. I really thought he cared about me, when actually he spent two years manipulating me. So I understand how you feel right now, I think. I know how easy it is to be overwhelmed by him."

"Except you're not the chancellor," Sorrow said. "My mistakes don't cost elections, they cost lives."

"He would have always won." Mael's words echoed Luvian's. "He doesn't play games he thinks he'll lose. That's why I was such a disappointment to him. He couldn't fathom that I wanted a family more than power. He can't understand that."

"What really happened, between you?" She knew Vespus's version, but knowing Vespus that could easily be more lies. More manipulation.

"Like I said, I wanted a family. I made it clear my goal was to come back here and build a relationship with you, and Harun. I didn't want to run for election, Vespus convinced me I had to. And when I tried to quit, he wouldn't let me. He threatened Beliss. . . He kept reminding me she was old. Frail. And when I called his bluff he had the Sons of Rhannon attack you in Adavaria."

Sorrow's jaw dropped. "What? No. . . He was behind that? How?"

Mael nodded. "Arkady told me. Vespus hired him to attack

216

you in Rhylla. He got the idea after what happened in here, in Prekara. That's how Arkady was able to get in and out of the castle complex – some of Vespus's other hirelings smuggled him in, and made sure your bodyguard didn't get involved. His job was to find you and scare you badly enough to make you quit the election race."

"Scare me? He held my head underwater, Mael, that's usually fatal," Sorrow snapped. "And he killed Dain, my guard."

"He didn't."

"Arkady told me so himself while he was attacking me. He thought she was Irris."

"That's proof he didn't do it – he knew who Irris was, from stalking you during the campaign. Again, he was just trying to scare you."

"Dain died."

"That wasn't him, I promise."

Sorrow gave Mael a long look. It was possible someone like Aphora, or her brother, Melakis, another of Vespus's lackeys, had actually killed Dain. Or maybe Arkady lied, not wanting Mael to judge him. Either way, it didn't change what he'd done to her, or the fact that Dain had been killed.

"Well, you'll have to forgive me, but experience suggests he's at least an aspiring murderer, and a liar." Sorrow crossed her arms.

Mael sighed. "I didn't come to argue with you."

"Then why *did* you come?"

"Because. . ." He looked away, not finishing his sentence.

He didn't elaborate, and Sorrow filled in the gaps. Because he thought she was his sister, and all the family he had left. Because he was lonely, and full of love, and he wanted to be part of something.

"I have another question," Sorrow said. "How did you end up here, with them?"

Mael smiled fondly, which startled Sorrow. "Luvian and Lawton found me after the election. Everyone swarmed around you and I left. Just walked out. No one tried to stop me." His voice wavered, but he continued.

"I went to a tavern to get a drink, and they were there, though in disguise – I didn't immediately go and join the enemy. I lost an election, not my mind." He smiled, and she gave a small one in return. "They came to sit with me and I proceeded to get hideously drunk at their expense. I don't remember much after that, but the next morning I woke up here, in this cottage. And Luvian wasn't disguised any more. I knew who he was, of course."

"That must have been one hell of a surprise."

Mael nodded. "Finding out his brothers were the Sons of Rhannon was the biggest surprise. But Luvian explained everything – about Vespus, and Lamentia. Then Irris found me, but – well, it didn't work out. I came back here."

Sorrow hung her head.

"We saw you at the ball, me and Irris. Something was clearly wrong between you and Vespus. So we decided we'd leave, and then plan to get you out. Luvian suggested the Sons of Rhannon as a scapegoat. He said even Vespus wouldn't see through that one."

"It was a good idea," she admitted.

"They're clever, the Rathbones. I get a headache every time I try to keep up with them." He glanced at her. "Which is good, considering we need a plan."

"I have a plan," Sorrow said. "Rathbone approved. But I need to talk to the others before I can put the final piece in place."

"Let's go then," he said, standing.

"Mael," she called, waiting for him to turn. "I really meant it when I said I wanted you to come back to the Winter Palace. I still mean it. I want us to be a family."

"OK," he said, nodding. "I'd really like that."

Warmth filled her. "Me too," she said. If it didn't matter that she wasn't a Ventaxis, then it didn't matter if he was, or wasn't one either. He thought she was his family, and that was good enough for her. From now on, he was her brother.

They headed down into the Point, making straight for the recreation room, where Irris, Rasmus, Luvian and Arkady sat in a semicircle, clearly waiting for her.

Sorrow and Mael took their places.

"I know what we need to do to stop Vespus." Sorrow looked at them all in turn. "But it's going to come at a cost." She turned to Rasmus. "The only way to stop Vespus is to seek help from the one person who has power over him."

"My aunt."

Sorrow nodded. "I'm going to write to Melisia and tell her what Vespus is doing. But that means I'm going to have to tell her about us, so he can't use it against me. One way or another, she's going to find out about us. I'd rather we controlled it."

Rasmus took a deep breath, and then nodded. "You're right," he said. Then again, in a stronger voice. "Absolutely right. And I agree. If it comes from us, I think she'll be more lenient. She respects honesty."

Sorrow gave him a sad smile. "Well, I'm going to ask her not to make our relationship public, in exchange for me not telling anyone that her half-brother killed my father, or revealing what Starwater can really do."

"What do you mean? It can't do anything, other than get you a bit drunker."

Sorrow shook her head. "Your father has been using it to experiment on Rhyllians with abilities. That's why he let you and Eirlys have so much. Because of your gifts. He wanted to see what you'd do with it. He was using you. Your father told me Melisia has hidden people with abilities who don't fit her vision of Rhylla. Rhyllians with abilities that might be dangerous. . . Imagine what your father could do with them if he gave them Starwater."

Rasmus looked outraged. "That's not how abilities work – you know that. They're natural, used only for good."

"Not always. Do you know what Taasas can do? What her ability is?"

When he shook his head Sorrow told him what Taasas had done to her. His mouth opened as she described the visions Taasas had shown her, the violence and the horror of them. The violation of them.

"Imagine how Astria or Nyrssea would react if they knew someone like Taasas existed. In Melisia's position I'd keep it hidden, too."

Rasmus nodded slowly, reluctantly conceding the point.

"There's more." Sorrow looked down, steeling herself. "He thinks your ability is on a par with Adavere's."

Rasmus laughed, but his face fell when Sorrow didn't smile back.

"I think, with Starwater, it might be. And it's my belief Vespus wants to use you, to use your ability, to control others. To do to them what it does to me. Soothe and seduce them into compliance."

Rasmus paled. "Don't threaten my aunt," he said finally,

220

his voice low. "Don't tell her you'll keep her secrets if she keeps ours. She won't respond to it kindly."

"That's what I said," Luvian added.

"Write to her. Tell her everything. Just don't try to bargain with her. And don't threaten her. I'll deliver it personally."

"Ras, no. You don't know what she'll do, and you know what the penalty is. I can send the letter with a bird, and you can stay here, safe, until she's decided."

"That won't help. She'll think it's cowardly. Besides, it's not about me. It's about my father. We have to stop him, and short of killing him this is the only way. More than that, it's the right way. And my aunt is fair. She'll treat me fairly. I don't think she'll have me executed."

"And if she tries?"

"Then we'll rescue him," Luvian chimed in. "Daringly."

"Arkady knows how to get in and out of the castle complex, remember?" Mael said. Arkady nodded, and Sorrow scowled at him.

Rasmus grinned. "I'll look forward to it."

"So," Irris said, still perched on the arm of Rasmus's chair. "We have a plan. You'll write to Queen Melisia and tell her that her half-brother is in the early stages of a coup. That's treason, so she has to have him arrested at the very least."

Sorrow nodded.

"What about the people who've been affected by Hellfior?"

"I don't know if Vespus has developed a cure," Sorrow admitted. "He said he'd try. I was hoping Melisia would force him to make one."

"I could try healing them," Rasmus said. "I don't know if my ability works in that way, but it's worth a go, isn't it?"

Sorrow and Irris looked at each other.

"It can't hurt," said Irris.

Sorrow thought rapidly. Melisia might not allow Rasmus to return to Rhannon after he'd given her Sorrow's letter. But neither could he go there before, because if Vespus realized what was happening – if he heard that the victims were waking and realized who was behind it – he'd punish them both.

"I don't know how we can do it," Sorrow said, explaining her worries to them.

"You're right," Rasmus agreed. "But I'm sure my aunt will let me try to help, if my father refuses to supply a cure. She might have me escorted by twenty or so guards," he added with a wry smile, "but she won't leave them all to die."

"All right," Sorrow said. "You're our Plan B."

"The ransom should be deposited tomorrow," Irris said. "Then you can go back to Istevar, while Ras returns to Adavaria."

Sorrow nodded again. There it was. With luck, and the Graces' favour, this would be over before Winterfest, and no one in Laethea would ever have to know the truth about her.

Except Irris. And Luvian. Sorrow owed them that.

"I need to talk to Irris and Luvian privately," Sorrow said. Mael looked sad, but rose, ready to obey.

Sorrow stopped him with a hand on his arm as he passed her. "I'm going to need a new senator for the South Marches once I fire Balthasar. Be on my Jedenvat?" She smiled. "Work with me to make a better Rhannon?"

Mael's face split into a huge smile. When he pulled her into a tight hug, she wrapped her arms around him and squeezed back, feeling his surprise and delight.

There was a sheen to his eyes when he finally let her go, but he was beaming, and he slung an easy arm around both

Rasmus and Arkady as they left. Sorrow's heart felt full, full of love for her friends, old and new.

Then she turned to the two people in the world she trusted most.

Remaining on her feet, she took a deep breath and began. "Last night Luvian and I went to Istevar, as you know. Specifically, we went to the Ventaxis Mausoleum."

Irris looked at Luvian, who nodded, confirming it. "Why?" she asked.

Sorrow's mouth was dry, her hands shaking. She clasped them together behind her back. "Because I'm not the real Sorrow Ventaxis," she said. "And Vespus knows it."

Neither Irris nor Luvian spoke, or moved. Both stared at her, identical expressions of confusion on their faces.

"But. . ." Irris stuttered after a moment. "But of course you are. I've known you since you were born."

"I wasn't born Sorrow Ventaxis," Sorrow told her. "I don't know who I am. Who I *was*," she corrected herself.

"Explain," Luvian said, his eyes sharp behind his glasses.

She told them everything, not stopping, or keeping anything back. She began with her grandmother, the hospital in the North Marches, the terrible crime the Dowager First Lady had committed. Even when Irris fell back against the chair, her hand at her heart, as Sorrow confessed Charon knew, even when Luvian slammed his fist down on to the mantelpiece as Sorrow explained how she'd realized who she was, she didn't stop, the confession falling from her like petals from a dying rose. The words kept coming, easier and easier, until it was time to say she'd moved the bones of the real Sorrow and hidden them.

Finally, the band in her chest had vanished. Finally, the

knots inside her had come undone. Sorrow had never seen snow, but she knew how it accumulated on mountains until spring, when it thawed and rushed to the sea in great rivers, and that was how she felt. The weight that she'd been carrying since she'd found out the truth about herself had melted, and was leaving her.

"I'm an imposter," Sorrow said. "The whole time we were trying to prove it was Mael, I was one."

Both Irris and Luvian stared at her, pale and stricken. Then Irris's expression closed, and she strode forward, pulling Sorrow into a bone-crushing embrace.

"You stupid, stupid, idiot," she hissed in her ear. "I'm going to kill you. And my father. You first."

Then another pair of arms wrapped around them both, and Sorrow found herself bookended by her two favourite people.

"I felt left out," Luvian said, somewhere near her left ear. "I hate feeling left out. It triggers horrific childhood memories. And I'm sorry."

"Why?" Sorrow asked.

"Because it was my lists that did this. If I hadn't got them, you wouldn't have realized and Vespus wouldn't have heard you. This is all my fault."

But before Sorrow could say anything, Irris, her voice muffled by Sorrow's shoulder, said, "The audacity of you trying to take the credit for the almost-downfall of Rhannon."

Then they were laughing, still clutching each other, delighted for reasons none of them could explain.

Eventually, the hysteria wore off, and they calmed, sitting in a small, tight circle, cross-legged like children, on the floor.

Irris was staring at her, as though she expected to see some change in her, as though what Sorrow had said should have altered her face.

"It explains so much," she said, still sounding stunned. "My father and your grandmother. Why he was so on edge in Rhylla. Why you shut down the morning of the election. Everything. And I would never, ever have guessed it."

"You should have told me what you were doing in the crypt," Luvian said, peering at her from over the rims of his glasses. "That can't have been easy."

"It was sad mostly. Really sad. It was only scary at the end, when I thought I was locked in for ever." She shot him a dirty look.

"I was only following your instructions," Luvian said sheepishly.

Irris looked thoughtful. "Poor Sorrow – other Sorrow, I mean. What a mess. I can't fathom how many things had to happen to bring us here."

Sorrow thought of all the potential strands of possibility out there, timelines where Mael was rescued, or had not fallen at all. Universes where Cerena had lived, the real Sorrow had lived. There was no way of knowing how any of them might have been.

"Well, I for one am happy with how it turned out," Luvian said. "I mean," he corrected himself, "I wouldn't have met you if things weren't this way."

"That's true," Sorrow said. "So, everything is awful, but we have each other."

The trio were silent for a moment, all lost in their own thoughts. Sorrow could feel a smile emerging, unable to contain her happiness at being accepted. They liked her anyway. Even though she wasn't a Ventaxis. They liked *her*.

"What are you grinning at?" Luvian asked.

"Just . . . feeling happy. Like you said. It's turned out well."

"You never know, it might even get better." His own mouth curved into a dangerous smile, and he gave her a slow wink.

Sorrow's face heated. "Maybe." She had to look away. "We'll see. Anyway, I suppose I should go and write this letter," she said.

"Use my cottage," Luvian offered. "You won't be disturbed."

"Thank you."

"I'll come and find you later," Irris said. "We should do something tonight. It might be the last time we're all together for a while."

It was a sobering thought. After tonight, Rasmus would be back in Rhylla and it was likely she'd never see him again. "Poor Ras," Sorrow murmured. "It seems unfair he's going to bear the brunt of this."

"He knows Melisia best," Luvian said. "But Irris is right. I'll go and see what stolen goods I can re-steal to throw us a little goodbye-for-now party."

He gave Sorrow another wink, and she knew he'd done it on purpose to fluster her.

Which it did.

"See you soon," he said, sauntering away.

"Interesting," Irris drawled deliberately, looking at Sorrow slyly.

"What is?"

"Oh, I think you know what, Miss Ventaxis."

Sorrow fled before her body combusted from embarrassment.

19

Joy and Sorrow

Sorrow returned to Luvian's cottage to write the letter, wanting space and quiet as she figured out what to say to the Rhyllian queen.

Searching for a clean sheet of paper, she opened a drawer in Luvian's desk and found the art supplies she'd bought for him in Ceridog. He'd placed them inside a box made of dark reddish wood, the lid inscribed with carved leaves. Hesitantly, knowing she was snooping but unable to stop, she opened the clay paints and found them used; she'd bought blue, red and yellow so he could mix his own colours, and he clearly favoured the blue most. It was almost gone. The paintbrushes were in the box too, clean, and dry, though flecks of paint on the handles attested to their use too, blues and greens and purples. Curiosity made her look for the sketchbook, but she couldn't find it, and once she found paper and a pen, she had no reason to keep rummaging through his drawers.

She sat down to compose her letter. She sucked the end of the pen thoughtfully, turning phrases over in her mind, and then she began.

She heard the front door open just as she signed the page, and looked up, expecting Irris. But it was Luvian who opened his bedroom door.

"Oh," he said. "Hello. You look very at home."

Sorrow suddenly felt shy. "I was just writing the letter to Melisia. I'm finished, actually. Oh – I used your pen. And paper. I hope that's all right?"

"It's fine. Use what you want. I just came to change my shirt."

She realized then his shirt was stained with some dark liquid. "What happened?"

"I dropped a bottle of squid-ink rum. I wouldn't get too close, it's not the nicest smell."

"I'll go."

"No, stay. Please." He opened his own small wardrobe and pulled out a shirt and some trousers, seemingly at random. "Carry on." He gave her a warm smile, and left.

Sorrow's stomach felt oddly fluttery, but she ignored it, and turned back to the desk, folding the letter in half.

When she opened Luvian's door, letter in hand, she found him standing in the courtyard, his back to her. He was shirtless, the old one flung over the back of one of the sofas, the new one in his hand.

He twisted at the sound of her startled breath, dropping the shirt, and swearing.

Sorrow stared at him. His olive skin was smooth, except

228

for a trail of hair leading down from his belly button into the waistband of his trousers, the sight of which made her stomach swoop. He was lean, and lithe, his shoulders broader than she'd thought. The thing that surprised her most was the silver bar through his left nipple. She couldn't stop staring at it. Rasmus's ears were ringed in silver – piercing was common in Rhylla: ears, noses, belly buttons. It was rare to find a Rhyllian who didn't have metal in their skin. . . But on a Rhannish person. . . Especially *Luvian*. . .

"You're pierced," she said. "You. You have a piercing."

Luvian crossed his arms over his chest.

"What, you think only Rhyllians like jewellery?" he said, his voice tight with embarrassment. "It was a dare, in my first year at university, and I'm too scared to take it out. All right?"

Sorrow flushed. "I wasn't judging."

Luvian bent to pick up the clean shirt and shrugged it on and Sorrow slipped out of the door, her heart beating fast.

"Ah!" Irris exclaimed, narrowly avoiding colliding with Sorrow. "I was just coming to find you." Then she saw Sorrow's expression. "Is everything all right?"

"Yes," Sorrow said hurriedly, shoving the letter in her pocket. "Let's go." For some reason the idea of Luvian coming out and talking to her was too much for her to cope with.

Mael, Arkady and Rasmus were already in the recreation room when Sorrow and Irris arrived.

Rasmus spotted them and made his way over.

"Hello, you two. Can I get you a drink?" he asked. "They have a nice Rhyllian vintage I happen to know went missing from Harcel's father's cellar a few years ago. Or there's some Merish viper-pear ale?"

Sorrow and Irris both took wine, and all three of them moved to where Mael and Arkady were talking softly. Arkady didn't look at either of them, his eyes remaining on Mael, leaning towards him, and it dawned on Sorrow that her would-be assassin might be nursing a bit of a crush on Mael.

Even as she watched, Mael gave Arkady the same open smile he gave to everyone.

Beliss might not have spoken his language, but she'd clearly filled him full of love, and the ability to be loved. Sorrow envied him that.

As though he'd heard her thoughts, Mael turned his gaze on her and held his hand out, inviting her to stand beside him. She didn't give herself time to refuse; she tucked herself beside him, only a little self-conscious as his arm came around her. It was a glorious feeling, to be part of something. To be his little sister. Sorrow made a silent prayer that if she ever told him the truth he'd be as understanding as Luvian and Irris had been.

Sorrow was so caught up in her thoughts she hadn't noticed Luvian arrive. He was standing by the drinks table, looking intently at the selection, as though deciding what to drink was an impossible task. She was about to excuse herself to go and talk to him, when Rasmus appeared at her elbow.

"Row, do you have a minute?"

"Sure," she said, slipping out of Mael's hold.

Sorrow followed Rasmus to a bench, pulling the letter out from her pocket.

"Before I forget," she said.

He held it in his palm, as though it weighed more than paper and ink, staring at his aunt's name written across the front. Then he nodded, and tucked it away in his tunic.

"Stars, this is hard," he began, running his hands though his hair. "Just . . . Luvian likes you. You know that, don't you?"

Sorrow's face burned, but she nodded. "I think so. Sometimes."

"And I think you like him too."

Again Sorrow nodded.

"What I'm trying to say is that I. . ." he said. "I like him. Not in the same way you do. I'm not about to challenge you for his hand."

Sorrow laughed nervously.

Rasmus continued. "He's a good person. And he cares a lot about you. So if you two did end up together . . . I'd understand. And I'd be happy for you." He took a deep breath. "I want you to be happy. He makes you happy."

"He pisses me off," Sorrow said.

Rasmus laughed.

"I'm grateful," Sorrow said. "But now isn't exactly the time for relationships."

Rasmus gave her a nudge. "If you're waiting for the right time, you'll wait for ever," he said. "So don't."

They were both silent for a moment.

"Is this weird?" Sorrow asked, unable to look at him.

"Yes. And no. It's what friends do," Rasmus replied. "And I told you I wanted to be your friend. Best friends. How we started."

"You don't have to be this nice."

"I know. Go after him."

Sorrow looked across the room and saw Luvian was slipping out of the door.

"Go," Ras said.

Sorrow left.

Sorrow turned the knob of the cottage door, relieved when it opened. She shut it quietly behind her, and took the few steps into the courtyard.

Luvian was sprawled across one of the sofas in a most un-Luvian-like fashion. He'd kicked off his shoes, his feet bare, a bottle of wine gripped in his right hand. He sat up when he saw her.

"Everything all right?"

She tried once, twice to reply. She wanted to tell him that she thought he was brilliant, that everything about him was brilliant. She wanted to tell him she trusted him, and that she was grateful every day she'd met him. She wanted to tell him she'd never met anyone who infuriated her more. And she wanted to kiss his stupid, arrogant mouth.

"Sorrow, what?"

Rasmus was right. There was never going to be a right time.

This was the right time.

Her heart was beating so hard it was painful, but she walked to him, kneeling down in front of him so their faces were level. Her gaze locked on his, she reached out, fingers shaking, and touched his cheek.

His mouth opened, his eyes wide behind his glasses, as he understood what she was doing.

She kept looking at him as she leant in, checking his reaction, braced for rejection. Then, her eyelids fluttering shut, she brushed her lips against his.

She heard the wine bottle hit the floor with a dull thud, heard it roll away, then his palms were cradling her face and he was kissing her back.

His lips were gentle at first, testing, as though he too wasn't sure of her reaction. To make herself clear, she moved a hand around the back of his neck, sliding her fingers into his hair. With the other hand she cupped his jaw, her thumb grazing his cheekbone.

He got the message, deepening the kiss, his tongue seeking hers, lips firm and sure now.

When she danced her tongue against his, he kissed her more furiously, his hands moving to her lower back. Her shirt – his shirt – must have ridden up, because his fingers brushed the bare skin at her waist and she shuddered, pressing into him. Luvian made a sound deep in the back of his throat, his grip on her tightening, his mouth moving with hers hungrily.

When she pulled away, dizzy for air, and looked at him, his glasses had fogged up completely.

She couldn't help laughing and he took them off, setting them aside.

"We're not done," he almost growled, pulling her back to him.

Fireworks went off in her mind as she kissed him again. He lifted her on to his lap, and she straddled him, knees either side of his thighs, his hands ghosting under her shirt, becoming ever more daring, moving higher along her back, over her ribs.

She pulled away from his mouth and her lips explored his throat and jaw, licking his earlobe before returning to his mouth, his lips greeting hers eagerly.

Sorrow felt consumed by the kiss, even as she devoured him, their mouths moving as though they'd never done anything but kiss, were never meant to do anything but kiss.

His thumb brushed the underside of her breast, and she sighed softly, leaning into his touch. She leant back and pulled the shirt over her head, tossing the unwanted garment on to the sofa opposite before turning to him once more.

Luvian's eyes were wide.

"Are you all right?" Sorrow asked, bewildered by his expression. She looked down at herself, puzzled. "Is there something wrong?" She fought the urge to cross her hands over her chest.

He swallowed. "No. Absolutely not. Everything is very, very right. It's just that... I've ... I've never..."

"Never... Ohhh." Sorrow couldn't hide her surprise. "That's OK. We don't have to do anything."

"There was never time, I was busy, and then my family..."

"Luvian," Sorrow said softly.

"I'm aware it's not a thing you can learn from books. Which is how I learn."

Sorrow bent forward and kissed his forehead. "Come on," she said. She climbed off him and held out her hand.

He obeyed her at once, following her with the air of a man who'd walk into hell after her if she asked.

She led him into his room, turning the gas lamps on low. Then she shut the door as he faced her, awed.

She took his left hand and placed it on her breast, both of them inhaling sharply as his cold skin met her warmth.

"We can stop whenever you want," she said.

"Unlikely," he whispered.

His touch was gentle, brushing a thumb lightly over her nipple, transfixed by the motion. Sorrow took his other hand and held it, her eyes closing as he stroked her.

When she felt his mouth on her they flew back open, and she looked down to see his tongue flickering lightly over her, lighting a fire low in her belly.

His eyes met hers, questioning, and she nodded, letting him know it was all right. He kissed a path up between her breasts, following the line to her throat, licking across her collarbones, copying the way she'd kissed his neck and chest, before claiming her mouth again.

As they kissed Sorrow unbuttoned his shirt, helping him take it off, before he pulled her against him. She could feel he wanted her and she moved her hips gently against him, making him moan.

Sorrow was light-headed with lust, and power, pulling him towards the bed, pausing only to push her trousers down over her hips, her underwear with it. Luvian paused and looked at her, his mouth open a little, reaching out to stroke her hip, dragging his fingers over her skin. Then he followed suit, fumbling with his fly before pushing his trousers down, stepping out of the puddle they left on the floor as they tumbled on to his quilt.

They lay against each other, body to body, both breathing hard. His pupils were dilated and in the dim light his eyes looked black, as though they could swallow her whole.

She wanted them to.

"We don't have to do anything else," she said again.

"As I said, unlikely," Luvian said, smiling faintly, his fingers keying down her spine.

Sorrow laughed softly. "Do you have a barrier?"

His face fell. "No. I don't. Graces, I don't."

Bitter disappointment coursed through her. "Oh. Oh, well. . . We can't then. Sorry." Her voice was soft, and sad, the need inside her demanding to be sated, even as she knew they couldn't.

"Don't be sorry. You're right." He pulled one of her hands to his mouth and kissed it. "It's fine. Just this is fine. More than fine."

She smiled at him sadly. "We can still kiss," she said, though it sounded more like a question.

He nodded, and then a wicked expression crossed his face.

"What?" she asked, not sure she wanted to know.

"We can kiss. I can kiss you. Anywhere."

Sorrow's brows shot up.

He raised a brow of his own. "I told you I've read books."

Before she could say anything, he'd rolled her on to her back, propped up on his elbows as he smiled wolfishly at her.

"Let's see if I can put it into practice. Be sure to give me lots of feedback. Loud feedback." He grinned. "How else will I learn?"

Then he lowered his head, making his way back down her body, licking her breasts, kissing her stomach, lower . . . lower . . . his hands gently pushing her knees apart.

Her hands fisted in the sheets and she closed her eyes.

PART THREE

I walked a mile with Sorrow,
And ne'er a word said she;
But, oh! The things I learned from her,
When Sorrow walked with me.

—Robert Browning Hamilton,
"I Walked a Mile with Pleasure"

20

All the World's a Stage

Considering she was blindfolded and tied up in a forest, Sorrow felt remarkably cheerful.

When she and Luvian had gone to find the others earlier that morning, ignoring a salaciously grinning Arkady, Irris told them the ransom had been paid and Rasmus had already left for Rhylla, carrying with him the letter that would condemn Vespus. It was time for Sorrow to go home.

A few hours later, she was waiting in the woodland she and Luvian had walked through just a few nights before, dressed in the same clothes she'd been taken in. Though her knees ached from kneeling, twigs and stones digging into her shins beneath the thin fabric of her trousers, Sorrow was happy for the first time since before the election. The past few days with her friends had done more to heal her than she'd known she needed, giving her back the fire Vespus had doused with his schemes. She was ready to take him on now. Itching to.

"Are you all right?" Luvian asked for the thousandth time, stroking her arm lightly.

"I'm fine," Sorrow said again.

He and Arkady had brought her there, watching over her until her rescuers arrived. Sorrow wanted to kiss Luvian, but she was too aware that Arkady was nearby, surveying the road for any approaching traffic. Instead she leant into him, joy sparking when he wrapped his arms around her and pressed a kiss to her forehead.

The night before they'd barely slept, too busy exploring each other. It was strange for her to take her time with someone, to be able to linger over skin and touch and taste, to experiment and be experimented upon. With Rasmus there had always been so much urgency, born of her near-addiction to his touch, and their fear of being caught. But with Luvian it had been slower: luxurious, even. His curiosity was endless; he wanted to know everything, master everything.

His arrogance, she had to admit, was on this occasion wholly justified.

Once, as the sweat cooled on their skin, she'd lain in his arms, toying gently with the bar through his nipple. "A dare?" she'd asked. "What kind of dare?"

"During the first few weeks," he said, "it was my first time away from my family, I was Luvian Fen, not Rathbone; I got drunk on it. Me and some of my dorm-mates were talking one night about things we couldn't do, because of the law, but wished we could. Obviously, growing up where I did, obeying the law was always more of an optional thing, so I couldn't think of anything I couldn't already do if I really wanted to."

240

Sorrow remembered something. "Wait. You once told me the reason you couldn't be an artist was because the option wasn't there. But surely if you could do anything you wanted. . ." She paused, waiting for an explanation.

"It wasn't the law stopping me," Luvian said gently. "It wasn't an option because my mother said it wasn't. I told you about the fallout when I changed from law to politics; I'd be sleeping with the fishes if I'd switched to art. Anyway," he continued smoothly, before she could say anything else, "when one guy said he'd get like to be pierced, like the Rhyllians, I copied him. Of course, it had to be somewhere no one could see. So. . ."

"Understood."

"In some ways I was lucky. Guess where the other guy got his?"

Sorrow laughed and placed a kiss on his chest.

They were quiet for a moment. "I still can't believe this is real," Luvian added, a few moments later.

"Why?"

"Because . . . Rasmus."

"We were over. Before I even met you," Sorrow said.

"I know. But if he's your type . . ."

"My type?"

"You know . . . tall, cultured. Handsome. Really, excessively handsome."

"Do *you* want to be with Rasmus?" Sorrow asked.

Luvian bit her shoulder and she laughed again, pushing him away.

She wasn't used to this side of him, hadn't considered he could be vulnerable, or unsure of anything. It made her feel powerful in a new, unexpected way. Sorrow propped herself up on one elbow. "I like you very much," she said. "Let me show you."

241

Arkady gave a low, trilling whistle, pulling Sorrow from the memory.

"A coach is coming." His voice was close by. "We need to go."

Luvian said nothing, and then she felt his mouth on hers, kissing her as though it might be the last time. Sorrow prayed to the entire pantheon of Graces that it wasn't.

"I'll see you very soon." He pressed his lips against her ear. "I promise."

Then he was gone.

"There she is!" she heard Dougray call a moment later, then the sound of footsteps, booted and heavy, running towards her.

Sorrow took a deep breath, bracing herself. This was it.

She was lifted and set on her feet, the bindings at her wrists cut free, the blindfold ripped from her face. Her faked relief was only half-pretence as she blinked into the light, trying to make out the faces of her saviours. She saw Arran first, his face severe with concern. As she adjusted to the light, she saw Dougray, his own expression somewhere between terrified and grateful. They stood back as she rubbed her wrists.

"Sorrow," Arran said, stepping towards her. "Are you hurt?" He turned around, as though expecting to see them darting away through the trees.

Sorrow had to bite back a smile at Arran's acting. He'd make a wonderful addition to the troupe she saw in the West Marches.

"I'm fine, Senator Day. Completely unharmed, I promise."

"Thank the Graces," Arran said, clasping her shoulders.

"Let's get you back to the palace."

She climbed into the carriage first, Dougray and Arran joining her, both sitting opposite, gazing at her with concerned eyes.

Dougray spoke as soon as they were on the move.

"Your Excellency, I apologize for what happened to you. I will accept any punishment you feel is fit."

Sorrow was taken aback. "I don't want to punish you."

"With all due respect, Your Excellency, you should. I have failed you in the worst possible way. Had anything happened to you, the fault would lie solely with me. I accept that, and the consequences of it."

Her heart went out to the man before her. She felt the misery rolling off him at the idea he'd failed in his duty, and wondered whether she should punish him a little, if only to appease his pride. But how? He really didn't deserve it.

"Dougray, I saw you fighting them off. We were brutally outnumbered. It wasn't your fault. I mean that. I won't let you hold yourself responsible for this."

"The Sons of Rhannon. . ."

"I don't want to hear any more of this," Sorrow said firmly. "I'm glad you're my guard and that's how you're going to stay. I trust you."

For someone who'd just been pardoned, he didn't look happy, and Sorrow realized it wasn't only guilt bothering him, but pride. His faith in himself had been shaken by what had happened, and it wouldn't recover easily.

They all lapsed into silence, and Sorrow leant back against the seat, closing her eyes. Now they were on the move, her nerves tightened as the countdown to seeing Vespus began. All her energies would have to go into convincing him that nothing had changed – that he still held all the cards. She'd need to keep it as simple as she could, tell him nothing that would make him suspicious...

"Sorrow? We're back."

Sorrow was startled awake by Arran. She hadn't even known she'd fallen asleep.

"Sorry. I was ... exhausted," she said truthfully.

The coach turned and Sorrow saw the palace, the white stone cast gold in the late autumn sun. And there was Charon, waiting by the door, his eyes marking the coach's progress with hawk-like intensity.

It wasn't just Vespus that Sorrow would have to put on a show for. Charon too would need reassuring.

Sorrow watched him through the window, his hands gripping the wheels on his chair tightly, his mouth a grim line, and all her apprehension towards him evaporated. Quite suddenly, she missed him desperately, his counsel and his comfort, and she wanted nothing more than to talk to him, to trust him again.

As soon as the coach stopped, Sorrow opened the door and tumbled out, straight into Charon's arms. He held her tightly, in that moment his actions purely paternal, not a hint of her stalwart vice chancellor to be found. And Sorrow returned it, trying to pour as many apologies and promises to do better – be better – into the embrace as she could.

When she pulled away and looked at him it seemed to her he'd aged ten years overnight, his face drawn, new lines around his mouth.

"Thank the Graces," he said, his voice trembling in a way she'd never heard it before, and for a moment she genuinely worried he might cry.

"I'm all right," Sorrow told him, remorse making her feel ill. "I'm fine, absolutely fine."

He looked her over as though checking for himself.

"I thought they were going to kill you," he said. "I thought we wouldn't see you again."

Sorrow kept hold of Charon's hand as Arran took the handlebars, pushing him in, Dougray staying close, even within the palace walls.

Arran guided them towards Charon's private quarters, the corridors mercifully free of anyone else. Sorrow hadn't been there since she was a child, but the rooms hadn't changed. His space was elegant and refined, the furniture all dark wood, gleaming clean. The floor was bare of carpet to help him move easily, and there were wide spaces between the tables and small sofas, the bookcases low, only three shelves high so he could shelve and organize his own books. Though Sorrow had never spent much time there, it was a place she felt instantly comfortable, because it was so very him.

"Arran, inform the Jedenvat that the chancellor is back, and in good health and spirits," Charon said, taking control of his chair and manoeuvring it opposite a small sofa.

"They're here?" Sorrow asked. "You recalled them?"

"I had to. In case... In case of the worst. Though they believe you were in quarantine at the Summer Palace. Tuva isn't here. She's broken her leg."

"Oh, poor thing. Is she all right? How?"

"A riding accident, I believe. She'll be glad to know you're back."

"Good to have you back," Arran said, smiling at Sorrow.

Sorrow looked at the clock on Charon's mantelpiece. "And tell them I want a meeting, two hours from now," she added.

"So they can see for themselves that I'm well. And also because I have something I want to propose."

Arran nodded, leaving Charon and Sorrow alone.

"Are you truly all right?" Charon asked. He looked her over, as though he could see what they might have done to her written over her skin. "They didn't harm you?"

She knelt down before him. "Truly. They treated me well, all things considered." Stars, this was hard. Sorrow could barely look at Charon as she spoke, staying as close to the truth as she dared. "I was fed, given access to a bathroom. I had a bed. I wasn't even tied up."

"I can't imagine what you've been through and I'm sorry I couldn't stop them."

Sorrow shook her head, not trusting her tongue. "I don't blame you. I don't blame anyone. It's over now. Let's not dwell on it."

"Of course. Of course you want to put it behind you. I've cleared your schedule, to give you some time to rest—"

"No," Sorrow interrupted. "Rest is the last thing I want. I need to get back on track, for everyone's sake. Being . . . there made me realize a lot of things. Mistakes I need to correct. For starters, I'm going to write to Irris and ask her to come home. Mael too. And I want to push forward with dismantling the Decorum Ward."

Charon stared at her. "Now?"

"Soon. Being taken has made me believe now more than ever that we need a reliable, trustworthy police force. Not a band of thugs who only rouse themselves at the promise of violence. I'm going to have a quick bath, write to the ambassadors and let them know I'm fine, and then see the Jedenvat. In fact, I'll raise it with them today, let them know my thoughts and hear what theirs are."

For a moment she thought he'd argue, but then he shrugged. "You won't be dissuaded, will you?"

She gave the gentlest smile she could. "No. But, I'm not going to rush into anything. I'm simply saying I'll talk to the Jedenvat about it. That's all for now. So, I'll see you in the Round Chamber in, say, an hour?"

"Sorrow." He hesitated, and she paused. "When you feel up to it, I'd like to talk to you. Since Rhylla, things have been strained. I know you've been avoiding me – and I hoped if I gave you time you'd forgive me for my part in … well, your past. But then you were taken, and I feared I'd not have chance to clear the air with you…"

"I *have* forgiven you," Sorrow said hurriedly, reaching once more for his hands. "And I hope you've forgiven me. You're right; I was avoiding you and I'm sorry for it. This time away has taught me what's important and what isn't. Me being angry with you for something you can't change – that isn't important. Rhannon is. We can't alter the past, but we can reshape the future. I want you by my side as I do that."

For the second time that day, Sorrow feared she'd make her vice chancellor cry, but Charon gave a swift nod, and swallowed. When he met her eyes, they were clear.

"Good. So, onwards."

Sorrow nodded. "Onwards. But seriously, after I've had a bath."

He gave a short laugh. "I'll be ready."

She left him in his sitting room, almost colliding with Dougray, standing directly outside the door. He followed her so closely to her room that she could feel the fabric of his tunic rubbing against hers, creating static that sent tiny shocks along her arms.

It soon became obvious that Charon and Dougray were the only ones willing to be close to her. A pair of servants polishing the banister on the main staircase blanched when they saw her, stepping back as far as they could, holding their breath as she passed. It puzzled Sorrow, who thought they'd be glad to see her back safely.

It wasn't until she reached her rooms and the maids looked terrified as she entered, one trembling and the other almost in tears as they stood, that she understood.

"I'm fine," Sorrow told them, as reassuringly as she could. "I don't have the plague. I never did. It was just a precaution."

But the fact she'd been near the disease was enough to frighten them almost beyond their wits.

"You can go." Realizing they'd be no good to her until they understood they weren't in danger, Sorrow dismissed them. Dougray, however, made no move to leave.

"I'm going to have a bath," she said.

The bodyguard nodded, but remained where he was

"I would like to bathe without my clothes on," Sorrow added. "And without an audience."

Dougray's skin turned cherry red beneath his tan cheeks. "I'll just check the bathroom."

He returned a moment later, satisfied that the Sons of Rhannon hadn't hidden in there, waiting to take his mistress again. "I'll be right outside," he said.

Sorrow locked the door after he'd left, and padded to her bathroom, placing the plug in the tub and running the water. She changed as it filled, shedding the clothes she'd been kidnapped in, and putting on a fresh tunic and trousers. When the bath was full, she turned the taps off and made a great production of splashing her hands in the water, hoping to give

Dougray the impression she had just sunk into the bath.

Then she tiptoed gently across the floor, into her wardrobe, reaching for the hole and opening the passageway. It was time to see Vespus.

21

Siphon and Reservoir

He answered the door the moment her knuckles tapped it, as though he'd been waiting for her. He gestured with his head for her to come in, and she did, once again entering the strange green world he'd created in her palace.

Taasas was on a swing made of vines, suspended from a canopy that had grown over the entire ceiling; Vespus had been busy since Sorrow had last been there. Stems undulated around the Rhyllian woman as she swung back and forth, as though they were vying for her attention. She was wearing yellow, and it made her china-doll skin look somehow paler. The Rhyllian woman smiled dreamily at Sorrow but made no move to stop, trailing pale toes through the mossy rug beneath her. Vespus walked to his table, clear of plants and cuttings today, and sat, gesturing for Sorrow to do the same.

"Where were you?" he said, his voice poisonous. "Really?"

Behind her Sorrow became aware Taasas had stopped swinging.

"I was at the Summer Palace, Vespus," she said. "Really."

His expression told her he didn't believe her.

"I'm telling the truth. The doctors in Inarz gave me gloves to wear made from this flimsy fish skin and my nails pierced it. When they spotted it, they panicked and told me I could be infected. I had to put myself into quarantine to satisfy them I wasn't about to infect half of the country."

Vespus raised an eyebrow.

"I could hardly tell them I knew I was fine, could I?" Sorrow sighed, sitting back. "I had to pretend it was possible I was at risk, and go through with the stupid isolation. I came here as soon as I could; my guard thinks I'm in my room, bathing."

"Hmmm," Vespus said.

"Believe me, Vespus, the last thing I want is to force you into doing anything rash," Sorrow said.

He gave her a sharp look, and then nodded, his shoulders relaxing. In turn, Sorrow's bones turned liquid with sheer relief.

"I don't suppose my son has written to you?" Vespus asked, staring at her.

Sorrow shook her head, feigning puzzlement. "Not unless he did while I was away. Why?"

"He's missing."

Sorrow kept her expression passive. "I'll see if he's sent anything when I go to my office."

Vespus shrugged. "Don't trouble yourself. I'm sure he'll turn up. I've asked some friends in Rhylla to keep an eye out for him."

She didn't like the sound of that. "Well, I just came here to

251

let you know I was back, and that I hadn't betrayed you."

"I assume we're going to continue with our plan. That I can begin work on my fence soon."

"Of course," she said, flattening her voice. "What choice do I have?"

"I do so hate when you make it sound as though I'm your enemy." He pulled a vial from the pocket of his vest and held it up to the light. It was full of a pale, oily-looking green liquid. "The antidote to Hellfior. I finished it last night. A single drop in a glass of water should be enough to wake each of them and guarantee a full recovery." He closed his fingers around it, and Sorrow stared at his hand, cradling the antidote.

"How do you know it works?"

His eyes narrowed as he smirked. "It works. I want the land, Sorrow. Once it's mine, the antidote is yours."

Sorrow reminded herself that his own son was heading to Melisia's castle in Rhylla, ready to reveal what Vespus was doing. She just had to hold her nerve a little longer.

But it was with gritted teeth she said, "I've already called a meeting this afternoon with the Jedenvat. I'll tell them about the fence."

Vespus smiled. "You see? It's so much better when we work together. We should celebrate."

Sorrow almost admired his nerve. "I really need to go."

"Nonsense. You can spare five more minutes for me, I think," he said, rising and walking to a small cabinet, where he withdrew a bottle of wine and two ornate glasses.

He filled them both, before raising his in a toast. She didn't return it, knocking the contents back in one mouthful.

It tasted like earth in her dry mouth.

"To us. And so we're done," Sorrow said. "You have your

land. You can grow your trees and leave the rest of Rhannon alone."

Vespus said nothing, swirling the wine around in the bowl of the glass, watching as it flowed perilously close to the rim.

"We're done," Sorrow repeated.

Movement behind her made Sorrow turn in time to see Taasas jump lightly from the swing, walking to Vespus and stealing his wine as she perched on his knee. The two of them looked beautiful together. Sorrow turned away, feigning interest in the swing, which was now unknitting itself, the vines retreating into the canopy.

When she turned back, Taasas had moved directly in front of her, and before Sorrow could stop her, she raised a hand and pressed it to Sorrow's cheek.

The world shattered and then remade itself, coming together like a kaleidoscope, the picture fragmented until finally Sorrow could see it.

She stood in the Winter Palace, dressed in white. Her gown was long, layered sheer panels that brushed the marble floor. She heard voices to her left and turned to see Irris, wearing a pink gown that exposed her freckled shoulders. She was holding a large posy of flowers: iris and roses and birds-of-paradise. Irris smiled at her and held out the bouquet and Sorrow took it, puzzled. Then Irris looked beyond her, gasped, and Sorrow turned.

Rasmus was walking towards them, dressed in an unusually formal green suit, a frothy cravat at his throat, a rose like those in her bouquet in his lapel, his hair half-up, exposing his ears and the rows of silver hoops and studs there. He smiled at Sorrow as he approached: a tender, hopeful smile.

Then he bent, and kissed her.

Sorrow jerked her face away from Taasas's hand.

"Don't you ever. . ." she growled.

"I thought you'd like it," Taasas said. "It was supposed to be an apology, for before. Now we're all friends."

There was something in the way she spoke that made Sorrow think she was damaged, broken in some kind of irreparable way. She didn't seem connected with the world around her, more ghost than woman. Sorrow wondered where Vespus had found her, or perhaps, where he'd kept her before, and for how long.

"I can try another one. Something from you. . ."

She brushed her finger against Sorrow's, and Sorrow caught a flash of grey, a glint of sunlight on the rim of glasses, and a wicked laugh, before she snatched her hand away.

"Call her off," Sorrow snapped at Vespus.

"Taasas, my love," Vespus said, luring the Rhyllian back to his side. She arched a brow, but listened, leaving Sorrow alone. "Let's finish the wine, shall we? I'm sure Sorrow has much to do."

Triumph gilded his every gesture, the slight flourish as he raised his glass to his mouth, the glint in his eyes when they met hers. Finally, after years – decades of plans and dreams – he thought he'd achieved his goal. That he had his land. He thought she was beaten.

Sorrow couldn't wait to wipe the smile from his face.

She made her way back to her room, turning alternately hot and cold with rage and the desire for revenge. She slipped into the cooling bath for long enough to wash quickly, then re-dressed in the outfit she'd worn to see Vespus. It was only as she braided her hair she remembered she hadn't held her breath in the bath. She was getting better, she realized.

254

Whatever trauma it had done to her, she was coping with it. Conquering it.

When she arrived in the Round Chamber, her councillors were thrilled to see her. Most of them...

"Sorrow. Thank the Graces you're all right," Bayrum Mizil said, moving from his seat in three steps, pulling Sorrow into a bear hug.

Balthasar tutted.

Sorrow turned to him. She had tolerated him too long.

"Is there a problem, Senator Lys?" she asked, her tone making it clear she hoped his answer was yes.

"Not at all. Am I obliged to embrace you, too?" he said.

"I'd really rather you didn't."

He frowned. She turned from him to Kaspira, who clasped her forearm and ask how she was. Even Eldon Samad, whose veins Sorrow had once thought were more sand than blood, shook Sorrow's hand vigorously, clearly glad she was home.

"Are you sure you should be doing this?" Bayrum asked her as they took their seats, his beside the empty place Tuva would have sat. "Don't you need to rest?"

"I'm fine, always was. But the same can't be said for the people of the North Marches, I saw that with my own eyes. We have some difficult decisions to make."

Sorrow used the great map on the Round Chamber wall to show them how clearly the infectious zone was marked.

"I spoke to the doctors there. Not a single case outside of this area," she said. "They think it means whatever is causing this illness exists inside there. Either the water, or something in the earth, or an animal..." She was painfully aware of Charon's eyes on her. "They believe that the source of the infection is local."

255

"So how do we stop it?" Kaspira said.

"We can't, without knowing what it is. We have to contain it," Sorrow said.

"How? A cordon?" Charon asked.

"Yes," Sorrow said, ignoring the look of shock on his face. "It's the best solution, for now. The only one."

A ripple of unease gently shook the room, and Sorrow braced her hands on the table, absorbing it.

"What choice do we have? If you have a better suggestion, I'm all ears. But otherwise, we need to evacuate the entire area, and seal it off."

"What if they bring it with them?" Samad asked as Kaspira and Bayrum nodded, and even Charon looked hesitant.

Stars, this was hard. Sorrow could scream with frustration. She *knew* they couldn't bring it because there was no plague. And there would be no evacuation, or fence; this was merely a pantomime she had to go through so Vespus would remain oblivious to her real plans. For him to believe everything was fine, the Jedenvat had to believe it wasn't. She had to convince them all.

"And their businesses? And lives?" Arran asked.

"The living can start again. The dead can't," Sorrow said, closing the matter. No one liked the idea, that much was clear. But there was no other solution. She watched as one by one they reached the conclusion she needed them to.

Knowing it would pass, Sorrow put it to the Jedenvat for a decision. Charon and Arran voted against, but the others voted for, even Bayrum, whose district was the one that would be decimated by it. He looked Sorrow in the eye as he raised his hand, and she felt her heart crack under the weight of his faith and trust. Once Vespus was gone, she'd dedicate her life to making sure his belief in her was justified. Sorrow would dedicate her life to making Rhannon the country she'd promised it could be. And be the chancellor she'd promised to be. At least on that, there was something she could do now.

"There's something else to discuss, something more positive, I think," Sorrow said, looking to Charon to gauge his response. When he nodded, she continued. "I want to disband the Decorum Ward." There was a collective indrawn breath, but she ignored it, and carried on smoothly. "Once things are under control with the plague I'm going to ask Captain Vine to consult with us to bring back the Lawkeepers from before Harun's – my father's – time."

Balthasar barked out a laugh, and everyone turned to him.

"I hope you don't expect him to agree to it," he said, mirth creasing his eyes.

"The Ward represent a past that I don't want to take forward into Rhannon's future," Sorrow said, meeting Balthasar's gaze. "I'm confident Captain Vine will understand that."

Balthasar smirked.

"I think it's an excellent idea," Arran said.

"As do I," Bayrum agreed.

Sorrow looked around the room. "Does anyone have any real objections or concerns?"

Kaspira seemed surprised, but shook her head when Sorrow met her eye. Lord Samad shrugged. Balthasar merely smiled, and Sorrow took it for a no.

"Good. I'll update you on the fence once I have more details."

Sorrow could have sworn Balthasar muttered something sarcastic, but when she looked at him he'd schooled his face to blank alertness, and she let it slide. She'd deal with him once

Vespus and Vine were gone.

Soon.

"I wonder about Vespus," Charon said in a low voice, at a subdued and sparsely staffed welcome home dinner later that night. Sorrow was already in a bad mood after one of the servants had practically flung her plate at her, covering her lap in rosehip sauce, in a bid to keep a healthy distance.

"What do you wonder?"

"If he'd still want the land, even now."

She'd turned to him, unable to mask her shock, but he began eating as though he'd said nothing at all, and Sorrow returned to her own meal, unable to taste a thing. It felt ominous that he'd mentioned it, and she wondered for a moment if he knew, or suspected the truth behind Hellfior. He couldn't though. And even if he did, Charon would never skirt around it – he'd ask her outright.

Sorrow wondered what she'd say if he did.

Six of Seven

The next morning found Sorrow in her office, drinking thick black coffee that made her heart judder pleasantly as she read her mail. There was no word from Rasmus, though Sorrow didn't know if he'd be allowed to write to her. It was possible she'd only know he'd delivered the letter when Vespus came to tell her that he was leaving. She offered a silent prayer to the Graces, and the stars, for Melisia's mercy for Rasmus. *Please let his aunt be just, and fair*, she begged.

Irris had written, to say she and Mael would make their way back to Istevar in the next couple of days. She also asked if she might bring another friend *"who urgently begs your pardon"*.

Luvian.

She still hadn't pardoned him.

What could she say, to clear his name without Melisia and the Rhyllians wanting to know how she knew he was innocent?

Then she realized she was being stupid – Melisia would be so preoccupied with Vespus she wouldn't be paying attention to Rhannish affairs, and if she did question it, Sorrow could tell her the attack had also been Vespus. As for the Rhannish, she could release a statement saying an investigation had proven Luvian wasn't one of the Sons of Rhannon – it wasn't even a lie.

Pushing the letters aside, she pulled out a clean sheet of paper and began to compose a pardon, only to pause as she heard a commotion outside in the corridor. Three loud, male voices, all apparently competing with each other for dominance. Dougray's voice she recognized, demanding someone stay where they were.

Could it be Vespus already?

Terror and joy mounting, Sorrow had barely risen when the door was thrown open, and Dougray managed to say, "Your Excellency, Captain Vine is here," before Vine appeared.

"Captain Vine, this really is most irregular," Charon said, somewhere in the corridor.

Sorrow didn't take her eyes off Vine.

He filled the door frame, his eyes locking on her, narrowing as they did. In his hand he clutched a piece of paper.

"Captain Vine, can I help you?" she asked calmly.

"Tell me you're fucking joking," Vine said, and Charon barked, "Captain Vine, control yourself."

Sorrow motioned for Dougray to let Vine in and placed her hands on her desk, using it to steady herself. Her heart was thundering behind her ribs, as both caffeine and adrenaline urged it faster.

Vine stalked towards the desk, standing before it, Dougray following close behind. He stood at the end, to block Vine from getting around to Sorrow. She doubted that would stop him. If he really wanted to get to her, he'd either vault over the desk or move it.

Charon wheeled himself into the room, swinging the door shut behind him with enough force that it slammed. Sorrow blinked in shock but said nothing, watching as he drew up beside Vine, breaking sharply, his face livid with rage. No matter that he was in a wheeled chair, he looked ready – and capable – of tearing Vine apart.

"Captain Vine, I command you to explain yourself. Now," the vice chancellor ordered.

"*She* needs to explain herself," Vine said, slapping the paper he'd been holding on to the desk, upsetting an inkwell. It was a letter, addressed to Vine.

"*She* is your chancellor," Sorrow said, iron in her voice. "You'd do well to remember it. And what exactly is it you hope I'm, what was it? – *fucking joking* about?"

Vine glared at her, but Sorrow turned her own attention to the letter. She moved her papers aside, otherwise ignoring the stain spreading over the surface, and picked it up.

She schooled her face into calmness as she scanned the note, her brows rising incredulously at the final sentence. "It's a note from a 'friend' to warn Captain Vine that I plan to fire all of the Decorum Ward," Sorrow explained. "And who is this 'friend'?" she said.

"Is it true?" Vine replied, his breathing shallow.

"No," Sorrow said. "I'm not firing anyone. But I am disbanding the Ward. They're redundant in the new Rhannon. We have no need to enforce a particular country-wide mood. We're not in mourning any more."

"We do more than that, and you know it. How exactly do you plan to keep the peace without us?" Vine was trembling now, not with fear, but with rage. The colour had drained from his olive complexion, leaving it grey.

Sorrow's pleasure in his obvious upset was visceral, a fire lit in her belly. Stars, it felt good to finally use her power, and not just to enact Vespus's plans. To finally be more than a puppet ruler. And she was ready for it. Ready to step out of Harun's shadow, ready to release herself from Vespus's manipulations. The only other dark spot in Rhannon was Vine. Now his time was up, and he knew it. What's more, he knew he couldn't stop her. She was the chancellor. She had her friends back, and Luvian. She had Charon and the Jedenvat. She had it all. And Vine had nothing. In that moment Sorrow realized she pitied him. The feeling was heady – so much that she had to bite back a grin of pure pleasure as she continued.

"Your 'friend' here has done you a disservice, Captain. He ought to have told you that the Jedenvat and I were going to consult with you on it."

"What makes you so sure it's a 'he'?" Vine asked.

"Figure of speech," Sorrow said. "Though, what makes you think it might not be? Do you know who sent it?"

"Of course not. I never said who I thought it was. I don't have any idea who it was."

But she noticed he wouldn't meet her eye, raising a hand to scratch his chin.

Satisfied, Sorrow continued. "It was never meant to undermine you, I agree that we need a peacekeeping force; my proposal is Lawkeepers, like those before the Ward. Agents of the country charged to uphold justice. Any of the current Ward who want to apply to become Rhannish Lawkeepers can. Everyone will need to be retrained and assessed for duty, and there will be a pay rise for those who successfully pass."

"And where will the money come from, for that? You keep telling me there's none."

"There's no money for the Decorum Ward," Sorrow said with finality. She didn't bother to answer any further than that. She was the chancellor; she didn't need to.

There was a silence, while she watched Vine mulling it over, his brow heavy.

"What does it mean?" he ground out. "For us. What powers will we have?"

He meant for himself. He might not have said it, but Sorrow heard it and it dawned on her he might actually quit. It was a wonderful thought. "The Ward will continue as an interim force, but their remit will be modified. They'll still have the power to place people under arrest, but not to sentence them or mete out any punishment. That will be for judges to decide, after peer adjudication."

"Can you skip the fancy words and tell me straight?"

"Of course. Simply put, the Lawkeepers' job will be to arrest citizens who are accused of breaking the law, and to maintain a general peace."

"Peace is another way of saying decorum, is it not?"

"It is." Sorrow smiled. "But the problem is the other ... connotations around the word 'decorum', these days. The Lawkeepers will be a fresh start. No more whipping. No more beatings. Any Lawkeeper who takes justice into her or his own hands will be treated as a criminal."

Vine stared at her, licking his fleshy lips, his brow furrowed. Sorrow had to fight not to turn to Charon, instead holding her nerve and waiting for Vine's response.

"So, you're stripping us of our powers?" he said finally, in a disappointingly calm voice.

"Not at all. As I said, you'll still have the power to detain people who break the law. But not using violence," Sorrow said.

"And if we're attacked?"

"Then you use only reasonable force to disable the threat. You set an example by behaving calmly and keeping everyone safe." She smiled. "Come, Captain Vine; this won't happen overnight. We'll do it district by district, beginning in the West Marches."

"Why there?"

"It currently has the smallest Ward, doesn't it? It seems the ideal place to trial it."

A dangerous silence bloomed between them as Vine mulled over what she'd said, and Sorrow waited to see if he'd give her the satisfaction she craved.

"Years of service to your father," he said at last. "Years. And after everything we've done during this plague. Putting ourselves right there, in the thick of it. After everything we did when the Sons of Rhannon attacked *you*. This is how you repay us."

Sorrow spoke before she could stop herself. "When the Sons of Rhannon attacked me and Mael in Prekara you stood and watched. You stepped in at the last minute."

"That's a Grace-damned lie," Meeren roared, his hand moving to the baton on his belt.

Sorrow tracked the movement with her gaze, then looked him dead in the eye, motioning for Dougray – who'd reached for his sabre – to stay where he was. Vine curled his hand into a fist and held it at his side.

"You've never liked me." Vine's voice was a rumble, the warning growl of a large cat.

"Rhannon is changing," Sorrow said, her own voice just as low. "You will change with it."

264

Vine smiled, an ugly curve more like a grimace. "And if I quit? Or is that what you want?"

"I want my country to thrive, Captain Vine. That's all. I'm giving you what you want. More money, and less duty. The two things you complained about. I should appreciate your support on this."

Meeren Vine gave Sorrow a look of pure hatred. She could feel the urge for violence like an aura around him, his need to squash her like an insect.

Sorrow kept her shoulders back and her face neutral, until Vine stormed out, Dougray following him.

"I really hoped he'd quit," she said, taking a shaky breath.

Charon was shaking his head. "You shouldn't provoke him. He's dangerous. And we need to discover who his source was."

"Balthasar," Sorrow said instantly.

Charon gave her a long look. "You're not letting your dislike of Senator Lys colour your thoughts, are you?"

"Who else could it be? Only those of us in the Round Chamber knew what my plan was. Tuva isn't here, I'm certain it wasn't you or Arran. Or Bayrum, for that matter. Neither Kaspira or Samad have any reason to. Only Balthasar."

"What reason does he have?" Charon asked.

"Reasons, plural," Sorrow corrected him. "One – he hates me. He has since I imprisoned him the night Alyssa died. And he knows I feel the same about him – he can't rely on me to promote, or support, or even tolerate him for much longer. Two – Vespus has rejected him. I noticed it at the ball here; Balthasar tried to talk to him, but Vespus ignored him. He had no use for Balthasar after he'd helped get rid of Harun, and that leaves Balthasar without a powerful ally. I think Balthasar went to Vine as soon as I said I'd disband the Ward, to buy his allegiance."

"You'll need proof."

"I have it." Sorrow nodded down at the note Vine had left behind. "It's his handwriting. The last line even says to burn it after reading, but Vine being Vine, he raced straight here to have it out with me, and left it behind. Idiot."

Charon rolled forward and lifted it gingerly, as though it might disintegrate. After a few moments, he nodded. "What do you plan to do?"

"Arrest him for treason and imprison him for the rest of his life."

When Charon didn't object, or argue, Sorrow felt another burst of glee. She could do this. She really could govern. No matter who she really was, she – Sorrow Ventaxis – could do this, and well.

"I'd like to make Mael the senator for the South Marches," Sorrow continued. "I think it would be good for him to have a role, good for Rhannon to see us working together."

"I thought you'd want Irris?"

"That would mean three Days on my council – it might cause some upset. Besides, I don't think she'd want it."

Charon inclined his head. "I believe you're right."

"Come," Sorrow said, walking around her desk. "Let's have some tea and draw up the plans I just told Vine I had ready. I doubt he's going to be able to keep his mouth shut for long, and it would be nice to have something solid to put in the bulletins."

The next morning brought Arran Day, flying into her room at first light, with Dougray hot on his heels. This time Sorrow wasn't prepared for it.

"What is it?" Sorrow scrambled to cover herself.

"Tuva Marchant's manse in the West Marches has been

attacked. Set alight."

"Is she alive?" They were silent, and she repeated again, her voice rising, "Tell me!"

"We don't know."

Vine.

Sorrow knew instantly that it was Vine.

She didn't bother dressing, throwing a robe over her nightgown and racing to the Round Chamber, where Balthasar, Samad, Kaspira, Bayrum and Charon were waiting. Tuva's empty chair now took on new significance, and dread pumped through Sorrow's body as she remembered the senator's broken leg. She wouldn't have been able to run from a fire. . .

Swallowing her fears, Sorrow slid into her seat and folded her hands together to hide their shaking. "What happened?"

"We're not sure." Charon's own fingers trembled, and when he saw Sorrow notice, he folded his arms. "All we know so far is Tuva's manse is on fire."

Sorrow felt sick. "Is Tuva all right? Do we know anything?"

Charon shook his head. "No word yet. The firefighters are working to get the blaze under control. They have every resource." He looked at her. "We have to hope that she got out."

Sorrow knew they all thought the same thing: that it was unlikely. That their friend hadn't made it.

"This was Vine," she said, her voice hard. "I want him arrested." She glanced at them all, leaving Balthasar until last. It was at him she looked as she said, "He came here yesterday, with an anonymous note, from 'a friend'. This 'friend' told him I wanted to disband the Decorum Ward and change them into Lawkeepers. He didn't take it well."

"Surely he wouldn't have attacked Tuva's place, though,"

Kaspira said. "What has she got to do with it?"

Sorrow turned to her. "I told him I planned to begin in the West Marches. Because it had the smallest force."

"And you think this is his response?" Kaspira asked.

Sorrow nodded. "I don't think it's a coincidence."

"I can hardly believe someone charged with upholding the law would stoop to this," Kaspira said. "A more likely culprit is the Sons of Rhannon."

"It's not the Sons of Rhannon," Sorrow said immediately. "I know it's Vine. I'm positive even the flimsiest investigation will prove it."

"And who's going to do that?" Balthasar said. "If it's the Ward you think committed the crime in the first place?"

Sorrow turned to him, tilting her head and staring at him. "If I were you, Senator Lys, I would think very carefully about your words right now."

"And what does that mean?" He was clever enough to look a little nervous, pulling at the collar of his tunic.

"You wrote to Vine telling him what my plans were."

As Bayrum gasped in outrage and Kaspira drew herself upright, staring at her neighbour, Balthasar's face darkened.

"I hope you have proof of this accusation, Chancellor."

"Oh, I do. I have the letter you sent. Written in your handwriting and left in my office after Vine had been. Contrary to your instructions, he didn't burn after reading, he brought it with him. Now do you deny it?"

Balthasar paused, as though debating whether to argue. Then he leapt from his chair, making for the door.

"Dougray," Sorrow called.

The bodyguard appeared in the doorway, grabbing the senator for the South Marches firmly as he tried to escape.

He'd been waiting for Sorrow's command ever since she'd briefed him on her way to the Round Chamber.

"Senator Lys is under arrest for treason, on my command," Sorrow said calmly. "Please see him to the dungeons. No, wait—" She remembered Vespus's trees at the last moment. "Have him taken to Istevar town and imprisoned in the Ward headquarters. I want Vine to know what happens to traitors."

"You can't do this!" Balthasar twisted, his features distorted as he spat the words at her.

Sorrow turned her back on him, on the whole room, pretending to study the map of Rhannon as Dougray dragged him away.

She waited until his outraged shouts had stopped before she looked back, to find all of her Jedenvat, save Charon, watching her with cautious eyes.

"I don't think we should say anything about Vine, publicly, at least," she said at last. "We don't want to send the country into a panic, especially not with the plague, and the evacuation. The last thing we want people to think is that their police are turning on them. On us. We're dangerously close to losing control as it is. I'll have some of the palace guards – people I trust – find and arrest him. Agreed?"

The Jedenvat nodded.

"I'll dispatch them as soon as we're done here."

"What about Tuva?" Bayrum asked. "What about her. She – she might. . ."

He stopped, shaking his large head.

It would normally have been Tuva who reached out to comfort him. The two had been thick as thieves for as long as Sorrow had been alive, and way before then. Now it was Arran who awkwardly patted his arm, meeting Sorrow's eyes as he did.

"I think maybe we should all try to get some rest," Charon said. "Hopefully by morning we'll know more. Sorrow, do you have anything else you wish to say?"

"No. Go, rest. If I hear anything else I'll let you know," Sorrow said.

One by one they filed out of the room; to Sorrow's surprise Lord Samad was the one who took Bayrum's arm and left by his side.

Sorrow remained, and Charon with her, while she sent for the captain of the palace guard.

"I want Meeren Vine arrested, in connection with the attack at the Marchant manse," Sorrow told the woman who appeared before her. The captain was somewhere in her early thirties, and looked capable of breaking a man's arm with a mere flick of her wrist. "But it needs to be discreet. The Ward mustn't know, or even suspect, until he's in custody."

"No, Your Excellency," the captain said. "I understand. Do you have any idea of his whereabouts?"

"I don't." Sorrow looked at Charon for confirmation. He shook his head.

"No matter," the captain said brusquely. "We'll find him."

Sorrow dismissed her and then stood, beginning to pace the room.

"You're not going to get any rest, are you?" Charon asked.

She didn't think she could sleep, not until she knew whether Tuva had made it. And she knew Charon wouldn't either. "Neither are you."

They stayed together, in companionable silence, waiting.

Just after sunrise, a message arrived from the West Marches.

Sorrow knew, as she took the scroll from the silver tray the servant presented her, that it wasn't good news.

She unrolled the scroll, scanning the message. Charon was watching, hope and fear in his eyes.

"Tuva is dead," Sorrow said. "She never made it out of her room."

There was a buzzing in Sorrow's ears, as if a wasp was trapped between her skin and her skull. She had suspected all along that Tuva hadn't made it, accepted it would be impossible for her to have survived. She was prepared for the worst. But the numbness that spread like a crack in glass, fracturing through her, made her realize she'd expected a miracle.

Sorrow sank back into her seat, closing her eyes briefly. "She had family?" she asked.

Charon took a moment to answer and when he did, his voice was hollow. "She had a sister."

"I'll write to her."

"I'll tell Bayrum," Charon said.

"Are you sure?"

He nodded. "Yes. You have plenty to do here." He gripped his wheels and turned his chair, leaving her.

Sorrow rolled her head, her neck stiff from bending over pages. She hoped that the smoke had got to Tuva first. What a horrible, terrible way to die.

Her thoughts turned to Vine, mutating from loss to fury. Stars, she was tempted to reintroduce the death penalty for this.

Sorrow went to her office and wrote to Tuva's sister, before making her way to her rooms to wash and change. She was absorbed in her thoughts as she walked the corridors, her mind aflame with plans of revenge.

"Sorrow?" A cool Rhyllian voice called her name and she turned to see Vespus leaving the ambassador's wing. "I was just coming to see you." He looked her up and down. "What's wrong?"

"Tuva Marchant died tonight. A fire, at her home."

Vespus looked genuinely shocked. "My condolences."

"Thank you. What did you want?"

"To tell you Taasas and I are leaving. My sister has written asking me to return home urgently."

Once she would have felt joy. This was what she'd wanted. This meant it was over. But as it was, all she felt was a numb sort of triumph and relief as she nodded.

"I hope everything is all right."

"As do I. Probably more of my son's nonsense."

"You said he was missing. . ."

"It seems he's been found," Vespus replied, then looked around. Checking to make sure they were alone. "I'll be back within two days. My trees are almost ready. I expect the evacuation to have begun."

"Vespus, I just lost one of the Jedenvat—"

"Which is terribly sad. But not my problem."

The numbness vanished, leaving a red mist of anger behind. She wanted to hit him. Her palm itched to, the muscles in her arm contracting as they demanded satisfaction. As though he knew it, his eyebrows rose, and he tilted his head, waiting to see what she'd do.

It felt as though it lasted for ever, even though it could only have been a few seconds. Sorrow mastered her temper and nodded. "Of course," she said. "Now, if you'll excuse me, I have work to do. Have a safe journey home."

Thank the stars. Thank the Graces and thank the stars. Rasmus had done it. He had got the letter to Melisia and she'd summoned Vespus there. Sorrow would never have to deal with his treacherous face again.

One and Another

Irris wrote to say she was coming at once, her and Mael both. They'd leave later that morning, and be in Istevar in time for supper.

Sorrow didn't like the idea of them moving through the country unguarded with Vine out there, but she fought the temptation to send an escort to meet them. A carriage with a guard – even an unliveried one – would mark the people inside as valuable, and potentially make them a target. And Vine, like Vespus, knew Irris was important to Sorrow. If he knew she was travelling, and vulnerable. . .

Sorrow stopped the thought in its tracks. Worrying would get her nowhere. There was nothing more she could do; she simply had to wait for Irris to arrive, and trust it would be all right.

She was supposed to be preparing a speech about the

fire, to reassure the people it was being investigated, and they had nothing to fear. A nonsense speech, as she thought of it, saying lots and yet nothing at all – classic politics. But she couldn't concentrate on it; too busy listening for Irris and Mael, too caught in imagining the worst. Finally, after staring at a blank page for an hour, she called it quits. She'd speak without notes – she was good at improvising; it was the more acceptable sister of lying, after all.

She abandoned her office, leaving a note for Charon explaining where she'd gone. Then she headed to the state gallery. It overlooked the main drive; she'd see the moment Irris and Mael passed through the gates.

Sorrow hadn't been in the state gallery for years; the last time had been with Rasmus when they were children, on one of their explorations. It'd been closed up during her childhood, on Harun's instructions, and she had always been frightened of it.

Not of the room itself, which was a long corridor, but the pictures on the walls of former chancellors, a dozen stern men staring down at Sorrow as she walked the room. Neither Reuben nor Harun was there, and Sorrow didn't feel inclined to have pictures commissioned. The Ventaxis ancestors all looked down at her from inside their gold frames, judging her, their eyes following her no matter where she stood.

But today she felt brave, and she looked at them, one by one. She was startled to see one looked a little like Mael. The same faint smirk, the same slight tilt to his nose. She moved closer to see who it was, not as surprised as she ought to have been when she saw it was Rohir – husband of Shira, whose tomb Sorrow had "borrowed". It made her stomach feel funny to see Mael in his features, an almost-answer to the question that

274

had plagued her for weeks. It didn't matter any more, whether he was or wasn't really a Ventaxis. She doubted Vespus would ever tell her, especially after Melisia dealt with him.

When the door opened, she expected it to be Dougray. But it was Charon.

He must have had someone carry him up the stairs, which Sorrow knew he disliked doing. Years before her grandmother told her Harun had sworn to put an elevator in the palace for him, after hearing the Merideans had invented one that worked with a rope pulley, but it had never happened.

"What's that look?" he asked, his frown matching hers.

"I'm going to have an elevator installed," she said. "For you."

He gave her a small smile. "Let's focus on Vine first, shall we? And what's this I hear about Vespus leaving again?"

"Queen Melisia summoned him."

"So he's gone, just like that, not waiting for a replacement to arrive? Sorrow, he's taking advantage of you."

She couldn't help it – she laughed.

Charon was scandalized. "It's no laughing matter," he said. "He's taking advantage of your age and inexperience, as well as this crisis with the plague, to not do his duty. He's supposed to be here representing his country and ensuring smooth relations between Rhylla and us. You need to make it clear this isn't acceptable. Actually, no, I'm going to be honest. I agree with Irris; he shouldn't be the ambassador at all."

"You let him come back in the first place," Sorrow protested.

"Because he was Melisia's choice, and I was preoccupied with the election. But I think you should approach her again and say you want a fresh start. In fact, Sorrow, I insist on it. Your father took long enough to listen to me about Lord Corrigan; I hope that you won't make the same mistake. Vespus is only interested in Rhannon in so far as what he can get out of it. You can't trust him."

Sorrow hesitated. The urge to come clean to Charon about Vespus – about everything – rose up in her. She'd told Irris, back at the Point, that she wanted to. There was no time like the present.

"What is it?" he asked. "You haven't trusted him with anything, have you?"

"Well . . . not intentionally. But I can promise Vespus won't be back."

"What are you talking about?"

"I've been keeping secrets from you," she said. "And the worst is that Vespus knows who I am. He knows you know, and he knows about Ras, too. He's been using it to blackmail me since the night before the election."

Charon closed his eyes, and Sorrow was frightened he'd fainted.

She reached for him and they snapped back open.

"Tell me everything."

So she did.

The sun had travelled across the sky by the time she finished, the day fading to late afternoon, the shadows moving like a changing of the guard. Charon had said little as she spoke, was pale as she finished her tale with the revelation that Melisia had called Vespus back to Rhylla.

"And even if he does say anything to try and expose me, the bones are gone and he has no proof. Melisia won't allow him to come back," Sorrow finished.

Charon nodded slowly. "And you haven't heard from Rasmus? Or Melisia directly?"

"No, not yet." Sorrow didn't understand why he sounded worried. "Do you think I should have?"

He paused. "Not necessarily. Rasmus would only have reached her yesterday; it's possible he hasn't had chance to write to you. Or that Melisia has forbidden him to. I'm just not convinced Vespus will give up that easily, especially given how close he is. Was," he corrected himself.

"Melisia won't let him out of her sight," Sorrow said. "Not where Starwater is concerned."

"I suppose—" Charon stopped and turned towards the window. Abruptly he rolled away, and Sorrow followed.

A single horse was galloping at speed up the driveway. The sun in her eyes, at first Sorrow couldn't make out who it was.

As the horse drew to a halt, Sorrow caught the rider's face.

Mael. With someone in his arms, a bright smear of blood on her face.

Irris.

Sorrow screamed for Dougray to help Charon, as both she and he sped from the room to the stairs. Her bodyguard carried the vice chancellor; Sorrow herself took his chair, her terror lending her the strength to lift it easily.

When they reached the door, Mael was carrying a pale and prone Irris over the threshold. She was unconscious, her blue tunic stained with blood from a gash on the side of her head, her hair sticky and matted with it. But there was no sign of any other injuries, and she was breathing.

"Give her to me," Charon demanded, and Mael placed Irris on his lap as Charon cradled her gently. "Take us to my rooms," he asked Dougray.

"Do it," Sorrow told him. "And send someone for a doctor. Tell them to hurry."

Dougray nodded, and took the bars of Charon's chair and began to push. Mael made to follow until Sorrow held him back.

"What happened?" she asked.

"We were attacked just outside Istevar town. Irris was hit in the head. I think the driver is dead."

Sorrow swore. She should have sent guards. She should have sent someone.

Fighting anger at herself, she looked Mael over. "Are you hurt?" Sorrow asked.

Mael shook his head.

Two of the palace guards – Sorrow recognized the faces but didn't know their names – came running from the direction of Charon's rooms.

"We're going to get a doctor, Your Excellency," one of them said, and Sorrow nodded.

"Let's go," she said, taking Mael by the hand and leading him away.

When they arrived at the vice chancellor's quarters, Irris was lying on Charon's bed, and he was beside her, leaning awkwardly out of his chair to hold her hand, the wheels preventing him from getting as close as wanted. Irris was still unconscious, and Sorrow watched her chest rise and fall. She felt impotent, and for want of something practical to do, she sent for tea.

It arrived almost immediately, the smell of mint permeating the room, and Sorrow poured herself a cup. It was sickeningly sweet, but the sugar gave her strength, and she finished the cup, pouring another.

It was then Irris woke.

At the sound of Charon's gasp, Sorrow almost dropped the pot, splashing hot liquid on to the table, as she put it down and darted to her friend's bedside.

Irris's eyes were dazed as she looked between them.

"Irris? Can you hear me?" Charon said.

She closed her eyes slowly, which Sorrow took to mean yes.

Irris raised a hand slowly to her head, touching the wound there, her fingertips red when she pulled them away.

"Where the hell is that doctor?" Charon growled, wiping his daughter's fingers on his own tunic.

"I'll go and look," Mael volunteered, but made it two steps before the door was knocked on, then opened, by a middle-aged woman carrying a brown doctor's bag.

She came to Irris at once.

"Hello, Irris. I'm Dr Majela. Can you talk?"

"Yes," Irris said softly.

"Good. I'm going to examine you now. I can see there's a wound on your head; can you tell me if you're hurt anywhere else?"

"Just there."

"All right. I'm going to have a look." She looked at Charon, nodding gently, and he moved his chair back, wheeling to the end of the bed so he could see what the doctor was doing.

She gently probed the gash, pausing when Irris gasped and winced.

"Apologies," Dr Majela murmured. "I'm going to clean it up, and make sure there are no fragments in there. It's going to sting. Will you hold her hand?" The doctor turned to Sorrow.

Sorrow looked at Charon, checking it was all right, before

easing past the doctor and perching delicately beside Irris.

Irris smiled, and Sorrow returned it, as the doctor pulled a bottle and some cloth from her bag. When she opened the bottle the sharp stink of carbolic acid drowned the smell of the tea, and both Sorrow and Irris wrinkled their noses as the doctor liberally splashed the liquid on to a cloth, then pressed it to the side of Irris's head.

Irris immediately swore like a mariner, and Sorrow laughed, stopping herself when she realized it was inappropriate. But when she turned to Charon to apologize, she saw his face had relaxed, his mouth soft with a smile, and Mael too looked thrilled at Irris's colourful language.

The amount of blood the doctor wiped away seemed never-ending, but after she was done, Irris's nails biting into Sorrow's hand with every wipe, the gash was small, a little under an inch in length.

"Head wounds always bleed a lot," the doctor said, depositing a final cloth in the bin Mael had brought over to her. "You've been lucky. An inch lower and it would have been your temple. It's clean, but it's going to need stitches and you're going to need someone to stay close to you for the first night."

"I'll take care of her," said Charon. "She can stay there. I'll sleep in my chair."

Irris began to protest, so Sorrow interrupted. "She can come to my room, with me. Or I can stay in hers?"

"Yes," Irris agreed. "Sorry, Father, but I'd much prefer Sorrow's help getting dressed and washing."

Charon's lips pursed but he nodded.

"Good. Now, I need to stitch that wound," Dr Majela said. The stitches seemed to pain Irris less than having the wound cleaned had, though Sorrow couldn't watch as the doctor threaded a needle with black ply and proceeded to sew Irris's skin together as though she was a torn gown.

"I'll be back tomorrow to check on you," Dr Majela said. "You'll have a scar, I'm afraid."

"I don't care about that," Irris said, making Sorrow smile.

The doctor repacked her bag and smiled. "See you tomorrow," she said.

Charon walked her out, shaking her hand in both of his as she left, before returning to the others.

"Is there any tea left?" he asked, and Mael got up to check the pot.

"Yes," he replied, pouring all four of them a cup.

He carried them over, one by one, and then sat on the end of the bed.

"What happened?" Charon asked. "Tell us everything."

"It was Vine," Irris said. "He didn't bother to cover his face."

Sorrow's blood ran cold. The only reason she could think of why someone wouldn't hide their identity was if they thought their victim would never be able to speak about it. From the way Charon's knuckles whitened on his cup, he'd reached the same conclusion.

"He attacked the carriage when we were a few miles from Istevar. He wasn't alone; there were three of them. A man and woman with him," Irris said. "They must have blocked the road, like we did—" Irris paused, and clamped her mouth shut, as Charon's eyes narrowed.

"It's all right. He knows about the kidnap," Sorrow told Irris. "I told him everything. I mean *everything*."

Irris visibly braced for a scolding, but all Charon said was, "We'll talk about that later. Carry on."

Irris gave him an apologetic smile, and continued. "I leant out and saw them pulling our driver down from the front. Then they came for us. I slid across the seat and got out of the other side and the woman gave chase, throwing stones and rocks at me. I made the mistake of turning and that's when I was hit. I didn't pass out straight away; I saw her lean over me, another rock in her hand. I think she meant to kill me, but by that time Mael had knocked out the man who'd tried to attack him. He felled the woman with one blow. Vine must have fled."

Mael nodded. "I unhooked one of the horses from the carriage and brought Irris straight here. There was nothing I could do for the driver."

"Lucky you were there," Charon said.

"Lucky Arkady taught me how to punch," Mael replied.

They all fell silent.

"I'd like to get changed, all I can smell is blood," Irris said.

"Of course," Charon agreed. "Sorrow, can you help—"

"Let me try," Irris said.

Sorrow stood, and so did Mael, moving either side of Irris to support her. She wobbled a little as she stood, but then smiled at her father.

"I'm all right. I really do just want to get changed."

"And then rest," Charon said firmly.

"And then rest," Irris agreed.

"Let's meet in my rooms for dinner tonight, just us and Arran; that way we'll be close while Irris rests, and we can talk," Sorrow said. "We need to make a plan about how to deal with Vine. And..." Sorrow took a deep breath. "I want to bring some others here. Specifically, one other person."

Mael and Irris exchanged smirks. Charon caught them, and glared at Sorrow. His brows shot up his forehead as he guessed. "The Rathbone lad."

Irris motioned to sit back down, so Sorrow and Mael lowered her on to her father's bed again, and waited for his verdict.

"You are legally an adult, and this is your house. Your country, even. But he is a member of a family who have caused nothing but trouble for your family, and Rhannon, for the past three generations."

"He's not like them." Sorrow regretted the words the moment they were out of her mouth, hearing the cliché ringing in them.

"He still sports the surname Rathbone."

"He doesn't need to. The world already knows I have a connection with him, as Luvian Fen. He can stay Fen."

"And if people look into him, trying to discover his pedigree?"

"Irris could find nothing on him, remember?" Sorrow looked at Irris, who nodded to confirm it. "If she can't, who else could?"

Charon looked thoughtful. "Be that as it may, there are those who know who he is, who would seek to exploit his connection with you. His family, for example. It will compromise you both. You need to think very carefully about pursuing this. For starters, there will be Kaspira's reaction if she discovers he's a Rathbone. Then there's the fact numerous members of his family are in prison. And Arkady is a thug."

Charon was right. No one would care that Luvian wasn't like the rest of the Rathbones. No one would care that he went to university to be something – someone – else. They'd only ever hear his name, as they'd only hear hers, and that would be all they needed.

Sorrow was aware, more keenly than ever, that her life

wasn't her own. Had never been her own, and would never be her own. She was born and bred to lead, whether she liked it or not. And she could be a great leader. She knew she could. She just wasn't sure what it would cost her. What it might cost Rhannon.

Irris yawned sharply, drawing everyone's attention back to her.

"Sorry," she said. "I think I'd like to lie down for a while."

At once Mael rose to help her, and Charon pushed his chair back to give her room as Sorrow moved to her other side.

They made it to Sorrow's rooms with no mishaps, Dougray clearing the corridors so they could pass unhindered. Mael left them to find his own rooms, and Sorrow dismissed the servants, surprised when they offered to stay.

"They've been avoiding me since I returned," Sorrow told Irris once they'd finally gone, and Irris was settled on Sorrow's bed, resting while the bath ran. "I suppose the need to find out what happened to you is more important than their risk of catching plague from me."

"Gossip is currency," Irris said. "And I just arrived bleeding, in the arms of your brother, on horseback, like a woman in one of Luvian's novels."

"You read them too?" Sorrow was surprised. Irris's taste tended towards the factual.

"Arkady wouldn't play cards with me any more. I got bored and Luvian offered me one."

"What did you think?"

Irris tried to arch a brow, forgetting she was injured and crying out.

"Serves you right," Sorrow said, not meaning it at all, heading to the bathroom and turning off the taps.

She helped Irris wash, then dress, before guiding her to bed and sitting beside her.

"I feel like I missed a lot," Irris said, reclining against Sorrow's pillows. "Catch me up?"

"You're supposed to be resting," Sorrow replied.

"I am. But I'm also perfectly capable of listening at the same time."

"Your father will kill me."

"I expect he'll kill me first. I can't believe you told him what we did. Go on, tell me what else you've done while I wasn't here to stop you."

Sorrow spent the next half an hour giving Irris the abridged version of what had happened after she'd returned to Istevar, marvelling as she realized it had only been two days. It felt like a lifetime. Irris was heartbroken over Tuva, her sadness swiftly becoming rage when Sorrow told her about Vine and his threats, though she perked up when she learned Balthasar was behind bars. And she was positively jubilant when Sorrow said Vespus was gone.

"Thank the Graces," Irris said after Sorrow finished, her eyelids fluttering heavily. "Rasmus did it. It's over."

"Almost. All I need to do now is arrest Vine, get the cure for Hellfior and distribute it, concoct some kind of story to tell the people of the North Marches so they feel safe going home, ask Mael to be the new senator for the South Marches, and restructure the Decorum Ward. Oh, and govern the country. Easy."

When Irris didn't reply Sorrow looked at her. She'd fallen asleep.

Sorrow watched her breathing until she was sure it was even, then pulled a blanket over her friend and walked to the window.

Arresting Vine was next on her list. The plan had been to do it quickly, and quietly, but that was before he'd attacked Irris and Mael. He knew they'd got away, and therefore that he'd been seen. Because of it, he'd be ready for whoever she sent now.

So ... what if she didn't send anyone? What if she made him come to her?

Sorrow chewed her lip as a new idea formed.

Sorrow knocked on the door of Charon's office.

"What is it?" He began to wheel towards her immediately. "Is it Irris?"

"She's fine. Asleep. Mael's sitting with her. I'm here because I have an idea," she said. "And you're not going to like it."

"Tell me."

"I wanted the guard to arrest Vine before everything became public, but it's too late now; people saw how Irris arrived, the staff will talk. Sooner or later it will become public knowledge he's wanted. And we don't know how many of the Ward are with him. Irris and Mael said there were two others, during the attack, but there could be more. I can't imagine the remaining Ward will jump at the chance to arrest him, because he's likely to kill anyone who tries. And I can't have half the palace guard searching the country for him, leaving us vulnerable here – in fact, that might even be what he wants. But we have to capture him, and soon, to stamp out the threat he poses. I'm proposing we lay a trap. With me as the bait. We don't wait for him to come for me; we make him come to us."

Sorrow thought of Beata Rathbone, saying she'd forge her own path. Sorrow would do the same. And Vine wouldn't know she was leading him by the nose until it was too late.

"Why am I not surprised?" Charon sounded resigned.

"I'm also proposing we get Arkady Rathbone to help."

There. *That* surprised him.

"Kaspira will be furious," Charon said, once he'd recovered from his shock.

"She doesn't need to know he's a Rathbone – no one does. It's not like she's ever seen him. We'll call him Fen, like Luvian. Kady Fen. The Rathbones hate the Decorum Ward – Vine, especially. He made life hard for them."

"Am I supposed to be sympathetic?" Charon asked.

"No, of course not. I'm just saying. Enemy of my enemy is my friend."

"No good can come of being friends with criminals."

"It's too late," Sorrow said. "We need muscle to take out Vine, and Arkady is muscle."

Charon exhaled a long-suffering sigh and rubbed the bridge of his nose. "Go on. How will this trap work?"

24

Enemy of My Enemy

"It's simple," Sorrow said.

She was back in her rooms, with Mael, Charon, Arran and Irris, who'd woken ravenous and refused to stay in bed while everyone else ate. The table before them was strewn with the debris of the dinner they'd just shared: capon stuffed with apricot and walnuts, cardamom bread and salted butter, fried plantain, wild rice, and bitter green salad. They were all full, and sleepy, save for Sorrow, who was brimming with energy.

"I need to go to the West Marches to pay my respects to Tuva. That's all." She set her chin grimly. "We head out in a carriage and – wait for Vine to attack."

"That's the plan?" Irris said.

"I did say it was simple." Sorrow smiled.

"What makes you so sure he will?" Arran asked.

"He won't be able to resist. But, as an added incentive, I'm going to write a statement for the circulars condemning his cowardice. I'm going to let all of Rhannon know he attacked you, and that he's wanted in connection with the fire at Tuva's manse. I want him on the run. And then. . ." She met Mael's eye and grinned. "I'm going to let Arkady loose on him."

Sorrow turned to Irris, who was smiling.

"And what do you think of this?" Arran asked his father.

"I'm just grateful to be included in your latest madcap plan," he said sternly. "Speaking of which," Charon said, "I covered the ransom. I want to know where my money is."

Irris raised her hand to the wound on her head and gave an impish grin as she said, "Ouch. I think I need to lie down."

Arran laughed, covering his mouth when Charon glared at him.

"I mean it," Charon said.

"It's in a safe account, don't worry, Father. I can have it back to you by the end of tomorrow. I promise." Irris reached for him, taking his hand. "Although I think I really do need to rest."

Charon grumbled but took the hint, and as Arran and Mael rose to leave, he pushed his chair away from the table, though not without leaving instructions to summon him if Irris felt even a little ill, and to remind them to keep the guards close.

When they'd been little, before Rasmus came, before Sorrow had her own rooms, Irris had often slept with her in the palace nursery. The two had curled up beside each other like speech marks, Irris rubbing Sorrow's back and telling her stories until the younger girl fell asleep. So it was a familiar, welcome feeling when they both slipped into Sorrow's bed, still fully dressed, propped up on their elbows, facing each other.

Irris looked like herself again, fully cleaned up, save for the gash, a dark stain between her eyebrow and hairline.

"So. . ." Irris said. "Luvian Fen. Or Rathbone."

"No. We're *not* talking about that," Sorrow said, fighting a grin.

"Come on," said Irris. "We used to talk about you and Ras. Tell me."

Something struck Sorrow then. "Why do we never talk about you and anyone?"

Irris gave a one-shouldered shrug and said simply, "I don't think I'm like that. I've never felt attracted to anyone, but then the only boys I knew growing up were Ras and my brother, so probably for the best." She smiled. "But even when I left here to study, I didn't think about meeting anyone, didn't hope to. I never have – I always just wanted to be an archivist. Never wondered who I'd marry, or be with. I'm starting to believe I'd be happiest on my own, with my work, and my family, and you and whoever you end up with."

Irris's words didn't surprise Sorrow. She'd always been eager to listen to Sorrow talk about Rasmus, but never once even hinted she'd like to meet someone – anyone, of any gender. When the occasional visitors flirted with her, she rebuffed them gently but firmly. Sorrow had assumed it was because they weren't good enough for her beautiful friend, and Irris knew it. But this made much more sense.

Irris narrowed her eyes at her. "Now tell me why Mr Rathbone can't hear your name without turning the colour of a plum."

Sorrow flopped on to her back.

"I didn't sleep with him," she said. "We couldn't. No protection."

"So..."

Sorrow turned to her and waggled her eyebrows.

Irris pulled a pillow from beneath her arm and hit Sorrow, exclaiming in pain as the motion jolted her head.

Sorrow sat up. "Are you all right? I mean, you deserve it, but are you all right?"

"I'm fine," Irris said, checking the stitches in her wound. "And not sorry. Though I do need to take that painkiller, my head hurts too much to sleep."

"I have to forgive you because you're injured, but I don't want to," Sorrow said, tucking the pillow under her own head and lying back down as Irris reached for the vial the doctor had left her.

"So ... I take it a good time was had by all."

Sorrow laughed.

"It was," she said. Then the heaviness returned, as she remembered what Charon had said. "But your father is right. As the chancellor I can't be with him, any more than I could have been with Ras. His father and brother are in prison, and let's be honest, it's a matter of time until the others end up there. The Jedenvat would be in uproar. It's impossible. Apparently I only like people I can never be with."

"If it's any consolation, I don't think it's on purpose. You weren't exactly festooned with choices either."

"Festooned" was such a Luvian word that Sorrow couldn't help smiling.

"I like him," she said. "And he likes me. But once again, it's not enough."

"Don't rule it out," Irris said, lying down gently. "With Ras it was impossible; it doesn't have to be with Luvian. Every point you've made is fair, but there's more to it – and him –

than his family. Don't tar him with their brush. Besides, it's like you said: he's a Fen as far as the world knows. Or ever needs to know."

Sorrow lay quiet for a moment, trying to put out the little fires of hope that had ignited inside her. It was hopeless. She couldn't ask Luvian to renounce his family – for all his joking it would hurt him. There was love there, between him and them. Odd, strange love, but then what family wasn't built on blood and shared madness?

She looked over at Irris and found that while she'd been thinking, Irris had fallen asleep.

Sorrow turned her bedside lamp off and lay down, eyes drifting shut. She was moments from sleep herself when she heard a faint scratching sound, coming from her wardrobe. Wide awake at once, she threw back the covers and sat up, straining to hear to it. There it was again, the sound of something dragging itself across the door.

There was someone inside it.

"Irris?" Sorrow whispered. "Irris?"

It was no use; the painkiller had put Irris into a deep sleep, and Sorrow wasn't about to ask Dougray to come and help – she didn't want anyone else to know about the passage.

Cursing herself for not having checked the room first, Sorrow lifted the lamp, leaving it turned off. Silent as the grave, she crept across the floor, listening to the scraping. Her pulse was out of control as adrenaline and fear coursed through her, feeding each other, but she gritted her teeth. She'd get them, before they could get her.

She reached for the doorknob and began a countdown in her mind.

Three . . . two. . .

She yanked the door open and swung the lamp in front of her.

It connected with nothing.

Sorrow pulled it back and turned the dial, releasing the gas and sparking it. She turned it all the way up, the light blazing, and peered into her wardrobe.

Empty.

Everything hanging as it should be, nothing moving, nothing bulging. No feet poking out at the bottom.

The hairs on the back of her neck rose as she heard the scratching again. It was coming from the passage.

But whatever it was must have known she was there. It must have heard the sound of the door opening, and the cry she couldn't quite contain. And still it scratched...

She paused and listened again. There was no rhythm to it, just the sound of nails, or claws on wood.

A rat?

She shuddered. She had no problem with them in theory, but she didn't want one in her palace. Near her bedroom.

Sorrow had to know.

She pushed the rails of clothes aside, revealing the false wall and pushing her finger into the hole, to release the hidden mechanism. With a click, the door freed itself and Sorrow opened it, stopping herself from screaming at the last moment.

Not a rat.

Thorns.

The passage was sealed.

A wall of thorns blocked it, wound tightly against each other. Still winding, moving slowly as if they were still growing. That's what was making the scraping noise: the sound of thorns scratching against the thin wood as they moved.

He'd done it to keep her out. To stop her from sneaking to his rooms while he was away. But why?

Had he left the antidote in there?

Her heart leapt with hope, and she tried to calm herself. He wouldn't have done that, wouldn't have risked it.

But then why else keep her from using the passage? He knew that diplomatic immunity meant she couldn't go to his rooms without his permission, which he wasn't there to grant. So in theory he had no need to block it.

All she had to do was wait for Melisia to send word about the new ambassador and she'd be able to have Vespus's rooms cleared. She'd be able to find the antidote; she wouldn't need to ask Rasmus for help.

Fighting the urge to get a sabre and cut through the thorns there and then, Sorrow closed the secret door and pushed the clothes back into place, covering it. They didn't mute the sound, the hollow passage acting as an echo chamber, and Sorrow could still hear it as she returned to bed.

She glanced at Irris, sleeping soundly and oblivious to the sound. Sorrow's eyes lit on the sleeping draught the doctor had left. She took a large sip, and closed her eyes.

Unsurprisingly, her night was fuelled by nightmares, each one worse than the last. She dreamed of the fire at Tuva's manse, of hearing Tuva's screams and not being able to get to her. Then Tuva became Irris, and Sorrow could see her, beating the glass of a window that would not smash as flames danced behind her. Then she was in the bath, Mael holding her head underwater as he asked a proud Arkady Rathbone if he was doing it right.

The final nightmare was the worst. She was with Luvian,

and he was holding a bundle over his shoulder, rocking gently. A baby. Sorrow knew with the certainty dreams bring that it was their baby, and when she looked again at Luvian she saw he was older, his jaw and cheeks shadowed with scruff, faint lines around his eyes. There was a ring on the third finger of his left hand, and she had a matching one.

"She's asleep," Luvian said, looking at Sorrow over his glasses. "Give her a kiss and I'll put her down."

But when Sorrow leant over to kiss the baby, she saw it was a skeleton, and the blanket now a thick silk shroud.

The baby opened its jaw and said, "Mama," and Sorrow had shot awake, her hands scrabbling at her throat as she gasped for breath.

She sat up, the cushions beneath her drenched with sweat, her quilt damp too. The clock over the mantelpiece revealed it was four, too early to be awake. Irris was still sound asleep, her breathing regular.

Sorrow stood, heading to the bathroom, and turned the taps on. A bath would help. Or if not, it would at least give her something to do. When she went to her wardrobe to get a fresh nightgown, it was silent, the thorns seemingly slumbering. As the bath ran, Sorrow looked out of the window, into the dark grounds. Everything was peaceful, quiet. The sky was pre-dawn dark, for once the stars hidden by clouds that promised rain later.

If she was lucky, by the end of the following day, all of her nightmares would be over. Vine would be in prison, Melisia would have appointed another ambassador. Life could return to normal.

She bathed and dressed, sending Dougray to fetch paper and ink for her, so she could write to Arkady and ask for his help, and draft her piece for the circulars. By the time Irris awoke to join her for a breakfast of buttery flatbread and soft-boiled eggs, Sorrow had sent both letters.

"Now what?" Irris asked.

"We wait."

For news from Rhylla. For Arkady. And for victory.

They didn't have to wait long. An hour later a message arrived from Vespus, resigning his post and saying another ambassador would be sent as soon as Melisia found a suitable replacement. The letter was perfunctory, terse even, not a word spared. All Vespus had said was that he wouldn't be returning to Rhannon as the ambassador and he apologized on behalf of Rhylla for the lack of notice. Sorrow imagined Melisia forcing him to write it, reading it over before allowing it to be sent, and the image filled her with joy. Vespus doing someone else's bidding. Vespus under someone else's control.

Sorrow danced around her room, Irris laughing at her from the bed, the pair creating such a noise that Dougray hurried into the room, only to be embarrassed as the two girls burst into giggles.

In a bid to redeem herself, Sorrow put on her most serious expression and explained her plan to trap Vine. Dougray assented gravely to an addition to the guard.

"It's nothing to do with you," Sorrow assured him. "And it's temporary – only until we catch Vine. You're still my main bodyguard."

"Of course," Dougray replied with a frown, as though he'd never doubted it, but his step was lighter than it had been since she returned.

She, Irris, Arran and Mael spent the day in Sorrow's

parlour, waiting for Arkady to arrive. And when he did, he brought a surprise with him.

Luvian was there too, his arms held behind his back by one of the palace guards, and Sorrow remembered the half-finished pardon on her desk.

"He arrived with him." The palace guard nodded at Arkady. "And insisted he be brought to you."

"That pardon would be excellent round about now, Chancellor," Luvian said, yelping as the guard tightened his hold on him.

"He's pardoned!" Sorrow said quickly. "Officially pardoned. Please, release him."

The guard gave Sorrow a dark look, but did as she asked.

Sorrow introduced Arkady to her bodyguard, and then finally allowed herself to look properly at Luvian. She wanted very much to slip her arms around him, press her face into his neck. The urge was almost overwhelming, and she had to cross her arms as she reached him.

"Chancellor," he said, eyes glinting behind his glasses. "Thank you for the pardon."

"You're welcome, Mr Fen. Sorry it took so long."

"Worth waiting for." He grinned, and Sorrow had the distinct impression he wasn't talking about the pardon at all. She looked back at Arkady, who gave her a knowing smile, and she scowled at him.

"Let me show you to where you're staying tonight. We've put you in the barracks—"

"Bad luck, runt," Arkady said, jostling Luvian.

"Don't call him that," Sorrow snapped, violently enough that Arkady flinched. "Let's go."

Sorrow had never been to the guards' barracks before – had never had a reason to. They were in the far west of the palace, through the kitchens, and above the cells, which made Sorrow think of the plants Vespus had left down there. She'd have to move them – no, she'd destroy them, she decided. That would be best. She assumed he'd taken the key with him, but Luvian would be able to pick the locks, she was sure of it.

As they walked on, the corridors filled with tantalizing smells; sautéed onion and garlic, something sweet and chocolatey, fresh bread and cinnamon. They were near the kitchens, another place Sorrow didn't know.

She'd never been the kind of child to sneak to the kitchens, because the food the poor chefs were required to cook was more trial than treat, so she was fascinated by the hidden areas of the place she'd grown up in. The passageways were white stone, unpainted, the floors tiled instead of boarded. The lamps mounted on the wall were the old, oil kind, so old that Sorrow hadn't seen them before. Servants moved rapidly, though they all stopped to goggle at her, Mael and Irris as the guard led them to the barracks.

Arkady and Luvian had been allocated private rooms, usually reserved for captains. They were sparse but comfortable, each with a single bed made with crisp white sheets, the corners sharp. Or at least they had been, until Arkady sprawled on it, claiming the room as his own.

"I suppose I'm next door," Luvian said.

"I'll come with you," Sorrow replied, desperate for a few seconds alone with him.

Arkady sniggered, and Sorrow wanted to murder him.

"Good idea," Luvian said stiffly, edging past Sorrow and opening the door.

Sorrow followed him, her blood lava.

The set-up was the same, only Luvian's bed was still pristine. She stepped into the room, and turned to close the door, hoping to buy them a moment's peace to talk. Instantly she became aware he was standing behind her.

His fingers moved to the tendrils that had fallen from the knot atop her head, winding them into curls.

Her mouth was suddenly desert-dry, her stomach tight.

"Hi," he whispered in her ear, sending a shudder along her spine.

"Hi," she replied.

His other hand crept to her waist, and he pressed his nose into her hair, inhaling. Then he kissed the tip of her ear, feather-light. Sorrow's eyes fluttered shut, her breath gone shallow.

"Listen," she said, catching herself. "We have to talk."

He released her at once, as though he'd expected as much, and sat down on the bed. Sorrow looked between the bed and the chair and then sat beside him, taking his hand. He looked miserable, like a dog bracing for a kick from a vicious master. He looked how she felt.

"I don't know how this works with us," she said. "Because of who I am, and who you are. Charon thinks—"

"You told him?" Luvian's eyes widened behind his glasses.

"I did. He pointed out that you're a Rathbone. And I'm the chancellor. The uproar if we were together would be huge."

"So we don't tell anyone," he said promptly. "You managed with Rasmus for two years, you can do it again."

"Is that what you want?" Sorrow asked. "To be a secret?"

"I would understand. But it might not be necessary. Remember, the world thinks I'm Luvian Fen. No one needs to know I'm a Rathbone. You couldn't dig up anything to prove it, so no one else would be able to."

It was what Irris had said, too.

"You'd have to give up your family. Even secret visits might be impossible."

He paused, then nodded.

"Even now. After everything they did for us?"

"Don't you want me to?"

"I can't make that choice, Luvian. You have to decide."

His eyes softened when she said his name. "I've decided, this is happening."

Sorrow laughed. "Think about it," she said. "I mean it. I'm not going anywhere."

"I should have just kissed you," Luvian grumbled.

Sorrow wished he had. She wished they were kissing now.

His hand rose to cup her face and she leant into it. When he pressed his lips to her forehead she fought to keep from claiming his mouth with her own. She'd wait for him to decide. And if he decided he wanted to be with her, she'd deal with Charon and they'd do it properly. No hiding or sneaking. Together, openly.

She realized she'd tilted her face a second before her lips would have brushed his and pulled away, sighing.

"So close," he said.

"You're a terrible person. Now I'm going to end up thinking about it all night," she admitted.

He grinned. "You could always distract yourself with the book I brought you."

"You got me a book?"

He nodded, and put his bag on the bed, rummaging through it until he found it. "Here." He handed her a parcel wrapped in brown paper, his smile widening as she took it.

300

"Oh, I almost forgot. My mother sends her love."

Sorrow's eyes narrowed. She hadn't got the impression Beata Rathbone thought very much of her, and definitely not enough to send her love. "Were those her exact words?"

"No... But reading between the lines, I'm sure that's what she meant. Come on," he said. "We've been in here for about five minutes. Let's not deprive Arkady of the chance to make many, many jokes at my expense."

Irris must have warned Arkady to keep his mouth shut, because he didn't say a word when they returned, barely noticing when they slipped back into the room. Although it might also have been because Mael was sitting beside him on the bed, their knees touching, and that seemed to be drawing all of his attention. Sorrow would ask Irris what – if anything – she knew, later.

They stayed another hour, filling each other in on what they'd missed. Sorrow was aware that for most of it Luvian watched her. He didn't look right in the small guard's room, in his freshly pressed navy-blue suit; miraculously wrinkle-free even after travelling for half a day. He looked like he ought to be in the palace, in an office of his own.

Too soon it was time to return.

They dined with Charon, down in his suite, and went over Sorrow's plan, until even Charon seemed satisfied. It was early when Sorrow left them, exhausted from the night before. Her servants had prepared her bed, and ten minutes later she was clean and changed, tucked up in bed. Beside her was Luvian's parcel.

Smiling, she opened it, laughing when she saw it was another romance. The cover illustration showed a bare-chested man holding a pale-skinned woman against him, her head tipped back, eyes half-closed. Sorrow read the back. This one was apparently about a highwayman who kidnapped a princess. She laughed again, and flicked through it.

She stopped when she realized some of the pages were marked, riffling back to find them.

Her entire body burned furiously hot.

Luvian had underlined the parts of the book where the characters were intimate, writing notes in the margins.

I'm not entirely sure I can contort my body into the necessary shape, so we might have to be a little flexible (pun intended) about how it works.
> *This sounds like A LOT of fun.*
> *As the more experienced one in this relationship, can you confirm this is possible? If yes, consider the challenge accepted. If no, consider the challenge accepted.*

Sorrow put the book down and kicked her legs, laughing aloud.

25

Vines

Sorrow slept better than she had since she'd been back, waking, washing and dressing before a servant brought her breakfast. She feasted on flatbread with grapefruit and pink peppercorn jam, then chose a cape to wear, thick enough to keep the chill off her as she travelled. She carried it in her arms as she made her way to the main hall, where Dougray stood rigidly to attention, along with Irris, Charon, Mael, Arran and Luvian.

Arkady was waiting in the carriage, had been hiding there for an hour already, having got in when it was still in the coach house. Anyone watching the front steps of the Winter Palace – and Sorrow had to assume someone was – would see just her and one bodyguard getting in.

Her statement had been published in the circular earlier that morning. She'd read it over breakfast, satisfied between that, and Balthasar's arrest, Vine would be itching to strike at her. Perhaps she'd been too hasty in arresting Balthasar – keeping him around to drip feed information to Vine might have been useful. But the statement would do the job, Sorrow was certain of it.

In it, she'd called him a coward and a fool, and sworn he wouldn't bully or frighten her. She'd chosen her words with care, every single one dripping with disdain for him. She was dismissive, rude. Stars, he'd hate it.

She imagined him seething as he read it, swearing revenge on her. It struck Sorrow then that both her enemies had links to plants; Vine by name and Vespus by nature, and there she was, caught between them.

"I wish you'd let me come with you," Luvian said as she joined them. "If anything goes wrong. . ."

"It won't," Sorrow reassured him.

"Your route takes you north out of Istevar, then west to Tuva's manse," Charon said. "From there you'll go to the temple to pay your respects, then home. Obviously we don't know when Vine's attack will come."

"Or if at all," Arran reminded them.

"I'll just have to keep going back out until he does," Sorrow said. Privately, she didn't think she would. Pride would force him to act sooner, rather than later.

They walked her to the carriage, and the first trickle of apprehension wormed its way down Sorrow's spine. But she pretended otherwise, hugging Mael and Irris, and shaking hands with Charon and Arran. Luvian helped her put on her cape, and she smiled at him, a thousand promises held in the curve of her lips, and he read every single one, his own mouth returning them five-fold.

She climbed into the carriage, surprised as ever by the sheer size of Arkady. Somehow a uniform had been found for him and it changed him; he seemed even taller, his bulk sharpened by it. He always looked threatening, but the crisp cut of the uniform honed his thuggish edges into something truly formidable, as though he was made of stone, or quartz, something unbreakable.

Sorrow didn't think she'd ever fully forgive him for attacking her in Istevar, but at some point there had been a shift inside her, and he'd stopped being an enemy, or even a threat. He was just Arkady.

The journey to the West Marches was a nightmare, not because anything happened, but because it didn't. Every time the carriage slowed to give way to another, or a pothole jolted the wheels, or one of the horses fretted, Sorrow's heart leapt into her mouth, her body readying itself to run and fight, only for the coach to continue on, the driver utterly unaware that his passengers were on the edge of their seats. She'd wanted to warn him what might happen, but Dougray suggested it was better to keep as few people as possible aware of the trap. When Arkady agreed, Sorrow reluctantly dropped it, but made Dougray promise he'd try to protect the poor driver if he could.

By the time they arrived in the village where the Marchant manse was, Sorrow's legs and jaw were sore from being locked for the entire trip, her teeth clenched as she climbed out of the carriage on shaking limbs. Not once had she relaxed, not once had the tension dropped. It was so bad Sorrow had almost wished something would happen, like a storm breaking the atmosphere in high summer.

The manse was a ruin.

Nothing remained, save a few of the outer walls, burned

black. The building had finally stopped smoking, and the shell of it was stark against the winter sun, scarring the landscape.

People had lain flowers at the gates, and Sorrow paused to read some of the messages. All of them said how loved Tuva had been, how greatly she would be missed. It made Sorrow tear up, and when she turned to look at Dougray his own eyes were misted and sparkling.

From the manse, they went to the temple, where Tuva would lie out for five more nights, as was the Rhannish custom. Seven nights in total, one for each Grace, before she'd finally be buried. Sorrow and the rest of the Jedenvat would attend the funeral then, but she'd wanted to come today, to say a private goodbye to the senator for the West Marches, who'd died because of her.

All temples were circular, in honour of life eternal, and there being no beginning and no end. Like most Rhannish buildings, it was made of white stone, and the ceiling was open to the sky, a huge central window letting light into the room. In high summer it would be terrible, like being trapped beneath a magnifying glass. But today, in gentle winter, it was pleasant enough to bathe in the sun's weak rays.

Sorrow stayed for a few moments, thinking about Tuva, remembering how warm she was, and how supportive. Sorrow wasn't religious, but she offered a prayer to the Grace of Death and Rebirth anyway, asking them to care for her.

The wintry sun was already starting to lower when she and Dougray left the temple to begin the journey home. It would take them hard east, before dipping south into Istevar.

Sorrow could almost sense Vine getting closer and closer. And it seemed Arkady could too, because when she got back in the carriage he was in the middle of pulling an impressive selection of knives and throwing stars out from under his tunic, collecting them in his lap, unstrapping even more from his ankles and upper arms.

Dougray's eyes bulged as Arkady examined his collection, seeming to sort them, before choosing four knives and four stars. He handed two of each to Sorrow.

"Just in case," he said, replacing the others. He stopped and looked at Dougray. "Want anything?" he asked.

Dougray shook his head mutely, and Arkady finishing concealing his weapons.

"Arkady?" Sorrow said.

He turned to look at her.

"Thank you."

He nodded, then peered out of the window.

Sorrow didn't think her aim would be worth much, so she pocketed the throwing stars but kept the knives on her lap, gripping the handles. They felt good, a nice size for her hands, and she realized that's what Arkady had been assessing them for: the right fit. He'd given her weapons she'd be able to hold easily. Weapons she'd be comfortable with.

Sorrow looked at him, but he was still scanning their surroundings, and she bit back more thanks, instead slowing her breathing, keeping herself calm. She'd be ready, when they were attacked. She'd put his knives to good use if she needed to.

A mile passed, and then another, and still nothing happened. Every now and then Dougray would peer out of the window, checking the road ahead and behind, but he saw nothing that disturbed him. And Sorrow realized she might have been wrong. That despite her attempt to goad Vine, he wasn't going to attack. Not then, at least.

As they drove into the centre of the Istevar town, Sorrow

offered Arkady his knives back.

"Keep them," he said gruffly. "I've got more."

Dougray looked scandalized, and Sorrow gave Arkady a small smile.

"Thank you."

He nodded, his mouth twisting in what might have been a smile.

"I think this afternoon—" was as far as Sorrow got before an impossibly bright light flashed outside.

Then she was out of her seat, flying through the air, colliding with Arkady, smashing into the ceiling, before they all fell to the right.

She slammed into Dougray, crushing him against the side of the carriage, one of the knives narrowly missing her eye as it clattered into her face.

A second later, the carriage hit the ground and shattered like a pumpkin, spilling its occupants on to the street, as screams ripped the air apart.

Instinct kicking in, Sorrow tested her limbs, surprised to find them all working, and pushed herself on to her knees to look around, something warm and wet dripping down her cheek.

To her left Arkady was getting to his feet, looking mercifully unharmed, eyes on Sorrow. Dougray appeared to be unconscious, blood on his own face. The driver was out for the count too, and the horses were dead, fallen in the road ahead of them.

People ran past, screaming and wailing, no one stopped to help, and Sorrow looked around, trying to get her bearings. It seemed they were on the main street, and a building had exploded.

Not just any building, she saw.

Ahead of her the Decorum Ward headquarters of Istevar burned. They'd been about to pass it, the poor horses bearing the brunt of it as the force ripped the carriage from the shafts and sent it careening through the air, back down the street.

She was lucky to be alive. A few seconds later. . .

"Shit," Arkady said.

Sorrow followed his gaze and saw three men, the lower halves of their faces covered, running towards them.

In the centre, shark eyes unmistakable above the scarf over his nose and mouth, was Meeren Vine. When he saw her, his eyebrows rose, as though he was surprised to see her, and Sorrow realized this wasn't an ambush meant for her – she'd just happened upon it. Neither of them had planned for her to be there during an explosion.

But it seemed Vine intended to make the most of it. He pulled the scarf down, showing his face, so she could see his satisfied smile.

Sorrow scrabbled around for Arkady's knives, spotting one a few feet away, the other missing. She dove for the one she could see and pulled one of the throwing stars from her pocket, gripping it in her left hand. She'd throw it if she had to, throw them both; the other was a comforting weight against her hip. She bent into a crouch, ready to fight.

Arkady stepped in front of her.

"Don't try to help," he said.

As Vine's men spread, Vine himself looked Arkady up and down.

"You're a big bastard," he called. "Bigger than me. But you know what they say about big bastards, don't you? They fall hard. You're going to rock Rhannon when I cut you down."

Arkady didn't reply, didn't move. He had his baton in one hand, just like those the Ward used, the other empty, despite the arsenal Sorrow knew he was carrying. Sorrow stayed back and ready, her eyes darting between the men, trying to read their body language, to predict who might move where.

Her fear seemed to have fled her; instead she felt focused, full of singular purpose, as though the world was moving a fraction slower than usual, giving her time to see everything.

She watched as the man on the left, middle-aged with salt-and-pepper hair, his girth owing more to flab than muscle, tried to dart around Arkady.

She saw Arkady's hand lash out, though it hardly seemed he had moved, clipping the man on the side of the head. He fell without a making sound, his eyes open, sightless. There wasn't a mark on him, but he was very clearly dead.

Vine and the other man paused, looking between each other, having a silent conversation.

Then they both rushed forward.

Vine went straight for Arkady, not even flinching when Arkady lashed out with his baton again. He was on him in a second, delivering a vicious punch to Arkady's jaw that sent his head lolling backwards.

It wasn't enough to fell him, though, and Arkady responded with a blow of his own, drawing a sickening crack from the centre of Vine's face.

Blood gushed from his nose and he leered madly, before lunging at Arkady and tackling him to the ground.

The two Goliaths held each other in a deadly embrace, keeping each other close while they delivered hit after hit, the force of each one devastating, rolling as they battled to win the upper hand.

Meanwhile his companion had stopped, his own rush faked, designed to confuse Arkady while Vine took him out. And with him downed, the other Ward had a clear shot at Sorrow.

Then her panic arrived, the world speeding back up, and Sorrow threw the star with her weaker left hand.

Annoyance and fear bit as it missed completely.

The man hadn't even dodged, as though he'd not expected her aim to be true, and he laughed as he moved in on her, his baton raised.

The second time, she didn't miss.

She whipped her wrist back and flung it into his face, catching him square on the cheek.

"Bitch," he hissed, lunging for her.

Then he was falling forward, as Dougray, miraculously awake, grabbed his ankle, sending him sprawling.

The moment he was down Dougray heaved himself atop him with a grunt.

"I've got him," he said.

"Tie him up," she ordered Dougray.

Dougray rolled off the man and began to restrain him.

Sorrow looked back to where Arkady and Vine were still locked in battle. Both of their faces were little more than meat, covered in blood, and as Sorrow watched Vine spat a tooth at Arkady. Behind them smoke billowed out of the Ward headquarters, the blaze inside raging unchecked.

Though the streets had emptied in the aftermath of the explosion, the people initially fleeing to save themselves, now they began to return, eager to help, and Sorrow's heart filled with gratitude for them, for their bravery.

Some rushed at Arkady and Vine, trying to separate them,

311

engulfing them in a tangle of bodies, while others set up a chain, passing buckets along to quench the flames in the Ward building.

The sound of hoof beats made her turn, and Sorrow saw horses bearing down on them, the riders in grey. The palace guard – her men – coming to the rescue.

And Luvian, eyes blazing behind his glasses as he galloped full pelt towards her.

He threw himself from his horse and pulled her to him, crushing her with the force of his embrace.

"Thank the Graces you're all right," he said, pressing kisses into her hair, his arms tight around her, even as he drew back to examine her for injuries. He touched her cheek where the knife had collided with her in the carriage, his fingers coming away red and sticky, fury darkening his features.

"I'm fine," Sorrow said, taking his fingers and wiping them on her clothes. Then she turned.

The brawl was finally over; Vine was on his stomach, face pressed into the cobbled road. And Arkady was standing, leaning a little but standing, citizens and palace guards noting his grey uniform and seeing nothing but one of their own in it, clapping his back and rubbing his arm, jeering at the prone body of Vine. Sorrow couldn't tell if he was unconscious or dead, and she didn't know which she'd prefer. She was just glad Arkady was all right.

He turned, seeming unsurprised to see his brother there, and nodded. Luvian nodded back, something fraternal and kind passing between them.

"We've got Vine," Sorrow said, her voice filled with wonder. "We really got him."

"We did," Luvian said.

They looked at each other, and both started laughing.

Vine, unfortunately still alive, was bound, to be taken to the Winter Palace, and locked up in the barracks. Thanks to his destruction of the Decorum Ward headquarters, and with Vespus still having the keys to the dungeons, it was the only place to put him. Sorrow disliked the idea of having him in her palace, but at least the entire palace guard would be on hand to keep an eye on him.

She looked at the ruins of the Ward headquarters, and realized with a start Balthasar had been in there. Surely Vine would have freed him before he blew it up? They were allies...

Sorrow walked over to where Vine was being bound.

"Did you release Senator Lys?" she asked.

He looked at Sorrow with his one good eye.

"Why would I? He was a snake."

Sorrow swallowed her shock. She'd hated Balthasar, but it didn't mean she wanted him dead.

"That's two senators of mine you've murdered in as many days," Sorrow said.

His mouth was a mess of cracked teeth, his lips split and swollen, and yet he grinned at her as though she'd just told the best joke in the world.

"Ignore him," Luvian murmured, and Sorrow did, raising an eyebrow at him before turning away, as though he wasn't worth her time. She didn't want her people to see her lose control.

A lead rope was attached to the bridle of a horse for his walk to the Winter Palace, Sorrow had to fold her arms to keep from slapping the horse's rump and sending it galloping off, Vine trailing behind it.

One of the guard approached her and bowed low.

"Your pardon, Excellency. Some of the guard were sweeping the area and found a carriage in a side street. It's full of quickfire. We assume it's Vine's."

"Stars." Sorrow shuddered. She could only imagine what Vine planned to do with that. "Take it to the palace and lock it in your weapons store. We'll decide what to do with it later."

"Very good, Your Excellency." The guard bowed and jogged away.

"Thank the Graces we got him before he used that too," Luvian said.

Sorrow nodded.

While a carriage was being sent for, and Arkady was being tended, Sorrow allowed a baker to usher her and Luvian into his shop, which had miraculously survived the incident. He guided them behind the counter, past trays of bread and cakes, and into the warm, sugar-scented kitchen, where he gave them hot wine and honey pasties, and wrapped blankets around their shoulders.

"For the shock," he said, though Sorrow didn't think she was in shock. On the contrary, rather than shutting down, she had energy to burn, enough that she almost suggested they walk back to the Winter Palace instead of waiting for the carriage.

The moment the baker disappeared into the recesses of the bakery, Luvian moved beside Sorrow, standing so close his body was pressed against hers. He put an arm around her, his fingers gripping her tightly, and she felt him shaking.

When she turned to him, questioning, his gaze was fierce and she stayed quiet, offering him a faint smile.

They stood there, Sorrow eating in silence, and Luvian holding her as though his life depended on it until the coach arrived.

"We'll be out in a moment," Luvian said to the guard who was waiting, and he nodded, leaving them.

Luvian took the cup from Sorrow's hand, placed it on the counter, drew her into his arms and kissed her.

There was a hunger in his kiss, a need born of more than desire as he pushed her back against the wall, pinning her there with his hips. She felt his glasses knock askew, but neither stopped to fix them, her fingers tight in his hair, pulling it harder than was kind. Not that he seemed to mind, as his tongue invaded her mouth, claiming her soundly.

Dimly, she realized fear was driving his need to kiss her, taste her, feel her mouth moving on his. Fear demanding this proof she was alive, and well.

Conversely, she felt almost giddy with life. She could feel the blood rushing through her veins, pulsing *alive, alive, alive* with the rhythm of her heart. She was aware of every inch of her body, both the bruises and scrapes from the explosion, and his hands on her, burning her in a different way. He was still trembling, violently, and when she stroked his arms, trying to soothe the shaking away, he kissed her more furiously.

They broke apart at the sound of footsteps, and Luvian straightened his glasses, his eyes glittering behind them, his breathing hard.

"The carriage is here, Your Excellency," one of the palace guard told them.

Sorrow thanked him, waiting for him to leave. Then she turned, giving Luvian a final, firm kiss, and followed the guard out to where Arkady and Dougray were waiting by the coach.

There was not an inch of Arkady's face that wasn't bruised, his lips and eyes swollen, gashes on his cheek, his nose clearly broken. But he tried to smile when he saw Luvian and Sorrow, even though it split his lip.

Sorrow walked over to him and leant up on tiptoe. Even then, she barely managed to reach his chin, kissing a corner of it gently.

"Thank you," she said.

He gave her a nod, and then reached out and patted her arm. She imagined it was somewhat like being gently mauled by a bear; even battered he had the strength to make her stumble. He was something, was Arkady Rathbone.

They had to call Dr Majela out again to tend to their wounds, and she dealt with Sorrow first. The cut on her face was shallow, and didn't need stitches, though it didn't stop Luvian from hovering over her, watching as the doctor cleaned it. Behind him Charon kept shooting dark looks, but he remained mercifully silent.

Arkady, as expected, was a mess. Both his nose and left cheekbone were broken, though he didn't seem to mind, announcing his nose had been broken twice before and he was still the best-looking of his brothers. His ribs and hands were miraculously unbroken, though when he lifted his tunic his chest and stomach were a patchwork of bruises, and the skin across his knuckles was split as badly as his lips.

Sorrow became aware that throughout Arkady's examination, Mael, who along with Irris and Charon had descended on Sorrow and Arkady the moment they'd got back, had grown stiller and stiller, until he resembled nothing so much as a statue beside him.

316

"I think that's everything then," Dr Majela said. "As ever, call me if there are any changes, or anything worries you. Otherwise I'll be back tomorrow to see what new injuries you have."

It took Sorrow a moment to realize the doctor was joking.

"Thank you," she said, smiling ruefully. "We'll try to stay out of trouble."

"I'll see you out, Doctor." Charon rolled over to the door. "Mr Fen, if you'll come with me I'd like a report of today," Charon said. "I need to begin the proceedings against Vine, your statement will be most useful."

She gave Luvian a small smile. "I'll see you tomorrow," she said softly.

They left, and Sorrow padded past Arkady and Mael, through to her bathroom, examining the cut on her face.

"We'll have matching scars." Irris appeared behind her.

"I don't know what Dr Majela thinks of us." Sorrow prodded her face, wincing at the burst of pain. It would bruise, she realized. Stars, she'd look a sight by the morning.

"On the bright side, we look a thousand times better than Arkady. And Vine," Irris said, turning away and returning to the others.

Sorrow gave herself one last look in the mirror, tilting her head. Maybe a scar wouldn't be so bad, she thought. A little rakish, something to suggest she wasn't just a soft-handed politician. That she could rumble with the best of them.

Irris appeared behind her again, eyes wide, a finger on her lips, her other hand beckoning Sorrow to follow.

To where Mael was kneeling before Arkady, cradling his face, kissing him.

"Ahem." Sorrow gave a loud cough, and grinned. Finally, a

317

chance to get her revenge on Arkady for his merciless teasing earlier.

"Mael, perhaps you should take Arkady back to your rooms to rest," she said, mischief lighting her eyes. "He doesn't look like he can manage the long walk to the barracks. In fact, he looks a little misty-eyed. Weak-kneed."

Arkady scowled at her, his face softening as he turned to Mael to see what he made of all this.

Mael was nodding, an answering grin in his eyes.

"Off you go then," Irris said.

Mael stood, moving to help Arkady, and Sorrow couldn't be sure, given the mess his face was in, but she thought he might have blushed.

"Be gentle with him," Sorrow warned Mael, and Arkady stuck two fingers up at her.

After they were gone, she dropped into a chair. "I need a bath," she said, and Irris groaned longingly.

"Me too. In fact, I'm going to do that right now. If I don't fall into the sleep of the triumphant, I'll come back?"

"Do. Although if I'm deep in the slumber of the victorious, leave me be." Sorrow walked Irris out, stepping into the corridor.

Dougray, who'd stationed himself at the end of the wing, moved at once to her side.

"I'm giving you the night off," Sorrow said.

"That's not necessary, Your Excellency."

"Nonsense. And it's an order, not a request. You were outstanding today. You deserve a good night's rest."

"But it's my duty—"

"—to do as you're told." Sorrow smiled to soften the order. "I promise you, I'm safe as houses here tonight. Go on. Relax."

He nodded, a frown creasing his brow, as though the idea of relaxation was alien to him.

Sorrow returned to her room, but hovered in the doorway, waiting until he'd exited the wing. She'd give him a rise, she decided. He'd earned one.

She walked through her suite, closing doors behind her, relishing the privacy as she rubbed her back. She'd thought she'd escaped the crash unscathed, but aches were blooming across her back and legs. She made her way to the bathroom, turning on the taps, and stripped off her tunic and trousers, twisting to examine herself

As she'd begun to suspect, bruises were forming, dark brown under her golden skin. She pressed on one before she could stop herself, wincing as pain radiated from it. A bath would help, she told herself.

Someone knocked her bedroom door and she caught up her clothes, throwing them on before she opened a door.

A servant stood there, bearing a letter on a silver tray. "Just arrived, Your Excellency. Marked urgent."

Sorrow snatched it up and turned it over, her heart stuttering as she saw the Alvus tree and three stars of Rhylla. The royal seal. Melisia's seal.

"Thank you." She dismissed the servant. She turned off the bath and walked to her bed, sitting down and tearing it open, her hands shaking. This would be Melisia's verdict on her and Rasmus. Rasmus's fate, and part of her own, were contained inside.

But it wasn't from Melisia.

It was from Vespus.

I warned you not to cross me, was all it said.

All of her joy and relief fled, replaced with dread.

Fiercely, she told herself to stop. He was in Rhylla, under Melisia's control. There was nothing he could do to her. Let him have his tantrum. Let him make threats. It didn't matter.

As she put down the letter, she heard that strange, shifting sound from her wardrobe.

Her heart started to beat faster, and her mouth turned dry as she rose and moved towards it.

Carefully, Sorrow triggered the release and pulled the door back.

The thorns had receded, leaving a gap she could pass through.

She paused only a split-second, but in that second the vines unfurled, snagging in her clothes and drawing her into the passageway with surprising force. She tried to scream, but another vine rose and wrapped across her mouth, muffling the sound.

She heard the door swing shut behind her.

Vines urged her on, pressing at her back, and she walked blind, with only the thorns to guide her, until the door on the other side swung open.

She was forced out, into the ambassador's corridor, and any thoughts she had of running vanished when she saw what lay ahead.

Floor to ceiling, everything was wrapped in vines, shrouded in them, thick and surging. They looked like snakes, or tentacles, twisting and seething around each other.

The only space they avoided was Vespus's door.

When Vespus had used his ability to alter the great hall at Castle Adavaria, it had been a magical, wondrous thing. But this was violent, and profane; nature made unnatural in a way Sorrow couldn't have imagined.

Then the door to Vespus's quarters opened.

She saw Rasmus, held like a fly at in the centre of the room, caught in a web of roiling green.

"Run," was all he managed before a vine slithered over his mouth.

26

A Patient Man

She turned, and tried to run, but it was too late. More vines caught her ankles and wrists, drawing her into the room. They carried Sorrow over the threshold, closing the door behind her.

The plants held her aloft opposite Rasmus, winding around her waist to hold her steady. She couldn't take her eyes off him, arms and legs held splayed by the vines, looking like nothing more than a sacrifice. His hair was tangled wildly, stems snarled through it, pulling it even as she watched, and he was shirtless, scratches on his stomach and arms where he'd fought his bindings.

Rasmus's eyes were wide, darker than usual. Unable to turn his head, he looked to the corner, back at her, then to the corner again. Struggling against her own ties, Sorrow twisted and her blood froze, her scream dying on her tongue.

Vespus, and Taasas. Sitting at a table, sipping from the

same two delicate glasses she and Vespus had drunk from just a few days before. Ignoring her. Ignoring Rasmus.

Sorrow's skin crawled as she remembered the nightmares she'd had.

Taasas had been there, while she slept. Watching her. Touching her. Infecting her mind with diseased dreams.

Now, they spoke to each other in Rhyllian, Vespus laughing softly at something Taasas said, and Sorrow couldn't help feeling embarrassed, as though she'd interrupted them.

Vespus was casually dressed in only a shirt and trousers, the sleeves once again rolled back, his hair in a knot atop his head. Opposite him, Taasas was dressed for a state occasion, in a long silvery gown hanging from thin straps on her birdlike shoulders.

Around them tendrils curled, undulating and waving like a green sea, tender compared to the viciousness of those around his son. As Sorrow watched they stroked Vespus's face and arms as though soothing him, leaves brushing over his hair with a silken whisper, lingering at his ears and neck. He seemed to take comfort in them, his eyes half-closed as they caressed his face, features smooth and untroubled.

They surrounded him like guards.

Despite his apparent calm, she could feel the rage coming off him, scorching her like summer sun. His fury was alive in the room, as though a third person sat with him and Taasas, ready to lash out. Sorrow felt it then: the blind terror. It robbed her of her voice.

Vespus turned. He looked at Sorrow.

Her insides clenched as his expression darkened, and the plants responded to his changed mood, rearing back and then clustering protectively around him, their leaves and tips

323

pointing at her like daggers. She had to fight to keep from wetting herself in terror.

Vespus looked at her, his head canted to the side. "Sorrow. For that is all she brings us."

As though his words had broken a spell, Sorrow found her voice. "What's going on? You were meant to be in Rhylla."

Vespus's lips curled into a silent snarl and his violet eyes darkened. "You told me once you weren't interested in sport, and neither am I." He picked up a piece of paper that Sorrow recognized as the note she had written to Queen Melisia. She began to shake then. She couldn't help it.

This seemed to please Vespus, who smiled, and held the note aloft.

"Imagine my surprise when my son was found almost at Castle Adavaria with this in his pocket," Vespus said, opening it up.

"*Queen Melisia,*" he read, and Sorrow closed her eyes. "*It pains me send bad tidings, more so because I now know that I should have written to you sooner. I had hoped, as we all do, that I'd be able to live up to the duty my people chose me for...*"

Taasas chuckled, the sound like a bell, and Sorrow struggled against her bindings, which only made the Rhyllian laugh more. Vespus's own lips curved into a smile that coloured his voice as he continued.

"*The night before the election your half-brother threatened to expose a secret I had, unless I granted him the land he's long desired in my country. It's not the first time he's acted against the interests of Rhannon with this aim in mind – as I'm sure you suspected, or perhaps even know – the last time he tried, his actions resulted in expulsion from his post. However, this time I believed I could stop him without embarrassment to either of our countries, so I played along with his demands, hoping that time would provide me with the means."*

Vespus paused and looked at her. *"So I played along. . ."* he repeated.

Sorrow couldn't look at him as he read on.

"I'm ashamed and saddened to admit I was unable to do so. Your Majesty, there is no disease in the North Marches, only a concoction of Lord Corrigan's designing, made to mimic one. At this time, Lord Corrigan intends for me to clear the land and give it to him as a farm for Alvus trees, with the intention of harvesting vast supplies of Starwater. He confessed to me, the night he first blackmailed me, that he believed he could do things with Starwater that would change the world. And I'm frightened that is what he means to do.

"I am writing to beg for your assistance, something I should have done a long time ago. But in order to do that, I need to be honest and tell you what it is Lord Corrigan holds over me. Your nephew, and my good friend, Rasmus has offered to convey this in person, which I am humbled by, and grateful for. I ask only your forgiveness and understanding, and to beg your aid in righting the terrible wrongs my naivety and inexperience have wrought. Yours, etc., etc."

He put the piece of paper down, and Sorrow's skin burned as though aflame.

"Clever, not to write it down. But ultimately not clever enough."

He picked up the glass and drank. As he did, the fingers of his left hand fluttered idly, and the vines around him danced in time with them.

Sorrow realized it was Starwater in the glass. Not wine. He was drinking it now.

"Did you think you could outwit me?" he asked. "Actually, that's unfair. You did well, and you might have won, had you not overplayed your hand. Your mistake was coming back to Istevar. You were seen, in the tavern you stopped in. It didn't take me long to understand why. You came back to move the skeleton, didn't you?"

The casual way he spoke chilled Sorrow to the bone.

The vines around him rose as he ground out, "You lied to me. In this very room. I thought we had an agreement. I really thought you'd understood what you might have gained from all this. But instead you play games. Kidnapping, grave robbing. You sent my son to my half-sister to beg for help. Did you think I wouldn't realize what was going on?"

"I had to try," Sorrow said. She made her voice steady.

Vespus studied her, then nodded. When he spoke again, there was respect in his voice. "I suppose you think you did." He reached for the decanter and freed the stopper, topping up his glass. "But you didn't. I want you to remember, whatever happens next, you made it happen. I told you I'd stop once I had the land. You chose to make this a war, not I."

"I was trying to save my country from you."

Vespus shrugged, and drained the glass.

As he refilled it again, she noticed something on his forearms: the veins darkening. Then she saw they weren't veins but roots, under his skin, green and spreading. The growth seemed to excite the plants around him, their dancing becoming more frenzied, their stroking of him more forceful. Taasas drew back, fear flashing across her face for the first time.

When Vespus looked at Sorrow, his eyes were green. Bright, luminous green – the colour of poison. She recoiled, and he laughed, lifting the glass. Sorrow didn't want him to drink it, didn't want to see what else he could unleash.

But he didn't drink it.

Instead he held it out, waiting for a vine to take it.

Rasmus began to thrash and moan behind his gag of leaves, and Sorrow twisted to see why, expecting to see thorns piercing his skin, or the fine hairs of nettles brushing against him, causing his agony. But she could see nothing, understood nothing.

Until Vespus raised his hands, and the vine holding the glass began to move towards Rasmus.

"Don't." She turned to Vespus. "Please, spare him. I'm begging you."

"Too late," he said, sounding almost sad about it, his emerald eyes glowing like starflies. "You had your chance. Twice you have defied me. There can be no third time."

"He's your son," Sorrow whispered, nausea roiling through her.

Vespus looked at Rasmus, and pain flickered over his features.

But then he shook himself, reaching for the leaves of one his plant sentries, stroking them.

"I have my plants, I have other children, and I can sire more. Taasas is young. And gifted," Vespus said, glancing at his wife, who was watching the scene with horrified fascination. "Rasmus, like you, made a choice."

Sorrow strained against her own bindings, but there was no use. There were creepers around her wrists and ankles, wrapping her waist. She could only watch as the vine holding the Starwater reached Rasmus, whose eyes were wild with terror as he struggled against his bonds, his head twisting this way and that to keep the vines from giving him the drink.

Finer shoots burst from between the thicker stems that held him, heading towards his face, and he bucked and writhed, trying to break away. But his father's will kept him prisoner as the smaller tendrils snuck beneath his gag, into his mouth.

"Stop it!" she cried. "Please!"

Vespus's gaze flickered to her, bored now.

"I hate that word," was all he said.

The sound Rasmus was making as the vines wound about him was mindless, unearthly, torn from him, no trace of the boy – of a person at all – in his cries.

Sorrow's screams died on her lips as the large vine gagging Rasmus peeled away, and she saw what they'd done to him.

The smaller shoots had pressed into every corner of his mouth, pulling back his lips, tilting his head as far back as it would go, opening his mouth and throat wide. And as Sorrow watched, the vine that held Vespus's Starwater snaked over to Rasmus, and emptied the glass into his mouth, the vines clamping over his nose and mouth to keep him from spitting it out.

He began to choke, but still the vines held him, and all he could do was swallow.

Starwater enhanced the abilities of those Rhyllians who had them. It made Vespus able to make plants do his bidding well beyond what they naturally should; it made the Rhyllian princess, Eirlys, able to conduct ice with her fingers.

It would make Rasmus, whose touch she already craved as a sedative, able to wipe every thought and feeling from her, except need. Need for his skin, and his touch. Something she was forbidden.

The moment she touched him, they were both doomed.

"You're a monster," Sorrow said, shaking with dread.

Vespus pocketed the letter as he stood, and walked past her to the door.

"I didn't have to be," he said, as he turned the handle to open it. "Now, Sorrow Ventaxis, I'm going to move my trees. I don't want them destroyed when the people come to tear down the Winter Palace in their rage against you. But don't worry, I'll be back soon. With company. You two enjoy yourselves in the meantime."

He turned to Taasas, who immediately pasted a huge smile on her face and held her hand out to him. Vespus took it, and left them.

Sorrow looked back at Rasmus, coughing as the shoots withdrew from his mouth, leaving it stained green. His eyes were almost as dark as his father's had been, barren when they turned on her.

"Forgive me," he said, tears streaming down his face.

Sorrow nodded, her own eyes flooding.

Then the vines bore her forward, to where Rasmus's skin waited.

The shoots snapped around her wrists forced her hands up to meet his chest, and she curled them into fists, hoping to lessen the impact of his touch, as his arms were bent against his will to embrace her.

And then it was over. No more pain, no more strife. She was floating, free as a bird, unbound by her skin and her mind and her role. She was nothing but sensation, it was like bathing in starlight, or velvet inside her mind: luxurious, sensual and decadent. She was free, so free.

Everything that had wracked her seconds before faded

329

away, leaving behind an ecstasy more intense than anything she'd ever felt before. There was no fear, no fright, and no pain. Instead there was only joy, and the need for more of it. She knew his body, knew the feel of his skin under her fingers, knew the scent of him, and that too gave her joy, she remembered it.

She pressed her face into his chest, listening to his wild heartbeat, ghosting her lips over the pulse there.

"Don't," he choked, and she looked up.

He looked so sad; why did he look so sad?

Puzzled, she pulled away from him, and frowned.

"What is it?" she asked.

"You're drugged. I'm drugging you. You have to stop," he said. His dark eyes fixed on hers. "Think of Luvian. You want Luvian."

But Sorrow didn't want to think of Luvian, or to stop. When she touched Rasmus nothing hurt. She basked in the feeling, allowing herself to float on it, her head falling back, eyes fluttering shut.

If touching him felt this good, then how would kissing feel?

She leant up, lips parted.

"Stop it," he snapped, and then a vine covered his mouth again.

He glared at her over the top of it, and something shifted in her mind. He'd never stopped her before.

Confused, she pulled her hands away, struggling against the vine that kept forcing her hands forward, until finally she lost patience, leaning down to the right and biting it. Sap coated her lips, and the vine recoiled.

Another immediately replaced it, but the bitter green taste of its life in her mouth, and the removal of Rasmus's skin bought Sorrow a second of clarity.

And in that second she raised her fist to her mouth and bit down, focusing on the pain. His ability – whatever it was that lived in his skin that called to her – rose instantly to ease it away but she bit down harder, over and over, refusing to be soothed, until tears sprang in her eyes and blood began to run between her fingers.

Think of Luvian.

Luvian, arrogant, irritating, irrepressible. Luvian, who would follow her anywhere, but only if he thought it wouldn't hurt her. Luvian who made her laugh. Who made her brave, because he believed in her enough for them both.

She thought of him and kept biting, nipping, gnawing at her own flesh, even as the vines lifted her tunic so the skin of her belly and her chest was flush against Rasmus's.

And she thought of herself, and Rasmus. Neither of them wanted this. They wanted to be friends, they'd chosen that.

Surely her will had to mean something? She fought for control over her own body.

It wasn't real.

"He's going to have us caught like this," Rasmus told her.

Again she nodded, still biting down on her hand, clinging to the clarity it brought her. She knew he was right. Better than Vespus telling people his son and the chancellor were breaking the most sacred law between their peoples. He would show them instead.

Without warning the vines dropped them, snapping back around the posts of the bed, as though they'd never been anywhere else. Sorrow landed on the bed, Rasmus somewhere beside her, the fog and need clearing from her as she sat up, pulling her tunic down.

331

She felt sick with shame and disgust.

"What happened?" Rasmus said, trying to sound normal.

"I don't know," she said slowly.

They looked at each other, and Rasmus's eyes widened. "Why did they stop?"

"Who cares?" Sorrow shot off the bed, trying the door handle, which wouldn't budge.

When Sorrow turned back, Rasmus was pulling on a shirt he'd found lying on a chair, buttoning it up hastily.

The plants began to recede, shrinking into their pots, the shoots withdrawing into stems, the life Vespus had forced from them with his intent restored to its natural state. Soon the room looked exactly as it had when Sorrow had visited Vespus there the morning the plague was reported. A room for a botanical enthusiast, nothing more.

"Do you think something happened to him?" Rasmus said.

Before Sorrow could reply there was a loud boom, and the room shook, the glass in the gas lamps tinkling as it rocked against the brass frames.

27

Endgame

"What was that?" Sorrow said.

"It sounded like an explosion."

She thought the same thing. Two explosions in one day. . . The hairs on the back of her neck rose. "We need to get out of here."

They tried the door again, but no amount of kicking or shouldering it would force it open.

"The sofa," Sorrow suggested, and the two of them lifted it, using it as a battering ram, though the delicate frame of the couch splintered on the first blow. There was nothing else in the room sturdy enough to use, not that they could lift. So they continued throwing themselves at it, until Sorrow hit her arm too hard and cried out, and Rasmus made her stop, pressing his hand to the injury and removing the pain.

As they rested, panting furiously, Sorrow thought she

could hear the faint sounds of screams, and she pressed her ear to the door, listening with all her might. But the sound had vanished, leaving silence, which somehow chilled her more.

They waited, Sorrow's heart pounding painfully in her chest, to see what would happen next. What had caused the booming they'd heard? Minutes ticked by, the two of them frozen like statues by the door, and no one came.

"We need to find a way out," Rasmus said finally, crossing to the windows. "I don't like this at all."

Unmindful of his father's work, he swept the plants on the sill to the floor and lifted the window open.

"It's too far," Sorrow said automatically. The sleeping quarters and the ambassador's wing were all on the third floor. The best they could hope for from a jump that high would be broken arms and legs.

"If we throw down the mattress, and the bedding, all of the soft furnishings?" Rasmus asked.

Sorrow walked to the window and peered down, vertigo sending her reeling away. "It's too far," she repeated.

He made to argue then stopped. "Someone's coming."

Sure enough, there were footsteps outside, then the doorknob rattled, and Sorrow and Rasmus took a step back, glancing at each other.

"Sorrow? Are you in there?" The voice was muffled by the thick wood, but recognizable.

"Irris. IRRIS!" Sorrow shouted, running to the door and slamming her palms against it. "We're in here."

"Stand back," Irris called.

Sorrow and Rasmus did as she said, as something large battered the door.

"Arkady," Sorrow murmured, smiling despite everything.

"Arkady's here?" Rasmus asked.

"Luvian too."

The door shook on its hinges and they both took another step back.

He surely wasn't in any fit state to be smashing doors down, but it didn't seem to bother him; on his next attempt the hinges burst and the door hung loosely from them, revealing Irris, Arkady and Mael.

"Rasmus?" Irris said. Arkady was looking between them both too, his puffy eyes narrowed. Poor Mael just seemed confused. "What are you doing here?"

"Vespus intercepted the letter," Sorrow explained quickly. "He had us both bound in here. How did you know I was here?"

"After the explosion the guards on our wing wouldn't let me leave. They told me to go back to my rooms and wait, but instead I went to yours. When I saw the wardrobe door open I assumed you'd gone through the passage, so I got Mael and Arkady and we followed."

"How did you get through the thorns?" Sorrow asked.

"What thorns?"

Sorrow looked at Rasmus, biting her lip. So the thorns, and the plants in the bedroom had withdrawn suddenly. . .

That couldn't be good news for Vespus.

"What exploded?" Rasmus asked.

"No idea. But I don't think we should hang around."

"We can leave through the ambassador's entrance – there won't be guards," Sorrow said, then paused. "Wait."

Realizing this might be her last chance, she ran to the cabinet and began to ransack it.

"Sorrow, what are you doing?" Irris demanded. "We have to go, now. He could be back at any moment."

"The antidote," Sorrow said desperately. "It might be here. It's a small vial, with a green liquid inside. Help me!"

Irris, Rasmus and Mael joined her, tearing through the drawers, while Arkady kept watch.

Finding nothing, Sorrow moved to Vespus's wardrobe and pawed through his clothes, checking his pockets, inside his shoes. There was a shelf at the top, and she jumped to feel if there was anything there, pulling down a thin folder, hidden at the back. She glanced through it briefly, in case the antidote was mentioned – a recipe, perhaps.

Instead, she saw Mael's name.

Some were letters, to Vespus. Going back over five years, the date was about all she could read of the cramped Rhyllian script. Not Vespus's writing. Someone writing to him, about Mael.

She flicked to the end of one and saw the name "Beliss" scrawled across the bottom.

Others were in Vespus's handwriting; notes, Sorrow assumed from the layout. Again, the only word she recognized was Mael. Until the last page.

When she saw her own name, crossed out heavily.

Every hair on Sorrow's body rose as she realized what they might contain.

The truth of who Mael was.

There was no time to look closer, so she took the papers out and stuffed them in the pocket of her trousers.

"Is this it?"

Sorrow dashed out of the wardrobe to see Mael holding up a vial of pale green liquid.

"Yes!" Sorrow cried, throwing herself across the room and snatching it from him.

"It was taped to the underside of the windowsill," Mael explained. "Beliss told me that's where he used to hide the potions he made as a child. I even found one in her cottage, once."

"Genius," Sorrow cried, and Mael beamed proudly.

"Let's go," Irris called from the doorway, and together they fled the room.

At the end of the passage, Sorrow listened at the door, faintly reassured when she heard nothing beyond. Screwing her courage together, she took a deep breath, and opened it.

Nothing.

The palace seemed spookily deserted when they all stepped out on to the upper landing. There was no one around, no servants, no guards on any of the doors. She hadn't expected to see any outside the ambassador's wing, for diplomatic reasons. But to see, nor hear, no one at all...

"There's no sign of anyone." Irris spoke Sorrow's thoughts, her voice coloured with confusion. "Not a sound."

"Maybe they've barricaded themselves in, after the explosion," Mael suggested.

Sorrow knew it was unlikely. Her guards would have run towards it, not away. Perhaps that's where everyone was. "All right. We need to find Charon. Maybe he knows what on Laethea is going on."

Sorrow and the others crept along the landing and down two flights of stairs, moving silently along the walls, listening all the while.

Footsteps ahead made them all pause, but the two servants who pelted around the corner were more frightened than Sorrow and her party were, dashing straight past them as though they hadn't seen them.

Sorrow exchanged a glance with Irris, and they moved forward more cautiously.

They followed the direction the servants had come from, cutting through the banqueting hall, moonlight falling in pale rectangles through the windows, lighting the way as they approached the council's part of the building. The room was ready to be used, as it always was, but tonight it was eerie to see the place settings laid out, as though just moments before they entered the room had been full of people sitting down to dine.

The silence was filling Sorrow with dread. It wasn't the quiet of the world at night. It wasn't even the slumbering of the old days, when the entire place had felt as though it was suspended in time. This was a predator's silence, a hunter's stillness. The night was watching them, and waiting. Every instinct in her body was screaming it at her; that they were in danger, that they needed to run and hide, go to ground and pray they weren't found.

She stopped outside the door, holding up a hand. "OK," she said, explaining for Arkady's benefit. "Through here are the Jedenvat's offices, my office, and the Round Chamber. We're going to—"

She paused, sniffing the air.

"Smoke," Irris said.

Sorrow reached for the door handle and snatched her hand back, gasping sharply at the heat she'd almost gripped.

As Rasmus reached for it, she smacked his hand away, and wrapped her own in her tunic, turning the handle.

A furnace roared the moment she opened the door, the fresh air sucked down by the flames and then belched at them in gouts of fire.

338

They all hit the floor and rolled, scrambling to their feet and darting back.

Sorrow watched as the flames began to lick the walls of the banqueting hall.

Anyone inside was dead. Her thoughts flew to Charon and Arran. They would be outside, she told herself.

"We have to go." Mael grabbed her arm, their time in Prekara re-enacted as they once again ran from flames. Back through the hall, out into the rear foyer. . .

"There!" someone called from above them.

Sorrow and the others turned to see a group of five men on the stairs, black scarves tied over their faces, batons in their hands. She saw the badges they wore, the fist over iron heart, and she knew who they were.

The Decorum Ward.

"Run!" Sorrow screamed, and they did, racing past the steps as the men turned to give chase, out of the doors on the other side and into one of the reception rooms. They skidded and slid across the polished parquet floor, panic rising as the men poured into the room behind them like locusts.

As they made it through the door, slamming it behind them as though it might help, Arkady lunged for an ornamental sideboard along the wall.

Understanding what he meant to do, Sorrow gripped the handle of the door, holding it as tightly as she could while the men the other side tried to turn it, slamming against it and jarring her teeth.

"Come on, come on, come on. . ." Sorrow chanted, sweat making the handle treacherously slick.

Mael and Irris ran to help Arkady as he huffed and heaved the sideboard to the door, Rasmus wedging his weight against the door alongside Sorrow. Even with the three of them pushing it, the antique piece of furniture took an age to move. Sorrow and Rasmus dove out of the way at the last minute, and the door crashed into the sideboard, keeping the men behind it from opening it fully.

It wouldn't buy them much time, but it would help, and they continued running, through the wide corridors, past paintings of scenery, past dark windows.

They made it to the west hall, racing to the side doors that would lead to the garden, when they were thrown open and a monstrous figure stood there.

Vine.

He was flanked by ten others, and he alone had left his face uncovered.

A face still raw from where Arkady had beaten him bloody. If it hadn't been for his frame, and the way he stood, Sorrow doubted she would have recognized him, one eye swollen completely shut, his nose little more than a smear in the centre of his face. His hair was matted with blood, and she could smell it from where she stood, the metallic reek of it soaked into his clothes, making him stink like an animal. When he grinned at Sorrow, there were gaps where teeth should be.

"You," said Arkady. "Want some more?" He looked as though it would be his greatest wish to go another round with Meeren Vine.

"This time I want the organ grinder, not the monkey," he leered at Sorrow. "Well, well, well. . . You're not as clever as you think you are."

"I'm still cleverer than you," Sorrow said. Though her throat was tight with fear at the sight of him, she balled her

340

hands into fists.

He saw the gesture, and his good eye glittered with amusement.

"Are you? Then how come you fell into my trap?" He grinned again, and Sorrow shuddered. "That's right, Miss Ventaxis. The attack in Istevar was all a plan to get me here, into the palace grounds."

Sorrow couldn't breathe. "You're lying."

"I'm not. I realized it was easier to get myself brought here and finish you all in one go, rather than picking you off one by one. You thought you'd set a trap for me, with your piece in the bulletin and gallivanting around Rhannon. You thought you were luring me. But really, I was hunting you. Getting you right where I wanted you. Right where I wanted to be."

Sorrow remembered the smile Vine had given her before he'd been taken away. She'd thought he was bluffing, trying to intimidate her. But it had been a true smile, of pleasure, because she'd done exactly what he wanted her to.

Vine had always meant to get himself arrested in Istevar, had always meant to be caught there. Because he knew that with the Ward's headquarters demolished, she'd bring him to the Winter Palace. The place he wanted to be.

He'd got her to let him into her home. To bring him within the walls, right in the heart of her palace. He'd even got her to bring the explosives in too, right there for when he got himself free. She'd given the order to have them locked away in the—

Sorrow realized then what had exploded. Why there were no guards.

He'd blown up the barracks.

Where the guards had been sleeping.

Where Luvian had been sleeping.

341

No. She shoved the thought aside, refusing it room in her mind.

"Now she gets it," Vine gloated. "Thank you, Miss Ventaxis. I couldn't have done it without you."

"So now you've come to kill me, and take my place?" she said.

Meeren laughed, the sound thick and meaty, rapidly becoming a cough. When he was finished, he spat blood on the floor between them.

"No. Not kill you. Arrest you. You, her" – he nodded to Irris – "them." His attention went to Mael and Arkady. "And tried, for crimes against Rhannon. Then I'll kill you."

She had not expected this, but she tried to keep her gaze level and her voice steady. "What crimes?" she said contemptuously.

"The same ones your family levelled against the royals. You remember, don't you, how the great Ventaxis dynasty came to power? You took down the monarchy. You rallied the people and you ended them. This is justice. It's come full circle. You're the same as they were, and now you have to go. Your crimes are neglect, avarice, corruption."

The only one she could honestly deny was avarice.

For a moment they were all silent and still, as though it were a dance and both parties were too shy to ask the other for their hand.

Then Vine lunged, and the dance began.

He went for Sorrow, but Arkady anticipated his move and threw himself sideways, knocking her to the floor.

She rolled away, only to find herself grabbed by one of the Ward, who punched her brutally in the temple, leaving her half-stunned and on her knees.

Before her Vine was kneeling on Arkady's chest, slamming his head back into the floor, over and over, while Mael screamed and tried to fight off the men who'd caught him.

Irris was being held by another man, his hand on her neck, her breathing ragged.

Rasmus was curled on his side, trying to protect his head, and as Sorrow watched one of the Ward kicked him in the stomach. He stilled, uncurling as his body relaxed and he lost consciousness.

Vine stood up and walked over to Sorrow, grabbing her by her hair.

"That's what a real fight with me looks like. Over in seconds."

Sorrow opened her mouth to reply, when something landed on her head.

And then another – small, sharp little pellets, the floor echoing with tiny taps raining down on them from the floor above; and all of them, even Vine and his people, paused to peer above them.

Vespus leant over the balcony, eyes glowing green, Taasas beside him.

Then Vespus raised his hands and the hall erupted with life.

As a shoot burst from out of the floor and grew within seconds, Sorrow realized the things he'd thrown were seeds.

Vine yelped in astonishment as a shoot wrapped itself around his neck, and released her. It pulled him to the ground as dozens of others did the same, binding him soundly.

Ivy, creepers and vines all wound through the hall, coiling around the Ward like serpents, leaving Sorrow and her friends alone as Vespus stood above them all, coordinating his plants

343

like a maestro with his orchestra.

Sorrow ran to Arkady as Irris moved to Rasmus, reaching him at the same time Mael did, both of them seeking a pulse.

"I can't find one." Mael's voice was a sob.

But Arkady Rathbone was made of sterner stuff than that, and Sorrow finally found his pulse, grabbing Mael's fingers and forcing them to his wrist so he could feel the truth of it himself.

"His stupid thick neck," Mael said, eyes shining, and without thinking Sorrow kissed his forehead.

"Stay with him," she said, skidding across the floor to where Irris was holding a moaning Rasmus.

There was blood on his face, and he couldn't straighten his body, in agony from the kick to his belly. Sorrow prayed to any Graces listening that nothing was ruptured.

She looked around and saw Vine was choking, the plants around his neck tightening, but still Vespus kept going, clenching his fist. Why was he helping them? Sorrow couldn't understand, staring at him.

Vespus's nose was bleeding, thick black blood streaming down his face, and it made the hairs on the back of Sorrow's neck stand up. Taasas was tugging his sleeve, but it was as if he couldn't see or feel her, newly emerald eyes blazing as he looked down at Vine.

Without understanding why, Sorrow said, "Stop."

Vespus either didn't hear her, or didn't want to, clenching his other fist as Vine and his men began to thrash, their bodies fighting to survive. They were dying.

So was Vespus, she realized.

She pushed herself up and made for the stairs.

"Stop," she screamed, taking the steps two at a time.

She didn't know why she was doing it – after what he'd just done to her, and to Rasmus. After everything he'd done to her, she ought to be glad to see him killing himself.

It was Starwater, he'd taken too much, using it to command the thorns, the vines that held her and Rasmus and now this. It was killing him, and still he wouldn't – couldn't stop.

He looked at her, his eyes glowing, blood flowing freely from his nose, from his ears. Then he staggered, and Sorrow caught him, Taasas at his other side as they lowered him to the floor.

Vespus locked his green eyes on Sorrow's. "Is my son alive?" he asked.

Stunned, Sorrow could only nod.

As though he'd been waiting for it, he went limp in her arms.

Then his eyelids flew open and Taasas screamed.

Where seconds before his eyes had burned green, now there were empty holes. Starwater, the same thing as Lamentia. Vespus had overdosed on it, just as Alyssa, Balthasar's wife, had the night before this all began.

Vespus began to convulse, his body shaking, his teeth rattling together as he shook, green froth foaming from his mouth.

"Do something," Taasas begged her.

Sorrow stared at her. What could she do? He was beyond any help.

"End it," Taasas whispered. "Please."

Sorrow placed her hand over Vespus's nose and mouth, covering it tightly, refusing to let go until he finally stilled.

She'd been wrong. It seemed she did have it in her to kill him.

"They destroyed his plants," Taasas said, reaching out to stroke Vespus's hair, when Sorrow finally removed her hand. "The ones in the dungeons. We were heading there when they blew up the barracks. They almost got us. They killed his babies. His life's work. His dreams. We checked – there was nothing left. Not even the tiniest seed." She stood. "They have to pay for it."

As Sorrow watched, Taasas rose. When she saw the small bottle in Taasas's hand, filled with crystal liquid, her breath caught.

"Don't," she whispered.

Taasas moved past her, descending the stairs. She uncorked her bottle and dropped the lid to ground, where it bounced in time with her footsteps as she walked, drinking the Starwater.

Vine and his men had recovered from Vespus's attack, stalking towards where Mael and Irris had assumed protective stances in front of the still prone Arkady, and Rasmus, who was struggling to his feet.

Vine looked at Taasas as she reached the bottom of the stairs, sparing a look of triumph for Sorrow.

"Where's your boyfriend?" Vine asked Taasas.

"He was my husband," Taasas said in her eerie, dreamy voice. "And he's dead."

"You have my condolences," Vine leered.

"And you mine."

Sorrow thought she saw something like fear cross his mangled features, but he forced out a laugh, looking at his companions until they laughed too.

"And what is it you can do, then?" he asked her.

"This," Taasas said. She dropped the bottle and pointed at Vine.

Sorrow watched him blink, as he found himself in whatever reality Taasas was showing him. Not just him. All of those with him, all of them were now staring around wildly, seeing things that weren't there.

Sorrow started forward, suddenly terrified that her friends would be affected, but to her relief they looked more bewildered than frightened. As Taasas walked around the Ward, never touching any of them, Sorrow slunk down the stairs. She helped Irris get Rasmus up and pointed at the front doors, before she went to Mael and Arkady. Arkady was still unconscious, so she took one arm, nodding for Mael to take the other, and between the two of them they began to drag him.

That was when Vine started screaming.

In fright, Sorrow dropped Arkady's arm and looked at where Taasas was still walking through the crowd, looking for all the world like a noblewoman taking an afternoon stroll. But the garden she walked through was made of bodies, all of them writhing on the spot, moving as one, swaying to and fro like flowers in the wind.

Only Vine was free of this macabre dance, whirling on the spot, seeing but not seeing. His focus seemed to be on his people, but Sorrow knew it wasn't their strange behaviour he witnessed, but something much darker.

Vine's screams grew louder, turning to shrieks as he suddenly stopped and looked down at his legs, his hips moving as though he was trying to walk, trying to escape. Sorrow watched a puddle of urine form at his feet, but he didn't attempt to step out of it, seemed to believe he couldn't, as his hips locked, then his shoulders, and finally his neck and head.

Then he moved with his men, his one good eye bulging in

terror, powerless to stop it.

As one, their hands rose and they paused, fingers splayed, arms akimbo, standing tall as a mighty oak. Like a child's game, pretending to be trees. Sorrow guessed what Taasas's vision was: Vine watching his men turn into trees, before he became one himself.

A nice tribute to Vespus. He'd appreciate it.

Then their fingers curled to become claws, their hands moving to their faces. To their eyes.

Sorrow knew what Taasas meant to do, and met her gaze.

Taasas smiled, and waved, before turning her attention back to the Ward.

And Sorrow grabbed Arkady's arm, not waiting for Mael to help, determined not to see how it ended.

28

New World Order

Sorrow didn't look back, and when Mael turned she barked at him to help her with Arkady. He didn't need to see it; no one did.

What made it worse was the silence; there should have been screaming. But Taasas's vision held the Ward so powerfully that they didn't know what they were doing.

A full-body shiver ran through Sorrow at the *power* Taasas held. Able to reorder the world as people saw it, lived it. Able to make them live a reality of her own design. Consciousness at her whim. It was no wonder Melisia wanted to keep those abilities hidden; war would be sure to follow if the world knew people like Taasas existed. If the world knew what could exist if Starwater ever got out there.

Irris came back to help Sorrow and Mael, and between the three of them they managed to get Arkady down the stairs, laying him gently on the path. He showed no signs of waking, but when Sorrow checked his pulse again it was still strong. Mael sat on the floor and lifted Arkady's head carefully into his lap.

She left them and went to Rasmus, sitting a little away, one hand clutching his ribs.

"I think they're broken," he said. His eyes were shadowy, his face paler than usual.

"Are you all right otherwise?"

He looked at her, violet eyes glassy with pain. "My father is dead, isn't he?"

She wondered if she should say she'd been the one to kill him, or at least finish what Starwater had started. She shuddered as she remembered how he convulsed under her grip, and how he'd slackened as she stole his life, his eyeless sockets staring blankly up at her.

No, she decided. All she'd done was end his suffering. And Rasmus didn't need to know the horrible details of his father's death.

"Yes. He overdosed on Starwater."

Rasmus let out a long breath, and closed his eyes. "I shouldn't be sad," he said. "Not after what he did to us."

"He was still your father," Sorrow said. "You can be sad. And he asked about you. He asked if you were alive. He seemed glad."

Rasmus shrugged, and she touched his shoulder gently.

"Listen, I need to find Charon and send for help. Are you all right here?"

Rasmus nodded, and Sorrow left him, beckoning Irris to come with her.

Smoke was choking the sky at the rear of the palace,

clouds of it obscuring the stars above, and it was towards it they headed. The two girls broke into a jog, almost colliding with a guard as they rounded the corner.

Sorrow's heart soared as she recognized her bodyguard.

Dougray, however, looked furious.

"Your Excellency. Where have you been? I went to your rooms and you were gone. The guards on the wing said you hadn't passed them."

Sorrow was too impatient to explain, or be polite. "It doesn't matter. Have you seen Lord Day?"

Dougray sputtered in outrage. "Yes. He's with the others."

"Which others?" Irris asked. "My brother? Mr Fen?"

"All of the senators are safe. And Mr Fen."

"He's alive?" Sorrow repeated, grabbing Dougray by the shoulders.

She released him almost immediately, as her stunned bodyguard nodded.

Irris and Sorrow looked at each other, and Sorrow felt hope at last fill her chest. How could they be so lucky? How could they be so fortunate that they all survived? She was cursed, *Sorrow was all she brought.* How had her curse not touched this?

She needed to see for herself.

"Are you hurt?" Dougray looked her up and down.

"Not us. Others are," Sorrow added. "My brother, Rasmus Corrigan, and Arkady – Kady Fen." Sorrow remembered his fake name at the last moment. "Can you send for the doctor?"

"I need to stay with you."

"Dougray, please."

He gave a tight nod.

"Thank you. They're outside the main hall. . . It's. . . It's not pretty in there."

351

Dougray gave her one last look, and began jogging away.

Sorrow clasped Irris's hand and began towards the fire.

As they got closer, the smoke thickened, making it harder to see. And when they finally reached the burning part of the palace, both girls stopped in shock.

The surviving palace guard were there, struggling to put out the flames, but Sorrow knew they wouldn't be able to save it. Almost the entire East Wing was gone: the offices, the Round Chamber. Charon's quarters were gone; high above, her own looked in danger of collapse at any moment.

The blaze was no longer raging, but still it smouldered, and every few moments Sorrow saw a red glint of heat from inside, like the opening of an evil eye to see if they were still there. When it did, someone quickly pointed it out, and vanquished it.

Guards, servants, and people in everyday clothes she didn't recognize were all working together to put the fire out, the fire service using pumps and hoses to suck water from the palace's ornamental lakes, directing it at the fire, chains of people passing buckets back and forth, doing their best to help. Sorrow found herself drawn into a bucket line, Irris beside her, passing water back and forth.

Soot settled on their skin, sweat running rivulets through it. Sorrow's arms and shoulders ached, but she kept going, mindlessly moving to and fro, until someone gave the all clear, and the line separated, moving forward a few feet and reforming, ready to go again. Sorrow and Irris were about to rejoin them when their names were called.

"Sorrow! Irris!"

They turned and saw Arran Day half-running, half-limping towards them.

"You're all right," he said, crushing both girls into his arms.

"We've been so worried. We thought you were safe in your wing, but the guards said you weren't there." Relief gave way to anger as he continued. "We couldn't find you anywhere. Where were you?"

He didn't wait for an answer, beginning to drag them away from the firefighters, but Sorrow stopped him.

"Wait," she said, pulling the papers from her pocket.

The truth about Mael. She was sure of it.

Sorrow folded them, making a thick paper dart. Then she threw it with all her might, into the burning building, watching it vanish into the flames.

A few people tutted at her for adding fuel to the fire, but she ignored them. A few pieces of paper weren't going to do any real damage and besides, it was her palace.

"All right," Sorrow said to Arran, who was watching her. "Let's go."

He led them through the gardens, to a small summer house.

Inside sat Charon and Luvian, talking in low voices. Irris rushed immediately to her father, but Sorrow remained in the doorway, staring at Luvian.

He wasn't dead.

The glass in one of his lenses was cracked, and it made her heart wobble. They sat crookedly too.

He saw her and gave her a faint smile. She walked over.

"Your glasses are cracked," she said.

"They're busted." He took them off and showed her, the arm on the left dented, hastily bent back into shape.

He put them back on and took her face in his hands.

"I punched someone," he said.

"Did you?" Sorrow raised an eyebrow.

"Yes. I think I broke my hand." He held it up to her. "Or

353

perhaps sprained it. It could be badly bruised. The point is I am never doing that again. My rumbling days are over."

Sorrow leant forward and kissed him. "Thank you for not dying," she said.

"My pleasure."

Charon cleared his throat and Sorrow touched Luvian's cheek, then went to her mentor.

She knelt before him and they hugged, Sorrow trying to convey her relief and her gratitude in it.

"I'm so glad you're both all right," Charon said, then pressed a kiss to her forehead.

Arran pulled over wicker seats for Irris and Sorrow, and the five of them formed a circle. Irris leant on her brother, who put an arm around her, and took one of Charon's hands in hers. Sorrow took the other. Luvian was sitting so close to her, she could feel his thigh against hers.

Charon told them he'd been in his rooms reading when he'd heard the explosion and had gone to raise the alarm, only to realize it was the barracks that had been blown up. He knew immediately it must have been Vine.

Two of the guards had evacuated Charon against his will, bringing him out to the summer house, leaving a guard with him. But one of the Ward had found them.

"That's when I became the hero of the piece," Luvian piped up, and to Sorrow's surprise Charon laughed and gave him a look that was almost fond.

Luvian picked up the story then.

"I heard shouts from the grounds. I found the guard struggling with one of the Ward. So I hit him."

Sorrow smiled at the pride in his voice. But Luvian didn't smile back.

He looked at her. "We were told you were safe in your quarters. It's the only thing that stopped me from coming to you. Clearly not the case. . ." His eyes asked a question.

Sorrow told them what had happened, sparing them some of the detail. She didn't tell them what Vespus had done to her and Rasmus either; it wasn't something she was ready to talk about – wasn't sure she'd ever be ready to talk about.

When she finished, they all sat in shocked silence. Luvian was gripping her free hand tightly.

"Where is Taasas now?" Charon asked.

"I don't know. Gone, perhaps back to Rhylla, to wherever Vespus found her."

"And he's dead?" Arran asked.

"Definitely. And if Vine survived" – Sorrow hoped he hadn't for his sake, as much as hers – "he and his men won't be a threat any more, either."

"You're safe then," Charon said. "Rhannon is safe."

"It is. And I have the antidote for Vespus's poison," she remembered, pulling the vial from her pocket. "One drop per victim, he said. Let's get it to the North Marches tonight. The people have waited long enough."

"What was that you threw into the fire?" Irris asked Sorrow.

Sorrow hesitated. "Letters, mostly. About Mael."

The atmosphere in the room tightened.

"What did they say?"

"I don't know, they were in Rhyllian. But I could understand enough to know they were dated before he came back. Years before."

"Why did you burn them?" Charon asked her. "They might have told us who he was."

"Because it doesn't matter," Sorrow said. It hadn't mattered for a long time. "Mael believes he's found his family, and that's true. He has. I'm his sister, and he's my brother. That's all we need to know. There's nothing else."

Charon nodded. "He's no longer a threat to you, anyway. It's over. You have the antidote, so we can give it to the victims." He rubbed his face tiredly. "We can get back to normal."

"Back to normal," Sorrow echoed. She wasn't sure why, but the thought made her sad.

They stayed in the summer house, out of the way of the commotion, until the guards came to tell them the doctor had arrived. Arkady was finally conscious, though barely aware of it. Sorrow gripped Luvian's hand tightly as he stared at his brother.

"He needs to go to a hospital," Dr Majela said. "That one too." She pointed at Rasmus.

"Go with them?" Sorrow asked Luvian.

"Of course."

He helped Arkady and Rasmus into a carriage and they vanished into the night.

"Ambassador Krator of Meridea has invited us to stay in her town house tonight," Charon said, returning from where he'd been speaking to a dark-skinned Merish envoy. The man smiled at Sorrow when he met her eye, and Sorrow returned it.

"Let's. We can relocate to the Summer Palace in the morning. After we've seen how bad the damage is."

They all looked to where the Winter Palace, once gleaming white, now stood blackened by smoke. Sorrow expected it to crumble at any moment. She didn't know whether she wanted it to.

She followed Charon, Irris and Arran to the coach the Merish envoy had arrived in, climbing in and settling herself.

356

There were people outside the gates from Istevar town, drawn by the fire and the noise, demanding to know what was going on.

"Wait," Sorrow said. "I need to speak to them. Show them everything is fine."

Charon gave her a proud smile and followed her down the winding path, Arran and Irris at either side of him.

The people cheered when they saw her, some of them reaching out as if to touch her. Their joy at seeing her alive and well choked her. That they cared about her at all choked her.

"As you can see, I'm all right," she said, and they cheered again. "Lord Day, Senator Day and Miss Day are all fine too."

More cheers, and Arran gave a small wave.

"I don't know the extent of the damage yet. There will be a lot of questions, in the days to come. A lot to discuss. But for now, I'd like you all to go back to your homes and rest. Tomorrow is another day."

As they broke into applause, she walked back up the drive, climbing into the carriage with her family.

Krator, Merish ambassador, welcomed them warmly, leading them to a room where food and drink were waiting for them.

Sorrow was ravenous, and she, Irris and Arran descended on the food like vultures. Within minutes they'd devoured everything: flaky pastries filled with spiced beans and rice, a deep red dip that made Sorrow's mouth feel cold when she scooped it up with fried potato skins, tiny sweet sausages that burst in her mouth, and glasses of cool, nutty milk, that the ambassador told them was made from plants.

She showed them to their quarters, first Arran and Charon, who'd share a room on the ground floor, and then up the stairs to where Irris and Sorrow would sleep. Sorrow looked longingly at the bed, before turning to the ambassador.

"This looks heavenly, but ... I have letters to write, and lists to make."

Irris, who had been about to sit on the bed, straightened.

"No, you rest," Sorrow said. "I need to write to Melisia, as soon as possible."

Irris nodded gratefully, lowering herself on to bed once more.

"It never ends, does it?" Krator said, giving Sorrow a wry smile as she led her to another to another room.

It was small, but it had a desk, and a clean stack of paper on it.

"Perfect," she said.

She wrote to Melisia and told her how Vespus had given his life to save her, Irris and Rasmus. She didn't mention he'd used Starwater, knowing the Rhyllian queen would be able to read between the lines as she described how he'd sacrificed himself. She didn't mention Taasas either. She explained Rasmus was injured, but would be fine, and she'd make sure he wrote to her as soon as she could.

Rasmus was safe now, she realized. Vespus had taken him before he had delivered the letter, so Melisia had no idea about him and Sorrow. He could go home, and be free. She knew she'd promised no more lies, but maybe this one, final lie wouldn't hurt. After all, the only people who'd been harmed by their being together was them, and they were finally at peace with it.

Sorrow wrote to each of her Jedenvat, telling them what had happened, and promising they'd be called to order soon.

Then she sat back, and rubbed her eyes. She had one more letter to write.

"You're resigning?" Charon stared at the piece of paper she'd handed him.

"I am."

"Why? Sorrow . . . this is your chance. Our chance. Vespus is defeated, the people from the North Marches will be cured. They can return to their homes. And Vine is dead; you can dismantle the Ward. We can really move forward, Rhannon can move forward."

"And she will. But not with me at her head. It's all in there," she said, nodding towards the document. "I want to change everything. I want Rhannon to start again. No more Ventaxis chancellor, followed by Ventaxis chancellor. And the Jedenvat should be chosen by the people. They should vote for the leader that best represents their community. Every five years, the whole of Rhannon will vote for one of the Jedenvat to become chancellor, and another to be vice chancellor. No one will be allowed to serve as either role more than two terms, to give all the districts a chance to be represented, and to make sure no one has chance to be like my ancestors."

"The current Jedenvat will hate it."

"I don't care. Besides, they can keep their homes and fortunes. I won't take those from them. Just their jobs. Which, if they're committed enough, they'll be able to convince the people to let them keep – Bayrum and Arran would be voted back in a heartbeat." She smiled. "The others will have to earn it."

"What about Mael? What if he decides he wants to be chancellor and the likes of Samad support him to keep their

359

jobs? What if they try to overthrow your orders?"

"He won't." Sorrow was sure of it. Like her, he'd never really wanted the job. Only to belong. And he did now. He knew it.

"Sorrow, I understand things have been nightmarish for you so far, but you need to think about this. . ."

"Charon, I've been thinking about it for months. I've told you all since the start I didn't want this job. I fought Mael for it because I didn't trust him. I thought I was the better option for my country. But now I see I don't have to be an option at all."

"You care about your people, though." Charon was staring at her as though he'd never seen her before. "You love them."

"I do. But I can serve them in other ways. I could become a nurse, or a professor, or a lawyer, or a firefighter. I could even run for senate one day, and win the chancellorship myself. I could do it on my own terms – I haven't decided for ever. But I have for now. The system is corrupt, and because of it I was corrupted. I want to make a difference, and I understand now I don't have to have the answers in order to do so. I can be part of the question."

She paused, and smiled. "I'm going to pass everything that's in that letter into law, and then stand down, but only after I've appointed you temporary chancellor in my stead."

"No—"

"Yes. I trust you to bring this vision to life. Only you. The rest of the Jedenvat will work with you for the next five years, helping you prepare Rhannon for the changes. Then they'll happen. We'll make the Rhannon we always wanted."

"And what will you do?"

"I don't know. I haven't decided. And I don't plan to for a

while, yet. I want to learn who Sorrow Ventaxis is. Maybe I'll find my birth family. Maybe I won't. Maybe I'll travel, or study, or start a circus troupe." She smiled. "I guess we'll find out."

29

Citizen Ventaxis

Sorrow sat on the steps of the Institute in the East Marches, her hands cupped around the coffee she'd illegally brought out with her. The sign on the door of the dining hall clearly stated that all food and drink must be consumed inside, but Sorrow had never really minded breaking the rules, big or small. Besides, she'd take the cup back once she was finished. No harm done. She just wanted a moment or two alone, to sit quietly and enjoy the dark, bitter drink.

"Miss? Miss? You need to bring that back inside, miss."

Sorrow smiled to herself – it had been nice while it lasted. She stood, turning around.

"Oh. Miss Ventaxis, I didn't know it was you. Please, feel free to stay where you are."

"It's fine." Sorrow smiled at the serving woman. "I ought to know better."

362

As Dougray gave her a look that unmistakably said, "I told you so," Sorrow followed the woman back into the dining hall, rolling her eyes at her classmates as she joined them, her bodyguard standing a discreet distance away.

"Well, you tried." Dorie laughed at her as Sorrow dropped into the seat beside her.

"It had to be done," Sorrow said. "I'm a student now. Rebellion and anarchy comes with the territory. I have to fight the system."

"How *is* the system?" Nataza asked.

Sorrow smiled coyly. "The system is fine. The system is picking me up this afternoon."

"Come on. We're going to be late," Dorie said, gathering her folders together.

Sorrow finished her coffee, and the three girls went off to their afternoon class, trailed by Dougray, who sat beside them and ignored them as they exchanged notes, and jokes, much to the chagrin of their professor.

She hadn't expected to find friends, didn't think she'd make friends easily. Certainly not given who she used to be. It was the first time in Rhannish history – Laethean history – that a chancellor had stood down and then announced she was going to university.

It had, predictably, caused an uproar, which was the reason Charon had insisted she keep Dougray as her bodyguard. They'd compromised that she'd keep him with her while she was at school, and when she travelled, but come the weekend, he was to take the time off and allow her to live a normal life. That was, after all, the point of stepping down in the first place.

There had been protests, accusing her of abandoning

Rhannon, and she'd suffered for the freedoms she'd already allowed the people – more than one editorial had appeared in the bulletins calling her reckless, and flighty, and implying the authors expected nothing less from a teenage girl.

Sorrow had refused to let Charon retaliate.

"No – they should be allowed to say what they feel out loud. Better that than whispering it in taverns."

Even when a small rebellion had attempted to rally, centring on Mael, Sorrow had continued to stay Charon's hand.

"Democracy," she'd said. "They're allowed to be angry with me. And they're allowed to express it."

Mael made it perfectly clear he wouldn't take the role, announcing he stood by his sister. And when disaster didn't immediately befall Rhannon, and the plans Sorrow had started in motion proved stable, the dissention died down. Now the biggest threat to her day were the gossip reporters, who liked to badger her fellow students and professors for titbits about her life as a student. She was, to her annoyance, becoming a kind of celebrity.

Luckily, her friends held the reporters in the same vein of disdain that she did. Now, three months into her first year as a student, she was enjoying it immensely, enjoying getting to know new people, enjoying trying things out, enjoying testing her mind on problems that would, at worst, result in a bad grade, as opposed to ruining a country.

So far, she'd attended law classes, art classes, history classes, literature classes – to both Luvian's and Irris's amusement – and even politics, though the lectures bore no resemblance to what she knew of it, and she already knew politics wasn't for her. Not yet, at least.

At some point, she'd have to decide which course she

was going to take. But again, not yet. She was still learning how to be a good student – obeying authority didn't come naturally to her, though she supposed that wasn't surprising, given that she'd *been* the authority until recently. Still, she was doing well – her grades were excellent, even if her work ethic sometimes lacked.

After the lecture was over, Sorrow waved goodbye to her friends and tripped out of the white stone building, heading across the university grounds to the gates.

Luvian was already there, waiting, and the frames of his glasses flashed in the sun as she approached and he saw her.

He took the few steps forward to meet her, holding out his hand for her book bag, and swinging it on to his back.

"My hero," Sorrow said.

"Shut up and kiss me."

She wound her arms around his neck and pressed her mouth to his, ignoring the whistles and whoops of her fellow students.

"Children," Luvian said as he pulled away, taking her hand.

"I'm one of those children."

He shook his head and gave her a mischievous smile. "No, you're—"

"If you say I'm all woman, I'm going to hurt you."

His smile became a grin and he remained tellingly silent.

They walked the mile back to the house in the East Marches that Sorrow had bought with her share of the Ventaxis fortune, chatting about their respective weeks.

"How are the renovations going?" she asked Luvian.

"Fine. The offices are done, I think Lord Day – Chancellor Day, forgive me – is planning to start working there next week, so I'll be there too. I get my own office, apparently. I've asked for a plaque for the door: Luvian Fen, Personal Assistant to the Chancellor."

"What did Charon say?"

"I dare not repeat it in front of your delicate lady ears. Have you seen Irris?"

"No, she's been busy this week. I wrote to her but she said she was really close to making a breakthrough on whatever she was working on, and she'd be in touch."

"Any idea what it was?"

"No, but last time she was this excited it was an old letter about a famine in Rhannon that lasted seven years, but wasn't recorded in the history books. So it could be anything."

"Classic Irris, she's a party in a person."

"Says the man who still runs the Luvian Andearly Rathbone Lending Library to this day."

"That reminds me, you have an overdue book. You'll have to pay the fine."

"What's the fine?"

He whispered something in her ear that made her face burn.

"There's interest if you're late paying too," he said, raising an eyebrow lasciviously.

Sorrow couldn't speak.

When they got back to her home, Luvian went straight to the kitchen to begin preparing supper, while Sorrow opened her mail. It was Sorrow's favourite part of the week – the two days when he didn't have to be in Istevar, but stayed with her. He reminded her frequently she could have gone to the University of Istevar if she'd wanted, and therefore seen him

366

every day, but she'd kissed his cheek and told him, "Absence makes the heart grow fonder." She needed this space, this time to focus on her studies. The first thing she had ever done just for her.

There were three letters for her, one in Rasmus's elegant script, one in Mael's equally beautiful writing, and one from Irris. She opened Mael's first.

Luvian brought her a glass of lemon water, and she sipped it gratefully. It tasted like spring.

"Mael wants to know if we'll go for dinner in Prekara next week," she said. "Arkady will be there too." From what Sorrow could tell, her brother and Luvian's were in a relationship, although neither of them were willing to discuss it with Sorrow or Luvian, no matter how hard they begged.

"It's private," Mael told Sorrow last time he'd seen her. "I don't ask you about Luvian."

"Mostly because we don't care," Arkady had added.

Sorrow smiled at the memory, and looked at Luvian, waiting for an answer.

He shrugged. "Can do. Oh, that reminds me – my mother wants to come and stay during the Spring Gathering."

Sorrow swallowed. "Here? With us?"

"Here, with us. She said, and I quote, 'It'll be interesting to see if the maverick keeps a better house than she did a country.' I don't think we can put her off any longer." He gave her an apologetic smile and returned to the kitchen, as Sorrow rolled her eyes.

Though the maverick was better than the puppet, she supposed.

Then she opened the letter from Rasmus.

He'd gone north, travelling to Svarta just before Sorrow had started university. They'd all had dinner together, at Melisia's Inn in Rhylla, toasting him, and each other. Sorrow and Mael had smiled at each other over the table, remembering the last time they'd been there.

Sorrow had no regrets about destroying the truth about whether or not Mael was a Ventaxis. She didn't need any evidence to prove Mael was her brother. He just was, and that was enough.

"Ras says they're preparing for winter there," Sorrow called through to Luvian. "Isn't that funny, that while we get ready for summer, up there it's getting colder and darker."

"We should go and see it one day." Luvian poked his head around the door.

"We should – is something burning?" Sorrow sniffed the air.

"No." Luvian disappeared back into the kitchen. "It's fine," he called. "They're supposed to be charred. That's the dish. Charred aubergine stew. It's my speciality."

Sorrow smiled and opened the third envelope. There was a second envelope inside it, the front blank. Irris had added a note.

She read it. Then she screamed for Luvian.

He was by her side in seconds, brandishing a knife.

He looked so ridiculous that Sorrow laughed. "I'm fine. But look. . ."

She held out the note to him. "It's from Irris. She found my parents. She found them."

Luvian stared at her. "Did you know she was looking for them?"

Sorrow took a deep breath. "Kind of. I'd forgotten I asked Charon to find them, so I could destroy any records to stop Vespus using them. Except I let him think I wanted to know because I was worried they had the plague. He must have asked Irris to look so I'd know, one way or the other if any of the people who died were my … were … you know?"

Luvian nodded, but said nothing, waiting for her to continue.

Sorrow looked down at the sealed envelope in her lap. "She says it's up to me if I open it, or not."

"And…"

Sorrow looked at the envelope and thought of Mael. And Arkady and Charon and Irris and Arran. And Luvian, standing beside her, waiting for her to decide. Her family. The family she'd cobbled together through love and pain, history, trust and sheer hard work.

Part of her wanted to know who her birth parents were and where she'd come from. She expected there would be times when the want of it followed her around like a ghost. Days when she fought with Charon, or watched him, Arran and Irris take each other for granted, and felt herself adrift from them. Nights when Luvian was bickering with Arkady, or lamenting his mother, sweetly ignorant of how she could never know what that was like. Then the envelope would tempt her.

And there was the urge to give her birth parents some kind of closure. To let them know what had happened, to close the book for them. Perhaps if Harun had had closure all those years ago with Mael, everything would have been different. But Sorrow understood now you couldn't change the past, only shape the future. It was the future she was interested in.

"I'll help you finish dinner," she said, rising.

She put the letter on the table, and reached for Luvian's hand.

Acknowledgements

We all know it takes a village, so thank you as always to my fellow villagers:

Claire Wilson, endless thanks for your wisdom and guidance. And to Miriam Tobin at RCW, for your support too.

To everyone at Scholastic UK, but especially my editor, Genevieve Herr, Lauren Fortune, copy-editors Peter Matthews and Jenny Glencross, and the PR and Marketing teams, who work so tirelessly to promote my books. And as always to Jamie Gregory. This is my favourite cover yet.

To the usual suspects – what a blessing it is to always have the same old names to thank. I love you all for your endless support, but owe special thanks to Emilie Lyons, Lizzy Evans, Steven Salisbury, Sophie Reynolds, and Sara Barnard. This time I really couldn't have done it without you.

Melinda Salisbury lives by the sea, somewhere in the south of England. As a child she genuinely thought Roald Dahl's *Matilda* was her biography, in part helped by her grandfather often mistakenly calling her Matilda, and the local library having a pretty cavalier attitude to the books she borrowed. Sadly she never manifested telekinetic powers. She likes to travel, and have adventures. She also likes medieval castles, non-medieval aquariums, Richard III, and all things Scandinavian.

She can be found on Twitter at **@MESalisbury**, though be warned, she tweets often.